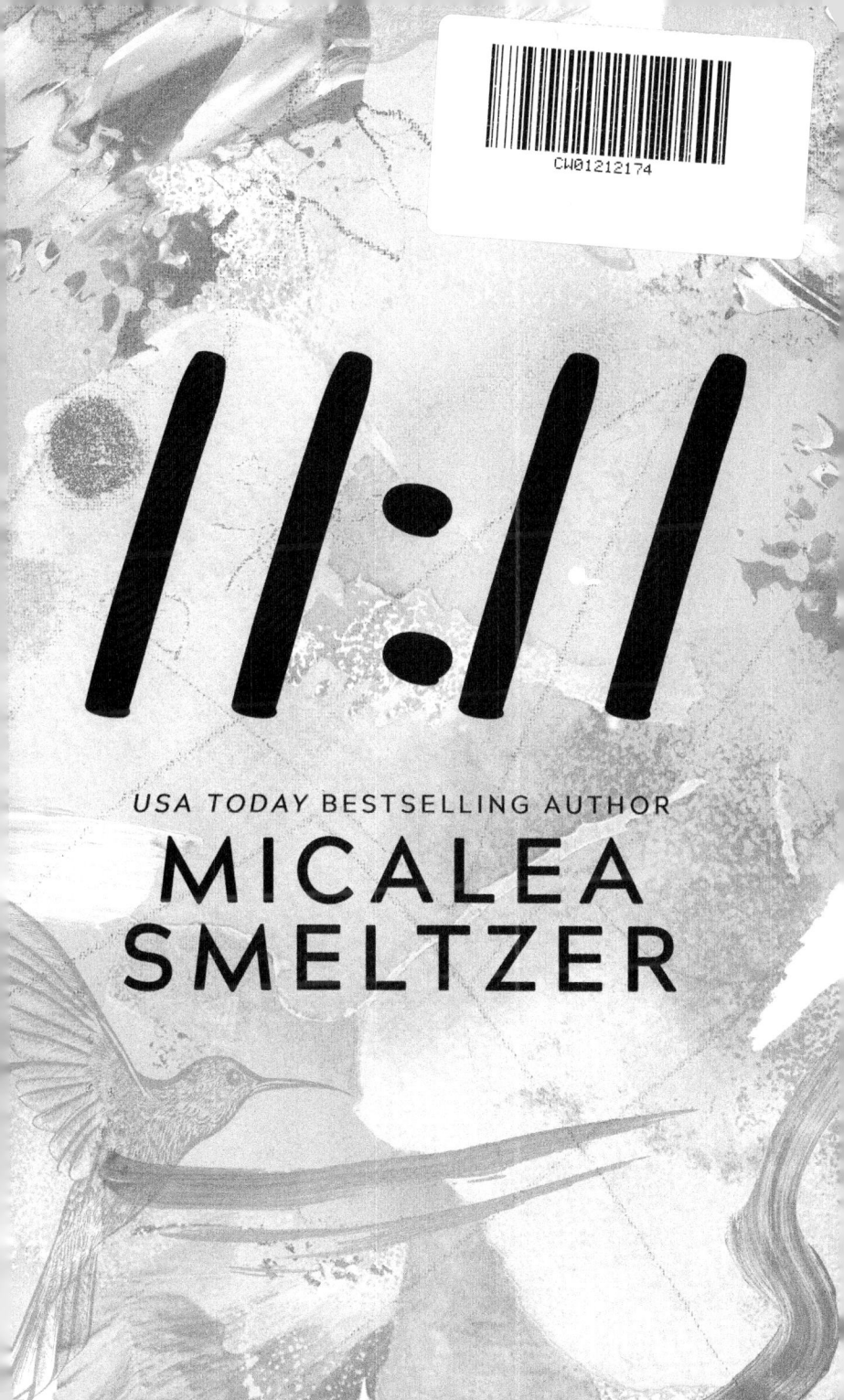

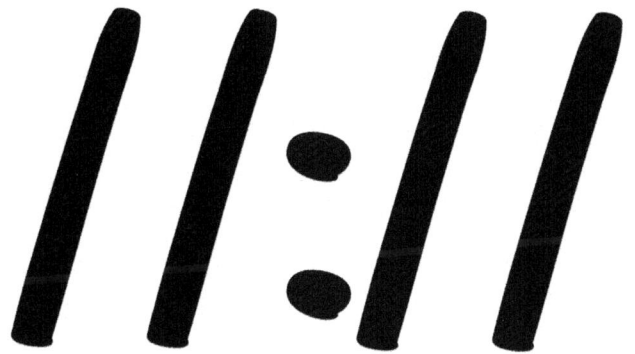

Make wishes on elevens.
Happy Reading!

© Copyright 2024 Micalea Smeltzer

All rights reserved. This book or any portion thereof may not be reproduced or used in any manner whatsoever without the express written permission of the publisher.

This is a work of fiction. Names, characters, businesses, places, events and incidents are either the products of the author's imagination or used in a fictitious manner. Any resemblance to actual persons, living or dead, or actual events is purely coincidental.

Cover Design: Emily Wittig Designs

Developmental Edits: Melanie Yu, Made Me Blush Books

Line Editing and Proofreading: VB Edits

Formatting: Micalea Smeltzer

*For the girlies who love a man in glasses.
You're welcome.*

PART ONE

one

I ease up on the steering wheel, my white knuckles slowly turning back to pink as I pass the city limit sign for Parkerville, Maine. A cross-country move in a U-Haul probably wasn't my smartest move, considering I hate driving and I've never been behind the wheel of anything bigger than a sedan.

Hiring movers and flying would've been the easiest route, but I wanted to do this on my own, and I needed this road trip to clear my head.

I left everything I knew in California, but with my divorce finalized, I couldn't stay there anymore. It no longer felt like home.

And more than anything, I need a massive change in my life.

The old me would've never quit her job, and she never

would have purchased a building sight unseen in a city she's never even visited.

That's right. Not just a house—a whole building.

The new me? She's desperate to break free of the confines she put herself in a long time ago.

I want new adventures. I want to do things I've never had the chance to do since I married young and put all my focus first into getting a law degree, then into my work. All that effort, and look what that got me. Unhappiness and a divorce, to boot.

Inhaling a shaky breath, I glance at the glowing green lights of the clock on the dash.

11:11

I close my eyes and make a wish.

I wish for this move to be the right thing.

Quickly, I focus on the road again, scanning my surroundings.

Maybe it's cheesy to wish on numbers, or on shooting stars, but I'll take all the potential luck the universe tosses my way.

As I navigate the unfamiliar streets of the small town, I send up a silent thank-you to said universe that it's nearly midnight. There isn't a soul around when I pull up outside the old brick building. The lower level will soon be renovated into an art studio, and the apartment on the second story is where I'll be living. I didn't see the point in buying a house when I discovered that little perk.

I sag against the steering wheel as I take in the details of the structure. When I purchased it, I knew it would need a lot of work, but knowing and seeing are two totally different things.

I'm once again grateful for the late hour as I attempt to parallel park the U-Haul in front of the building. If there were bystanders milling about, witnessing the chaos as I back up, pull forward, readjust, and back up again, I'd probably be panicking. It takes a solid fifteen minutes before the truck is mostly in its designated spot. Hopefully it's parked well enough to keep me from earning myself a parking ticket on day one. The last thing I want is to introduce myself to the town by breaking the law. That would be my luck since it's been in the shitter lately.

With the truck parked, I shoot off a text to my younger sister, Izzy, to let her know I've made it.

Almost immediately, my phone vibrates in my hand. I accept the FaceTime call with a swipe of a finger, knowing I must look terrible. I've been living out of hotels for the better part of a week. It's a fifty-hour drive from my old home to my new one, so I decided to take my time.

Plus, driving the U-Haul for long stretches of time was terrible for my anxiety.

Izzy's face pops up on the screen, her hair slicked back in a sleek bun. Her makeup is flawless, her lips a vibrant blood red. The room she's in is dim, but from the look of the background, she's in a booth at a restaurant.

"Late dinner?" It's after eight for her.

She shrugs, making her off-the-shoulder top slip just a little lower. "It's for a video."

Izzy started vlogging at sixteen and quickly gained a

massive social media following. At twenty-five now, she's created an empire using her name and personality alone.

"You didn't have to call me," I say, stifling a yawn. I'm ready to hit the bed, except my bed is in the back of the truck, so that won't be happening any time soon. At least I had the forethought to buy a sleeping bag on my trip here.

"Turn on the light or something, goober. I can't even see your face," she chides playfully, resting her chin on her fist.

"Oh, right." Obediently, I flick on the light above me.

"Put a little cream under your eyes tonight. Your dark circles are giving vampire and not in a cute way." She winks.

"Ha, ha." I fake laugh and rub my eyes, but I can't stop the small smile creeping up my face. "That's what I was going for."

She leans a little closer to the screen. "Actually, it's a bit Robert Pattinson in *Batman*."

I survey myself in the small video window and cringe. She's not lying. "I forgot I had makeup on."

"Clearly." She giggles. She leans to one side, almost off-screen, and takes a bite of something I can't see. "Don't forget to take it off. Skincare is important. Remember what I told you—oil cleanse first and then face wash."

I snag my tumbler from the cupholder and bring it to my mouth, only to discover it's empty. Great.

"Yeah, I remember." I didn't remember. I have way too much on my mind to be concerned about the order in which I should use the skincare products Izzy forced me to buy. "I better go so I can get some of my things inside. I'll call you tomorrow."

"Okay—I just wanted to see you. I miss you." She frowns, and her eyes fill with tears. Izzy lives in LA, so even before my big move, we were still separated by several hours, but now we're on opposite coasts.

"I miss you too. Once I get settled and open the studio, you should visit. You could vlog it." As much as I hate being on camera, the exposure could do wonders for me.

She fiddles with the gold chain around her neck, fighting a smile. "You never want to be in my vlogs."

I shrug. "That was before."

When I was a lawyer and married and wasn't worried about making ends meet.

She tilts her head and her eyes swim with sympathy.

My stomach sinks at the expression. I don't want her to feel sorry for me. *I* don't want to feel sorry for me. I've already grieved my marriage. It's over, done with. Chase is in my past. My family doesn't understand my need to move so far away, but a fresh start, a total clean slate where no one knows me, is what I need in order to heal.

"Right," she finally says. "I'd love that when you're ready."

"Love you, Izzy-Tizzy."

She rolls her eyes at the nickname and sticks her tongue out. "I love you more, Via-Mia. Text me when you're settled so I know you haven't been hacked up by some small-town ax-murderer and fed to the pigs."

I huff a laugh. "That was a very specific scenario, and now I'm terrified, so thank you for that."

"You're welcome. Bye." She holds up two fingers in a peace sign, then the video cuts off.

Silence fills the cab of the truck. It's a stark reminder. It's only me now.

It takes far too long to muster the energy to drag myself out of the truck. My legs are stiff, and my bladder is screaming at me. I've had to pee for a solid thirty minutes, but I refused to stop when I first felt like I needed to pee.

"The keys should be around here somewhere," I mutter to myself, heading to the front of the building.

The real estate agent said she'd leave them under the gnome flowerpot. I thought she was joking until she sent me a picture. At first, I couldn't believe she was just leaving keys to a whole building under a flowerpot, but then I realized that small towns do things differently. That, and she laughed at me when I asked if someone would use them to break in.

Now that I'm standing in front of the dilapidated building, I understand why my question was so laughable. I looked through photos of the place before making the purchase, but now that I'm here, I'm certain the photographer used one of those beauty filters. In the glow of the old-fashioned streetlamps, the brick building looks like it will topple over if a wolf shows up and huffs and puffs a little too hard. Kind of like me, ironically.

There, beside the door, is the gnome flowerpot, as promised. I pick it up and slide the key ring out of its hiding spot. There are two keys, one for the front of the store and one for the apartment upstairs.

Staring down at the keys, I let myself have a brief *what the fuck?* moment.

I can't believe I'm doing this.

Closing my fingers, I form a fist around the keys so the grooved edges dig into my palm. It hurts a little, though far less than my mangled heart. It's fitting. A new beginning should be a little painful. Growing pains are natural. Keys in hand, I decide here and now to embrace each one.

Feeling a little lighter, I head to the front door and let myself in.

But as I look at the space, my new beginning, my heart falls. "Oh, fuck."

It's even worse in the light of day.

Hands on my hips, I scan the store space, feeling absolutely helpless. Anxiety seizes my chest at the sight of all the dirt, dust, and grime that will need to be scrubbed away. I'm going to need a hazmat suit. Seriously. This place is probably full of rodents and bugs. It's a hoarder's dream. The entire space is filled with stacks of newspapers, a mountain of odds and ends, and broken furniture.

The bright spot in all of this is that the apartment above is in much better shape. From what I can tell, its last inhabitant at least knew how to keep the place clean. It'll need some sprucing up, sure, but that's nothing in comparison to the task I'm currently staring down.

I have no one to blame for this but myself. The real estate agent warned me this place would need some TLC.

She probably could have elaborated, but I also could have asked. Frankly, I was afraid that if I delved too deep, I would chicken out. And I refuse to chicken out.

I pull my phone out of the back pocket of my jeans and tap on the Notes app so I can start making a list of what needs to be done.

Priority number one: get a dumpster here ASAP. Next, hire a contractor to whip this place into shape. I'll also need to find the nearest home store and buy new appliances. The refrigerator and stove in the apartment are relics from the eighties. If there's one thing I love to do besides create art, it's cook, so updated appliances are a must.

Satisfied with the start of my list, I put it away and decide to ignore the mess I have to wade through for the moment. Right now, I need breakfast, and since I have no food, I'm hoping there's a diner or restaurant within walking distance.

Out front, in the daylight, I take a look at my surroundings. My store looks to be in the middle of the old town. And between the buildings across the street, I get glimpses of the water. The atmosphere is idyllic. Most of the original brick buildings are well kept, unlike the one I purchased, and though the town is small, it's vibrant. Passersby are chatting with one another, each wearing a smile. Several stores have their front doors propped open, and the florist on the corner is displaying bouquets out front.

I smile to myself as I continue down the street, already feeling certain this is where I'm meant to be.

This simple community feel doesn't exist in San Francisco.

Up ahead, *Norma's Diner* is painted in yellow block letters on the side of the building.

As if on cue, my stomach growls.

When I push the door open, the bell above rings, signaling my arrival.

And every eye in the place homes in on me.

I freeze beneath the curious stares, my heart lodged in my throat. From the wide, unblinking eyes, one would think I look like I crash landed from an alien planet, but when I dip my chin and assess myself, I don't find anything wrong with my jeans or my black turtleneck.

"Can I help you?" a woman behind the counter asks, her gray hair pinned back. "You look lost, dear."

"No." I shake my head, breaking out into a sweat under the scrutiny of all these patrons. "Not lost. I wanted to get breakfast." I wring my hands, willing them to stop trembling.

She examines me for a long, silent moment. "All right," she finally says. "Grab a table wherever. I'll be there in a second."

I shuffle past occupied tables and slide into a booth in the back corner. My butt has barely settled on the ripped pleather seat when conversation resumes. I hadn't realized how silent the dining room was until this moment. I tilt my chin so my hair falls forward to shield my face, because despite the conversation now buzzing, I can still feel people looking at me.

I've never experienced this kind of guarded attention before, having only ever lived in and visited big cities where no one bats an eye at strangers.

The woman who spoke when I entered approaches, menu extended, tapping the plastic cover with long red acrylic nails.

"You're not from around here."

It's a statement, not a question, but I answer anyway. "No, I just moved to town."

I swear there's a collective gasp in the diner.

"You moved here?" She looks me up and down. She's not judging, at least it doesn't seem like it. Her head is tilted to the side and her brows are high, making her look perplexed more than anything. "To Parkerville?"

Gently, I take the menu she's still holding out and clasp it to my chest like a shield. "Yes. I bought the store down the road. It used to be a consignment shop."

"Oh, yes." She nods. "We noticed it had sold."

Around us, patrons murmur in agreement, obviously eavesdropping on our conversation. My shoulders cave in at the attention.

"Didn't know it had gone to an out-of-towner, though." She puts a hand on her hip. "What brought you to Parkerville?"

I clear my throat and go with the simple truth. Small towns are known for nosy people, right? So they'll find out eventually. Might as well hear it from me. "I got divorced and needed a change."

"How'd you find this place?"

I blow out a breath, resigned to enduring this interrogation. If I don't, I may never eat. This woman is obviously in no rush to take my order. "Lots of Google searches. I was looking for a change. Somewhere completely different, and I love the water. This seemed like the right fit."

"Hmm." She taps her long red nails against the table. "You're not planning to fix that place up, then turn around and sell it to an out-of-town corporation, are you? What about luxury apartments? If that's the case, I have news for you: we don't want to be a destination town. We like things the way they are."

My stomach twists at the accusation. "No, that's not my plan at all." She's being rather rude, so the last thing I want to do is open up about my plans, but I stick with the theme I've got going so far—open honesty. I've read people enough over the years to know it'll be in my favor. "I'm turning the storefront into an art store—a place where people can come to paint and draw, all kinds of things like that, and I'll be living in the apartment above."

She regards me for a moment longer, a smile slowly spreading across her face. "In that case, welcome to Parkerville. I'm Dolores. What can I get you to drink?"

I rest my arms on the table and heave out a breath, exhausted but grateful that the inquisition is over. This kind of confrontation is exactly why I left the courtroom. I might be good at making my case, but it doesn't mean I like it. "A coffee with cream and sugar would be lovely to start."

"Coming right up." With another tap, she's gone, making a beeline to the counter for my coffee.

With her retreat, the conversations around me resume once more.

I'm just settling on the veggie omelet when Dolores returns, and once I've placed my order, I fix my coffee with the right amounts of cream and sugar. That first tentative sip from the steaming mug is nirvana. Closing my eyes, I savor the taste of real coffee. The gas station sludge I've been subsisting on hasn't been doing the job. Wrapping my hands around the mug, I let it warm me from the outside in.

It's strange to think that I'm home now. This is the beginning of my new life. The biggest risk I've ever taken. I left behind a high-paying job and my friends and family for a future filled with uncertainty.

Even so, this feels like the right decision.

This is where I belong.

At least for now.

three

Covered in a sheen of sweat, I haul out the fifth trash bag of the day. It's a fight to get it up and over the edge of the dumpster that was delivered this morning. I've been here for a week, and I've barely made a dent in the disaster of the storefront. There's no point in calling contractors for quotes when the space is so cluttered it's impossible to see the floors or most of the walls. I could've hired someone to clean up, but I'm trying to be careful with my money. It's going to cost plenty to get this place updated, so I'll do all I can on my own and save my money for the bigger projects.

I tug off my heavy-duty gloves, wiggling my bare fingers to bring life back into them, and brush my hair away from my damp forehead. Sitting on the curb beside the dumpster, I take a minute to suck a few breaths of fresh fall air into my lungs. The smell in the building is more than a little gag inducing.

Tipping to one side, I pull my phone from my back pocket, unsurprised to find nothing waiting for me. Izzy is the only person from my old life that's bothered to contact me since I left California. Even my own mother is ignoring me. Why? Because she loved Chase. In her eyes, *I'm* the one who failed.

I didn't give him what he wanted, so he moved on to greener pastures.

You should've tried harder. Fix this.

I would've if I could've, but the negative pregnancy tests were piling up, and my body was failing me—failing us.

I couldn't get pregnant, so he found someone who could.

His secretary.

So fucking cliché.

I laughed when he told me. Hysterical, hiccupping chokes of laughter. If I didn't laugh, then I'd cry. Not only can she give him a baby, but she's only twenty-five. I shouldn't have been so blindsided. He's a man, after all. But we'd been together for so long. He was my *best* friend. And then he went and pulled the rug out from under me. He'd been cheating on me for months, and I'd been too lost in the pain of trying and failing to get pregnant and drowning in a massive workload.

With a thumb, I tap on the messages icon and click on my mother's name. She's read the one I sent the morning after I arrived. It was a quick check-in, letting her know I'd made it and I was safe. She didn't even offer me a thumbs-up.

She'll get over it eventually. Although at this point in my life, I'm not sure I care. I've put my parents' happiness above mine for way too long. They're the sole reason I became a lawyer. I never had an interest in it, but they pushed me down a traditional career path. And I let them because I wanted them to be proud of me. Don't get me wrong, I did enjoy family law, but it wasn't my passion.

Standing, I tuck my phone back in my pocket and tug my gloves on. Then, with a fortifying breath, I pull my shoulders back and return to the danger zone.

Maybe my mom is right to be mad at me. This *is* crazy. I don't know what I'm doing—running a business, teaching art. I've always been artistic, and it was my safe space when I was growing up. My dream was to go to art school, but I was constantly being told to pick a more practical career. When I made the decision to quit my job, the thought of going back to my artistic roots settled my spirit in a way nothing ever had. While this might be a wild idea, it's the right choice for me.

Picking up a fresh trash bag, I shake it out and pick up a wad of soiled, ripped paper towel. The movement disturbs a mouse, sending the little thing rushing past my booted foot. The scream that rips out of my throat is hilariously high-pitched. I've seen the mouse droppings. I knew it was likely I'd find a live one, but knowing and seeing are two different things. My heart races behind my rib cage.

Call pest control. I add the task to my mental checklist so I can add it to my real one later.

Blowing out a breath, I tip my head back and inspect the exposed beams crisscrossing the ceiling. This place really does have good bones. It's got potential. It's worth it. These are all things I've been reminding myself of for days.

This will all be worth it in the end.

"YOU GOT ALL OF THAT IN THERE BY YOURSELF?" My sister is slack-jawed, taking in the space as I hold the phone out and rotate it, panning the apartment.

"Um ... sorta."

She arches a brow as I tap the screen to flip the camera. "What does 'sorta' mean?"

I prop the device up against the sugar canister on the kitchen counter and pick up my cup of coffee. Closing my eyes and forcing my shoulders to relax, I take a generous sip. "A couple of locals saw me struggling and helped out."

With a snort, Izzy scoops up her little white fluff ball of a dog. He's a Maltese named Wonton. "LA could never. You're more likely to get robbed than to get help."

"Unfortunately, true." I take another sip of coffee, brewed in my Nespresso—a relic from my old life.

"The place is cute," she goes on. "What plans do you have for it?"

I look over my shoulder at the plain wall behind me. "I

was thinking I'd do funky wallpaper there. The whole place needs a paint job and new flooring is a must."

The apartment is in much better shape than the store below, but it needs more updates than I originally thought. The bathroom is a total gut job. The water pressure sucks and the toilet only flushes half the time. I'm pretty sure what I thought was a design on the tiled walls is actually mold. I'm probably living in a total health hazard. So not only will I have contractors quote the downstairs renovation, but I've decided I might as well get started up here too, rather than waiting. I plan on being here for a long time, so this place needs to be livable. And if I ever decide to rent it out, I definitely can't do it like this.

"It'll be really cute when you get it all done." Either she's just putting on a brave face for my sake, or she can really see the potential. "Let me know when I can come visit."

I snort. "That'll be a while." My to-do list is endless.

"I can always come stay in a hotel."

"There are no hotels here." Not the kind she's used to, at least. "There's a motel that looks straight out of a horror movie, and there's an inn. That's it."

"Ooh, an inn?" She claps Wonton's paws. "That sounds cute. Maybe I could vlog it."

"You really think your followers would want to see this place? Parkerville isn't exactly a destination getaway." I think it's cute and idyllic, but that doesn't mean others will.

She lifts one shoulder. "Content is content. I can make anywhere a destination. You know that. But enough about me. Do you have any fun plans for the weekend?"

I snort. "Plans? Izzy, I haven't had plans since before I got married."

She sets a wiggling Wonton on the ground and leans in closer. "You owe it to me. It's Friday, go out tonight. Do something crazy."

"Something crazy?" I wander to the sink with my empty coffee cup and rinse it out. "Like what?"

"I don't know. Go to a bar. Kiss a handsome stranger. Get out there, Via. Live life. You deserve it."

I *had* thought about going out tonight, but there's no way I won't feel awkward. I don't know a soul in town, and the thought of a rehash of the diner experience makes me break out into a cold sweat. There is a bigger town about twenty minutes away. I could go there.

My heart lifts a little at the prospect of getting out. Life has been lonely since I arrived in Parkerville. "Maybe I will."

Izzy's smile is nearly blinding. "No maybe about it. You're going. You still have that green dress, right? You know which one I'm talking about?"

Of course I know. I bought it when I was with her. My intent was to wear it for my anniversary. Except by the time the date rolled around, Chase and I were separated.

"I kept it," I admit, ducking my chin. It was expensive, so I probably should have returned it, but it's gorgeous. I considered it, but in the end, I couldn't part with it. I haven't had the opportunity yet, but I deserve to get to wear that dress. Fuck that slime bag Chase.

"Good." She grins, rubbing her hands together like a

villain in a cheesy superhero film. "Wear it. It makes your tits look great."

"Izzy!" I bark out a laugh.

"What? I'm only speaking the truth. If you weren't my sister, I'd motorboat you in that dress."

I bury my face in my hands and smother a laugh. She's only trying to make me feel better. Chase dashed every ounce of my confidence. Sometimes, at my lowest moments, I still hear his voice in my head telling me he's not attracted to me anymore.

"Don't chicken out on me, Via. I mean it."

"Fine," I agree, pulling the long strands of my dark hair back into a ponytail. I secure it with an elastic and pull it tight. "I'll go."

She does a happy dance, then wags a finger at the camera. "I'll know if you don't. I'll be tracking you on Find My iPhone."

"Okay, stalker."

"Have fun, Via. That's all I ask. You deserve it."

Fun. I'm not sure I even know what that is anymore.

four

I almost don't recognize my reflection.

It's been so long since I've bothered to do my hair or put on makeup. I poke my cheek just to be sure the woman staring back at me is, in fact, me.

I snap a selfie and send it to Izzy.

Barely ten seconds pass before she responds. The woman is always glued to her phone.

> Izzy: Hot babe! Wife me up! <heart eye emoji>
>
> Izzy: The dress is a 10/10 and so are you
>
> Me: Thanks.
>
> Izzy: Where are you going??
>
> Me: A bar called Monday's.

I pull up the address on Google Maps and forward it to her before she can ask for it.

> Izzy: If you go home with a guy, text me. Just in case he's a murderer
>
> Me: I'm definitely not going home with anyone.
>
> Izzy: NO
>
> Izzy: You have to
>
> Izzy: Get laid
>
> Izzy: I'm begging you
>
> Me: You're begging your sister to get laid? That's weird.

A heartbeat later, my phone rings in my hand. Shaking my head, I answer. I put her on speaker and set the device on the counter so I can inspect my lipstick in the mirror. The lighting in the bathroom sucks, and I'm afraid I missed a spot.

"You know what I meant," Izzy gripes. Wonton barks his agreement in the background. "You're newly single. Your vagina needs a spiritual cleanse after that fuckwad."

"A spiritual cleanse?" I throw my head back and cackle. "Are you implying I need to douse my vagina with holy water?"

"*Yes.* You were with Chase for what? Eight years? It's time to get under, over, and all around someone else."

"It feels weird." My stomach knots, and my reflection

frowns back at me. "I haven't gone out like this in so long." I bite my lip to hold back the words threatening to escape. That I never thought I'd have to again. Though I'm sure it's implied.

"Listen," she goes on, "you may not even find a cute guy at this place. I don't know how these small towns work. Hallmark makes it seem like there's a hot guy on every street corner, but I doubt that's true." She chuckles. "All I'm saying is that *if* there's a cute guy, and *if* you hit it off, then you should see where it goes. Whether that's a one-night stand or a date or just someone to drink a beer with. You're allowed to let loose."

I swallow past the lump that's formed in my throat. "I know that."

"Do you?"

I sigh, putting my makeup back in my bag. "I do, but it's not that easy for me. Like you pointed out, it's been a long time since I was with someone other than Chase. I'm not familiar with this whole hookup culture thing like you are."

She snorts. "I feel like I should be offended, but I'm not. I won't keep you any longer. Have fun. Do what I would do."

I laugh. "That's dangerous advice."

"I know. Love you, sissy."

"Love you too." I end the call and grip the stained porcelain sink. It's only me and my reflection now. "It's just a bar. Food and drinks. You can do it."

Before I can talk myself out of it, I tuck my slim wallet into my bra. I keep my phone in my hand and take the stairs. Out front, I climb into my new Nissan Altima. I sold my Mercedes before I left San Francisco and used the money to pay for the Nissan outright. The Mercedes was practically new, and maybe I should have kept it, but once I saw it for what it really was—a gift from Chase because he felt sorry for cheating on me, though I didn't know it at the time—I wanted it gone.

I blast music on the way to the bar in an effort to drown out my thoughts. If I chicken out and turn back now, Izzy will hop on the next flight to Maine just so she can scold me in person.

I can't even remember the last time I was in a bar. College, maybe?

And here I am, back at the starting gate. Single and confused. I'm not even sure who I am or what I want. Since my divorce, my thoughts have revolved around getting out of California. I did it. I'm here. But beyond working on the store, I don't know what comes next for me.

I haven't given dating any thought, really. Not out of any sort of loyalty to Chase, because fuck him, but because I'm not sure what I want. I *think* I'd like to find love again someday, but for now, being unattached feels like the best idea.

It doesn't mean I can't put myself out there, though.

I'm severely out of practice, so why not brush up on my skills?

I wasn't kidding when I told Izzy I knew nothing about hookup culture, but I'm determined to be open-minded about it.

It's been a solid six months since I had sex, and before

that, it was sparse. Chase and I had always had a good sex life ... until we didn't. I thought it was a rough patch. I thought we were busy with work and life and that physical affection had taken a temporary back burner. And I was so wrong. The physical affection wasn't there, because he was giving his to someone else.

You're overthinking this. Go to the bar, sit your ass down, and order a drink. What happens beyond that doesn't matter.

I blow out a pent-up breath.

I can do this.

The bar parking lot is packed. I circle a few times before I end up parking in a patch of grass. Saying a silent prayer that I don't get ticketed for it, I pluck my phone from the cupholder and head inside.

I'm hit with the yeasty smell of beer the second I open the door, along with the sounds of raucous conversation and rock music.

The interior is mostly wood—floors, walls, and the bar itself—with empty beer bottles dangling from the ceiling for decoration. Interesting. Drum-like lights spread throughout the space give off a golden-orange glow, casting heavy shadows. It gives an almost intimate feel despite how packed this place is.

I suppose it was naive to think that a bar in Maine wouldn't be crowded. Clearly, I haven't been out in the world enough.

Striding up to the long u-shaped bar, I search for an empty stool. The only one available is in one of the darkest corners, near the end on the right side, but that works for me. I can lurk in the shadows to people watch.

I sit, tugging at the hem of my dress. I'm not used to showing so much skin. Within moments, a bartender makes his way over to me.

He leans against the counter, the sleeves of his black tee hugging thick, tattooed biceps. He's good-looking with dark, slicked back hair and a beard. His eyes are dark too, a warm shade of brown.

"Hey," he raises his voice over the music. "I'm Jesse. What can I get you?"

"Oh ... um." I hadn't even considered this part. I'm not a beer connoisseur. Chase and I were much more into wine, spending a lot of weekends at wineries near our place. "What do you recommend?"

He smirks a little at that. "You trust me?"

"Right now, I think I have to," I admit, wrinkling my nose.

He holds up a finger and picks up a plastic sample cup. "Hold on." Spinning on his heel, he swaggers to the beer tap and returns with a small sampling.

Tentative, I take it from him and bring it to my lips. "Mm." I hum. "That's really good." It has a slight citrusy flavor. "I'll take that."

He raps his knuckles against the shiny wood bar top. "Coming right up...?" He arches a brow.

I blink at him, confused by his hesitation.

Oh. *My name.* Wow, I am so out of practice.

"Via."

"Via," he drawls, a smile tugging at his lips. "That's different."

"My mom liked the name Olivia," I blurt out over the clash of drums. "But she wanted something more unique."

"I like it." He grins, his eyes sparkling as he looks me over. They linger a little too long on the swell of my breasts. He's cute, more than cute, actually. Possibly a contender if I'm really going to do this. Step out of my box and go home with a stranger. Though from his swagger and the easy way he flirts, I wonder if this is a regular thing for him. There's nothing wrong with it if that's the case, but the idea is intimidating.

He wanders down the bar again, and when he returns, he slides a full glass in front of me. "What else can I get you? Food?"

"Do you have a menu?"

With a nod, he grabs one from behind the bar. "Flag me down when you're ready." With a wink, he's off, going to tend to other customers.

My phone vibrates on the bar top before I can take a look at the menu. With a huff, I shake my head at my sister's name lighting up the screen.

> Izzy: Any prospects?

> Izzy: Should I Amazon Prime a box of condoms? Do they have same-day delivery out there?

> Izzy: Even if they do, they probably won't make it in time but it's the thought that counts

With a sigh, I tap out a response.

> Me: Maybe. The bartender is nice looking, but he seems a little too sure of himself.

> Izzy: Don't overthink it

> Me: I'm going to order food. Leave me alone.

> Izzy: Fine fine

I turn my phone face down so that if she continues texting, I won't be tempted to read her messages. Then I scan the menu. I don't want anything too greasy, since it might upset my already nervous stomach, but I don't want to be the chick who sits at a bar and eats a salad either.

The next time Jesse is in my vicinity, I wave for him.

He comes right over and props himself up against the bar, hitting me with a flirtatious smile.

I wait for my stomach to dip or for my heart to race. Nope. Zilch. Not a thing.

At least I'm trying. It's the thought that counts, right?

"Can I get the grilled chicken sandwich with mayo on the side?"

"Sure thing." He takes the menu from me and puts it back behind the bar. "It'll be a bit of a wait. The kitchen is backed up."

I wave. "It's not a big deal."

With another smile, he turns and heads to the computer to put my order in.

Across the bar, a chorus of raucous cheers breaks out. I squint, searching for the cause of the commotion. It only takes a moment to pinpoint it. Ten or so young-ish guys, probably in their early twenties, are stationed around a table, enjoying a night out. The guy on the end, clearly the center of attention, raises a shot glass to his mouth while his friends cheer him on. His dark hair is rumpled, like he's been running his fingers through it. Black-framed glasses sit on his nose, and his angular jaw is dotted with stubble.

He's gorgeous, but more than that, he's magnetic. Something about him draws me in and refuses to let go. Maybe it's his crooked smile, or the way he effortlessly commands attention. Whatever it is, it feels like he's sucked every ounce of oxygen from my lungs.

He takes the shot, and his friends cheer even louder. When he slams the glass down on the table and throws his arms up in the air, he's immediately approached by one of his buddies. This guy is wearing a shit-eating grin and holding another full shot glass out to him. The man of the hour throws his head back and laughs. As he turns to his friend's offering, his eyes collide with mine.

In a rush, all the air is forced back into my lungs. I gulp it down greedily, like I was pulled underwater unprepared and have finally made my way back to the surface. I'm trapped in his gaze, unable to break eye contact. He doesn't turn away either, and as the seconds tick on, my cheeks heat with a mix of discomfort and desire.

His friend throws his arm around him, jostling the mystery man and breaking our connection. Finally, he looks away. The moment he does, I come back to myself and drop my eyes.

Holy shit.

I felt more in those five seconds than I have in a long, *long* time. My skin is heated and my mouth has gone desert dry. Bringing my beer to my lips, I tip it back and wave to get Jesse's attention. I order a glass of water, making a concerted effort not to look in the guy's direction again.

My eyes don't want to listen to my brain, though. The next time I find myself peeking over at him, he's wearing a black headband that reads *Happy Birthday*, and he's shaking his head at his friends.

I can't hear their conversation, but I can read the lips of the guy closest to him when he says, "You know the rules."

Suddenly, the good-looking man with messy dark hair is watching me again. He grins, a dimple popping out in his right cheek, and points at me.

His friends all swivel to look in my direction.

When he winks, I melt into a puddle beneath the stool.

Oh my God. Is this my main character moment?

I want to pick up my phone and text Izzy, but I refrain. This is crazy anyway. The bar may be dark, but it's obvious this guy is a lot younger than I am. He might be cute, but I can't go there. Can I?

No, of course not.

I'm being foolish. He probably wasn't even looking at me in that way. I'm so out of practice I'm reading more into it than what's there.

Jesse appears and places a glass of water on the bar in front of me, then points to my mostly full beer. "You don't like it?"

"Oh, no, it's good. I'm just not a big drinker. It'll take me a while." I smile at him, a flirtier smile than I'd normally give.

He slips a straw onto the lacquered bar top beside the glass. "Ah, gotcha. I'll go check on your food. It shouldn't be much longer."

"Thanks." I rip the paper off and stick the straw in my water glass. In a matter of seconds, I've gulped down half of the water, and by the time I set it down again, I'm considerably cooler.

I'm so focused on hydrating that I'm caught off guard when the stool beside me scrapes against the hardwood floor and a body drops into it.

"Hello."

I don't know *how* I know it's him, but I do.

Slowly, so I don't give myself whiplash, I turn to the left to take in my new companion. The grin he's got trained on me isn't cocky in any way. He's not looking at me like he's certain he can get me into bed. In fact the way his lips quirk up a little more on one corner is sweet, almost shy. His glasses slip down his nose when he scoots a little closer to the bar, and as if it's habit, he uses an index finger to quickly push them back into place. His eyes are a beautiful shade of emerald green with gold flecks, and his dark lashes are ridiculously long. Why are the best lashes always wasted on men?

I can't even be mad. This guy is so beautiful, he deserves them. He looks more like a model who should be living it up in LA than a small-town guy in the middle of nowhere, Maine.

Angling forward, he clasps his hands on the bar in front of him. His skin is pale and dusted with dark hair that does nothing to camouflage how veiny his arms are. God, every bit of him is a work of art. He's the kind of man the great sculptors of the Renaissance would weep over.

When I follow the line of his arms up to his shoulders and then to his face, I realize he's grinning at me. Shit. I've been silently checking him out like a man-starved freak.

"Hi," I finally say, my cheeks flaming.

"Lost in thought?"

"Yeah." I latch on to the excuse he's given me. "Sorry about that. I zone out sometimes. This isn't normally my scene." At least the last part is true.

"I'd ask if I could buy you another drink, but..." He tips his head at my mostly full beer.

"Are you even legal?" I blurt stupidly. *Of course he's legal, Via. He was just taking shots with his friends.*

He points to the ridiculous *Happy Birthday* headband he's still wearing. "As of today, yes."

"Prove it." The words are far more coy than I intend.

Grinning—and causing that dimple to flicker into existence—he pulls a worn black leather wallet from his pocket and takes out a driver's license. "Check it out." He slides it over and flicks his fingers at it lazily. "I don't have anything to hide."

"Reid Astor Crawford," I read out. "Birthday ... today. Twenty-one-years old." I gulp at that last part.

He wasn't lying.

Twenty-one.

I turned thirty-two a month ago.

That makes him eleven years younger than me.

Ironic. That it's my lucky number.

"Satisfied?" He quirks an amused brow.

I hand him his ID and lift my chin. "I suppose."

His smile only gets bigger. "What's your name? It's only fair now that you know my whole name." He cocks his head to the side, waiting.

I clear my throat. "Via. I'm Via."

"So, if I can't buy you a drink, Via, then can I buy you dinner?"

I try to smother my smile. "Shouldn't I be the one offering to buy you dinner, since you're the birthday boy?"

God, I want to text my sister so badly. I need her help to make sure I'm doing this right. Is this flirting? I think it is. At least, that's what I'm going for.

"I'll be more than happy to pay for your meal tonight, but I was thinking we could set a time to go on a real date. What do you think?"

"I think that's ... very forward of you." And impressive, the way he's not beating around the bush, if wholly unexpected. "Are all guys your age like this?"

He tugs on the collar of his tee, giving me a glimpse of a thin silver necklace hidden beneath. "Like what?"

"So sure of yourselves."

He shrugs. "I don't have anything to lose if you're not interested, *but*," he draws out the word, that adorable smile of his making my stomach dip, "I have something to gain if you are."

Oh, he is *smooth*, like the creamiest peanut butter.

"Okay, let's pretend I say yes to this date. What would it entail?"

With one brow cocked, he looks me over. "Why don't you say yes and find out?"

I angle closer and am immediately hit by a whiff of his cologne. It's clean and woodsy, like a bright summer's day. How is it possible to smell so good after throwing back shots in a crowded bar like this?

"I'm not really looking to date," I admit, biting my lip.

His focus falls to my lips, and his tongue slides out the tiniest bit to wet his lips. "What are you looking for?"

"I'm not really sure. Some fun, I guess."

With a chuckle, he drops his chin and shakes his head. "At least you're honest."

I realize then that my food has been sitting in front of me. Jesse is on the other end of the bar, so it's likely been sitting here for a while. I snag a fry and nibble on the end of it, confirming that they're still mostly warm.

"You're the one with a tattoo that says temporary." I tap the inside of his forearm where the word is spelled out in a small typewriter-style font.

He booms a laugh. "Temporary, but not for the reason you think."

I bite into another fry. "Explain then."

He traces his finger over the word. It's small. Looking at it now, I'm surprised I even noticed it.

Fine. I caught sight of it on one of the many times I checked out his veiny arms.

"I wanted the reminder that life, all of this," he waves a hand to encompass the world around us, "is all temporary. I want to cherish every single day." Sobering, he clears his throat. "My mom died when I was young. I guess you could say that her death had quite the impact."

Heart aching for him, I lay my hand on top of his.

His eyes widen and dart to mine at the contact.

"I'm sorry. I know that's cliché, but I mean it."

"Thanks." He turns his hand over, palm up, and loops our fingers together. Again, he's so damn *smooth*. "Now tell me something about you. Something that isn't so happy."

I don't even have to think, and I'm strangely interested in what his reaction will be. "I'm recently divorced."

Huffing out a breath of air, he shakes his head. "Your ex must be an idiot."

Tendrils of warmth work their way through me. He didn't balk or fumble for an excuse to walk away. "What makes you say that?"

"Because you're fucking gorgeous and nice to talk to. If I had a woman like you, I'd never let her go."

The look he gives me is pure sex and something more, something deeper that has my thighs clenching together.

"I'm thirty-two," I blurt out.

He puts his free hand over his heart. "Thank God, we're both legal."

A stunned laugh escapes me. "That doesn't bother you? That I'm older than you?"

"No." There isn't an ounce of hesitation in his response. "Does it bother you that I'm younger?"

With a gulp, I survey him, getting lost for a heartbeat in those uniquely green eyes. Shaking myself out of my stupor, I dip my chin. "Yes."

His smile returns. "Good."

"Good?" I rear back. "How is that good?"

"It means you're thinking about me in less than decent ways." He moves in so close I can feel the heat radiating from him. "Am I wrong?"

I don't respond, but it's answer enough.

Unfazed, he sits straighter again, keeping his hand locked with mine. "Are you still hungry?"

I shake my head. "No."

He stands, finally releasing his hold, pulls a few bills from his wallet, and sets them on the bar.

"I—what are you doing?" Throat suddenly tight, I look from the cash to him and back again.

"Come home with me." He smiles. "You are the one who said you wanted fun."

My heart races, pounding a furious rhythm against my breastbone. This is what I came for, yet at the first suggestion of a night of no-strings fun, I'm chickening out. Partly because I didn't think I'd actually find a worthy prospect, but mostly because the last thing I expected was to be propositioned by a guy more than a decade younger. A guy who, I have to admit, makes me feel more attraction than my husband managed to do during our final year of marriage.

"What about your friends?" I'm grasping at straws here, searching for an excuse to walk away.

He tips his head toward the table where he and his buddies were celebrating before he approached me. "What friends?"

I crane my neck to look past him, and sure enough, they're all gone. I open my mouth, and when I can't formulate another excuse, I snap it shut again.

"Come on, Via, what do you say?" He leans in, his mouth pressed to my ear. "Don't overthink it. Everything is temporary anyway. Me. You. The stars in the sky. We're all just a blip. Take the risk. I'm worth your while."

My breath catches at the sincerity in his tone. Trembling, I stand, taking in how much taller he is than me. He has to be at least six-three. At five-nine, I tend to tower over other women, and Chase was only a couple of inches taller than me. So this sensation, feeling small, like I'm being swallowed whole by his body, is new for me.

That alone sends a strange thrill through me and bolsters my courage. A single word swirls through my mind.

One word.

Four letters.

"Okay."

five

Outside the bar, I do an awkward shimmy, hit with indecision. Should we take my car, or his, or do we go separately? If we go separately, will I chicken out and head for home instead?

As if sensing my panic, Reid slides a hand down my arm and gives my wrist a light squeeze. "I'm parked over here." He tilts his head toward a restored black Mustang. I'm not familiar with classic car years, but this one is probably from the sixties, maybe the seventies.

"Wow, that Mustang is beautiful."

He peers down at me, brows raised. "You know your cars?"

He unlocks it, then opens the passenger door for me.

"Not really, so don't get too excited." I slide into the car.

It smells like a combination of Reid and clean mint, no

doubt from the pack of gum sitting in the cup holder.

His chuckle is warm. Bracing a hand on the roof of the car, he hovers above me. "I'll take what I can get. Do you know who makes the Mustang?"

I arch a brow. "Ford."

"Fuck." The low, hungry growl that escapes him sends a wave of desire through me. "I think I'm in love."

He closes the door and rounds the hood. When he's settled in the driver's seat, I put a hand on his thigh.

"Wait." Beneath my palm, his leg his warm and firm. The heat of him instantly soaks into me. "I should drive. You've had more to drink than I have. Oh my God, you have to be so drunk. This is so bad. I can't ... I'm taking advantage of you in your inebriated state."

Panic heats my veins. This was such a bad idea. I'm going to kill my little sister for suggesting it.

I scramble for the door handle, but he grasps my hand to halt my movements.

He looks me up and down, his eyes heated. "You want to ... drive my stick?"

My heart stutters in my chest, and my jaw drops open in shock. And then I laugh. "Smooth. Real smooth."

He chuckles. "I'm glad you're amused. I'm not drunk, by the way."

"But I saw—"

"I took one shot. That was it." He starts the car, and the engine purrs to life. "My mom ... it was a drunk driver. The last thing I want to do to celebrate my birthday is get wasted."

"You're not drunk? You're sure?"

He wets his lips, his focus fixed on me. The expression on his face is full of nothing but honesty and heat. "Not even close."

My heart squeezes in my chest as I hold his gaze. "Are we really going to do this?"

His eyes twinkle with humor. "Do what? Go to my place and play Candy Land? What did you think we were going to do?" He rests his forearm on top of the steering wheel and shifts so he's looking at me full-on, a chestnut brown strand of hair falling over his forehead in the process.

I itch to reach over and brush it away, but my nerves hold me back.

"You can go, Via. I won't hold it against you."

Somehow, I know he won't, but despite my nerves, I know I'll regret it if I get out of this car and leave.

"I don't want to go."

A slow smile quirks his lips, making that delicious dimple wink at me from his right cheek. "Good."

I PAUSE IN THE CENTER OF REID'S APARTMENT, suppressing a laugh. "Oh my God, you really do have Candy Land." The game is spread out over a simple wood coffee table.

He locks up behind us and tosses his keys on the

kitchen counter. His apartment is tidy and far nicer than mine. It's not at all what I'd expect of a guy his age.

He stuffs his hands in his pockets and rocks back on his heels, suddenly shy as he watches me take in his space. "Yeah, my niece was over earlier. I was babysitting."

"That's sweet of you."

Hands still deep in his pockets, he shrugs his wide, muscular shoulders. "She's a good kid."

We stand about five feet apart. It's not awkward, per se, but there's an underlying tension between us. Seconds tick by, the air growing thicker. My stomach twists when he doesn't make a move. He's watching me, stance casual and expression patient, like he's waiting for me to make the first move. He knows I'm nervous about this, so he's putting the ball in my court. It's cute, sweet. I appreciate that he's not trying to paw all over me and drag me to bed. That's probably how most guys his age *would* behave. What makes Reid so different? His upbringing? Or is this just who he is?

I take a step closer. Then another. With a deep breath, I garner my courage and close the rest of the distance, until I'm standing before him but we're not touching.

"Hi." I smile up at him.

His lips quirk. "What are you doing, Via?"

"I'm not sure."

"Hmm," he hums. Slowly, he lifts a hand, index finger extended, and brushes my cheek. When he pulls away, he keeps that finger up for me to see. "Eyelash. Make a wish."

My stomach flutters at his request, and I bite back a smile. "No." I shake my head. "You're the birthday boy."

"All right." He twists his lips back and forth in contemplation, then he closes his eyes and blows the lash away.

When he opens them again and homes in on me, the desire swimming in them steals my breath. It makes me wonder what he wished for. I want to ask, but that defeats the purpose.

"Wish made," he whispers. "Now what?"

My breath is shaky, and so is my hand as I reach up and wrap it around the back of his neck. His skin is soft, warm. The hair on his nape tickles my hand. God, he's so tall. Popping up on my tiptoes, I move in closer. Before our mouths touch, his hands are on my hips, helping to stabilize me.

Chase will no longer be the last man I kissed.

That's my last thought before my mouth is on his.

I thought kissing someone new after eight years would be strange, but it's not. He tastes minty, like the gum he popped into his mouth on the drive here. He doesn't take control, but he does kiss me back. The low groan in his throat alone has my nipples tightening.

I open my mouth against his, and he deepens the kiss, his tongue caressing mine. Suddenly, I find myself grappling to get closer, gripping the soft cotton of his shirt like it's the only thing keeping me afloat. With a smile against my mouth, he slides his hands down my hips to just below my butt and lifts me effortlessly. My legs instinctively circle his waist. It forces my dress up, exposing my ass and the black thong I put on earlier. Not that he can see it. Yet, anyway.

He turns and sets me on the counter. I like this change in position, how it puts me closer to his height. His hands are on my thighs, bare now since my dress his hiked up to my hips, but he keeps his thumbs a careful distance away, not pushing. He rubs them in slow, soothing circles against the sensitive flesh there and kisses me lazily, like we have all the time in the world.

Thoughts of Chase invade my mind again. This kiss is unlike any he gave me in the last year of our marriage. For months and months, every time he kissed me, it felt like a duty rather than passion or need.

But Reid kisses me like I'm the tastiest beverage on a summer day and he can't get enough. Until now, I didn't know how much I'd missed this—being wanted, desired.

"I've never done this before," I admit on a gasp.

He pulls away, lips quirking in amusement. "Sex?"

"No." My cheeks heat, and I swat playfully at his bicep. "I've ... never had sex with a stranger. A one-night stand. Whatever you want to call it."

I didn't realize I'd lowered my head, but suddenly, his finger is beneath my chin, lifting my head up so I'm forced to meet his gaze. "Neither have I."

My heart tumbles in my chest. "Seriously?"

He dives in and kisses my neck. "Nope. But when I saw you across the bar, I knew I'd regret it for the rest of my life if I didn't talk to you."

I push him away, heart hammering even harder than it has been since my lips first connected with his. "Why?"

I'm pushing it. This is supposed to be a no-strings night

of fun, and here I am hitting him with question after question. But rather than waving them off and rushing to get to the naked part, Reid indulges my inquisitiveness.

"Because you were sitting there with this lonely look in your eyes." He brushes a thumb along my jawline. "I wanted to be the reason you didn't feel that way anymore."

Overwhelmed by his earnest expression and the depth of his response, I stare into his green eyes. "That's the only reason?"

With a mock-wince, he gives my thigh a squeeze. "And your tits look fucking amazing in this dress." The groan that escapes him then is low and guttural. He closes his eyes and breathes in through his nose, then lets it out slowly. "Sorry." He blinks his eyes open. "I have to be honest." The boyish grin he gives me has my stomach dipping. "Now tell me," he leans in, brushing his nose against the curve of my ear, "what did you think when you saw me?"

I press my lips together, my face heating once again.

"Tell me," he coaxes. "Be honest, Via. Do you want me for my body?"

I throw my head back and laugh.

He watches, lips parted like he's captivated by the move.

"My first thought," I hold up a finger and wag it, "was that you're gorgeous."

That dimple, I'm certain, is going to be my undoing flashes at me, and his eyes glimmer behind his glasses. "I knew you wanted me for my body. What was your second thought?"

"I was impressed by how you commanded attention. I

don't know if you're aware of it, but I'm..." I bite my lip, holding the words inside.

He cups my face in his left hand and runs his thumb over my lips. "Care to finish that thought, angel?"

I inhale a shaky breath, skimming my hands beneath his shirt. His stomach is smooth, hard, defined in a way that feels like it's come from more than the gym. He shivers at my touch and presses his forehead to mine.

"I'm not the only one who couldn't take my eyes off you."

He pulls back a fraction and regards me, flames flickering in his eyes.

One heartbeat.

Two.

"You're the only one I saw." With that confession, he slams his lips to mine.

This kiss is different. Hungrier, desperate, like he's unleashed something in himself.

I moan when he grips my throat, angling my head back. With his other hand, he finds the zipper at my back and guides it down. The sound it makes when he lowers it is almost indecent. It's the promise of what's to come, but it's also a reminder that I'm about to share myself with a man who's not my husband.

He places a gentle kiss beside my ear. "Is this okay?"

"Yes." I lean back, lifting my arms up.

He takes the invitation, slipping the dress up past my stomach, then my breasts, and tossing it to the tile floor. I contemplate it for a moment, the splash of green fabric against the gray of the tiles, hit with the need to recreate the effect in a painting. Thoughts of the color combinations I would use to create the exact shade of green swirl in my mind.

I'm brought back to reality by his low groan.

Oh. Propped up before him, I'm naked but for a thong. For an instant, I'm hit with the urge to cover myself.

It dies quickly when I get a good look at Reid.

Eyes roving over every inch of me, he swallows hard. "Let me look at you." His voice is raspy with want and he's palming his now hard cock over his jeans, biting his lip as he takes me in. Emboldened by the pure desire in his expression, I lean back on my elbows, giving him a better look. *"Fuck."*

"Touch me."

His eyes flare with heat. With a hand at the back of his shirt, he yanks. The way his abs flex with the removal of the garment is a special kind of torture. I'll be replaying that image in my brain for a long time to come.

He takes me in, eating up every inch, a groan rumbling in his throat. Looping his fingers into the sides of my underwear, he wiggles them past my hips and lets them join the growing pile of clothes.

"Lay back." The command is sharp and full of need.

Swallowing back the nerves working their way up my throat, I obey, shuddering when the heated skin of my back meets the cool countertop.

I gasp when he clutches my legs and pulls me to the edge of the counter. *"Reid."*

The shocked squeak quickly morphs into a moan when he pushes my thighs apart and shoulders his way between them. When his mouth meets my core, the muscles in my stomach flex. I'm reeling. I don't know what I thought he planned to do, maybe just go straight to sex, but this is a welcome surprise. One my body is craving. God, I've been dying to be worshipped like this for so, so long.

He expertly works his tongue against me, going down on me with an exuberance I've never experienced. He makes these noises, small groans of pleasure, that send desire flooding through me.

I can't remember the last time I was this turned on. Maybe that perhaps that should make me sad, but sadness is the last thing I feel in the moment with Reid.

Twenty-one-year-old Reid, who has more skill with his tongue than should be possible.

"Fuck," I cry out, throwing my arms out in search of something to hold on to.

I settle for the strands of his hair and rock my hips against him. He groans in response, working his tongue against my clit. Without slowing, he peers up, focusing on my face. My skin flushes, not from embarrassment, but the pure lust gazing back at me. It's the way every woman hopes to be looked at by a man, like an object of pure desire. Something to be worshipped, not possessed.

"You taste so good, Via. You have no idea." My whole body hums at the compliment. I jolt when his fingers join the party, stroking my folds. "You're so wet for me already.

All this just for me." He pulls his fingers away and brings them to my lips. "Suck."

The request is filthy. The idea of tasting myself is … strange.

"Don't get shy on me now," he coaxes. "Not when my tongue has been all over this sweet pussy."

Heart racing, I open my mouth and suck his fingers clean like he requested.

"Good girl," he growls, biting his lip to contain his victorious smile.

Lowering his head, he licks and sucks at me, bringing me back to the edge in a ridiculously short amount of time. He makes it seem so easy. Until this moment, orgasms have been elusive, experiences I've had to work hard for yet only enjoyed every once in a blue moon.

He holds tight to my thighs, keeping me spread open even as the intensity of his movements urges them to close. I might have bruises come tomorrow, but I welcome the idea and relish the reminder of our night.

"I'm close," I gasp. "Don't stop."

He hums in answer and keeps working his tongue against me at the same pace, proving he's an exceptional listener and building me up to that glorious crest. I grasp his hair harder and tug, back arching off the counter when I fall apart. Pleasure zings through me, taking over. I ride out the wave, lost to the intensity.

If he could do that with only his mouth, I can't imagine what else he can do. My body is languid, limbs loose, when he plucks me off the counter and holds me close.

Still unsteady, I wrap myself around him and lay my head on his shoulder. "That was..."

He presses a kiss to my cheek. "I know."

He carries me to his room and lays me on his bed. The covers are soft against my back and smell of laundry detergent. Watching me with his tongue pressed against his cheek, he undoes his belt with one hand.

I gape, mesmerized by him. How the hell did he do that and why was it so fucking hot?

"You have another tattoo?" I blurt at the sight of dark ink peeking out over the top of his jeans.

He follows my gaze, popping the button on his jeans in the process. "Oh, yeah."

"What is it?"

His eyebrows inch up his forehead. "You don't want to see it?"

"Oh." I blush, crossing my legs. "Right."

With a smirk, he works his zipper down. When he's discarded his pants, he palms himself over his black boxer briefs, still watching me with pure hunger. A small trail of hair travels from the bottom of his navel down beneath the band of his underwear. I still can't see the entirety of the tattoo.

"I can't see it yet," I whimper.

He grins. "Sit up. Look for yourself."

Obediently, I rise up, surprisingly steady. Though he's virtually a stranger, I can't deny that in Reid's presence, I feel comfortable, sure of myself.

Easing the edge of his boxer briefs down on the side, I

reveal the tattoo. It's an intricate design of a hummingbird—the details absolutely stunning. With one finger, I trace the edges of the design. "What inspired this one?"

"My mom, again," he chuckles, rubbing at the back of his head. "They were her favorite."

"It's beautiful." Truly, it's one of the nicest tattoos I've ever seen.

"I drew it."

My heartbeat stutters. "You did?"

Looming above me, he nods and pushes his glasses back up.

"You like art?"

"Yeah." He swallows thickly. "It's always come naturally to me."

"Something we have in common."

A slow, sure smile spreads over his lips. "I have a feeling we have a lot in common."

It's on the tip of my tongue to tell him I'm not sure about that, especially considering our age difference. Before I can, he grasps my chin between his thumb and forefinger and angles low to kiss me. He takes his time, his tongue moving languidly against mine despite the insistent presence of his hard cock between us.

Emboldened by his reaction, I grip his length through his boxer briefs. My lungs seize and I nearly choke on my tongue at his size. He's long and thick, bigger than I'm used to. I edge down his underwear to free the tip and rub my thumb along the smooth crown and over the slit, spreading pre-cum around.

Releasing my lips, he straightens and watches, homed in on where my thumb rubs back and forth. A shiver runs down his spine. "Fuck, angel." His hips buck, desperate for more, and his eyes flutter closed.

Pride washes over me. I'm barely touching him, yet he's so obviously affected. I push his underwear down, freeing him fully, and to my own embarrassment, my jaw unhinges in shock.

I knew he was big, I *felt* it, but with his cock bobbing in front of me, I'm at a loss for what the hell I'm supposed to do with this behemoth.

"It's too big," I squeak.

Stroking himself, Reid throws his head back and laughs. "God, Via, you really know what to say to make a man feel good."

I gape up at him. "I'm not trying to flatter you. It's huge."

He bites his bottom lip, obviously suppressing more laughter, and cups my cheek tenderly. "I'll be gentle."

Overtaken by an unfamiliar bravery, I press my lips together and look up at him through my lashes. "What if I don't want you to be?"

"Via." My name is a low, delicious rumble that vibrates through my body and makes my skin pebble.

Without stepping away, he slides the top drawer of his nightstand open and pulls out a condom. Magnum, of course.

He rips the foil open, but I hold up my hand before he can remove it. "Can I?"

With a single brow arched, he hands over the opened packet.

My fingers shake a little as I slip it out. Once we do this, there's no going back. I'm moving on and I *want* this. I want it to be with Reid too. Age difference be damned.

Without second-guessing myself, I slip the condom down his considerable length.

He leans down, his body hovering over mine so that I'm forced to lie back. His lips find mine again, and he smiles against my mouth. "I love kissing you."

"Mm," I hum, stroking my thumb against his stubbled cheek. "That so?"

His nose brushes mine, and he guides my head back until my throat is exposed. He kisses his way down my neck, between my breasts.

I keep expecting him to get carried away, to move straight to the actual sex, but Reid continues to surprise me in the slow, gentle way he worships my body. Rather than singularly focused on his pleasure, he seems to only get more turned on by indulging me.

"Yes." He drawls the word, swirling his tongue around my nipple.

As much as I appreciate his patience and devotion, I'm *this* close to begging him to fuck me senseless. If his goal has been to wind me up and make me beg, it's working.

He moves to my other breast and lavishes the same kind of thoughtful attention. When I wiggle impatiently under him, he laughs, his breath skating across my sensitive skin.

"Relax." He pushes gently on my pubic bone, urging my

hips back down to the mattress. "It's my birthday and I want to savor my dessert."

Who am I to argue with that logic?

He peppers kisses all over my breasts and torso and works his way back up to the sensitive skin of my neck. "God, Via," he growls, his breath a tickle against my skin. "I haven't even felt your pussy on my cock yet and you're already making me lose my mind."

"Please," I beg, skating my hand up his bare back and stopping at his neck. "I want you..."

He hums, brushing his nose along my cheek. "You want what?"

I bite my lip and close my eyes, mustering the courage I need to go for complete honesty. "I want you to fuck me." The words are a barely audible whisper. I'm not used to asking for what I want.

"Fuck." He rises up and considers me. "When you ask me so nicely it's hard to say no."

He snags a pillow and silently urges me to lift my hips. When he has me how he wants me, he guides the tip of his cock to my entrance. I gasp at the hard, insistent press of him, and splay a hand over his stomach. I'm not sure if I'm signaling for him to wait or begging him to do it.

He presses against me but doesn't enter. "Are you okay?"

"Yeah," I pant. "Just ... be careful. I'm not trying to flatter you when I say you're big. This is ... I'm not used to that."

He smirks, pure male satisfaction settling on his face,

and kisses the corner of my mouth. "I'll be gentle. You set the pace."

"Okay."

He works his way into me, inch by delicious inch, until he's seated fully inside. I'm certainly not a virgin, but it takes my body a moment to adjust to his length and thickness. When I saw Reid tonight, I saw a man who's cute in a boy-next-door kind of way. Never would I have expected him to be hiding a whole anaconda in his pants.

With a hand flat against the mattress on each side of my head, he holds his weight above me. His eyes drift down to where we're joined and he hisses out a low curse. "Fuck, look at us, angel. Look at the way your pussy grips my cock. It's like I belong inside you." He kisses me long and slow. "Tell me when you're ready. Tell me what you need."

I nod, wetting my lips. "You can move."

Eyes driving shut, he lowers his head. "Thank fuck."

Slowly, he pulls out of me, then he's plunging back in. The move lights me up from head to toe.

Gripping my hips, he guides me to meet him thrust for thrust. I bite my lip to keep a moan from escaping. I've just met this man, and already, I'm addicted. He's like a drug I'm suddenly sure I can't live without.

He cups my breasts, pinching my nipples with enough pressure to send pleasure zinging through me.

"Reid?" I pant his name, my breath gone.

The tendons in his neck strain. "Yeah?"

"Hold my hands down and fuck me hard."

I blush at my request, but dammit, I'm thirty-two. It's about time I asked for what I want.

He flashes a crooked grin and does exactly as I asked, pinning my hands above my head. I moan at the sensation the slight change in our position creates. Like this, his pelvic bone pushes directly against my clit. Once he finds a rhythm, he fucks me harder, faster, quickly hurtling me toward climax.

I flex my fingers, and as if he can read my mind, he grins and tightens his hold by clasping our fingers together.

"I'm close." I squeeze him tighter. "Oh my God. Right there. I—" My body shudders, shaking with the tremor of the orgasm that rips through me. It's so intense that my eyes roll back as I cry out.

His mouth claims mine, silencing the sound. For a moment I forgot that we're not the only people in existence. Reid certainly has neighbors.

He fucks me through the aftershocks of my orgasm, quickly building me to another. I claw at his hands, lost in ecstasy, but he holds tight. I'm on the cusp of another orgasm when he pulls out and releases his hold on me. Bereft, I gasp, but I don't have a chance to protest before he's guiding me over on all fours and lifting my hips so my ass is in the air.

"This okay?"

"Yes—*oh my God.*" I clutch at his sheets, searching for purchase, some way to hold myself together. This new position is everything I need and more.

I cry out in surprise when he spanks me. In response,

my pussy floods. With an approving grunt, he does it again, slapping my other butt cheek. When I spasm around him, he grips both globes in his big hands and squeezes. I wiggle against him. He's so deep like this. There's no way I won't be sore come tomorrow, but I don't care.

"Fuck, angel. You're so fucking perfect."

Grasping my hips, he sets the pace. I lower from my hands to my forearms and moan at the way his balls hit my clit.

"Yes, yes, *yes*. Reid, I—" And then I'm coming again. This orgasm is so strong that my whole body shakes and I lose control of my limbs.

Reid loops an arm around my stomach and supports me as I ride out the waves.

Holy shit.

I don't know whether he's just that good or whether our chemistry is truly this incredible. Either way, I've never come this many times during a single round of sex. Reid's endurance is unreal. I'll probably spend most of tomorrow icing my poor vagina. Not that I'll mind. This is more than worth it.

When I've mostly recovered, he pulls from my body and urges me to lie on my side. I comply, my brain mush and perfectly willing to do whatever he wants. He lies behind me and pulls me flush to his chest. Lifting my right leg, he rests it on his, opening me up to him. Instead of sliding home, he reaches around me and rubs my clit.

I whimper at the sensitivity, and he stills.

"Do you want me to stop?"

"No," I blurt, tilting my head back. "No, please don't stop."

He nods once and resumes his circling of my delicate bundle of nerves. When he stops this time, I mewl in protest, but then he's guiding his cock back to my pussy. His sheets are a tangled mess from my clawing and yanking, because holy fuck, I'm so full. My body doesn't know quite what to make of the size of him, but I'm not mad about it.

He's slower this time, gentle in the way he rocks his hips against mine. His left arm snakes under me, gripping my breast.

"Reid," I pant, practically begging.

For what, I'm not sure.

I tilt my head back, taking in the way his hair falls over his forehead, how his lips are parted in pleasure.

He regards me in return, a moan rumbling in his throat. "You're so hot." He dips his head, capturing my mouth in a searing kiss. "I'm close. You?"

I nod, not having enough oxygen to form words.

"Ah, fuck." The fingers of his right hand tighten around my hip. "You feel amazing. I—" He groans, clearly fighting to hold out longer.

"I'm right there," I encourage.

He slides his hand down from my hip and finds my clit again. One circle, then another, and I'm falling apart, my limbs practically going limp. When he pulls from my body, a whine escapes me at the loss.

I watch, my vision slightly blurred, as he stands and rips

off the condom. He fists his cock, working it in hard strokes, his focus locked on me, his eyes heavy with lust.

"I want to come on your face," he confesses, the words a rasp.

"I—" I'm taken off guard. The filthy words are in direct contrast to Reid's sweet, boy-next-door appearance. It's not something I've ever done before. On my breasts or stomach, yes, but not my face. But I find myself nodding eagerly, turned on by the dirtiness of the request. "Yes."

His eyes widen and his lips part in surprise, but a heartbeat later, his jaw goes rigid in determination.

I slip out of the bed and kneel in front of him. It's such a vulnerable, submissive position, especially with someone I only met a handful of hours ago.

"Fuck, Via. You have no idea how hot you are. God, just look at you." He works his fist faster over his dick. "Almost," he warns, giving me a chance to back out.

I tilt my head back and stick out my tongue. Jaw clenching, he squeezes his eyes shut and moans as thick jets of cum spray my face. I'm not sure exactly how I feel about it, but I don't hate it either. The way he looks at me, covered with the evidence of his orgasm, is sexy as hell.

He helps me up from the floor, his expression pure heat, and scoops me up and over his shoulder. With a swat to my ass, he declares, "Shower time." Then he's striding to the bathroom and depositing me in the stream of hot water. And once we've scrubbed each other clean, he drops to his knees on the tile and goes down on me again.

six

"Ugh." My body aches, sore all over like I did a full-body workout. *What the hell did I do to myself?*

The question is followed by an onslaught of memories of last night. Gasping, I blink my eyes open and take in my surroundings.

This isn't my bed.

This isn't my room.

And this certainly isn't my apartment.

Sunlight streaks in through the half-open blinds. I turn to the bedside table, searching for a clock, but there isn't one. My companion is nowhere to be seen, but noise from another part of the apartment filters in through the closed door. When I shake my head to clear the haze of sleep, the first thing I notice is the smooth croon of Frank Sinatra. A wave of surprise hits me at the realization. This twenty-one-year-old guy is listening to Frank Sinatra?

My body protests when I slip from the bed. I didn't intend on staying the night, but after the shower and another mind-blowing orgasm, Reid led me to his bed and begged me to stay. When he wrapped his big body around mine, I was helpless to leave. As good as the sex was, just being held by him healed some pieces inside me that had been broken for a long time.

Now that I'm faced with the consequences of my actions in the light of day, I wish I'd insisted he take me back to my car.

You're an adult, he's an adult. There's nothing wrong with consensual sex.

Even so, I've never done this kind of thing. It shouldn't feel all kinds of wrong, but it does, and I can't magically alter my brain chemistry to think differently.

I'm not normally one to rifle through people's things, but since my clothes are nowhere in sight—because we left them scattered in the kitchen last night—I do a quick search of Reid's dresser. At the top of one drawer, I find a t-shirt that blessedly falls to my thighs.

On tiptoe, so as not to alert Reid to my movements, I make my way into the attached bath. When I'm met with the sight of myself in the mirror, I have to slap a hand over my mouth to stifle the terrified shriek that works its way up my throat.

I look *terrible*.

My hair is a certifiable rat's nest. Lips? Puffy and

swollen and at least two sizes bigger than usual. My neck is red from his stubble and—

Oh my God, I have a freaking hickey, like I'm an uncontrollable, lust-filled teenager.

Izzy will be so proud.

I say a prayer of thanks when I discover a hairbrush on the counter. Gently, I smooth it through my unruly locks, untangling the knots as I go. It takes a bit to work through all of them, but when I'm finished, I look a heck of a lot better. His toothpaste sits on the counter too, so I put a dot of it on the end of my finger and scrub my teeth the best I can.

I dally around a little, avoiding the inevitable, but my bladder is screaming, and once I flush, he'll know I'm awake.

Unable to hold it any longer, I take care of business. After, as I'm washing my hands, I study my reflection. "Stop being a wuss."

I brush my hands down the front of Reid's shirt and blow out a breath. Then, with a small whistle and a flick of the bathroom light, I head out.

The moment I ease the bedroom door open, the greasy, salty scent of bacon hits my nose. My stomach rumbles loudly. Thankfully the vinyl playing from the living room masks the sound.

The apartment is small, so in a matter of a few steps, I'm standing in the middle of the open living space with a full view of Reid. He's standing at the stove with his back to me, his muscles flexing when he flips the bacon. A pair of loose shorts hangs off his slender hips.

"You're cooking breakfast?"

He turns around, wearing an easy grin. "Yeah, I, uh … figured you might be hungry after last night." Red blooms across his cheekbones. "I mean, I know I am."

In the light of day, a shyness has settled over Reid. "I'm almost done with the bacon, and I have eggs ready to be scrambled."

Plagued by a sense of discomfort, I tug on the end of his shirt. In response to the movement, he lowers his chin, taking in my bare thighs, his eyes flashing with heat.

"You didn't need to cook breakfast for me."

"It's no big deal."

I bite my lip. "I should really get back home."

He considers me for a moment, his expression somewhere between a frown and a smile. "You don't have to run away from me."

I look down at my feet. The polish is chipped and missing completely on a few toes. I can't remember the last time I had a pedicure. Regardless of how long it's been, the polish that's left behind is hanging on for dear life.

"I'm not running away."

Oh, really?

"You sure about that?" He arches a brow and turns back to the stove to remove the curled pieces of bacon from the pan.

I sigh, wringing my hands together, warring with

myself. Finally, realizing there's no good way out of this, I say, "Breakfast will be great."

It's not that Reid is trying to keep me trapped here, but I need to put on my big girl panties and be an adult about this. He's handling this with far more maturity than I am.

"Where are my clothes?"

He peers over his shoulder and points to the coffee table. Last night, the Candy Land board and pieces were scattered across it. Now, only my neatly folded clothes sit atop it.

"I washed them."

Hit with a pinch of confusion, I swing my head in his direction so fast I nearly give myself whiplash. "You washed my clothes?"

"That's what I said." He turns a chuckle into a cough, like he knows I wouldn't find it amusing if he laughed at me right now. "I was doing a load this morning anyway. It's not a big deal."

My one-night stand washed my clothes. What the fuck?

"Thanks." I tiptoe across the room and scoop my thong up first. Without preamble, I slip it on. When I glance behind me, Reid is watching, tongue practically hanging out of his mouth. For now, I'll leave his shirt on. I don't feel like contorting my body into the tight dress. "Do you need any help?"

He piles the bacon onto a plate and nods to the loaf of bread on the counter. "Want to pop a couple of pieces of bread into the toaster?"

"You got it."

We work together easily in his small kitchen. When the

last song plays and the arm of the record player lifts, Reid runs over to flip the vinyl.

"I can't believe you have a record player."

"You can't beat the sound of vinyl. It's superior, and I'll die on that hill." He pushes his glasses up his nose.

"How'd you get into it?" I prop a hip against the counter and watch as he resumes the eggs. The arm porn I'm being treated to is pure perfection.

"Into records?" He glances over, scraping a spatula around the edge of the pan. "They've regained popularity recently, but I fell in love with the sound because of my grandparents. They have an extensive vinyl collection. My grandpa buys my grandma a new album for every holiday."

"That's beautiful."

Chase and I never collected anything of sentimental value together like that.

I eye his setup and consider what it would look like if I did something similar in my apartment. I love music, and the idea of painting with a record playing in the background has a dreamy appeal.

The toast pops up, startling me. Shaking out of my daydreams, I find the butter in the fridge. Once Reid has pointed me in the direction of the silverware drawer, I spread the butter on the slices and cut them in half diagonally. My stomach rumbles again. This time I'm close enough to Reid that he hears.

He chuckles. "Someone's hungry, and here you were trying to run out on me."

"Shut up." My tone is playful as I hip check him.

Once he's plated the food, we sit at his breakfast bar together.

I'm having breakfast with my one-night stand.

As far as I know, the majority of one-time encounters are nothing like this. Reid is baffling. He's twenty-one, but incredibly mature. Especially for a guy. God knows they don't mature as fast as women.

Silence descends upon us. It's not awkward, but it makes me a little twitchy. We know each other in a very intimate way now, yet we know almost nothing about topics outside of the bedroom.

"Did you grow up in the area?" he asks, cringing instantly.

I laugh. "No, I was born and raised in California. I moved to Parkerville recently."

His eyes widen. "No way. That's where I grew up. My dad still lives there."

I smile down at my plate of food. "Small world."

"The smallest. You'll have to check out Ms. Kathy's donut shop. Her donuts are incredible."

"I will. Which one should I try first?"

He tears off a bite of bacon and chews, head tilted like he's mulling over the choices. "They're all good. The matcha is a crowd favorite, but I love classic flavors best. You can't go wrong with a plain old glazed donut. The blueberry cheesecake is incredible too." He smacks his lips, like the thought alone has him salivating.

"Blueberry cheesecake sounds delicious." I push my eggs around with my fork, trying not to hoover up every bite on my plate. When I'm hungry, I tend to scarf my food down ridiculously fast.

"It's out of this world. You have to try it."

I swear I'm living in an alternate reality. I'm sitting across the table talking about donuts with this guy when I should be hightailing it out of here.

When we're finished, Reid handwashes our dishes, and I dry. He goes about things in such a leisurely way, like he's not at all bothered by having a strange woman in his space.

When the dishes are clean and put away, he leans back against the counter, crossing his arms over his chest. "Do you want a cup of coffee? I have a Keurig."

The way he says *I have a Keurig* has me pressing my lips together to stifle a laugh.

"Reid." I draw out his name in careful amusement. "Why do I get the impression you don't want me to leave?"

He swallows thickly and sticks his hands in his pockets. "Because I don't."

My stomach flips at the surprising, yet simple, honest answer. "Why?"

His chest rattles with a sigh. "I have a feeling that once you go, I'll never see you again and I'm not looking forward to that."

What? I struggle to wrap my head around his confession.

"And," he goes on, "I have a feeling if I ask for your number, you'll say no."

Heat rushes to my face. "You're right." There's no point

in beating around the bush. "I would say no. I ... this," I wag a finger between us, "isn't something I do."

He adjusts his glasses. "Stand in kitchens and talk to guys?" His lips dance with amusement.

"You know that's not what I meant," I mutter. Suddenly hit with memories of last night, I duck, letting my hair hide my flaming face. God, I'll still be thinking about it when I'm old and gray.

"I know." His voice softens. Stepping in close, he cups my elbows and ducks down to meet my eyes. "It isn't something I typically do either."

I inhale a shaky breath, fighting the urge to look away. "Okay."

He frowns. That's clearly not the answer he wanted. I *want* to believe him. He seems sincere enough, but there's no way a guy Reid's age who's *that* skilled in bed isn't getting laid often. I'm okay with that. Sort of. I have to be. It's not like I'll ever see Reid again. This will be nothing but a distant memory for both of us one day.

"Okay," he repeats, his warm touch disappearing from my skin. "I'll take you back to your car, then. If that's what you want."

I jerk my head in a small nod. It's not what I want, but what choice do I have? My time with Reid has to come to an end eventually, so I might as well rip the Band-Aid off and get it over with.

Why, though, is doing this so difficult? I don't know him. I couldn't tell you his favorite food or his favorite color, yet when I leave, it feels like I'll be abandoning a piece of myself.

That's downright nuts.

I've always been a logical, level-headed person. My God, I'm a lawyer—*was* a lawyer. But there's nothing rational about what's happening here.

Reid maneuvers around me, swiping his keys off the counter. "All right, angel. I'll take you back to your car."

I dip my chin and avert my gaze. "Thank you." I tiptoe my way over to my clothes and scoop them up, then head to the bathroom to change. I hate putting the dress back on. It's such a ridiculous thing to wear in the light of day, but what choice do I have?

Once I'm changed, I give myself a quick moment to catch my breath before I open the door.

Reid is waiting for me in the kitchen, typing away on his phone. "Good to go?" he asks, looking me up and down, lust in his eyes. He looks away quickly, like he doesn't want to get caught, but it's too late.

My heart stumbles in my chest and my cheeks warm. Every one of our interactions, whether intentional or accidental, bolsters my confidence. "Yeah, I'm ready."

We don't say a word on the drive back to the bar, and I don't fight it when he reaches over and laces our fingers together, bringing our joined hands to rest on the shifter. I'm craving the touch as much as he is.

When the bar comes into view, my stomach plummets.

This is it. Goodbye.

He pulls into the lot and parks beside my car. It's the

only one there. Ironic, since the lot was packed to the brim last night.

The engine is a rumble in the background, the two of us sitting in silence, afraid to speak.

Swallowing, I carefully extract my hand from his. The loss of his touch is like a gust of cold air.

Reid sighs, running his now empty hand through his tousled locks.

"I need to go." My words are soft. I hate to speak them into existence, but I have to. I'm being ridiculous.

He nods woodenly, clearing his throat. "Okay."

Still, neither of us moves for the space of a few heartbeats. Finally, he makes the first move. He heaves his door open, and I follow suit, though I fumble with the unfamiliar handle. Before I figure it out, he's there, swinging it open for me.

The sadness lingering between us is heavy. It's the feeling one might get when visiting a new place and falling in love with every aspect of it, all the while knowing the trip will end and the chance to come back is near nonexistent.

Standing in front of him, I exhale a shaky breath.

"Bye, Reid."

He swallows, watching me silently. I take a step to the side, to move closer to my car, but then his hands are on my cheeks and he's pressing me against the side of his car. A moan escapes me before I can put a leash on the sound. It's cut off abruptly, though, when his lips are on mine. He devours me in a kiss that sends tingles all the way down to my toes.

Holy hell.

With a final tender kiss on the end of my nose, he releases me.

"Goodbye, Via." His voice is nothing more than a rasp.

On shaky legs, I cross over to my car and slip into the driver's seat. I fumble against the keyless start button, but after the second try, the car roars to life. I try to ignore the tall, looming presence watching me drive away, but it's pointless. Unable to fight the pull, I glance in the mirror one last time. Reid lifts two fingers to his forehead and dips them in a wave, like he senses my attention.

As I turn out of the lot, I catch sight of the clock on the dash.

11:11

Dammit.

seven

I had no intention of giving Izzy all the details of my time with Reid, but when she sends me a FaceTime request that evening, I get a giant case of word vomit, and I can't spew the words out quick enough.

"Wait, wait, wait," she chants, holding her hands up. "I can't wrap my head around this." She pinches her brow. "You did *what?*"

I peek at her from between my fingers. Halfway through my explanation, I slapped them over my eyes to shield myself from her scrutiny. "I'm not saying it all again."

"I think you need to."

"No." My tone is equal parts authority and embarrassment. "I never meant to tell you all of that in the first place."

"Ugh." She throws her head back. "Indulge me here,

Via. I wasn't sure you would even go through with it, but look at you. Not only did you go home with a guy, but you went home with a hot younger guy who—"

"Shh," I hush her, my cheeks flaming. I'm not a prude—at least I don't think I am—but I planned to keep Reid to myself. A secret I could hold tight to and look back on with fond memories.

Her shoulders deflate. "Fine, I'll let it go." The *for now* is implied. "Now that you've been thoroughly fucked, what are your plans for the rest of the day?"

"Izzy!"

She cackles, flicking her hair over her shoulders. "Sorry, I had to. Seriously, though, what are you up to?"

With a sigh, I survey my apartment. "I might go to the hardware store and pick out paint."

"Ooh, what color are you thinking?"

"I'm not sure yet. I should probably just pick up paint samples today."

"Good idea." She nods, holding a tube of lip gloss. She uses the camera as a mirror, swiping the sticky-shiny stuff onto her lips. "I'll send you a few Pinterest board inspiration pics."

"You don't need to do that." There's no telling what she'll send. My best guess is either stark white spaces or neon colors. There's rarely an in-between. "I know you're busy." Between posting on her social media, filming, and editing content, she's always up to something.

She waves her hand dismissively. "For you, it's not a problem. I better go, though. I have a nail appointment."

"Bye, I love you."

"Love you, too!" She blows air kisses at me before ending the call.

When her voice no longer fills my apartment, the weight of loneliness settles on my shoulders. I like time by myself, but there's a vast difference between having a little much-needed alone time to decompress and being entirely alone.

I hadn't actually planned to go to the hardware store, but I *do* need to paint this place and make it my own, since I'll be here for a good long while.

Throwing my hair up into a ponytail to get the half-dried mess out of my way, I take a quick look at my reflection in the bathroom mirror. I've looked better, but the ripped jeans and oversized long-sleeve t-shirt will have to do. I don't have the energy to change. If Reid were here, he'd probably smirk at the state he's left me in.

I swipe my car keys off the kitchen counter and head down to my car. I'll get coffee while I'm out too. Maybe even a donut.

***

THE HARDWARE STORE IS ONLY A HANDFUL OF MILES away. One of the perks of a small town, I suppose. I'm used to battling traffic for an hour, only to go a few miles.

Purse slung across my body, I step into the store. The door makes a merry chiming sound when I enter, and the cashier gives me a kind smile.

"Hi." He lowers the newspaper he was reading. He's on the shorter side, with thinning gray hair. "Is there anything I can help you with?"

"I was going to look at the paint."

"It's straight in the back of the store." He points. "Can't miss it."

With a smile and a nod, I head that way, my sneakers squeaking loudly against the linoleum flooring as I go.

The paint area is small, but it'll do. I pick up a few card swatches and compare them. All the while, my phone vibrates over and over in my pocket. The messages are no doubt Izzy's promised inspiration photos. I ignore them. While I appreciate the thought, I want my place to be a reflection of me.

With paint samples in hand—or basket, since I'm getting so many—I make my way back to the register.

The man behind the counter smiles as he removes them from the basket. "Someone's going to be doing a lot of painting."

"You have no idea," I laugh. Eventually, there'll be all kinds of painting going on in my art store.

"Home improvement?" He slides one of the samples into a paper bag, then another.

"Sort of. I just moved to town. I'm renovating a building and living in the apartment above."

"Oh." His eyes widen. "That's quite the project."

"You have no idea."

"Do you have a contractor lined up to do the renovations?"

"Not yet." I adjust the strap of my purse so it's no longer digging into my shoulder. "I haven't been in town long enough to reach out to any."

He smiles and scans another sample. "I have some recommendations if you'd like them."

"Yeah, of course." Truly, I'd be grateful for them.

"I'll write down their names and numbers before you go. Around here we all know one another." He points to the card machine, signaling that it's ready for me. "Most of the local contractors buy their supplies here, so I know them well."

"I don't come from a small town." I type in my debit passcode. "But I'm already loving the community vibe here."

Even after my encounter at the diner.

"This is a great town. Good people. We look out for each other. I'm Gary." He holds out a hand.

I slide my palm against his. "Via."

"It's nice to meet you, Via."

I smile at the older gentleman. "Likewise."

Once he's tucked my receipt into the bag, he passes it to me. Then, with a finger in the air, he says, "Let me write down those numbers for you."

Taking a step back, I assess the swatches on the wall. The sun is setting, so the lighting isn't the best. I'll have to live with whatever color I choose in all hours, though, so I might as well get a feel for them.

At the moment, the olive-green swatch is speaking to me the most, but I don't want to marry myself to a single choice just yet.

Ha. *Marry*. What a joke marriage turned out to be.

I snort, then immediately groan. Clearly, I'm tired if I'm laughing at my own pathetic thoughts.

When I'm hit by a second yawn in a matter of minutes, I decide to call it a day, though I suppose I should fix myself a quick meal before heading to bed since I haven't eaten since breakfast with Reid. I was anxious to get the samples I'd chosen on the wall when I left the store, so I didn't bother to pick up any donuts.

The state of my fridge is pathetic, so pizza it is.

The guy on the phone takes my order and gives me a less than enthusiastic "delivery will be thirty minutes" before hanging up.

I showered this morning, but I managed to get paint all over myself, so I hop in for a quick wash before my dinner arrives.

The fatigue I was already feeling settles fully into my bones by the time I finish. The exhaustion plaguing me is a feat, considering the water jumped from hot to cold and back again at random intervals, shocking my system each time.

Just as I'm pulling a sweatshirt over my head, there's a knock on the door.

I swipe some cash from my wallet and hand over

enough for the pizza and tip to the driver in exchange for my veggie cheesy goodness. My mouth waters, my stomach coming to life.

I eat my pizza on the couch, watching videos on my phone like a pseudo iPad kid, since my TV isn't hooked up yet.

Or internet, for that matter.

Tomorrow, I'll get things scheduled and call the list of contractors Gary gave me. This is going to be a long project, so the sooner it gets started, the sooner I can get the store up and running.

eight

The first two contractors who come by to give me quotes are a bust. Both are overpriced, and neither is willing to even show me photos of their work, which does not give me confidence in their abilities.

I'm beginning to think Gary did me dirty, but then the third and final recommendation he gave me pulls up to the curb in a red work truck with ladders strapped to the top.

I say a silent prayer that this guy won't be a jerk and that he's at least somewhat knowledgeable in his field.

My hopes are slim at this point, but I step out of the shop and plaster on a smile as he gets out of his truck and rounds the front.

"Hi, you must be Ms. James."

"That's me." I nod. "You can call me Via."

"Derrick." He pushes his hair back and assesses the

outside of the building. "I was surprised when I heard this place had sold." He smiles over at me, his eyes crinkling at the corners. He's a handsome man. Probably about ten years older than me, with dark hair that's peppered with gray. He seems vaguely familiar, but I can't put my finger on why. "I've always seen potential here. Should we head inside and discuss what you have in mind? Jessica mentioned that you plan to turn it into an art store."

Jessica was the woman I spoke to when I called to schedule a quote.

"Yes, it'll be an art studio, a place where people can relax and paint or take classes if they're interested in learning."

"You're an artist, then?" He arches a brow, almost like he's impressed.

"I suppose."

He chuckles. "You suppose? What does that mean?" He crosses his arms over his chest, and I can't help but notice how fit he is. I guess he'd have to be with such a physically demanding job. Then again, the other guys were paunchy in the middle. They looked more like the kind of men who delegate work rather than get their hands dirty.

"I've always loved art, and I'm good at it, I think." I wrinkle my nose. "I always wanted to pursue it but grew up being told I should choose a more practical career path. So I got a law degree instead. And I stuck with that until…" I shrug, letting the rest go. There's no need to give this stranger all the sordid details of my miserable life.

He lets out a low whistle. "That's quite the switch."

"You have no idea," I mutter.

With a smile, I open the door to the store and gesture for him to step inside.

The last guy *tsk*ed when he saw the place and muttered comments about the amount of work it needs.

In contrast, Derrick peruses the place carefully and quietly, taking inventory of the current state and writing down notes.

He's quiet for a solid ten minutes before he turns back to me. "Other than the basics—painting, new lighting, that kind of stuff, what's your vision?"

Sticking my hands in the back pockets of my jeans, I inspect the space for the hundredth time, seeing it in my head so perfectly it's like the work has already been done.

"I would love to do some sort of wash on the concrete. It's going to get paint on it anyway, so nothing fancy. Over there, I want to do built-in displays with lighting above so I can showcase students' artwork. Oh, and back here." I grasp his forearm in my excitement and tug him along after me, but I quickly drop it when I realize what I've done. "Back here," I repeat, "I want shelving for supplies. A craft corner over here for kids and—" I take a breath and let out a laugh. "Sorry, I'm getting carried away."

I pull my hair back and secure it in a bun at my nape to give my jittery hands something to do.

He taps his pencil against his paper. He's been taking notes the whole time. "Keep going." He cracks a smile. "Your enthusiasm makes me excited about the potential for this project."

"All right, then." I continue my trek around the space, and he follows. "Over here, a counter with a register. Back here would be more storage for canvases and supplies."

I can't wipe the stupid grin off my face. This move, the massive change I'm making, wasn't an easy decision, but I can't deny how happy this vision makes me. This is what I was always meant to do with my life.

Derrick listens attentively as I go on, inserting his thoughts now and then. I'm worried about the cost of some of his grander ideas, but at least he's interested in my vision.

After showing him the apartment as well and what needs to be done, I walk him to his truck.

"I'll get you a quote in about a week. You have my number if you need me or think of anything else we didn't go over today." He opens the passenger door and drops his notepad and pencil onto the seat. Then he turns back to me. "This place ... it's going to be a lot of work. I won't sugarcoat things, but there's potential. A lot of it."

My chest expands and a wistful warmth envelops me. "I think so too. That's how I ended up here in the first place. Thanks for coming to take a look."

He cracks a crookedly endearing smile. "Of course. We'll talk soon, Via."

He heads around to the front of his truck and climbs into the driver's side. When he pulls away from the curb a moment later, I watch him disappear down the street. Then I turn on my heel to walk back up to my apartment.

I snag my paint-stained overalls from where they hang over the bathroom door and change into them, then get back to work on what I've decided will be the focal wall in my living space. An olive-green background with subtle white flowers. The flowers are so small it'll take me at least a week to finish them, but it'll be worth it in the end. I wanted a design detailed enough to look like wallpaper without having to deal with actual wallpaper. This way, if I change my mind, I can easily paint over it. Plus, it's the kind of mind-numbing project I need right now.

I get in the zone painting, and the next thing I know, it's almost dinnertime.

When I check the time, I let out a curse and quickly pack up my paint and supplies. Technically I don't need to hurry. My only companion tonight will be myself, but I'm determined to have dinner at a restaurant I found on the water a few towns over. I never used to go out to eat on my own, so I've added it to the list of things I want to change. I need to be comfortable on my own. There's a certain level of loneliness that comes with picking one's life up and moving away from everything familiar. And that loneliness only makes me more determined to get out and do new things.

Fresh out of the shower and smelling like my favorite vanilla-scented body wash, I scour my closet for an outfit. Halfway through the rack, I freeze when I catch sight of the dress.

The dress I originally bought for Chase. The one that only carries memories of Reid now.

I bite my lip at the phantom sensation of his hands on my body.

Stop it, I silently scold myself. *You have to stop thinking about him.*

Easier said than done. To say Reid made a lasting impression on me is an understatement.

Pushing the dress to the side, I grab my favorite pair of jeans—the kind that are worn and soft and hug my curves in all the right places—off the narrow shelving unit. Then I swipe through my tops and snag a white tank and a beige sweater.

I dress quickly and head out before I can change my mind. Despite my vow to get comfortable doing things on my own, the sentiment is new and still a little uncomfortable.

The restaurant is thirty minutes from Parkerville, so I put on an audiobook to help pass the time and to keep me from dwelling on things I shouldn't.

The distraction doesn't last for long, though. Halfway through the drive, a notification pops up on the screen, causing my heart to lurch painfully in my chest.

It's a text message from Chase.

What the fuck? We haven't spoken or communicated in any way since the divorce was finalized. We've had no reason to. As awful as it sounds, our relationship was severed in one clean cut. There's not a single thing connecting me to him anymore, and there certainly isn't anything left to say.

I hate that I'm tempted to pull over and check his message. What he has to say shouldn't matter. And it doesn't, but dammit if curiosity isn't about to kill this cat.

Tightening my grip on the wheel, I focus on the road ahead and the words pouring from the speakers. I will not be distracted by my ex-husband.

I find a spot near the entrance and vow to continue ignoring the message from Chase. So, with my head held high, I step inside the restaurant and boldly tell the hostess I'd like a table for one on the back deck.

As I peruse the menu, more than one entrée stands out. I determine then and there that I'll have to come back to try more. The deck is surprisingly warm thanks to the outdoor heaters. Not even the breeze coming off the water makes me chilly.

I take a delicate sip of the wine I ordered when my server stopped by to introduce herself and watch the calming sway of the water around me. I didn't spend a lot of time near the water when I lived in San Francisco. It wasn't something Chase enjoyed, and since we were both so busy with work, when we did have free time, we'd spend it together. How futile that effort seems now. I'm well and truly over him, but that doesn't mean the betrayal doesn't still hurt. I'm working on it, one day at a time. Eventually, just like my feelings for him, the sting of it will disappear too.

When my seafood scampi arrives, I dig in, enjoying my alone time and dinner.

I manage to forget about the text message until I'm climbing into bed later that night.

Once I'm settled, I pick up my phone to set my alarm,

the notification is there, taunting me. So I pull a deep breath into my lungs and click on it.

> Chase: I miss you.

I squeeze my eyes shut and close out of the messages app. I won't indulge him by responding. He doesn't deserve it, and fuck him for thinking it's appropriate to send a statement like that.

He ruined us.

He knocked up his secretary.

Therefore, *he* deserves to wallow in the mess he's made.

nine

"He did not!" Izzy gasps. She claps a hand over her mouth with such force she scares poor Wonton right off her lap. Instantly, she disappears from view to apologize profusely to the dog. When she returns, she's shaking her head with her lips pursed like a disapproving mother. "I can't believe he had the audacity to text you, let alone tell you he misses you." Is it weird that her words warm my heart? She's more irate than I am.

"He's a man. That's all they have. Audacity in spades."

"I'm going to drive up there and castrate him."

I give an amused laugh as I arrange my new dishes in the cabinets. If the clanging of the glass bothers Izzy, she hasn't said.

"I don't need you to do that."

"I know, but *ugh*. I cannot believe him. What a dick. I want to give him a piece of my mind."

"Why would he say that?" I flick a piece of hair from my eyes and sigh. "Because things aren't going well with her?" I don't like to say *her* name. She and Chase are equally at fault. She knew he was married. She knew *me*, specifically. God, what a fool she must've thought on the rare occasions I showed up to have lunch with Chase. How smug she must've been knowing what they were doing behind my back.

Izzy picks up the phone and wanders into her kitchen.

"Probably," she says, filling a glass of water from the sound of things, "because he realizes now that you're a fucking catch. He knows he had the best and now he has to deal with his ridiculous consolation prize."

Her response makes me laugh. It feels good to find some sort of amusement in this mess.

"I'm serious. I just read a blog post about this. The author wrote about how men can have eighty percent of what they want and need in a partner yet seek out that other twenty in another person. In the process, they lose the eighty, but they don't figure that out until it's too late and all they're left with is the twenty. Twenty." She wiggles two fingers at me. "I guess the point is that men are stupid."

I snort. "You've got that right."

"You're not going to respond, right?"

I scoff at my sister. "God, no."

"Good. He doesn't deserve it."

"I know." God, I'm so lucky to have her on my side. She

was just as hurt and blindsided as I was when the truth came out. I think she had looked up to us, hoping she'd find herself in a relationship like ours one day.

"So," she begins, sitting at her kitchen table, "are you going to call the bar hottie?"

My cheeks flush at the mention of Reid. "I didn't get his number, remember?"

"You could look him up on social media."

I gape at her. "I'm not going to go FBI stalker on my hookup."

"Why not? I do it all the time." She sticks her tongue out when I blink at her in horror. "Don't look at me like that. Guys can be psycho. I'm just doing my due diligence."

I drop onto the couch and curl my legs under me. "Dating is so different now. I have trouble wrapping my head around it."

"It's bleak out here." She takes a sip of water. "God, that sounds terrible, especially when I'm trying to motivate you to get out there and date, but it's tough." She pouts.

My heart aches for her. She deserves the world. She deserves a man who loves her for who she is, not what he can get from her. Since her social media influence has grown, an abundance of men and women have tried to get close to her so they can mooch. It has to be maddening, never knowing whether someone's intentions are genuine.

"You'll find your person."

Her eyes meet mine through the screen. "You will too."

I lower my head. The idea of dating, doing the whole

marriage thing again, is absolutely exhausting. I don't even want to think about it.

"You need to call Mom," she says, changing the subject. "She misses you."

I bite my lip. And I love her. Sure, my parents were strict when we were kids, and they might be the reason I strayed from my passion in life, but they're good people. Talking to them, though, has been hard. It broke their hearts when I packed up my life and moved across the country. Not because *I* left, but because I walked away from my career and the life I had built.

"I will."

"Today." The tone she affects is one my baby sister rarely uses with me. She knows she has to add this stipulation, or I'll continue to put it off.

Stuffing my head under a proverbial rock and pretending the world doesn't exist is all well and good. Sometimes it's even necessary, to take that much-needed mental break, but the problem is that the things I've been avoiding stay there and continue to pile up.

"I'll call her as soon as we hang up."

"Good. Bye, love you!"

"Wai—"

The screen goes black. That little...

Izzy: CALL HER.

I pinch the bridge of my nose. I did say I'd do it.

So I scroll through my contacts and tap on her name

before I can talk myself out of it. I spoke to my parents when I arrived in town, but haven't since because I'm a sucky daughter. Sure, they could call me, but that's never how it goes.

She answers after the second ring. "Oh, Via, it's so good to hear from you."

"Hey, Mom." Hauling myself up from the couch, I go in search of my duster so I can busy myself while we chat. "What are you up to?"

"Not much. Just working on a puzzle. Your dad is playing golf."

"Tell him I said hi and that I miss him."

"I will. How's Massachusetts treating you?"

I press my lips together, torn between laughing and screaming. "It's Maine, Mom. I'm living in Maine."

"Maine, Massachusetts, Montana, Mississippi—all those M names blur together for me. Anyway, how's Maine treating you?"

"I love it." It's impossible to keep the sheer happiness out of my voice. I've fallen so in love with Parkerville. With Maine itself. "It's beautiful here. You and Dad will have to visit."

"Or you could come back here."

I sigh. I knew that was coming. "Yeah, I'll visit, but you could come see me too. There are a ton of cute shops and restaurants. You and Dad would really like it. There's a cute inn around—"

Her heavy sigh reverberates against my ear. "It's a lovely

thought, dear, but at our age, I don't see us traveling across the country like that."

Their age? They're sixty and in excellent shape. It has nothing to do with age. They don't *want* to come here or be a part of this life I'm making. They're convinced this move is temporary. I'm not sure how to make them understand that I didn't move to Maine on a whim.

"If you ever change your mind, then you know where to find me." I cringe at the words spewing from my mouth. Pathetic.

"When do you think you'll make your way back here for a visit?"

Seriously? For a long moment, I let silence settle between us and collect my thoughts. "Mom," I say carefully, "I just left." I've been gone a month at most.

"Yes, but surely you plan to come back for the holidays. You could stay with us from Thanksgiving through Christmas, or even New Year's."

My heart sinks. She means well. There's no malicious intent behind what she's saying. Even so, it hurts, because this line of questioning means that each time I talked to her about my plans, she wasn't listening.

"Renovations will be underway by then, and once they start, it will be impossible for me to get away."

She clucks. "That's right," she says, like she's already tuned out. "Maybe we can see you for Christmas."

"Yeah," I sigh. "Maybe."

"I'll let you go. I'm sure you're busy."

Shoulders slumped, I nod, even though she can't see me. "All right, love you, Mom."

"Love you too."

When she disconnects the call, I stare down at my phone in stunned silence. I wish I could say it doesn't sting, her blatant refusal to come to Maine to see me, but it does. I want to show her that my life here matters just as much as the one I built in San Francisco, if not more, because this one is entirely my doing. But I can't force them to come any more than they can force me to go back.

With a quick text to Izzy, I let her know I did my daughter duties and spoke with mom, but I leave out what a disaster of a conversation it was. She doesn't need to be dragged into it. She'll only feel bad for pressuring me to make the call in the first place.

But she can't control our parents any more than I can. It's not worth getting upset over. I learned a long time ago it's easier to let the disappointment roll off my back than to wallow in it. I've wasted too much time over the past year, longer even, feeling sorry for myself. No more of that. The new and improved Via is going to shake off all the negativity.

ten

Despite the small size of the town, every time I get out and explore, I find something new. The little bookstore is tucked around a corner, out of sight of the street. What alerts me to its presence is a sign hanging above the door. It's a cutout stack of books painted in bright colors. I wander down the alley to see if it's open.

The door creaks loudly when I push it open. The hinges definitely need a dose of WD-40. My breath catches at the inside. Every surface is covered with stacks upon stacks of books. Mostly old, with yellowing pages. Inhaling the familiar scent of paper, I step farther inside, closing the door behind me. The store is narrow but deep.

"Hello?"

A banging sound comes from the lone hallway to my

left. "Hi!" The reply is loud and frazzled. "Hey, you, get back here!"

I scan my surroundings, confused about whether she's speaking to me. When a large tabby cat goes running past me with a dead mouse in its mouth, I get my answer.

The girlish shriek that flies from my lips is downright embarrassing. Even more embarrassing is how I suddenly find myself on top of the table used to house the ancient register. The cat turns back and stops below me, swishing its tail and staring me down with round green eyes.

"Don't you dare," I warn, a note of hysteria in my voice. I might cry if it jumps up here.

Just then, a woman darts around the corner and scoops up the cat. "Bad, Tremaine. What have I told you about killing mice? You're really trying to live up to your name, aren't you?" With a sigh, she opens the door and shoos him out. "Out with you."

I stay where I am, frozen on all fours on top of the table.

"Ugh." She shudders. "I wish he'd stop doing that. I suppose it's my own fault for naming him after the wicked stepmother in *Cinderella*. You can get down from there now." She wiggles a finger.

"Does he do that a lot?" My heart rate finally slows as I climb off the table.

If she's bothered by me using her table as a means of escape, she doesn't show it.

She blows out a breath that ruffles her blunt blond bangs. "Every day."

I wince. "Gross."

"Sadly. But I'm used to it." Eyes narrowing on me, she snaps her fingers. "You're the lady who just moved to town, right? Olivia?"

I wince at the use of the word *lady*. God, it makes me feel far older than my thirty-two years. "Via," I correct. "And yeah, I'm the newbie."

"Well, welcome to Whit's Books. I'm Ella, not Whit. Whit's my grandpa." She sticks a hand out.

I slip my palm against hers and shake. "It's nice to meet you."

"What kind of book are you looking for? Anything specific?" She sways, practically dancing behind the counter.

"Not really. I didn't even realize there was a bookstore here."

"Yeah, we're kind of hidden."

"Do you..." I look around, taking in the selection. Most of the books around us are war related or political. "Do you have any romance books?"

She snorts. "Grandpa Whit doesn't believe in romance books. He says they're the devil's backbone. Grandma Mabel, though?" She arches a brow and crooks a finger.

Obediently, I follow her to a closet secured with a padlock.

She pulls out a key, and when it's unlocked, she swings the door open to reveal a selection of romance books. "She loves them. Take a look."

She steps back, letting me peruse the shelves. The selection is limited, but there are some newer titles I recognize.

"If you're interested," she says from behind me, "we have a book club of sorts."

I look over my shoulder. "Of sorts?"

She laughs, tucking a short strand of hair behind her ear. Her stylish blunt bob and bangs suit her. "We *do* read the books, but sometimes we forget to discuss them. Often it kind of devolves into a gossip session."

"Oh?" It's on the tip of my tongue to say no, that I'm not interested. Only, on second thought, it sounds like the kind of thing that could help me make connections and build friendships. "Sounds like fun."

"Cool. I'll get you a card."

She disappears, leaving me alone with the closet of locked-away romance novels. I pick a few that sound good, then meet her at the register.

She beams at the books clasped against my chest. "Good, you found some. Here's that card." She passes me a business card emblazoned with *Ladies of Parkerville Book Club (No Men Allowed)* on it. Below the name of the club is an address and a phone number. "We always meet at Lucy's house," she explains. "She's single and has the space for all of us."

"How many members are there?" I set the stack of books down so she can ring them up.

"I can't tell you the exact number, but anywhere from six to ten of us are usually there. It varies each week."

"Week?" I blurt. Aren't book clubs typically a once-a-month thing? Weekly seems excessive.

"Yeah," she giggles. "Like I said, it's usually more of a

gossip session. It's a great excuse to take a break from husbands and busy lives and just have girl time. Good food and wine too."

"Hmm." I tuck the card away. "Sounds fun."

But then again, maybe it only sounds fun since I'm starved for friendship.

"We're meeting this Saturday if you want to join."

"What book are you discussing?" I use air quotes around discussing. "I don't want to be completely out of the loop."

"Actually, you've got it right here." She taps the book on top of my stack. With a grin, she pulls out a brown paper bag with the store's name stamped across it. When she's rung up each book and placed it inside, she takes the cash I offer her. "I really hope you'll come."

Holding my hand out, I take the change. "I'm going to try."

I have no reason not to. The only thing that would keep me from attending is my own insecurity. I never used to feel weird about making friends, but since losing all my supposed friends in the divorce, a new vulnerability has shrouded me. After all, I wasn't the one who broke up our marriage. But at the end of the day, Chase was far more comfortable being the life of the party than I was.

"Good, I'll tell the girls. It was nice meeting you, Via. I ... uh ... wish we hadn't had the incident with Tremaine." She winces. "Hopefully next time will be better."

With a laugh, I pick up my bag. "It was interesting, that's for sure. I'll see you."

The second I'm out the door, I gasp at the ice-cold rain

that pelts me. Where did this come from? Hunching my shoulders, I run down the alley, back toward the main street and my apartment. My teeth chatter as my feet slap against the pavement. At least I wore my tennis shoes.

Too lost in my thoughts of getting back to my apartment, I don't see the massive roadblock on the sidewalk—said roadblock being an actual person—until it's too late. I slam into him and nearly go sprawling to the ground, but a big hand grasps my arm, preventing me from eating asphalt.

"Whoa, are you okay?"

I blink water from my eyes at the sound of the familiar voice. For a split-second, my brain is convinced it's Reid, but the timbre is too deep. When the man lifts his head, his face comes into view. Beneath the large brim of his raincoat hood—at least one of us was prepared for this downpour—Derrick is studying me.

"I'm fine," I huff, breathless. My heart is beating a mile a minute, and I'm still processing how I managed not to hit the concrete.

He releases me and nods toward his truck. "Hop in."

I'm tempted to say no. My apartment isn't *that* far and I'm already soaked. But I don't have it in me to turn down the offer. So with a deep inhale, I agree.

He opens the passenger door to let me in, then jogs to the driver's side. In one quick move, he throws his hood back and slides in. With the key in the ignition, he turns on the heat to full blast.

I shiver and inspect my books. Luckily, in my mad dash,

I clutched the bag against my chest in such a stranglehold that not a single drop of moisture reached them.

Derrick watches me with an amused smile.

"I had to make sure the books were safe," I defend, setting the bag on the floor between my feet. "Clearly," I motion to myself, "I didn't check the weather."

Note to self: Check the fucking weather app before leaving the apartment.

He chuckles, shaking his head. His hair is slightly damp, as if he didn't get his hood pulled up in time. "The weather in Parkerville can change like that." He snaps his fingers to drive home his point. "There's an old sea story about this place."

He looks over his shoulder and pulls away from the curb.

"Well," I prompt, "are you going to tell me this tale?"

He rubs his jaw. "The legend says that long ago, there was a fisherman who promised his wife he'd stop returning to the sea, but—"

"Let me guess, he didn't keep his promise."

He smiles over at me, eyes crinkling at the corners. "Of course not, and his wife was a descendant of sirens. You know what those are, right?" I nod, so he continues. "The legend says she cursed this town, made the weather impossible to predict so he could never leave again."

I arch a brow. "That's it?"

"Uh, well, it ends with him going out anyway. While he was at sea, a storm destroyed his ship, and he never came home. From then on, he belonged to the sea, since he loved it more than her."

"That's…"

"Depressing?" he supplies, pulling up outside my building.

"I was going to say badass. Women are powerful."

His laughter fills the cab of the truck. "I guess you have a point there."

"Thanks for bringing me home." Already, the rain is lessening, but I appreciate not having to run the rest of the way home in it.

"No problem."

I grasp the door handle, but before I can climb out, he clears his throat, garnering my attention.

"I'm sorry I haven't gotten a quote to you yet. I've had some personal things going on. Family stuff, you know?" He winces. "That sounds like such a bullshit excuse, but it's true."

"Don't worry about it. Send it over when you can."

He gives me a closed-lip smile. "Thanks for understanding."

Outside the windshield, the dark clouds part and the sun breaks through, shining through the mist and forming a rainbow.

"Would you look at that," he muses. "I told you it changes quickly."

So does life. But I keep that comment to myself. No need to bring my cynicism out right now.

"Thanks again." With a grateful smile, I climb out of his truck.

"I'll see you around, Via." He tips his head at me.

He pulls away as I start up the stairs to my apartment. Once I'm inside, I change into cozy sweats and pull this week's book club pick out of the bag, then let myself get lost in someone else's world for a little while.

eleven

Parked in front of a cute two-story white house, I fight back the nerves rattling around in my stomach. Meeting new people never used to bother me, but now that I'm living the slower, simpler life in Parkerville, it makes me queasy. I still feel out of place here, like the stench of California follows me wherever I go. It's a preposterous state of mind, but logic doesn't always dictate our emotions.

"Stop being a little bitch," I mutter to myself. "They're just a group of women. That's all."

I inhale a full breath, then blow it out slowly and climb out of the car. With my tote bag over my shoulder, I straighten my top, still summoning my courage.

The curtain shifts in the window near the door, making my left eye twitch with the desire to count how many people are peeking out at me. Instead, I keep my chin held high and my gaze forward. I school my face into what I hope is a pleasant expression—not too smiley, but no resting bitch face either.

Raising my fist, I knock.

Instantly, a muffled "it's unlocked" comes from inside.

I give myself one last second to internally freak out before I put my brave face on. Commanding a courtroom for a case? No big deal. But stick me in the middle of a small-town book club/gossip group, and I melt down.

"Hello," I say, taking in the group of women. "I'm Via, I moved to town recently and Ella told me about book club." I look around, searching for the familiar face. The women staring back at me range in age from what appears to be early twenties to eighties. My stomach knots when I don't see Ella.

Before I can turn around and bolt, though, she pops out from what I assume is the kitchen.

"Via!"

Relief floods my system at the chipper greeting.

"I was just telling everyone about you." She wipes her hands on a dishrag and slings it over her shoulder as she approaches. Without hesitation, she wraps me in a surprising hug. "I just put cookies in the oven, and we have charcuterie boards in the kitchen if you want to grab a plate. Let me introduce you to everyone."

Grabbing my hand, she tugs me farther into the room where everyone's seated.

"This is Lucy." She points out a dark-haired woman with

graying roots. "She graciously lets us take over her house for these events. Then we have Cassandra, Susan, Anna, Jessica, Tammy, and finally, that's Glenda in the corner pretending to nod off. Don't be fooled. The old bat is always listening."

"I heard that. I'm old; not deaf." The old woman cracks an eye open and scrutinizes me.

Ella nudges me with her elbow. "What did I tell you? Now, come on. Let's get some food in you. Wine too." She yanks me in the direction of the kitchen, causing me to catch the toe of my shoe on the rug. Blessedly, I catch myself before I face-plant in front of everyone. "I'm so happy you decided to come."

Whether I'm in agreement with that sentiment remains to be seen.

"Wow." The spread on the island is extravagant. Cheeses and crackers and veggie and fruit trays cover every inch of the countertop. "You guys really go all out."

She snatches the dishrag off her shoulder and drops it to the counter. "What can I say? We love wine and food."

"And good books," Lucy pipes up from behind me.

"And great sex!" someone yells from the other room—someone who sounds suspiciously like Glenda.

A bubble of laughter escapes me, and Ella grins.

The ease with which they interact is refreshing.

"Don't let them scare you off." Lucy passes me a plate. "Please, help yourself to whatever. If you don't like wine, I have beer and soda in the refrigerator."

"Wine is perfect," I assure her, turning to show her my

tote bag. Scrawled along the front in bold serif letters are the words *Read. Wine. Repeat.*

With a gasp, she grabs the sides of my bag. "Oh my God. This is perfect. We all need one."

Ella takes a peek at the tote. "Most definitely. Where did you get it?"

I add a couple of crackers and cheese to my plate. "Etsy. That website is incredibly dangerous for me. So many cute things."

"It really is." Lucy picks up a cracker and nibbles a corner. "I can waste hours browsing."

"Bring your gossiping selves back in here so I can hear!" Glenda calls out. "I can't turn my hearing aids up any more, and you know I'm nosy."

With an amused sigh, Ella shakes her head. "At least she admits it."

When I've loaded my plate, I follow the women into the living room.

"Cookies will be ready shortly," Ella says, taking a seat on an ottoman. She points to a chair, motioning for me to sit as well.

Lucy joins the others on the couch. "Should we discuss the book?"

Glenda grunts. "I'd much prefer to talk about what brought our newest member to town."

All eyes shoot to me. Shoulders hunching, I sink as deeply into the chair as I can, wiping crumbs from my mouth in the process. Naturally, they put me in the hot seat the second I stuff my mouth.

Come on, Via. You wanted this small-town life.

Every person I've encountered has been curious about my arrival, so I should've expected this. I don't have the same kind of privacy here that I had in my old life.

"I got divorced," I answer, and leave it at that.

Glenda narrows her eyes. "Did he cheat on you? Real men are shit. Gotta stick to the fictional ones. They're great." She holds up the book we're supposed to be discussing, flapping it around.

So much for keeping the answer simple.

"He did, actually." Surprisingly, the words don't sting as much as they used to.

The ladies gasp and *tsk*, telling me I'm too good for him anyway, even though they've never met the guy.

"With who?" Lucy asks, bringing her glass of wine to her lips.

I wince at the reminder of how cliché he is. "His secretary."

There's a collective gasp.

"He didn't!" Ella exclaims. "What a dick."

Glenda shakes her head. "Men."

Over the next hour, I find myself spilling every detail of my life to these women. I've never considered myself an over-sharer, but it's all too easy to talk to them. In the midst of my storytelling, I end up seated on the floor, hands on the coffee table, while Jessica gives me a full gel manicure, because, in her words, I deserve to be pampered. She has a small nail salon in her home, and based on the quality of the work she's done thus far, she'll have a repeat client in me.

By the time my story is done, so are my nails—painted an olive green with gold star accents—and it's time to go.

Though I was a wreck at the beginning of the night, I leave feeling utterly refreshed. I make plans to return next week, and also take Ella up on her invitation for lunch in a few days. In one fell swoop, I think I've found a whole tribe.

twelve

I'm beginning to enjoy my time alone.

There are times when I feel lonely, but for the most part, it's not nearly as horrible as I thought it would be.

I walk up and down the aisles of the nearest art store I could find. It took almost an hour to get here, and I'm not pleased with the selection. But there's an itch just beneath my skin, an urge I need to satisfy to get a painting out of my head. The one of my dress splashed against Reid's kitchen tiles.

I shouldn't be thinking about Reid, let alone creating a constant reminder of him, but I have to. It's been a long time since I've felt this passionate about a piece that's taken shape in my mind.

I pull a canvas from the shelf. I've vetoed the last two, and with a look at this one, I know. I'm not going to find the quality I want here. So I'll have to make do. With a sigh, I put this one back and go back to the last large one and finagle it into the cart.

The paint selection is slightly better, but still not great.

I don't want to get too many since I plan to order better quality supplies soon, so I pick out enough colors to bring my vision to life.

Once I have brushes, I head to the checkout. I don't want to get carried away and buy more things than I really need. I pile everything on the counter, being sure to give the girl at the checkout a pleasant smile. She's too busy chewing her gum and staring at her phone to notice or return it as she monotonously scans my items.

Once I've paid, I stick my supplies in the back seat. Behind the wheel, I take a deep breath, finding myself strangely melancholy. These moments hit me from time to time, but I've learned to roll with it.

Loading items in the back seat triggered the emotion, I'm sure. The empty space when I opened the door made me think about the lack of a car seat. Years. I tried for years to get pregnant. Dropping my head back against the seat, I close my eyes. Immediately a vision appears in my mind. That first negative test. The memory follows—the disappointment, though I didn't think much of it, and the words I said to Chase: "It usually takes a few tries."

So we tried.

And tried again.

And again.

There were two miscarriages along the way. Devastation

is an emotion too mild to describe the way I still feel about them. How I always think about them near what should've been their birthday and also when I lost them. I wonder often about who they would've been, what they could have become if my body hadn't betrayed me.

It wasn't my fault—my inability to get pregnant or stay pregnant—but that doesn't make the losses easier to cope with. It's impossible to be prepared for the anger that comes when one's body commits such a betrayal, when it refuses to participate in what's seemingly the most basic experience a woman goes through.

When I found out about Chase's infidelity, I sobbed in our bed, convinced that it was all my fault, since I couldn't give us a baby.

Izzy quickly sorted me out, reminding me that the only person to blame for Chase's indiscretion was Chase himself.

But I wasn't exactly logical in those early stages.

I was grieving my marriage, the loss of my future, like it was a real, tangible being.

After another minute, my heart feels a little less heavy and the tears that had welled ebb, so I start the car and head home. There's no point in dwelling on the past.

I pull into the alley behind my building and wrestle the large canvas out. There might be some grunting involved, but thankfully, I'm alone back here.

Just as I've crossed the threshold of my apartment, one plastic bag breaks. Tubes of paint and brushes scatter, and several items roll under the couch. With a groan, I squat and peer under the couch, bracing myself for what else might be lurking beneath it. Lucky for me, all I find are a few dust bunnies, not a mouse or—*gag*—a cockroach.

I scoop everything up and spread them out on the coffee table, then shuffle to my room to change my clothes. What I'm wearing is far from fancy, but I am fond of the light blue sweater I tugged on this morning.

Once I've donned my overalls, I turn on music and settle myself in front of the canvas. For a long quiet moment, I stare at it. Get a feel for it. Then I squeeze a few colors onto a paper plate and get to work on underpainting with an orange-brown shade.

When I start adding in the shapes and shades of Reid's kitchen tiles, my brain cycles through snippets of that night.

I wanted to wipe memories of that night—of him—out of my mind. But Reid has proven to be unforgettable.

With every stroke of my brush, I feel a phantom touch, his hands on my bare skin.

As I swirl the colors on the paper plate, I remember the way his mouth felt on mine, how he kissed me like I meant something.

I thought it would be easy to put thoughts of him out of my mind. He was a one-night stand. That's all. But Reid has seeped his way into my marrow, and not because of the mind-blowing sex, but because of the genuine sweetness with which he treated me.

With my base down, I set the canvas aside to dry before I go in and add the details of my dress on the floor. When I'm done, the subject of the painting shouldn't be obvious, but I'll know. And once it's finished, if I'm lucky, my brain will flourish with creative ideas that don't revolve around Reid.

I wash my hands, and once they're free of paint, I search my fridge for suitable dinner options. Everything I find feels like too much effort for one person, so I boil a pot of bowtie pasta. When it's done, I add butter and a sprinkle of parmesan cheese. Sitting down by myself to eat is one of the few things that's bothered me since the divorce. Chase and I didn't eat every dinner together, but most. A pit forms in my gut at the notion of doing this alone for the foreseeable future.

My phone rings when I'm halfway through my dinner.

"Hey, Izzy," I answer, putting the call on speaker.

"Hey," she replies, the sound of her car blinker in the background. "I'm on my way to the gym and thought I'd give you a ring. What are you up to?"

"Eating dinner." I stab a noodle and hold it aloft. "I was painting before that."

"Painting your apartment or…"

A chuckle escapes me. "I was painting an art piece."

"To sell?"

I wrinkle my nose. "I'm not talented enough to sell my art." *But you think you're talented enough to teach others?*

My shoulders sag. That's not the case either.

My mission is to open a place that allows people of any age to come and paint or draw or sculpt—whatever their preferred medium is—and have fun with it. I'll be there to offer support and advice and lead classes, but my goal is to support artists along their own journey, not preach about what might be considered right and what might be considered wrong.

When Izzy huffs out an annoyed sigh, I can all but guarantee she's rolling her eyes at me. "Via, you're more than good enough."

"You've never seen my art," I remind her. I haven't done much over the years, and on the rare occasions I did, my creations stayed in my sketchpad.

"You're amazing at everything you do. I'm sure this is no different. Send me a picture of it."

"It's not done," I mutter around a mouthful of noodles. The old Via would've never spoken with her mouth full of food, but the new Via gives no fucks. It's refreshing.

She sighs again. "Then show me when it's done."

"Sure."

"Mom was talking about you today."

I freeze, my stomach going leaden. "She was? What did she say?"

"The usual." Izzy sighs, though it's mostly drawn out by the sound of a horn honking in the background.

"That doesn't sound good."

"She's just worried about you," she says, her tone turning defensive.

I'm cautious when I talk to her about our parents. Her upbringing with them was vastly different from mine. I was —*am*—the oldest. The pressure is different. Plus, they tried and tried for years to conceive after I was born. Izzy is their little miracle, therefore she can do no wrong, and she's always gotten away with more.

"I know that," I reply. "I know she's upset about the move, but I'm not going to suddenly change my mind and come back."

"She says you don't want to visit."

"I didn't say that." Though I'm sure she picked up on my reluctance. "But I just moved. I need time to get settled, and renovations will be a pain, not to mention time-consuming. I can't just hop on a plane and fly back to California any time Mom thinks I should. My life is here now."

With a heavy exhale, I stab an innocent piece of pasta harder than necessary.

"I get that," Izzy says.

Does she, though?

"Could you try to give her some hope or something?"

Heart sinking, I press my lips together. "I'm not going to lie to her."

Besides, my mom doesn't actually miss me. I *wish* that were the case. Then I'd be more apt to consider visiting sooner. With my mom, though, it's all about control. It doesn't matter that I'm a fully functioning adult and have been for more than a decade now. She doesn't approve of my decisions—walking away from my job, the divorce, moving, none of it. She thinks if she can get me back home for a visit, under her roof, she can convince me to step back into my old life. Like slipping on a pair of old, beloved jeans.

Only, they're not beloved. Not anymore. They're the wrong fit. The wrong cut. Just ... *wrong*.

From here, I can see they always were, but for so long, I

thought they looked nice. My friends and family told me they did too. So I convinced myself they were perfect.

Izzy taps her nails against the steering wheel in the background. "I know you and Mom have a ... unique relationship."

Understatement of the century. Things could be worse, sure, but my relationship with my parents is far from ideal.

"But she does love you."

I stare down at what's left of my pasta, my appetite gone. "I know she does."

But...

The but is what Izzy doesn't get. It's what my mom doesn't get. Izzy, like always, doesn't know everything. For my whole life, I've felt compelled to protect her, and part of that responsibility includes keeping the ugly details from her. She doesn't know about my infertility—neither do my parents—and I didn't tell her about how our mom blamed *me* for Chase's infidelity. How she told me I should've done more because, clearly, I wasn't giving him what he needed. How she lectured me about not fighting hard enough. As if I wasn't devastated by his betrayal.

"Did you hear me?"

"Huh?" I shake my head free of my thoughts. "No, sorry."

"I have to go, but just ... maybe try to *talk* to her. Let her know how you feel."

Does she think I haven't tried? Over and over for years?

"Yeah, I'll do that," I say instead. "Enjoy the gym. Love you."

"Love you too. Bye."

When the call disconnects, I set my phone down beside me. The rest of my dinner ends up in the trash, and after a shower, I crawl into bed, doing my best not to replay the conversation in my mind.

thirteen

I nearly choke on my morning coffee when I open the email from Derrick and click on the quote. I thought I was prepared. The other contractors' quotes were even higher, but the number staring back at me still gives me heart palpitations.

But this was inevitable. I prepared for this. I'm just being a chicken.

I read over the email, noting the details he's laid out for the work. He's broken down the approximate cost for building materials and labor, and he's given me a detailed timeline. Six months if things go smoothly. Nine if they run into unexpected issues. It could be worse, I suppose. In less than a year, I can have this place open and running.

Blowing out a pent-up breath, I pull my hair into a

ponytail. Then, before I can second-guess myself, I type out a response of acceptance and hit Send.

With a whoosh, the email disappears.

Then I pace. Worrying my lip, considering sending a second *just kidding* email and scrapping the whole plan. The almost finished painting in the corner catches my eye, forcing me to stop and take a breath.

This calls for a sweet treat. In the end, that's the only decision I let myself make. I grab my purse and leave. It's better than staying here and quietly freaking out. If I'm going to spend that kind of money in one fell swoop, I deserve a sugar high and maybe a bottle of wine to crack open later.

I still haven't tried the donuts Reid mentioned. I've been avoiding the shop out of a ridiculous fear that once I try them, I'll lose some last piece of him. It might be the most pathetic thought I've ever had.

He was a one-night stand. One I desperately need to get over.

The only reasonable explanation for my hang-up is that I don't do casual hookups. This assessment makes me feel marginally better.

I stop off at the grocery store first for a bottle of wine. The most expensive bottle in stock is twenty dollars, which just so happens to be in my budget since most of my savings will go to the reno. I'm not sure why I'm freaking out so badly. I knew what I was signing up for when I bought the place.

As I check out with the wine, the cashier gives me the

side-eye. I guess purchasing wine at nine in the morning *is* a bit strange. And I probably look a tad unhinged.

"Thank you," I say, flashing a smile as I take the paper bag from her.

"Mhm," she hums, the sound oozing with judgment.

It isn't until I'm stepping through the front door that I realize I'll now have to carry my wine with me to the donut shop. By noon, the whole town will probably think I'm a drunkard. I wish I was kidding, but every day, I overhear new gossip about someone in Parkerville. I can't yet put names to faces, but that'll come with time.

I could take the wine back to my apartment first, but if I do that, I'll probably convince myself to stay home, and I really want a donut. My sweet tooth is practically crying out for sugar.

Sucking it up, I continue my trek around the block to the shop.

My heart stutters an out-of-rhythm beat when it comes into view, like Reid might be there waiting for me. It's so stupid, the way my body still reacts to the mere thought of him. It liked everything we did that night a little too much.

If I were honest with Izzy about how much I still think about my hookup, she'd tell me I was crazy, but then she'd tell me that the best way to move past him is to do it again with someone else.

If I thought that would actually work, I might consider it. However, I don't think there's any forgetting Reid.

Luckily, no one is inside Ms. Kathy's Donuts but Ms. Kathy herself. Hopefully this means reports of my bag containing a lone bottle of wine will be limited. I order half a dozen, a mix of the glazed and blueberry cheesecake.

The smell of them taunts me on my walk back home.

I lock the apartment door behind me and set my goods on the counter. When I flip open the box, I can't help but rub my hands together like a greedy little gremlin. The blueberry cheesecake is calling my name. Closing my eyes in an effort to better savor the flavors, I take a bite.

I'm not sure I've ever had a donut this good. Reid wasn't kidding.

After another bite, I set it on a plate and pick up a glazed one. The second the flavor registers on my tongue, I throw my hand up in exasperation. Damn, it's just as good. This might become a dangerous addiction for me. I can imagine it now, me showing up to the bakery every day for some of this goodness.

My phone rings, and I'm not surprised when it's my sister FaceTiming me. It's become an almost daily occurrence. When I lived in San Francisco, we never talked this much. For years, we've talked once every week or two. Ironically, the distance between us has made us closer. The fear of falling out of touch is much more prevalent with me across the country.

"Hey." I prop my phone against a vase and pull out a stool.

I'm over my frustration regarding the call earlier in the week. I know her concerns come from a good place.

"What's on your face?" is the first question out of her mouth.

"My face?"

"By your mouth."

"Oh," I brush crumbs from my lips. "I was trying donuts from a local place. They're amazing."

"Ugh, donuts sound so good right about now. How dare you tease me like this?"

Laughing, I take another bite—not to rub it in, but because I simply can't resist. "You could come visit," I singsong.

When she suggested the idea of coming shortly after I moved, I wasn't gung ho about it. Not because I didn't want to see her, but because my apartment was in shambles. I've still got a lot of work to do here, but now that I've settled in and have had a chance to fall in love with the town, I love the idea of her coming.

"Ooh," she trills, rubbing her hands together like a supervillain in a corny kids' movie, "are you okay with that?"

"Definitely." I slide the donuts away so I'll leave them alone. The attempt is probably futile, but I get points for trying, right? "I think you'll enjoy it here. I don't think you want to crash on my couch, though, so the inn is probably the best fit."

A half smile quirks her lips. "I'll look at my schedule, but I could probably come soon. Maybe around Halloween?"

My heart lifts at the prospect of seeing her in just a few weeks. I wouldn't label myself as homesick, but if being people-sick was a thing, I'd definitely fall into that category.

I don't miss California at all, but my sister? I miss her loads.

As if I have a schedule to check, I hum, smiling at her responding giggle. "I'm free whenever you are."

She lets out a high-pitched shriek. "I can't wait."

When we've finished our call, I take another bite of donut, then close up the box and hide it away. By hide it away, I mean I stuff it in the farthest corner of the kitchen counter and pretend I won't be sneaking more bites later.

In the corner of the room, my almost completed painting taunts me. I think, subconsciously, I've been avoiding those final details, the ones that will make it obvious—to me, at least—that it's meant to be a dress on a tile floor.

But I *want* to see it finished, and in order to do so, I need to pick up my paintbrush and get it done.

I change into my paint-splattered overalls. I bought them years ago for a trip. Chase, of course, questioned the purchase, since, in his words, they were boring. Now, covered in various colors, they're certainly not *boring*, but while they're a constant work in progress to me, he'd probably see them as something better suited for dumping in the trash.

Stop thinking about him. He's in the past.

It's hard, though, when Chase was such a big part of it.

I sit on the floor in front of the canvas, pulling my supplies closer to me. I'm pleased with how it's turning out, how the strokes of paint look. It's absurd that I settled here and have plans to open a store when I've ignored my artistic side for years, but this is exactly why. I want people like me, people who have been told their art isn't good enough or that they should be more practical, to have a space to let loose. Art doesn't have to be perfect. I don't think any artist is ever entirely satisfied with a project.

Once I've got my colors mixed, I get to work on those final touches I've been too chicken to add. I'm still not sure what I'll do with it. It's too personal to sell, but too *something* to hang on my own wall. Or maybe I should push past my fear and hang it up. Think nothing of it. I'm the only one who will understand its significance anyway.

I pull up my music app and put on a slow jazz playlist. From there, it doesn't take long to get in the zone. I focus on making sure every detail in my mind is represented, and by the time I sit back, finished, several hours have passed. I wipe my face, no doubt smearing a streak of gray across it, and admire what I've created.

It's not perfect. It's not even *close* to a masterpiece. But it's mine. And in a way, it's Reid's too, even though he'll never know. Thoughts of him swirl—what he's doing right now, if he's been craving donuts since our conversation—but I suck in a deep breath and quickly shove them all out the window. What Reid is up to is none of my business. He's probably already forgotten about me.

fourteen

Propped up against the side of my car, I watch for my sister. She'll be hard to miss at such a tiny airport. Anticipation claws at my throat. It still feels unreal, that she'll be here any moment, and it likely won't sink in until I can wrap my arms around her. And squeeze her so tight she'll probably wish she'd never come in the first place.

The doors slide open again, and in response, my feet do an awkward little jig. But it's all in vain. It's not her.

I check her text again.

> <fifteen minutes ago> Izzy: Landed. See you soon, Via-Mia.

I wait, my worry mounting every minute I don't see her, but finally, she strolls through the doors looking like she stepped straight out of LA, which I suppose she has. Her dark hair is pulled back into a slick, purposeful bun, and she's dressed in head-to-toe black. She's wearing a pair of heeled boots, and her makeup is flawless.

"Via!" She runs toward me. Behind her, her suitcase bounces so viciously I cringe and hope she doesn't have anything breakable inside.

Her perfume engulfs me, a fruity, fresh scent that reminds me of the beach and warm summer days.

"I can't believe you're here." A treacherous tear leaks out of the corner of my eye.

"I can't either!" Her voice is a high-pitched squeal. "It's cold here. I should've had my coat with me."

I open my mouth to lecture her, but she taps me on the forehead and grins.

"Don't worry, it's in my suitcase. Sorry it took me so long to get out of there. I had to take a call."

"Everything okay?" I pop the trunk and take her suitcase. When I lift it, I nearly keel over. "Jesus, Izzy, what do you have in here? A whole-ass child?"

She laughs, twirling her hands through the air. "Don't be ridiculous." It takes the two of us to get it in the car. "And yes, all is fine. My agency called to discuss a new brand deal. It could be a big thing." She bites her bottom lip, her eyes reflecting nerves and excitement. "I would be the face of a makeup brand. I can't say which. I had to sign an NDA to even speak with them." She rolls her eyes like their dramatics are ridiculous.

"Izzy." I pull her in for another hug. "That's big. *Huge.* I'm so proud of you. We have to celebrate."

I'm not sure *how* we'll celebrate since nothing in the area even remotely resembles what she's used to in LA, but surely I can think of something.

"Yeah?" she asks, almost shyly.

"Absolutely. A nice dinner, maybe?"

She wrinkles her nose. "What about something more ... I don't know, unique to the area? Authentic? Something that's not LA-esque."

Stunned, I blink at my sister a few times. I never would have expected a comment like that from her. She *loves* LA.

Once we're in the car with the heat cranked up—since Izzy can't stop shivering—I rack my brain for ideas. It takes a minute, but it comes to me. "I have something in mind. Are you okay getting a little dirty?"

She grins back at me. "Always."

"I LOVE THIS PLACE!" IZZY SAYS, CRACKING A CRAB leg. At the sound, her eyes bulge with manic delight.

I haven't had the opportunity to try the crab shack on the pier until now, but it's been on my list of places to check out. It's a hole-in-the-wall kind of restaurant. The walls and ceiling are covered in dark paneling. The air in here smells like Old Bay seasoning and stale beer mixed with a few decades' worth of grime. Izzy doesn't mind it one bit. We're seated at a long, shared table that's covered in a white plastic tablecloth and piled high with mountains of crab legs and shrimp.

Izzy hams it up with the man beside her, who has long hair, a beard, and hands the size of plates. His resemblance to J.K. Rowling's description of Hagrid from *Harry Potter* is uncanny. It's like he walked right out of the novels themselves.

Adjusting her plastic bib, my sister beams at me from across the table. "Best dinner ever."

My chest gets tight with affection. "I'm glad you like it."

"Like it?" she scoffs, dipping a bit of crab into the lemon butter sauce we're sharing. "I *love* it."

She puts away an impressive amount of food for someone so tiny.

I can't keep up, and by the end of the meal, I feel like Violet Beauregarde from *Charlie and the Chocolate Factory* after she chews the gum and turns into a giant blueberry. "My stomach hurts."

"Really?" Izzy cocks her head to the side, reapplying her lip gloss while we stroll across the lot.

Well, she strolls. I'm dragging my feet through the gravel because my body feels thirty pounds heavier. I think the butter got to me.

"I feel fine."

She looks fine too. Fresh as a daisy.

Is this what happens? The thirties hit, and suddenly one's body is incapable of handling the abuse it's been used to taking? Is this why I conk out after a single glass of wine in the evening?

Oh, God.

Now's not the time for an existential crisis. I need to get Izzy to the inn, and then I can have a breakdown.

I hit the unlock button on my key fob, and my headlights flash, lighting up the darkened lot in response.

"I can't wait to see your apartment." She snaps her seat belt in place, ignoring my groan when I drop into the driver's seat.

Maybe I should've test driven an SUV or two before purchasing another sedan, because climbing in and out of a car this low to the ground isn't exactly easy. I'll have to take up yoga to keep doing this comfortably.

"Trust me," I slide the seat belt across my body, "it's not much."

"But it's *yours*."

The way she says it makes me smile. She's right. It is mine, all the way around. I bought it, and I've single-handedly begun to make it a home.

"I haven't asked…" She smooths her hands over her perfectly styled hair. "But did Chase ever text you again?"

I back out of the parking space and head for the road. "No."

Thank God. I don't want to deal with him. His message was absolutely ridiculous. *I miss you*. Like he's done nothing wrong. He *cheated* on me. He got another woman pregnant. He's still with her, as far as I know. It's unforgivable in my eyes, but he's selfish enough not to care.

I didn't see it in him at first—the selfishness. But after my life blew up, I started to see things for what they were. I was annoyed at myself at first, for not recognizing the signs. But I guess that saying is true. I was too close to see the forest for the trees.

"It's okay if you're still sad, you know."

I stifle a snort. "Trust me, I've closed that chapter. I'm over it. Resigned is more like it." Quickly, I survey my sister, who's wearing a sympathetic expression. "I deserve better."

"You do. Speaking of better," she turns down the volume, "I'm still mad at you for not getting that guy's number."

My grip on the steering wheel tightens. "He was twenty-one."

"And?" She taps her foot on the floor of the car like she's irritated.

A humorless laugh escapes me. "You need more reason than that?"

"I see it as a nonissue. It doesn't have to be serious. Get out there, have great sex with a younger guy, and leave it at that."

I huff a breath. I get where she's coming from. I do. But that's not who I am. One hookup was out of my comfort zone. I'm not sure I can bring myself to do it again, even if it was with Reid.

"I appreciate your concern about my sex life—"

"No, you don't." She laughs.

"But I'm more of a dating kind of woman."

"Then go on a date," she singsongs. "That's your next

challenge. While I'm here, you have to go on one date." She wags a finger in my periphery. "I'll even set up a dating profile for you."

"Oh, God. Don't even joke about a dating profile." I shudder at the very thought. "I'm not doing that."

"Fine, then will you at least go on a date? There have got to be eligible bachelors out here somewhere. Hot fishermen, maybe? Or a sexy farmer or two?"

With a scoff, I shoot her a skeptical glance. "I'm not saying yes."

"But you're not saying no. I'll take a maybe."

Pinching the bridge of my nose, I turn down the lane that leads to the local inn. In the photos online, it looks idyllic. Lots of land and grazing farm animals, horses, water access, and a great view of the lighthouse in the distance.

Izzy quiets, taking in the long driveway lined with trees in a multitude of colors.

"This is going to look great in my vlog," she muses, tapping her bottom lip. She's probably running through the clips she'll create and the angles she'll use. "Do we have plans for tomorrow?"

"Nothing of importance."

"Via." She sighs my name. "*You* are important."

I laugh. "I just meant that I thought we could take it easy since you had a long flight. I know you want to see the store, but this is your warning. It's ... a mess." That's putting it lightly. "Especially since they started work this week."

The inn comes into view when the drive makes a curve, but she's too busy watching me to notice.

"I don't care about that. This is your home now, sis. Once I'm gone, when you're filling me in on your days, I want to have visuals of all the places you go."

With a groan, I put the car in park in front of the large home. "Ugh. Don't make me emotional. I hate crying."

Leaning over, she wraps an arm around my shoulders. "As your little sister, it's my job to put you in your feels. I'll see you in the morning, okay? Love you." She smacks a loud, glossy kiss to my cheek.

Luckily, we're saved from having to wrangle her suitcase out of the trunk when a young guy steps out of the inn and heads straight for the car. I pop the trunk and sit in my car long enough to watch Izzy take the stairs up and toss a wave my way.

My sister is in Parkerville. Having her here puts me at peace, even if she's going to pull me into all kinds of shenanigans.

fifteen

Izzy grasps my wrist and yanks me down the hall with so much force I stumble and have to slap my free hand against the wall to keep from falling over.

"What the hell, Iz?"

She releases her hold on me, and instantly, blood flow returns to my hand. "You didn't tell me your contractor was that hot?"

"Who?" I ask stupidly, rubbing at my arm. The girl has an iron grip. "Derrick?"

"Yes, Derrick." She hisses at a volume so low I can barely make it out over the cacophony of hammers and other tools. "He's gorgeous, fit, has a great smile, and he owns his own business." She ticks every detail off on her fingers. "He's perfect."

I blink at her, confused about where she's going with

this. In my defense, it's early and I haven't had coffee yet.

"Perfect for what?"

She flicks my forehead.

"Ow." I rub at the spot. "That hurt."

"*Perfect for what?*" She mimics me in a deepened tone. "For a date, you dummy."

I practically gasp at the suggestion. "I'm not going on a date with my contractor."

With her hands on her hips, she glares at me. "And why the hell not? He was checking you out. He's clearly into you."

I hold an open hand out in the direction of the power tools threatening to give me a headache. "Um, because he's my contractor. I have to work with him."

Izzy swats at my worries like a pesky fly. "What's the big deal with one date? If it goes well, you can go on another. If it's a bust, then no harm, no foul. You're both adults."

How is it that my sister so easily makes things sound vastly easier than they are? "No."

"Oh, come on. You promised you'd go on a date while I'm here." She pouts her lips at me like a petulant child.

I lift my head and jut my chin in response. "I made no such promise, and I won't be suckered into this."

Her sullen expression morphs into a bright smile. "It'll be fun!"

"For who?" I counter, crossing my arms over my chest.

"*You!*" She bounces on the balls of her feet. "I'll ask Derrick for you if that's what you're worried about."

I open my mouth to shut her down, but a deep voice

speaks up from behind me before I can get the words out.

"Ask me what?"

My lungs seize and my eyes threaten to bug out of my head. *Don't you dare*, I mentally command Izzy, but when have little sisters ever listened?

Grasping my hand, she spins me around. "Via was just telling me that she'd love to ask you on a date, but she's shy."

I squeeze her hand so hard she'll no doubt be left with the crescent-shaped marks with my nails. I cannot believe her right now.

Derrick's eyes flash in surprise. "Oh?"

Ugh. I want to melt into the floor. Embarrassment bubbles in my stomach.

"You're single, right?" Izzy goes on, filling the silence. "She's not interested in being a home-wrecker."

Right now, is when I wish the ground would open up and swallow me whole.

Derrick chuckles, running his fingers through his salt-and-pepper hair. "Yeah, I'm single."

"*Perfect*." Izzy draws out that single syllable. "So is she."

With that, she practically shoves me at the man and runs away like a little troll.

Suddenly, I regret extending the invitation to visit.

Stifling a cringe, I swallow past the lump in my throat and collect myself. "I'm so sorry about that. My sister can be—"

"I have to admit, I wanted to ask you out, but I didn't want to come across as unprofessional."

"Wait." I gape. "What did you say?"

He repeats himself, wearing an amused smile. "If she pressured you into it and you don't really want to, it's okay. I won't be offended."

"I—I mean, yeah. Okay." *Why am I so uncool about this? Get your shit together, Via. We're adults. We can go on one date and keep things professional if it's a bust.* "I would like that." My voice is stronger this time. Thank God for that.

"Are you free tonight?"

"Tonight?" I parrot. *Tonight?* "Yeah, I'm free." Izzy and I haven't made plans yet, and if I turn down his offer, she'll probably kill me.

"I'll pick you up at seven, then?"

Pulling in a breath, I nod. "Seven is great."

He grins, eyes twinkling. I'm not stupid. I can tell he's attracted to me. Izzy's right; I've caught him checking me out once or twice. The question is, am I attracted to him?

"Rub your lips together." Izzy holds my chin between her fingers, scanning my face to make sure the makeup she's spent the last hour doing is impeccable.

I do as she asks. "How do I look?"

She leans back and grins, clearly pleased with her handiwork. She should be. She's been the resident makeup artist for me and her friends since she was twelve. A lot of the videos she posts are makeup tutorials.

"You tell me." She grasps my shoulders, encouraging me to turn to the mirror.

I suck in a breath when I catch sight of my reflection. Sure, I do my own hair and makeup most days, but I don't possess even an ounce of Izzy's skills. My skin looks glowy in a healthy, not oily way. The bronzer makes it look like I've spent more time in the sun than I actually have. My hair hangs in loose waves, with a small section clipped back loosely from my face.

Hesitant, I brush my fingers against my cheek. "I look…"

"Hot. You look hot." Izzy crosses her arms over her chest and nods when our eyes meet in the mirror. "All you need is a dress, and I have just the thing."

She grasps my arm and tugs me out of the chair, and I obediently follow. Her suitcase lays open on the bench at the foot of the ornate bed. She convinced me to get ready here so she wouldn't have to lug all her makeup to my apartment.

While she digs through her suitcase, I hold my breath. She'll either pull out the perfect outfit for the occasion or something completely scandalous. The odds are pretty evenly matched.

To my relief, she extracts a long black sweater dress and holds it up triumphantly. "Tada. Do you like it?"

I rub the fabric between my fingers. "It's perfect." It will hug my body instead of swallowing it while keeping me warm.

"I have a jacket that will look nice with it too." She

passes me the dress. "And shoes."

In the bathroom, I slip the dress on carefully so I don't mess up my makeup and hair. Izzy would fuss at me if I messed up her hard work.

The fabric clings to me like a second skin. I feel good in it. Confident.

I *know* I'm not responsible for Chase's infidelity. I've known it for a long time. Regardless, my confidence took a hit after I found out. I questioned everything about myself. Was I not pretty enough? Smart enough? Was our sex life that bad? Was *I* bad in bed?

The blame I pinned on myself for *his* choices was all-consuming. It took time to identify what I was doing, and when I did, it was an eye-opening moment.

Izzy knocks on the door. "How long does it take you to put a dress on?"

With a turn of the knob, I let her in. "How do I look?" I twirl around, an almost girlish giggle bursting free. I might have been coerced into this date, but I still enjoy getting dressed up and having fun with my sister.

Besides, Derrick is a nice guy. I'll probably have a good time.

As long as I can push away the concern that creeps over me when I remember that I have to work with him after this.

Izzy clasps her hands under her chin. "You look amazing."

She's pulled out a pair of black velvet booted heels for me, and as I put them on, she gasps. "Oh my God, I almost forgot. You need jewelry." She scurries over to the dresser and rummages through her jewelry case. After a moment, she comes back with a long gold necklace and a couple of rings.

It feels weird slipping the rings on. I've never been a jewelry person, so, for years, the only adornments I wore were my wedding ring and studs in my ears. I left the ring behind for Chase to find. I didn't want it anymore and it was a final fuck you to him.

After Izzy helps me shrug into a brown suede jacket, she takes a step back to admire her handiwork. "God, I'm good," she congratulates herself. "Some people might say black and brown don't go together, but in my opinion, it's a top-tier combo."

Knowing that if I don't leave now, I'll be late, I pull her into a hug. "I might hate you for this, but thank you."

She laughs, hugging me back. "That's what sisters are for."

Out in the small parking lot, Izzy watches me climb into my car and start the engine. When it's running, she silently mimes rolling down a window, and when I follow her instruction, she says, "Call me when you get home. I want all the details."

I shake my head and laugh under my breath. "Of course you do."

"Have fun." She spins on her heel and all but skips back into the inn.

God, I wish I had even a smidge of Izzy's free spirit, but the expectations our parents had for her were vastly different from the ones placed on my shoulders. I'm okay with her being the favorite. She's my favorite person too. She lights up a room in a way most people can't.

On the drive back to my place, I blast music in an unsuccessful effort to drown out my thoughts.

Dating after divorce is normal—whether one jumps in right away or waits—yet I'm still struggling with the idea. Though my issue has less to do with actual dating, and more with feeling out of touch with dating culture. The world has changed a lot since I was in the dating scene. I'm not *old*, but man, am I starting to feel like it.

Back at home, I almost immediately catch myself pacing the short length of the living space. I force myself to sit on the couch, but then my legs jiggle with nervous, pent-up energy.

It's just a date. Relax, Via.

It's easier said than done.

My phone vibrates in the pocket of Izzy's jacket. I nearly fall off the couch in an effort to yank it out. It's probably Derrick telling me he's canceling. Before I can even check the screen, I'm waffling between feeling relieved and annoyed.

The internal debate is pointless, though, because when I finally pull it free, my sister's name and contact photo flash on the screen.

> Izzy: Don't freak out. Just have fun!
> Love you!

With a chuckle, I shake my head. Sometimes I swear we

have some sort of sibling telepathy.

> Me: This is all your fault, remember?

Izzy: You'll thank me later!

Just as I'm headed to the kitchen for a bottle of water—I need something to do with my hands—there's a knock on the door.

I shuffle over and grasp the nob but force myself to take a deep breath and fix a smile to my face before I open it.

The light at the top of the stairs flickers behind Derrick, momentarily distracting me. When I force myself back to the moment, he's watching me, wearing a soft, open expression. His hair is still damp from a shower, and his light beard is freshly groomed. The woodsy smell of his cologne is warm and subtle.

I realize belatedly that I'm standing there staring at him like an idiot. "Hi."

He smiles, holding out a bouquet of flowers I hadn't noticed. "These are for you."

Roses. Lovely, if a bit predictable.

"Thank you. These are wonderful." I take them and bring them to my nose. "Come on in while I find a vase."

He'll be doing some renovations up here, so he's already seen the place. Even so, I straightened up before I headed to the inn to meet Izzy. It only takes me a minute to pull down a vase, fill it with water, and pluck the flowers inside. When I turn back to him, he's wearing an amused smile.

My cheeks heat at the attention. "What?"

"You were dancing."

Horrified, I slap a hand to my chest. "I was?"

"Yeah." His smile widens. "Humming too."

"Oh, God." I bury my face in my hands. "That's embarrassing."

With a chuckle, he brushes his fingers along my forearm, and I lower my hands. "It was cute."

"I have this stupid song stuck in my head."

"What's the song?"

"I'm not sure." My sister played it all day. "I'll have to ask her. It was this electronic dance song—not the kind of song I usually listen to—but it was catchy."

I pat my pocket to be sure I have my phone, and grab my purse, then head for the door. With a hand hovering at my lower back close enough that I can feel the heat, Derrick follows.

"What kind of music do you normally listen to, then?"

"I love anything by Hozier. He's my favorite."

Derrick frowns thoughtfully when we hit the bottom of the stairs. "I don't think I've heard of him."

I name a few of his more popular songs, but Derrick continues to shake his head.

"No, doesn't sound familiar."

"Not even 'Take Me To Church'?" This is blasphemous. How has this man not heard of the greatness that is Hozier?

"Um…is he, like, a religious singer or something?"

"Oh, no." I throw a hand in the air, teasing. "This just won't do."

"Play something for me on our way." He opens the

passenger door for me, and once I'm safely inside, he jogs around the front of the truck. When he gets in, he passes me the auxiliary cord plugged into his dash. "Hit me with it."

I pull up an entire list of songs from all of Hozier's albums. If Derrick is handing over the control of music, then I'm going to take full advantage.

Obviously, I start with 'Take Me To Church,' sure that once he hears it, he'll recognize it, but not even a hint of familiarity crosses his face.

"This isn't bad." He taps his fingers to the beat against the steering wheel. "What about his other songs?"

I put on my personal favorite, 'Movement,' next. Derrick doesn't seem to hate it, so I'll give him points there, though he isn't overly enthusiastic, either.

Halfway through the song, I turn the volume down low. "What do you like to listen to?"

He hesitates, tugging on the collar of his flannel beneath a heavy denim jacket. "Country, mostly."

I laugh and scroll through Spotify to find a country playlist. "I should've expected that."

"What does that mean?" He chuckles.

"I don't know. I guess you give off that kind of vibe." I nod at him. "The flannel, for example."

He's very much giving Luke from *Gilmore Girls*.

He eases the truck to a stop at a light and glances down. "This is what gave it away?"

Raking my teeth over my lip, I shrug. "Stereotypes exist for a reason."

The light turns green, and with a wink, he turns back to the road. "I'm going to take a long look at my closet when I get home."

"Where are we headed?"

Small talk with Derrick is surprisingly easy. It doesn't feel at all stiff or awkward.

"There's an Italian restaurant not far from here. I haven't been before. It's fairly new. For around these parts, anyway." He shoots me a playful smile.

"What's fairly new?"

"It's been here a couple of years, maybe?"

I gape at him. "And you've never been?"

He makes a right at the next stoplight. "I ... I tend to keep my head buried in my work, so I don't always realize how much time has passed."

"I understand that."

For the past year, maybe even two, my life has been on autopilot. Only now does it feel like I'm waking up from it.

"You said your divorce is pretty recent, right?"

I wince. "Finalized recently? Yes. But it's been over for a year. Longer on his side of things, I guess." Miraculously, I manage to keep the bitterness from my voice. I'm over him, and I've moved on, but that doesn't mean the pain has gone away completely. "What about you?"

He clears his throat, keeping his eyes on the road. "My wife passed away."

I study his profile, searching for lingering sadness, but his expression is relatively easy. "I'm sorry." There is no good response to a confession like that, so I keep it simple.

"It was a long time ago."

I spot the restaurant up ahead, or what I assume is the restaurant, and my suspicions are confirmed when he turns into the lot.

"It was a drunk driver."

My heart aches for this man. "That's awful…" Again, I keep my response short.

"It's okay." And it is. He looks genuinely at peace. "This town is like family. They helped me raise my kids. Now they're both adults with their own lives."

"How many kids do you have?"

"Two. A girl and a boy. They're twenty-five and twenty-one. I have a granddaughter too."

I suck in a breath and almost blurt out something stupid like *how old are you?* but manage to bite down on my tongue before I can make a fool of myself.

"I was eighteen when my daughter was born," he goes on, like he knows exactly where my brain is at. "I'm forty-three."

Eleven years older. Huh. Interesting.

"Does that bother you?"

"Your age or the kids?" This time the words do escape before I can think them through.

He chuckles, rubbing his hands over his jeans. He's nervous, which is oddly endearing. "Both, I guess." The smile he shoots in my direction is shy, but his eyes are shadowed with trepidation.

"No," I answer honestly. "It doesn't bother me."

At least, I don't think it does. The goal of this date, for

me, was the practice, putting myself out there. I didn't go into it with the hope of something serious in mind. But maybe Derrick...

I push the thought away.

"Good. That's good." His smile is a little surer this time. "Wait here," he directs, holding up a finger.

He shuts the engine off, plucks the keys from the ignition, then hops out of the truck with an ease I'll never master at my much shorter stature.

As he rounds the hood, I slip my seat belt off, and when he opens the door, I take his offered hand.

Inside the restaurant, the hostess leads us to a table near the window right away. Outside, wind stirs the slowly dying leaves in a small whirlpool-like pattern. I should be paying attention to him. Instead, I'm quietly panicking that tonight means far more to him than it does me.

"You do like Italian food, right?" Derrick's question pulls me back to the present. Across from me, his cheeks are tinged the slightest shade of pink. "I should've asked." He hangs his head, almost like he's ashamed. "If you hadn't guessed, I'm not good at this."

"This, being talking?"

My joke hits the way I hoped it would, and some of the tension eases from his shoulders. "I don't date much," he supplies, fiddling with the edge of the menu. "I'm a bit out of practice."

I smile, finding his unease makes me feel better about my own. "This might come as a surprise, but me too," I whisper conspiratorially.

"That..." He flexes his fingers on the table. "That makes me feel better."

"Why don't we relax and enjoy dinner together? No pressure on either of us. This can be practice."

"Practice?" He runs his fingers through his hair but abruptly pulls his hand away and drops it like he's realized his nerves are still getting to him.

"Yeah, since neither of us are used to dating."

He tilts his head and presses his lips together like he's mulling over my proposal. "Okay."

Dating is never easy, but jumping in headfirst like this is panic inducing, at least for me.

When the waiter comes, we order a bottle of wine to share, and when he's gone again, Derrick clears his throat and sits a little straighter. "I'll only have a glass since I'm driving."

"We can always take an Uber back." I give him a smile, hoping to put him at ease, then dive into the basket of bread the waiter left behind. I skipped lunch because I was too nervous to eat.

Derrick laughs like I've said the funniest thing ever. "Uber? In Parkerville? Yeah, we don't have that here."

"Oh." I cover my mouth with my hand while I chew. "I didn't think about that."

"What part of California are you from?"

I tuck a piece of hair behind my ear, immediately cursing myself because I don't want to mess up the hard work Izzy put into curling the strands. "San Francisco."

"I bet your life there looked a whole lot different from this."

The waiter returns and uncorks the wine. I wait until he's filled our glasses and taken his leave to continue. "Yes, life here is vastly different."

"But you're liking it?" He sounds doubtful. Maybe I should be offended by that, but it really was a huge change, so I suppose doubt is reasonable in this situation.

"Yeah." I pick up my glass and bring it to my lips. "This place already feels like home, though. Does that sound strange? It's nothing like what I'm used to."

He shakes his head and picks up his glass of water. "Not at all. There are places that our souls are called to. Had you been here to visit? Before you decided to move?"

"Actually, no." I dip another small piece of bread into the oil. "I found the town online while researching the best places to live on the East Coast. I wanted to settle somewhere coastal, and this fit. Maybe it was crazy of me, but I took a risk and bought the shop sight unseen. Then I loaded up my belongings and I didn't look back."

Derrick leans forward, creating an intimate little bubble where it feels like only the two of us exist. "Do you mind if I ask about your divorce?"

"No." I wipe my fingers on the napkin draped over my lap and blow out a breath. "I'm okay talking about it."

"Was it bad?"

I wince. "It wasn't amicable, if that's what you're asking."

"Did you want the divorce or...?"

Pursing my lips, I take a minute to mull over the easiest way to answer. "I initiated the divorce, but no, I didn't want it. I … I was very much in love, or what I thought was love." A self-deprecating laugh flies out of me, loud enough to earn me a few funny looks from nearby diners. "He cheated on me, and I knew I could never forgive him, even if he'd wanted my forgiveness—which he didn't. People who can—forgive, I mean—and move past it are a lot stronger than I am. He got another woman pregnant, and so…" I trail off with a shrug. "That was that."

Derrick clasps his hands on the tabletop and frowns. "I'm sorry."

"Don't be. I'm so much better off now. I finally get to be the person I was always meant to be. I'm following my own dreams rather than someone else's for the first time in my whole life. It's strange, but that makes it all worth it."

He nods. "I get that. Sometimes we have to go through something awful to finally take a risk on ourselves. I started my business after my wife passed. It's something I'd always wanted to do. It was scary as hell going out on a limb to make it happen, but it's paid off."

I take a slow sip of wine and set my glass down. "And you love what you do?"

He leans back in the chair and drums the fingers of one hand on the table. "Very much. That doesn't mean it's been easy, though. We've had some rough years, income wise, but it's been worth it."

I'm not sure there's a romantic connection here, but we could be friends, and that's something. Izzy will be disappointed at the lack of spark between us, but despite being coerced into this date, I'm enjoying it.

Derrick insists on paying the bill, and I thank him profusely on the way to the truck.

"What kind of man would I be if I didn't pay for my date's dinner?"

I shrug, clutching my bag to my chest. Halfway across the lot, a piece of gravel gets lodged in the bottom of my shoe, so I bend to dig it out, using Derrick's arm to keep myself upright. "I don't know. Lots of people split bills these days. I just didn't want you to think I expected you to pay for me."

Once the gravel is out, I release my hold on his muscular forearm. Just as he's opening the passenger door for me, his phone rings in his pocket.

He hesitates for a heartbeat but ends up pulling it out of his pocket. "I need to take this."

I settle in the seat and straighten my skirt. "No problem."

With a nod and a soft smile, he shuts the door and steps a few feet away to answer his cell. While he's busy, I check my own phone, expecting a string of texts from Izzy. Surprisingly there's only one waiting for me.

> Izzy: I hope you have fun. You deserve it.

I don't reply. If I do, she'll be chomping at the bit for details, but I've already promised her a thorough rundown when we meet for breakfast tomorrow.

Looking troubled, Derrick ends his call. He runs a frustrated hand through his hair and practically stomps back to the truck.

He hefts himself inside with a grunt. "I hate to do this to you, but do you mind if we drop by my place before I take you home? It's on the way, and there's something I have to take care of sooner rather than later." His hands are vibrating, like he wants to wrap them around someone's throat.

Despite the visual, I don't feel any fear. It's easy enough to recognize his anger and near panic have nothing to do with me.

"That's fine. Seriously."

Neither of us speaks on the five-minute drive to his house. I swear he holds his breath and doesn't let it out again until he pulls into the driveway of a Cape Cod–style home that's so cute it makes my teeth ache. It's clearly a loved home. The way every inch has been taken care of is noticeable even in the dark.

He curses and glares at a run-down red car in the driveway. Its paint is peeling in places and there's a coat of rust on the hood.

"Who's—"

Before I can get the question out, Derrick is climbing out of the truck.

Based on his demeanor, I should stay in the truck, but instead, I find myself undoing my seat belt. The brick pathway that leads up to the front of the house is freshly cleared of leaves and other debris.

In his haste to get inside, Derrick left the front door ajar, so I let myself in. The entry opens straight into a living area. A leather couch faces a TV set, and the coffee table is covered in puzzle pieces. There's a soft pink blanket on the floor beside it. Muffled shouts echo through the house, one of which sounds like Derrick. I eye the staircase, wondering if I should interfere or if my presence will only make things worse.

Footsteps to my right have me spinning in that direction.

"Via?"

The sight before me steals all the breath from my lungs.

Reid. What the hell is he doing here?

"Reid?" Stunned doesn't even begin to cover how I feel.

Was his car outside?

I didn't notice it, but then again, I don't know if I would have put two and two together, even if I hadn't been focused on Derrick as he stormed into the house.

"What are you doing here?" He asks the question like *I'm* the one who's out of place here.

"I ... I was ... on a date?" I stutter. I can't wrap my mind around what I'm seeing. Reid is here. Standing right in front of me.

"A date?" With a frown, he pushes his glasses back into place. "Then why are you in my dad's house?"

My stomach drops, and I swear every ounce of blood in my body drains right out of me.

"Y-your dad's house?"

Why is my voice so high and squeaky?

"Wait." Reid shakes his head and roughs a hand down

his face. "My dad was on a date too…" His eyes narrow on me and his jaw goes rigid.

The pieces are coming together for me too, even if the scenario unfolding here is horrifying.

"You were on a date with my dad?"

The yelling above us gets louder, and we both look up at the ceiling like it'll transform into a window that will show us what's happening up there.

Reid grabs my wrist, sending a shot of electricity zinging up my arm, and tugs me into the kitchen. When he lets me go, he flexes his hand at his side like maybe he felt that zap too.

"I was," I finally answer him. "We were leaving the restaurant when he got a call and said he needed to stop by his house first."

Reid's perfect, pouty lips dip into a frown. I know I shouldn't, but I can't help thinking about all the pleasure that mouth brought me. I wrap my arms around my midsection in a vain attempt to hold myself together. This is the kind of turn of events no one could've expected.

With a pained grimace, he rubs his jaw, almost looking betrayed. "My *dad*, Via?"

"I didn't know he was your dad," I hiss. "How could I?"

Those intriguing green eyes that drew me to him the first moment I saw him are locked on me. Although, tonight, his dimple is missing.

Izzy's not going to believe any of this.

"You really didn't know he was my dad?"

"No," I spit out the word like it tastes bad on my tongue.

"Do you really think I would've gone on a date with him if I did?"

Reid looks me over, his jaw working back and forth. "No, I don't." He blows out a weighted breath. "This is fucked up, though."

"Yeah." I drop my gaze to my bootie-covered feet. "It really is."

He hooks a finger under my chin, sending a shiver running down my spine. He opens his mouth, but before he can speak, the yelling cuts off and several sets of feet stomp down the stairs.

"Dad—stop," a female voice pleads. "He's my boyfriend."

Reid and I quickly move back into the living room, and a heartbeat later, Derrick and two others appear. He's disheveled and still fuming. The scrawny guy he's manhandling toward the door has stringy, greasy hair that's plastered to his head under a black beanie. The young woman has tear tracks racing down her cheeks as she follows behind.

"He's a piece of shit is what he is, Layla. I've told you time and again that he's not allowed in this house."

"My sister's boyfriend," Reid whispers.

Derrick hasn't realized I'm in the house yet.

"Let go of me." The guy tugs against Derrick's hold, to no avail.

"I go out for one night, Layla. *One night*, and you do this?"

Layla rounds on her brother, finger pointed. "Did you

call him?"

Reid throws his hands up and raises both brows. "Wasn't me." He shuffles closer, and under his breath so his sister can't hear, he says, "Only because Lili beat me to it."

Who's Lili?

"If it wasn't you, then who was it?"

Her question is answered a moment later when a little girl no more than five or six tiptoes into the room and clings to Reid's leg. "I called grandpa."

Layla looks about two seconds away from blowing up, whether at the little girl—her daughter?—or the situation itself.

That's when Derrick spots me. When we make eye contact, he sucks in a breath and his eyes go wide.

I swallow past the lump in my throat and give him a small shrug. I should've stayed in the truck. Things would be a lot less complicated.

With a sigh, Derrick looks at his son. "Would you mind taking Via home?"

Reid meets my eyes like he's trying to gauge whether I'm okay with this request.

I give the tiniest of nods to let him know it's fine. It seems like Derrick is going to be occupied for a while.

"Not a problem."

"I'm sorry," Derrick mouths.

I give him a reassuring smile. "It's okay."

Outside, Reid leads me down the street to where his Mustang is parked at the curb. I definitely would've recognized it if we'd passed it.

He opens the passenger door for me. Once I'm seated, though, he doesn't walk away. He stands on the curb, gripping the doorframe, hesitating like he wants to say something. But after a moment, he shakes his head, closes the door, and walks around the front of the car. The whole way, his lips move like he's muttering to himself.

The driver's door opens with a slight squeak and he slides onto the leather a little less smoothly than he did the night we met. Hand hovering to put the key in the ignition, he blows out a breath.

Neither of us says anything for a long moment. With a shake of his head, he slips the key in the ignition and cranks the engine. Finally, he looks over at me.

My breath catches in my lungs, freezing there like my body has forgotten the ability to perform the basic function.

"I thought I'd never see you again." His voice cracks with a heartfelt emotion that takes me by surprise. "And then I do. But it's because you're my *dad's* date. How fucked up is that?"

Heart lodged in my throat, I rub my hands over the soft material of my sweater dress. "Very."

There's no sense in denying it. Regardless of whether I knew or not, it's fucked up.

Reid cocks his head to the side, assessing me. Can he see straight through me to the internal conflict brewing inside me? Can he sense the epic meltdown waiting for me just around the corner?

The streetlight casts shadows across his face, lending an additional intensity to his expression as he regards me.

God, I wish I could read his mind right now.

As if he can read my thoughts, he puts it out there. "Is it wrong that I really want to kiss you?"

My stomach flips over itself, and I blurt out the first thing that pops into my head. "Why?"

He rubs his lips together, fighting a smile. His dimple flashes at me for the briefest of seconds. Damn, I desperately want to coax it back out.

"Because I haven't stopped thinking about the taste of you since that night."

I blink at him, stunned into silence. Guys like him just don't exist, and yet he's sitting right beside me.

We watch each other, frozen in place, waiting for *something*. I'm not sure what.

One of us moves. It might be me, but I'm not sure. All I know is suddenly his mouth is on mine and I'm sighing in relief, like my body has been longing for the taste of his lips since the moment we parted. The feel of his mouth on mine is even better than I remembered. He kisses with a reckless desperation that makes me feel more desired than I ever have.

His fingers delve into my hair, holding me to him while he works his mouth against mine. I open for him, and his tongue flicks lazily against mine like we have all the time in the world and we're not making out in his car like teenagers. He tastes minty, like the gum he chewed the night we met, and I'm suddenly grateful I plucked a mint out of the bowl on the way out of the restaurant.

Reid angles my head back, peppering open-mouthed

kisses down the column of my neck. I squirm against him as goose bumps crop up in his wake. He laughs, his breath a gentle caress.

My body comes alive beneath his touch, the same way my creativity sparks with a brush in my hand. It's never responded this quickly before. My nipples are two hard points pressing against the fabric of the dress, practically begging him to take notice.

His lips return to mine, slower this time. Softer. And the hand in my hair slides to the back of my neck. Gently, he massages there, like he knows that, although I'm very much enjoying the kiss, I'm also quietly freaking out.

I was never supposed to see him again.

And my body, the treacherous wench, isn't supposed to want him like this.

But here we are, and I don't want to tell him to stop. The chemistry between us is far more explosive than I've ever experienced before. It makes me wonder if what I felt for my ex was even real.

Reid pulls away from me slowly, still holding the back of my neck, and we both struggle to regain our breath. My brain feels fuzzy, like I can't string together my thoughts, let alone speak words aloud.

"Where do you live?"

I blink at him, trying to clear the cobwebs from my brain. "What?"

He grins, and that damn dimple appears, making my heart swoon. "I need to take you home."

"Oh." I lick my lips in an effort to right myself. It's difficult with his hand still clasped around me. His touch sends wave after wave of goose bumps slithering down my spine. "Right."

Once I rattle off the address, he finally releases me and puts the car into gear.

"How'd you end up on a date with my dad?" He's suddenly far more at ease. Like he's no longer bothered by our encounter. Like it's not the most horrifying thing to ever happen to me.

"My sister." That's all I manage at first, though I realize quickly it's not nearly enough of an explanation, so I clasp my hands in my lap, sit up straight, and gather my wits. "She's in town visiting, and your dad's company is doing the renovations to my store and my apartment. She set us up."

He nods, lips pressed tight. "I see."

Does he? Because I'm still trying desperately to process this unexpected turn of events.

I watch the houses passing by us through the passenger window. It's easier to look outside than to focus on my reality. I'm sitting beside my one-night stand. The man I walked away from, sure I'd never see him again. I'm a wuss. I know that.

Beside me, Reid clears his throat, but I can't face him. I press my hands between my knees to stop them from shaking and keep my gaze averted to hide the tears welling in my eyes. I'm so overwhelmed in this moment that I'm about two and a half seconds away from bursting into tears. This is not how I expected my night to go. I blame Izzy.

Stupid, meddling little sisters.

"Stop freaking out."

I whip my head, *Exorcist* style, in his direction. "I'm *not* freaking out."

He arches a brow at me before quickly returning his gaze to the road. "Yeah, definitely not." Sarcasm bleeds through his words.

"How can you be so cavalier about this?"

Great, now I sound hysterical.

He snorts, rubbing at his jaw with his left hand. His right is still firmly wrapped around the wheel. "I really didn't think I was being that way."

I take a deep breath and close my eyes for a brief moment while I center myself. "I'm sorry. I…" I pull my hands out from between my knees and flex my stiff fingers. "I just don't know quite how to handle all this."

I'm usually the calm, cool, and collected one in any stressful situation. But when it comes to Reid, that's not the case. Maybe because, when he's near, my body reacts so viscerally to him that it's impossible for me to formulate normal, coherent thoughts.

"It's an unusual situation," he agrees. "I don't like that you're freaking out about it. We're both consenting adults. It doesn't have to be a big deal if we don't want it to be."

I close my eyes again, breathing in through my nose and out through my mouth. How is it that the twenty-one-year-old is the sensible one in this situation? He makes it sound so easy. And maybe to him, it is. But I don't *do* this kind of thing. I don't have sex with strangers, and I *certainly* don't go out on dates with their fathers.

Except I did.

But I didn't know.

In what feels like a blink, his mustang is cruising to a stop in front of my building. I fought so against giving him more than the basics about myself during our first encounter, and now all that has gone out the window.

He shuts the engine off and undoes his seat belt.

"What are you doing?" I blurt out the question so fast the words are slurred together.

His tongue slips out to moisten his lips. It's not meant to be enticing, but oh boy, my body did not get the memo. Not if the way my thighs clench together is any indication.

"I'm walking you to your door..." He hesitates, giving me hooded bedroom eyes. Intentional or not, the look sends a bolt of heat to my core. "Like a gentleman."

At those words, I'm flooded with memories of the very un-gentlemanly things he did to my body. Oh yeah, the eyes thing was one hundred percent intentional.

I narrow my own on him, a silent warning to cut out whatever it is he thinks he's doing. *Nothing* is going to come of this.

His face splits into a grin, and his green eyes twinkle with humor. I have to bite my lip to suppress a moan. Dammit, this guy is way too sexy for his own good.

Raising his hands in mock innocence, he presses his lips together to stifle his smirk. It's pointless; that impish grin has moisture flooding between my legs anyway.

"I ... I'm not so sure that's a good idea."

It doesn't matter how much I tell myself nothing is

going to happen when my body doesn't seem to get the memo.

How his smile grows even bigger, I'll never know. "Afraid you can't resist me?"

That little...

I stick my chin in the air. It's a haughty gesture, but I can't bring myself to care. "I can resist you just fine."

The way he cocks his brow seems to say *"We'll see about that."*

When he slips out of the car, I fumble with my seat belt in an effort to get out before he can open my door.

It's all in vain. He beats me to it, and when I finally unbuckle myself, I practically tumble out of the car onto the road.

"Whoa." Reid steadies me with a gentle hand on my arm before I can eat pavement. "Are you okay?"

"I'm fine." I chew on the words and spit them out between my teeth.

I shouldn't be mad. It's not his fault I find him utterly irresistible.

Reid wiggles his fingers. "Take my hand, Via. I don't bite."

Resigned, I obey. But only because his car is low to the ground, and I don't want to make an even bigger fool of myself. He helps me out, but once I'm steady on my feet, he doesn't let go. I try to tug my hand free, but his grip only tightens in response.

"Reid," I warn.

"Via." His tongue rolls around each syllable, drawing

them out.

We stand beneath the glow of the streetlight, locked in a stare off.

In resignation, I break first and tug him around the building to the staircase that leads up to my apartment. At the bottom of the rickety stairs, he stops short. "These need to be replaced."

"I'm aware. It's on the list, along with new wiring and new floors. New everything, to be honest." I let out a hefty sigh. It's overwhelming to contemplate. I might've cried myself to sleep last night at the thought of it all.

"You bought the whole building?"

"I did. I plan to open an art studio downstairs, and I'm living up here." I tap on the door to my apartment as we reach it. "It needs work too."

"An art studio, huh?" He tugs that full bottom lip between his straight teeth, instantly sending my thoughts back to the kiss in his car.

I *want* to kiss him. I shouldn't. I *won't*. But I want to, and that's the scariest fact of all.

"That's right, you like art too."

"Mhm." He nods, a brow raised thoughtfully. But an instant later, he's chuckling and shaking his head.

"What? What is it?" I narrow my eyes, willing him to tell me before my mind spirals and I come up with all kinds of scenarios.

He squeezes my hand, reminding me that we're still connected. I'd forgotten. That's how scarily right it feels.

"I ... uh ... I work for my dad part time. I also work as a

mechanic. Anyway," he runs his free hand through his hair, "when you said art studio, it clicked. I'm scheduled to start on this project on Monday."

My chest gets tight, and instantly, my hands become sweaty. Reid and his dad? Here? Together? "No."

There's no way I can handle Derrick *and* Reid all in one room.

One, I went on a date with.

The other I fucked.

Father and son.

Oh my God.

I long for the earth to open up beneath my feet and swallow me whole. Put me out of my misery.

This scenario keeps getting worse and worse.

"Via?" He says my name in a way that makes me think it isn't the first time.

"Yeah?" My voice is shaky, and panic crawls up my throat, threatening to suffocate me.

He steps closer and cups my face. *"Breathe."* He takes a deep breath in, encouraging me to mimic him. "That's it, angel. Breathe for me." When I start to gain control of my breathing again, he gives me a small smile. "Good girl."

"Y-You-You're going to be working here?"

His only response is a single nod.

I blow out a breath as unshed tears sting my eyes. "Oh boy." Is the universe laughing at me right now? I kind of feel like it is. This has to be a cruel cosmic joke. I lower my head and fight back the tears. I'm filled with the sudden need to walk off my stress, but there's nowhere for me to go.

The space at the top of the stairs is small, and with both of us in front of the door, I'm stuck. "I can't believe this."

Reid's pointer finger is a gentle but persistent press beneath my chin.

"Don't freak out. Please. I hate seeing you like this."

I flex my fingers at my sides. "I'm trying not to."

And failing epically.

"I'm not going to say anything to my dad, if that's what you're worried about. I don't believe in kissing and telling."

"I..." I shake my head, the curls Izzy meticulously styled beginning to fall flat. "I didn't think that."

Did I?

No.

I just don't know that I can handle the fallout of this reality.

"Everything will be fine," he says gently. "Go inside, shower, and go to bed."

My lips twitch with the desire to smile. I shouldn't like that he's bossing me around, dammit.

"This doesn't have to be a big deal." He leans in and presses a gentle kiss below my ear. "Night, Via." He pulls back, but with an "oh," he quickly ducks close again and brings his lips to my ear. "I can fuck you better than my dad ever could."

My eyes go wide and my throat closes up. Stunned by his audacity, all I can do is watch, frozen as he descends the stairs. When he reaches the bottom, he turns back to look up at me and winks.

That little...

PART TWO

sixteen

Via

After a failed attempt to sneak into the inn—which was locked up tight for the night—and numerous unanswered calls to Izzy, I came home and crashed face-first into my mattress. I didn't even bother to change out of my clothes or remove my makeup.

That's how utterly exhausted I was after all of last night's happenings.

Slowly, I blink my eyes open. They're stuck together by copious amounts of mascara and eyelash glue. Something skitters across my cheek, and with a shriek, I smack at it, only to discover the culprit is a fake eyelash that became dislodged.

Ugh.

I roll over onto my back. I feel hungover, even though I only had a glass of wine with my dinner last night.

Dinner.

A date.

With Derrick.

Who is Reid's *dad*.

With a groan, I cover my face. It takes a solid five-minute mental pep talk before I'm ready to pull myself out of bed and stumble into the shower I desperately need.

I'm not normally one for long showers, but I spend forty minutes scrubbing myself from head to toe at least three times over. Brushing through the wet strands of my hair, carelessly letting water gather on the cracked tile floor beneath my feet, I steadfastly ignore the persistent ringing of my phone.

No doubt it's my sister. The sister who was nowhere to be found in my time of need. The one million missed phone calls probably have her worried, but she can wait until I've better sorted myself out.

After I've applied lotion and light makeup, I pull on a simple pair of jeans and a black sweater. Only then do I check my phone.

It's all Izzy, just as I suspected, and one text from Derrick apologizing for last night.

I cringe at that. His apology is far from necessary. Not when I know what his son's penis looks like. Not when I—never mind.

Oh my God, I hate myself.

Bracing for the inquisition, I call Izzy back.

Unsurprisingly she answers on the first ring. "Jesus, Via-Mia, it's about time you answered. I wake up to a thousand missed calls, and then you go MIA? Do you need bail money or something?"

"Not exactly." I pace the length of my bedroom, my stomach already sinking. All of the nerves I thought I had worked out of my system are returning.

"What is it, then?"

I twirl a lock of half-dried hair around my finger and breathe through a wave of panic. "I'd rather talk to you in person."

"Okay, come pick me up. We can go to that cute little diner on Main Street. I'm *starving*."

"Don't they serve breakfast at the inn?"

She huffs, the sound crackling down the phone line. "Yeah, but I wanted to have breakfast with my sissy, especially after I looked at my call log. I thought someone died."

"I'm sorry." I am. Last night, I didn't consider what she would think when she woke up to that many missed calls and desperate text messages. "We can pick up food from the diner and eat at my place."

"Why?"

"Because," I drawl, "this town is full of Nosy Nellies, and I'm not about to say what I need to say in a place with so many ears."

She's quiet on the other end for a moment, then bursts into raucous peals of laughter. "Was the date that bad? Is that what this is about?"

I sigh and drop to the end of my bed. "Just you wait, Izzy. I'll be there in ten."

My sister gapes at me, her fork hovering halfway to her mouth. The bite of uneaten pancake falls from the end of her fork and lands with a splat in her to-go container.

"I'm going to need you to repeat that." She popped up on her knees on the other side of the coffee table when I got to the part where Reid appeared in Derrick's living room, and she's been inching higher since.

I nearly choke on my sip of orange juice. "Oh, please don't make me say it again." The grimace I shoot her is not because the juice is sour.

"I just ... There's no way I heard you right."

I press my lips into a thin line and drop an elbow to the table. "You did. Trust me."

"The guy you had a one-night stand with is Derrick's *son*?"

With a long breath in, I search for a little inner peace. Too bad that well's all dried up. Slowly, I let the air back out. Am I stalling? Totally. "Yeah."

"Whoa." She sits back on her butt and crosses her legs under the table. I'm not sure why we chose to sit here instead of at the breakfast bar. "This is a lot to process."

"How do you think I feel?" I force myself to take a bite

of my egg sandwich, and miraculously, my stomach doesn't revolt.

"It's not the worst thing in the world. There's no way you could have known, so there's nothing to feel guilty about. It was just a strange set of circumstances." She shrugs like it's really that simple. "Wow," she mutters, "I guess this really is a small town."

With a groan, I wipe my mouth with a napkin. "This is a mess."

Calling this a mess is the understatement of the century, but I'm at a loss for words when it comes to the clusterfuck I've found myself in the middle of. The stupid part, the thing I don't voice to my sister, is that I wonder if I'm being punished. I finally took a risk, did something out of my comfort zone by hooking up with Reid, and now I'm forced to deal with the fallout.

"It really could be worse." Izzy lifts one shoulder in a dainty shrug. "I mean—" The words are garbled around a massive bite of pancake. She holds up a finger and chews. Once she swallows, she goes on. "You could've fucked them both."

I almost knock our food off the coffee table in my haste to slap a hand over her mouth. We're alone, so there's no one to overhear, but I have the urge to shove the words back in there and make them disappear.

"Don't even joke about that." I lower my hand and sit back with a whimper.

Ugh, now I definitely don't want to eat.

"Why? It could've happened."

"But it didn't, and I had no plans to even kiss Derrick on our date, so sex was already off the table."

Izzy arches a single dark brow. "Sis, sex is always on the table."

Rubbing my temples, I say a silent prayer that I don't end up with a migraine.

"Anyway," she spears another bite of pancake, "we need to pick up some candy."

"Candy? Why?"

She stares at me in abject horror, eyes wide and lips parted, and clutches her napkin in her fist like she wants to chuck it at me. "Via, you can't be serious."

"What?" I ask, glaring down at the sandwich I wanted so badly but can't eat thanks to my little sister and her uncanny ability to ruin my appetite.

"Halloween is tomorrow."

Oh.

"I know."

Now she's slack-jawed as she scrutinizes me. "You know and you're unbothered? We have to get candy for the trick-or-treaters!"

Dammit. I'm definitely going to end up with that migraine.

"No one's going to come to my door." I point at said door to drive home my point. "It's up a set of stairs in a sketchy alley."

Izzy frowns and sets her fork down. "We should spruce that area up while I'm here. Add a patch of fake grass and a little table and set of chairs." She snaps her fingers.

"That easy. It could be so cute. But I digress." She sighs deeply. "There's a Halloween event in the middle of town. It starts at five. The sign at the grocery store said to bring candy."

Tilting my head, I narrow my eyes on her. "When did you go to the grocery store?"

"This morning. I explored town while *someone* was sleeping in."

I stick my chin in the air. "I was trying to sleep away my trauma."

She cackles, tossing her hair over her shoulder. "And Mom and Dad think I'm the dramatic one. We're going to the Halloween event, whether you like it or not."

PRACTICALLY THE WHOLE TOWN IS GATHERED TO celebrate Halloween. This time of year, it gets dark early, so though the event is just beginning, as the sun has already set by the time we head inside the community building. Armed with far too many bags of chocolate, thanks to Izzy, we navigate our way through throngs of people to one of the candy stations.

I'm not sure how she managed it, perhaps the magic of Amazon Prime, but she produced costumes for us seemingly out of thin air. Hers is a flapper style dress with a headband—simple but cute. For me, she chose what I *think* is a slutty rendition of Red Riding Hood. I had to put a pair of tights on beneath the dress and pin the top so my boobs weren't spilling out.

"Hey!"

"Who's that?" Izzy asks, squinting at the woman who's waving and heading our way.

The Lady Tremaine costume is elaborate, right down to the cat in her arms. I have to slap a hand over my mouth to hold in my laughter.

"Ella," I answer my sister, tugging her toward my friend. "She works at the bookstore. She's the one who invited me to book club."

We reach Ella in no time, and I make quick introductions. It's no surprise that they become fast friends. Within minutes, Ella is insisting Izzy join us for book club night before she leaves.

"Your sister has the book for next week. She's probably plowed through it already." *Guilty.* "So you can borrow hers."

"Sounds fun. I'd love to vlog some. Do you think anyone will mind?"

Ella shrugs. "I doubt it, but fair warning—there is no controlling what comes out of Glenda's mouth."

"I'm going to grab a drink," I mouth to my sister as I slip away from the two of them.

I say hi to a handful of people along the way. With every passing day I spend in Parkerville, I'm greeted by more.

When I finally make it to the refreshment table on the far wall, I swipe a donut that's clearly from Ms. Kathy's and take a bite of the delicious blueberry—of boo-berry for tonight, according to the label—goodness.

Eyeing the drink options, I scoop up a cup decorated with ghost stickers and the bottle of Dr Pepper.

I nearly tip my entire cup over when a husky male voice whispers, "I'll have what you're having."

I don't have to turn to look to know it's Reid.

"You want soda?" I reach for another cup but leave my hand hovering above it.

"Not what I meant, angel." He swipes at my lip with a thumb, pulling a gasp from me, and comes away with blueberry frosting. When he brings it to his mouth, licking it away, he flashes a set of very realistic vampire teeth.

The sight makes my knees wobble. "W-What are you doing?" I stutter, scanning our surroundings to see if anyone near us witnessed what he did.

Surprisingly, no one is paying us any mind. Instead, all focus is on the kids who are playing a rowdy game at a booth nearby.

"I wanted a taste," he reasons, filling a cup with orange soda. He makes a face after the first sip. I can't imagine the blueberry frosting left on his tongue complements the orange flavor very well.

Once again, I scan the crowd. "Is your dad here?" Even in costume, I think I would recognize Derrick.

"Nope." He pops the *p*, stepping so close I can feel the heat radiating from him. "Why are you here? This is for kids."

"I'm with my sister and niece. Why are you here?" he

counters, his focus wandering to where my top is pinned to minimize the amount of cleavage on display.

"My sister dragged me here."

"Is she five?"

I sigh, knowing exactly where he's going with this. "Add twenty years to that."

He gives a low chuckle. "Via, I thought this was for children."

He grasps my wrist, sending a zap up my arm. Can he feel the way my pulse jumps at his touch?

"There's something I want to show you."

"Show me?" I blurt, confusion swirling in my mind.

"Mhm." I shouldn't like the way he's examining me, dammit. "It's this way." He gives my wrist a tug, pulling me away from the table and my Dr Pepper.

Ugh, and my donut. RIP boo-berry donut. You will be missed.

He hauls me toward a closed door just outside the room and peers over one shoulder, then the other, before pulling it open and striding down the long hallway on the other side.

I have to practically run to keep up with him.

I pull in a breath, ready to complain about the speed at which he's jerking me along, but I let it out again in a whoosh when he comes to an abrupt stop outside yet another closed door. He yanks it open and pulls me in after him.

"Is this what you—"

My question is cut off, because suddenly his mouth is on

mine. It's a shock to my system, but oh boy, does my body respond. My fingers have a mind of their own when they twine in his hair. It's hard, slicked back from hair gel, but that doesn't stop me. He nips at my bottom lip, and my mouth opens in response. I whimper when his tongue swipes gently against mine, eliciting a low rumbling in his chest.

He wraps a hand around my throat, thumb on my chin, and guides my head back, deepening the kiss in a way that makes my knees go weak.

But he's ready for that too.

He lifts me easily, and my legs wind themselves around his waist. His erection presses against my center, persistent and demanding, encouraging my hips to grind against him of their own accord. He's unleashed a deep yearning inside me. I'm not thinking about our ages or his dad. Instead, all I can think about is how good he'd feel inside me again.

Maybe my brain is taking a back seat on this endeavor because he took me by surprise. I wasn't even expecting to see him tonight.

He sinks his teeth against my neck, the points of his elongated canines digging into the tender expanse of skin.

"I wanted to fuck you so bad the other night," he confesses, his voice husky. His lips skim over mine for the briefest of moments. "Spank your ass raw for going on a date with my dad."

"I-I didn't know." A small cry escapes me when he rocks his thick erection against me. I don't know what's wrong with me, but I'd give anything for our clothes to slip away.

"Unknowingly or not, I want to mark you so you remember which Crawford you belong to."

My lips tremble beneath his kiss. *Why do I find that so fucking hot?*

"Would you like that, Via?" He slips his tongue past my lips, the move mimicking the way he fucked me that night.

I nod, which only makes him chuckle.

"Use your words, angel."

Smart Via would shove him away, walk out of this ... whatever room we're in, and act like this never happened.

Stupid Via wants to be fucked very, very much.

Despite my shock over this whole fiasco with Reid and Derrick, there's no denying the powerful chemistry that exists between the two of us.

"Y-Yes."

He skims his hands down to my hips, rubbing lazy circles over the thin fabric of the cheap dress with his thumbs. "You want me to fuck you?"

I nod again, whimpering like an ensnared animal when his hand moves beneath the dress. All that's left between us is the tights and my thin pair of underwear.

He lingers there, giving me another chance to say no if I'm unsure about this. I appreciate it, but it's unnecessary.

Sometimes being stupid can be very, very fun.

"Fuck me, Reid." I tack on his name so it's clear that I'm here with him in this moment.

Will I regret this? Probably. Not because I don't want it, but because I *shouldn't* want to have sex with Reid again. It's pure selfishness, and that's so foreign to me. But for years I put everyone else before me. My parents, my sister, my friends, *Chase*, and look where that got me.

Now I'm learning that it's okay to put myself first every now and then. If that means letting the twenty-one-year-old son of my contractor fuck my brains out, then so be it.

"Thank fuck," he all but growls, setting me on my feet.

He takes a step back and pulls a pocketknife from his pocket. Before I can ask him what he's doing, he kneels on the ground and gently parts my thighs. It's dark, dark enough that my eyes have barely adjusted in the time we've been in here, but his teeth flash in a grin so bright it's hard to miss a second before he grabs my tights at my crotch and slices right through them.

He doesn't stop there.

My panties are still in the way, so he makes quick work of slicing those too.

"You could've taken them off," I protest, my voice annoyingly weak, just like my knees. "This was hardly necessary."

White teeth flash at me again. "This is way more fun." He kisses my now fully exposed pussy—literally pecks a kiss on the sensitive skin like it's my mouth.

As he stands, the sound of his zipper sliding down is loud in the silent room. He strokes himself. He's still cast in shadow, but his rough movements are impossible to miss, and the sound of his hand working over his cock? Each slide up and then back down sends another wave of liquid heat to my core. I whimper at the memory of how his thick cock felt sliding into my pussy.

He rips a condom open, the sound almost jarring.

"You brought a condom?" I should be glad he has protection, not annoyed, but I find myself feeling irrationally jealous over some phantom mystery girl he might be carrying condoms around for.

"Just the one." He smacks a kiss to my lips. "And only because I saw you the other night."

My heart stutters in my chest. "Did you expect this to happen?"

He lifts me, and once again, my legs know exactly what to do. When I'm wrapped around him, he lines me up with his latex-covered cock. "No," he admits, hovering *right there*, teasing me with his proximity while leaving me guessing when he'll pull me onto his cock. "But I hoped."

He thrusts into me hard. The sudden intrusion has me screaming more from surprise than actual pain. My pussy is drenched. I've been wet since the moment I heard his voice at that wretched refreshments table.

"You feel so fucking good, angel. Your pussy squeezes me so tight."

My inner walls quake around his solid length. Hell, my whole body quakes. I grasp his shoulders to steady myself, praying he doesn't drop me.

He laughs, the vibrations that work their way through me nearly making my eyes roll into the back of my head. "I'm not going to drop you."

Oops. Did I say that out loud?

My head lolls back against the wall as I ride the wave of pleasure.

I can't believe I'm doing this. My sister is down the hall, along with half of the residents of my new hometown.

But I don't care—and that might be the most glorious thing to ever happen to me. For all my life, I've cared too much about everyone else and not enough about myself.

Tugging at my top, he frees my breasts, causing the pin to pop free and ping against the floor. I doubt I'll ever be able to locate it.

"Fuck, your tits are perfect," he practically growls. He closes his mouth over one pert nipple, licking and sucking, never slowing the thrust of his hips. "I wish I could see your skin right now," he muses, voice husky. "I bet you're flushed the prettiest pink."

He adjusts his grip on me, deepening the angle of penetration in the process. That's all it takes to send me flying off the edge of the orgasm cliff. I squeeze my eyes shut, and he presses his mouth tight against mine in a bruising kiss to quiet my screams. The orgasm goes on and on, and when it finally ebbs, I go practically limp.

"Not so fast." He uses the wall to support me so he can grasp my hands and pin them above my head. "I'm not done with you yet."

I whimper at the devilish promise in his words.

Our fingers twine together, pressed there like that, and despite how exhausted I already feel, I meet him thrust for thrust. Biting down on my bottom lip, I hold in a cry as another orgasm builds. I don't know what the hell his dick is made of, but it must be full of magic orgasm juju or something. My body has never responded like this before.

"Feel the way I fuck you?" His lips brush my ear, eliciting a rush of tingles. "How good it is? How your pussy was made for me? I'm going to ruin you, Via, the same way you've ruined me. No man is ever going to make you feel this good. Not the way I can."

I want to protest, to fight him on that proclamation, but I can't find the words. Frankly, I think he might be right.

He adjusts so he's gripping both of my wrists with one hand. Then he skates the other down my body and finds my clit. He rubs his thumb against the sensitive bundle of nerves, and even in the dark, I know he's smirking at me.

"Oh, fuck," I curse a moment before the orgasm hits me.

I sag against his body when he releases my hands, but he's quick to grab on to my hips. His thrusts are hard, fast. Impossibly, a third orgasm builds. I go over, and he's right behind me, shouting my name into the damp skin of my neck.

We stay like that for several long moments before he sets me down and we go about righting our clothes. It's a much easier process for him, especially when I'm tucking my breasts back into my dress and he's pulling my neckline down again and grasping them, testing their weight. He rubs his thumbs over my sensitive nipples, and when I mewl in response, he shoots me a cocky grin.

"Reid," I practically beg, "I need to get dressed."

"I prefer you naked." Angling in, he presses a kiss to my cheek. "I love that you're going back in there with your pussy out just like this." His fingers skim over the slit he cut in my tights and panties.

"Ugh, don't remind me." I push at his shoulders, but he doesn't budge. "I'm going to have to go home."

"Mm," he hums, kissing along my neck. "Is your pussy sore?"

"*No*," I lie.

"Are you going to regret this?" His tone has gone serious, and from what I can make out, his expression is hard.

"I—" I duck, avoiding his scrutiny. "I don't know."

He tips my chin up and presses a gentle kiss to my lips. "I hope you don't."

Taking a step back, he lets me fix my dress. There's no chance of finding the pin in what I now realize is a highly organized storage closet.

Smoothing my hands over my hair, I groan. Dammit. It's a mess of tangles.

"Let me help."

I almost protest, but he gently turns me around and smooths those long, sensual fingers through the strands. He twists it at the base of my neck and secures it with an elastic. Once he's done, he gives my ass a light swat.

"You carry hair ties around with you?"

With a shrug, he opens the closet door. I blink rapidly at the sudden intrusion of light. Thankfully, like before, no one is in this part of the building.

The door clicks shut behind us.

Out in the hall, Reid holds up a wrist and tugs on a black elastic wrapped around it. "I have a sister and a niece. I've learned to be prepared." His expression is soft now, as he reaches out, tracing a single finger over my cheek like he can't help but touch me. "Can I have your number?"

My stomach flips at the unexpected question.

My surprise must show plainly on my face, because he chuckles.

"Why?"

"So I can call you. Text you. Whatever." He flashes that adorable, crooked grin, causing that damn dimple to wink at me. "Only if you want."

Do I want?

I look away, wringing my hands. I *shouldn't* want to give him my number. That first night, I specifically made sure there was no way he could contact me. But it seems futile at this point. He knows where I live. He's going to be *working* at my place come Monday.

I wet my lips and give him a single nod. Without missing a beat, he pulls out his phone and passes it to me. If he notices the way my fingers tremble as I type in my number, he doesn't comment on it.

Once I've passed the phone back to him, he quickly types out a text. "Now you'll have mine."

I hate the way my heart swoops over the idea of having Reid's number.

What is wrong with me? I'm like a giddy teenager being noticed by her crush.

His hand hovers at my waist, guiding me back to the correct door. The warmth of his touch disappears a second before the door opens.

"I'll see you soon, Via."

With that husky promise, he heads to the right, leaving me to search the crowd for my sister. Luckily, I don't have to look far. As I scan the crowd, I find her dashing toward me.

"There you are." Her frown is full of genuine worry. "I've been looking everywhere for you. You went to go get a drink and disappeared."

"S-Sorry," I stutter. "I went looking for a restroom and got lost. This place is surprisingly large."

The lie sounds believable enough to my own ears.

She narrows her eyes on me like she isn't buying what I'm selling. "Are you feeling okay? You're flushed."

I latch on to the excuse she's unknowingly given me. "Actually, I'm feeling a bit lightheaded. I don't think I've eaten enough today and it's getting to me."

Guilt eats at my gut as she looks me over, wearing an expression of gentle concern. I hate lying to my sister, but I'm not ready to tell her about what happened with Reid.

"All right." She loops an arm through mine like she thinks she needs to hold me steady. "Let's go. We'll grab food on the way."

I let my sister guide me out of the community center and to my parked car.

I don't even argue when she takes my keys and drives.

I'll tell her about tonight eventually, but just ... not yet.

I kind of like that it's a secret between Reid and me. Like it's ours and no one else's.

seventeen

Reid

My alarm blares, waking me from the best fucking night of sleep I've had in weeks.

Via.

Is it pathetic that my first thought upon waking is of her?

Absolutely.

With a groan, I slam my hand over the alarm to shut it up. Then I drag my sorry ass out of bed. Normally, I hate Mondays. Worst day of the week if you ask me.

But this Monday might be my favorite day in a long time.

All because of a certain stunning woman.

Not that I can acknowledge her in the ways I want while at work. Not only would it be entirely unprofessional, but I'm pretty sure she'd kick me in the balls if I tried. She's just as aware as I am of the insane chemistry between us, but where I want to jump in feetfirst and explore it, she needs time.

I can respect that.

It still blows my mind. The odds of the job I'm scheduled to start today being hers. Her going on a date with my dad. All of it. When I saw her in my childhood living room, I thought I was having a seizure or a waking dream. I was certain she wasn't real.

But she very much was.

I didn't plan to fuck her on Halloween night. Honestly, I was surprised she went along with it. But damn if I'm not elated that she did.

And my biggest takeaway from that night?

This thing between us? It's not one-sided.

I turn the shower on, then pee while I wait for the water to warm. Showering is pointless, considering I'll be covered in sweat and wood dust by lunchtime, but it's a necessity if I want to be fully alert.

Stifling a yawn, I step beneath the spray. "Ah, fuck." Shit, it's still cold. I should've checked it first. Looks like I'm going to have words with my landlord *again*. If it's not icy cold or boiling hot, then there's no water at all. The complex is decent in general, so the whole thing is uncalled for. Especially with what I pay.

Until recently, I lived at home, but I couldn't take living

with my dad anymore. Not him specifically. The issue is my sister.

I love her, and we've always been close. We kind of had to be. For years it was the three of us. Dad, Layla, and me. We called ourselves the three musketeers when Layla and I were kids.

But the minute she met Brandon, things changed.

He's a piece-of-shit alcoholic drug addict who treats her like garbage.

They've been in an on-again, off-again relationship since middle school. If only they had ended things permanently when Layla got pregnant with Lilibet. Her conception—unplanned, of course—happened during one of their many breakups. To this day, Layla has never admitted who Lili's father is. She knows, I can see it in her eyes, but she won't tell us. I don't know whether she's protecting the deadbeat from us or from Brandon.

It isn't until I'm finishing up that the water turns warm.

Figures.

It doesn't take me long to get ready for the day. I throw on a pair of cargo pants, a long-sleeve Henley, and a black sweatshirt with my dad's company logo across the back. As I'm lacing up my boots, I eye my phone and consider texting Via.

I've never been like this before.

It's not just the sex, even though it's phenomenal. I'm intrigued by her. I genuinely want to get to know her, but she's skittish. Our age difference freaks her out, yeah, but I don't think that's the whole picture.

"Don't be such a little bitch," I mutter, unplugging my phone from the charger.

I type out a quick text.

> Me: Want me to bring you coffee?

The second I click Send, I cringe. That's the best I could come up with? *Want me to bring you coffee?* I'm a fucking embarrassment.

I run my fingers through my hair and pace while I wait for her to reply. When I hit the other side of my room and turn, the time catches my eye. Shit. It's early. She might not even be up yet.

A heartbeat later, though, my phone lights up.

> Via: Don't you think it would be weird if you brought me coffee? As far as anyone else knows, we barely know each other.

Blowing out a breath, I point at myself in the reflection of the cracked mirror leaning against the bedroom wall. "You're a fucking idiot."

> Me: Right.

> Via: Why do I get the impression you're nervous?

Do I go for honesty or play it off?

Without giving myself time to overthink it, I type out a quick response and tap Send.

> Me: Because I am.

> Via: Don't be. Skip breakfast. I'm getting donuts for everyone.

> Me: You're incredible.

> Via: So you tell me.

We exchange a few more casual messages before I head to the kitchen to get the coffee started. I get to skip trying to scrap some semblance of breakfast together thanks to Via.

While I wait for my coffee to brew, I scroll through my social media apps, responding to comments from friends, and then check my email. I work for my dad part time, and I spend the rest of my weekdays working for my best friend's dad, who owns an auto shop.

I don't like construction work, even if I'm good at it. It was hard not to be. I spent my childhood helping him, so I was bound to develop a knack for it. But Mr. Vasquez can't afford to pay me a full-time salary at the repair shop, so for now, this is the best I can do.

I enjoyed tinkering with cars with my grandpa before he passed. The restoration side of things is my favorite aspect. Probably because it sparks my passion for art to life. Getting to bring an old car back to life? There's nothing quite like it.

My coffeepot makes an obnoxious noise to let me know it's finished, so I pull a ridiculously oversized gas station travel cup from the cabinet and add in my favorite French vanilla creamer, stifling one yawn after another. My friends make fun of me for my love of creamer, but who wants to drink bean water without it? A little sweetness never hurt anybody.

After a hefty swallow to check the coffee to creamer ratio, I nod to myself.

Perfection.

Stifling another yawn—I fucking hate early mornings; being up before nine is a crime—I grab my keys, then I head out to my car. As I approach, I drop my head back with a groan at the thick layer of frost covering the window.

If I'm late, my dad will have my head.

I'M NOT LATE—THANK FUCK FOR SMALL MIRACLES. With another gulp of coffee, I snag my hard hat from the back and tuck it under my arm. I parked down the street to avoid the risk of getting a nail in my tires, but that means I get to walk in the cold.

My breath fogs the air, just another reminder of how quickly the temperature drops here on the coast. I love Maine, and I couldn't imagine living anywhere else, but damn if the cold doesn't still get to me at times.

Each step brings me closer to a donut and Via, and that's all I need to stay motivated.

The old building needs more than just some TLC. This is an entire overhaul job. I can't see the potential, but my dad wouldn't have taken the job if he didn't think it could be transformed.

The front door is propped open, meaning at least one of the guys is already here. I toss my hand up at Joe when he comes out with a load of scraps to throw in the dumpster.

Inside, I home in on Via, who's standing in the back of the room. My body sensed her the second I was in her proximity, just like it did on Halloween and the first night we met.

It's this weird, magnetic connection. An unexplainable tug of recognition. She must sense me too, because her eyes find mine almost immediately. I hold my breath, anticipating the freakout that's bound to happen now that she realizes I'm in her orbit.

But a heartbeat after our eyes lock, she surprises me by smiling and waving me over to the waiting boxes of donuts. My stomach rumbles, half from hunger and half from the desire to cup her face and kiss her that washes over me.

I can't do that, but man, do I think about it.

None of the other guys are around when I approach her, so I give in to the grin fighting to break free.

"My sister is here," she whispers in warning when I get close.

I give her a small nod. "Is my dad here yet?"

She shakes her head. "I overheard someone say he had to stop by the lumber yard first."

"Donuts, hmm? Ms. Kathy's?"

"Of course. Someone told me they were the best around." She's wearing a small smile, and the soft spot at the base of her throat flutters quickly, like maybe she's nervous. The way she doesn't quite seem to know what to do with her hands, clasping them, then putting them on her hips, confirms my suspicion.

Finally, she settles on crossing them beneath her breasts.

That move forces my focus to dip low so I can appreciate the way they push against her sweater.

She groans, dropping her hands back to her sides.

Dragging my attention back up to her face, I shove my glasses up my nose. It doesn't matter how many fucking times I get the stupid things adjusted, they never stay in place.

"Sorry," I tell her sheepishly. "Couldn't help it."

"Sure," she drawls.

"You smell good." The thought escapes me before I can rein it in. Standing this close to her, I lose control of basic functions, like the ability to filter thoughts.

She tries not to laugh. "Thank you."

Determined not to make a fool of myself again, I clear my throat and scan the selection of donuts. "Lots of choices." I'm sure the guys appreciate the selection. I certainly do. "I'm usually partial to blueberry," I muse, tapping my bottom lip like I'm seriously contemplating this. "But I had the best-tasting one I've ever had just a few days ago. It was just a bite. Barely a bite."

Her eyes are wide as she listens to me.

"More of a lick, you could say. I'm not sure if I'll ever have one as good again. Maybe I should go with a glazed so I'm not disappointed. What do you think?"

Her throat works with a swallow. "I ... I'm partial to the taste of blueberry."

Fuck. I love getting her flustered. "You want me to take a blueberry one?"

"I bet it would taste good on you—I mean f-for you," she quickly stutters.

I suck in my cheeks to keep from kissing her. She's not even trying to be alluring; she just is. "All right." I reach into the box. "Blueberry it is."

Winking, I take a massive bite. Then I walk away from her before I make a fool of myself.

Well, more than I already have.

eighteen

Via

"That's him?" Izzy whisper-hisses, her grip painful on my wrist as she yanks me back toward the store.

I dig my heels in. We're supposed to be walking to the diner for lunch. "You don't need a second look."

"Oh, yes I do. Stay here, you wuss. I'll pretend I dropped an earring or something." She's already tugging one out of her lobe.

"Stop it," I beg. "You can see him when we get back."

She rolls her eyes, but thankfully drops her hands, leaving her earring in place. "Fine, but only because I'm starving. I desperately need a burger. But if you think we're not talking about this, you're mistaken, missy."

"I figured."

When we step inside the diner, the same woman who interrogated me on my first visit indicates for us to grab a booth.

"I love this place." Izzy already has her camera out, filming clips for her vlog. I'm anxious to see how she edits everything together once she's gone. Not that I'm anywhere near ready for her to leave. She might be nosy and meddling, but I love having her around. This is the most time we've spent one-on-one since I lived at home.

I've made it my mission to try something new every time I come until I've ordered everything on the menu, so I take my time perusing the choices. Normally I settle on one entrée at every dining establishment I frequent and never deviate, but I've already broken out of my comfort zone by moving to Parkerville, so I might as well branch out in other ways.

Like fucking guys eleven years younger than you in supply closets.

I still haven't told Izzy, and I'm not sure I will. It feels too scandalous, even if she's probably done far worse. Izzy's never been quiet about her sex life.

Thankfully she waits until we've placed our order to launch into her interrogation.

I know I'm in for it when she lays her hands flat on the table. "*That* was the son?"

Stalling to give myself a moment to pull it together, I reach for my glass of water. She narrows her eyes when I take a sip. She knows exactly what I'm up to.

After I've swallowed, I pat my lips with my napkin and place it in my lap. Then I pull my shoulders back and force myself to look her in the eye. "Yeah, that was him."

Her jaw drops. "Via!" She hisses my name loud enough that more than one patron turns to look at us.

I want to crawl beneath the table and disappear. I've never liked attention, and that's one thing I don't see changing, even as I continue to challenge myself to do things that make me uncomfortable.

"You didn't tell me he looked like *that*."

"I mean … it's kind of hard to do him justice," I whisper, drawing a doodle in the condensation on my glass.

"You can say that again." She fans herself. "He'd give most of the male population in LA a run for their money, and that's saying something. All the pretty people move there."

"Like you." I flick my rolled-up straw wrapper at her. Laughter bubbles out of me when it lands in her hair.

Frowning, she disentangles it from her straight dark strands. "Yes, like me." The sarcastic response is paired with a batting of her lashes.

While I wait for her to launch into another round of questions, my phone buzzes in my pocket. I fish it out, my heart leaping in my chest, thinking it might be Reid.

It's not. It's the last person I expected it to be. The last person I want it to be. My grip on my phone turns my knuckles white.

> Chase: I want to talk.

"What is it?" There's an edge of panic in Izzy's tone. Just like that, she can sense the change in my mood.

In answer, I pass my phone across to her.

She glowers at the message. "The audacity of that cheating, mistress-impregnating fucker."

I take my phone back before she can type out a strongly worded reply to my ex-husband. I *hate* that his random messages leave me shaken like this. After our divorce was finalized, I mostly put him out of my mind, thankful I'd never have to deal with him again. Now he keeps popping up out of nowhere like I'm trapped playing some sick, twisted game of Whack-a-Mole. I should've blocked him a long time ago, but I couldn't bring myself to do it. I *could* do it now, I suppose, but I stupidly want to see how long it'll take him to give up.

Across from me, Izzy's face grows redder, like the more she thinks about Chase and his audacious text messages, the angrier she gets.

I hold up a hand to stop the vitriol she'll no doubt spew when she opens her mouth.

"I love that you want to stick up for me. I really do. But it's not necessary. I'm over him. I can promise you that."

Sadly, it took sleeping with Reid for me to realize just how over him I truly am. Our sex life was lackluster, and he was controlling and manipulative most of the time. I deserve better. I know that now more than ever.

An annoyed breath gusts out of her. "I want to give him a piece of my mind. He *hurt* you. You wanted a baby more than anything—"

My heart squeezes painfully in my chest at the

reminder. I have to grip my napkin in my lap to keep my hands from shaking.

"And he just..." She trails off, probably noticing the expression on my face.

I don't like talking about my inability to get pregnant. In hindsight, I'm thankful I never did. He was the last person I should've created a family with. But that doesn't diminish how badly I wanted—*want*—to be a mom. I can't just snap my fingers and get pregnant. That's been made clear. But it's still the one thing I want most. And Chase, the bastard, stole my dream and gave it to someone else. *That's* what hurts.

Ironically, we'd scheduled an appointment with a fertility specialist so we could pinpoint where the trouble lay and find out what, if anything, we could do. Obviously, we know now there was absolutely nothing wrong with his swimmers. Nope, just me.

In the middle of the divorce, I went to the specialist on my own. Even though my marriage was ending, I wanted answers. The verdict? I have poor egg quality. They said it was the cause of my early-stage miscarriages too. My body knew the problem and took care of the issue naturally. Poor ovarian reserve is what they called it. They said it's *normal*. As if that word would somehow bring me comfort, even as I was told I'd never have a healthy baby on my own. I could use an egg donor. That was their solution. But I don't know that I'd ever be interested in going that route. There are other options, at least, for becoming a parent.

Izzy wraps a hand around mine on top of the table. "I'm sorry."

I squeeze her fingers. It's on the tip of my tongue to tell her it's okay, but I hold back those words. Because it's *not* okay. I have to stop downplaying my feelings to make it easier for everyone else.

We eat our food mostly in silence. When we do talk, it's about her vlog and her upcoming brand deals.

"I think he's good for you," Izzy says when we're headed back to my building.

"Who?" I ask, like I don't already know to whom she's referring.

She loops her arm through mine. "Reid."

A humorless laugh escapes me. My mood is gloomy now, thanks to Chase and my worries about never having a family. "Why do you think that?"

She tilts her head and hums. "This morning, when I showed up? I've never seen you smile that big. I know it was because of him."

I shake my head in vigorous protest. "That's not possible. We've … I … I don't *know* him."

She shrugs. "Sometimes, even if you don't know every detail about a person, they can light up your soul."

I look over at her, my breath catching. "Where did you get all this wisdom from?"

With a laugh, she pats my arm. "I'm not sure if I would call it wisdom. I think it's a romantic heart."

"Yeah," I agree, stifling a laugh of my own. "That makes way more sense."

nineteen

Reid

The microwave beeps, signaling that my dinner is ready. Thank fuck for leftovers.

Fork in hand, I pull the plate out. I know it's going to be too hot, but does that stop me from digging in anyway and scalding my tongue?

Nope.

In my eagerness to see Via, it never even crossed my mind to throw food in a cooler. That's how much she rattles me. Even now, I want to text her.

If my friends knew how often she's on my mind, they'd think I lost my mind and tell me to play it cool. They'd swear that the way to get a girl is to play disinterested. I call bullshit on that. But then again, Brandon has been a complete asshole to my sister for years, dragging her along and driving her nuts when he doesn't respond, and she's still on the hook.

But that's not the kind of person I am.

I hate mind games. They're a waste of fucking time. It's so much easier to be clear about my interest. Though most people, apparently, don't share my mindset.

Food in hand, I head to the couch and get settled in. I click on Netflix, then navigate to the show I've been watching.

On the cushion beside me, my phone rings, and my sister's name flashes on the screen.

I consider not answering. She probably wants to chew me out again. She's still pissed about Dad coming home and kicking out Brandon. She knows he's not allowed in the house, but I guess she thinks rules don't apply to her.

Despite her awful piece-of-shit boyfriend, we've always been close, so ignoring her feels wrong.

I swipe to accept the call and put it on speaker so I can keep eating.

"What's up?" Better to cut to the chase if she wants an argument.

"Hey." Her tone is subdued, hesitant. Maybe she isn't still pissed after all. "Could you watch Lili for a few hours on Saturday? I was offered an extra shift, and I really need the money."

"Yeah, no problem."

I'll never say no to hanging out with Lili. She's way cooler than most people I know. When my sister got pregnant, we both still lived at home, and I was worried about what it'd be like having a kid in the house. But the minute I visited the hospital and held the little sucker in my arms, I was a goner. It did take some time to adjust to having a screaming newborn around, but she's way more fun now that she can have a full-on conversation.

Lilibet has all of us wrapped around her finger, and she knows it. She certainly uses it to her advantage any time she can. She saw a commercial about Home Depot's kids' classes once, and the next thing I knew, my dad was taking her to learn about tools and build all kinds of junk once a month. They still do it. She's so proud of the pins she earns and sticks on her apron each time she completes a class.

"Thank you, thank you, thank you," my sister chants, her voice breaking up from bad cell service. "You're a lifesaver."

I swallow the bite of food I'm chewing and clear my throat. "How many hours?"

"I'll work lunch to close. You can drop her off at Dad's around five, though."

"Where's he going to be?"

"Not sure. Just said he was busy."

I bristle. Normally, I wouldn't think twice. I don't keep tabs on my dad's whereabouts, but what if he's going out with Via again? I don't think she'd agree to another date with him after our encounter on Halloween, but how well do I actually know her? If he asked *before* we discovered this convoluted connection, would she go through with it out of politeness?

"Are you okay?" Layla asks. "You got really quiet all of a sudden."

"Yeah." I stuff another bite into my mouth. "Totally fine."

"You really don't mind watching Lili?"

"It's not a problem. Swear."

Once I end the call, I stare at my phone, my mind still scrolling through scenarios. I shouldn't do it. I *know* that. But I type out the text message anyway.

> Me: I'm still thinking about how good you taste.

I LIE AWAKE IN MY DARKENED ROOM AND WATCH AS 11:10 turns into 11:11.

I've been in here for an hour, yet sleep evades me. I can't stop thinking about Via. Every time I close my eyes, I see her. Some of my visions are tame—her in that tight pair of jeans and sweater she wore today—while others are entirely X-rated.

Grabbing the pillow from the other side of the bed, I cover my face with it and groan.

I have to be back at her place bright and early. I need to go the fuck to sleep.

But it's clearly not going to happen anytime soon.

Throwing off the covers, I haul myself up and stomp

around my room, yanking on clothes. Swiping my car keys, I head out the door. Once I'm in the car and the engine is rumbling, I turn on the radio to drown out my racing thoughts. If I drive around for a while, then maybe by the time I get back, I'll be ready to sleep.

As if on autopilot, my car heads toward Via's place and parks on the street.

Don't do it.

She never responded to my text, not that I expected her too. I wished I could take it back as soon as I sent it. I have no doubt it was too much to say to her.

Don't do it.

But of course, I fucking do it.

Yanking the key from the ignition, I pull my hood up to block against the icy rain coming down from the dark sky. It's after midnight now. The last thing I should do is knock on her door like a complete psycho, but logic doesn't reach my brain.

The stairs leading up to her door are slick, and I nearly wipe out when I'm about halfway up. It's probably a sign from the universe telling me to turn my ass around, but do I heed it? Not a chance.

Shoulders hunched to ward off the cold, I knock. She's probably in bed. If she doesn't come, I'll leave, and she'll never know I was here to begin with.

Before I can force my feet to take me back down those icy steps, there's a squeak inside, the sound of a cornered animal.

I lean my head against the door and inwardly curse.

Dick move, knocking on a woman's door in the middle of the night.

I type out a quick text.

> Me: It's just me.

I wait, listening to the footsteps on the other side of the door, and move back a second before the lock clicks.

"Are you crazy?" Via asks as she comes into view. Her hair is piled on top of her head in a haphazard mess of strands. "You nearly gave me a heart attack."

"I didn't mean to scare you."

"Well, you did." She looks around, wrinkling her perky nose at the disgusting weather. "You might as well come in."

I'm not going to turn down her offer. It's cold as fuck out here.

Stepping inside the warmth of her apartment, I rub my hands together, yet the chill lingers in my bones.

Via locks the door behind me and pulls her robe tighter around her body. "Despite my better judgment, I let my sister talk me into watching a horror movie tonight, and then you knock on my door at"—she squints at the clock on her microwave—"a quarter past midnight. I thought I was about to be murdered." She hisses the last part. "What the hell were you thinking?"

I scratch at the back of my head. "I guess I wasn't thinking."

She crosses her arms over her chest, making it obvious she's not wearing a bra.

"You definitely weren't," she chides, smoothing her hair down. "Did you leave something downstairs, or…?"

I shake my head and shrug off my hoodie. "That's not why I came."

"Then why are you here?"

"Figured that was obvious, Via."

Her nipples pebble against the fabric of her top when I say her name. With a huff, she tugs her robe tighter around her body.

"Did you get my text?"

I know she did. It showed read.

She closes her eyes and looks away. "What are we doing, Reid? Because this," she flicks a finger between us, "it's a lot."

"Intense, you mean?" I itch to reach for her, but I don't want to push her too hard, too fast, so I keep my hands to myself.

"Sure. Whatever you want to call it."

It really is hard to put into words, this thing between us.

Intense.

Otherworldly.

I could list a dozen more descriptors that come to mind.

"Don't let it scare you," I practically beg.

She lets out a humorless laugh and wraps her arms tighter around midsection, like she's holding herself together. "Too late for that. I was never supposed to see you again." She practically whispers the last part, like it's a confession or a plea.

The words strike me right in the heart.

"Is…" I breathe through the pain that lances my chest. "Is that what you want? I can leave right now. I'll ask my dad to put me on a different project. I—"

She grasps my wrist, cutting off my words. Her eyes are wide when I look down at her, her lips a sweet berry red color.

"No. that's not what I want, but…" She maintains eye contact, but for a moment, she doesn't speak, like she's sorting through her thoughts. "You have to understand how wild this is for me." She flicks a freshly painted nail between us. "It's been a long time since I was free to make choices for myself," she goes on, her voice growing stronger. "I don't want to rush things just because … just because…" She drops her gaze to the floor.

"Via?" I put a finger beneath her chin and gently guide her head back up. "Care to finish that thought?"

She swallows, steeling her shoulders. "Just because I like you."

I grin, and God, do I want to kiss her. "You like me?"

She rolls her eyes and takes a step back. "Don't let it go to your head. I like lots of people. My sister. Ms. Kathy. Ella from the bookstore and—"

"And me."

"Yeah." She sighs softly and drops to the couch. "And you."

Via's affection feels like a monumental win already.

I sit on the coffee table in front of her. The room is small, so there's little space between the pieces of furniture. Our legs touch when we sit like this, but I don't think she minds any more than I do.

"It's okay to like me."

"I know that," she huffs, adjusting her robe when it dips over one shoulder, exposing the strap of her camisole.

"It's even okay to desire me."

I can't help but smile at the way her eyes go wide. Via is a tightly wound woman who clings to control, but around me, she's not. Selfishly, I love that I rattle her. I love that when she's around me, she's just a little unwound.

"I desire you."

She licks her lips in response to that comment, but she turns away, like it doesn't affect her.

"Do you?" I ask her. "Desire me? You can be honest."

She turns back and meets my eye. Then she absolutely shocks the shit out of me. "I wouldn't have had sex with you in a closet on Halloween if I didn't."

Fuck, I want to kiss her sassy mouth.

So I do.

I give her enough time to turn away if she wants, but again, she surprises me by clasping her hands behind my neck and tugging me to her.

"Just fucking kiss me, Reid," she breathes against my mouth.

I don't hesitate.

When the hottest woman you've ever seen tells you to kiss her, you fucking do.

It's always explosive with us. Never just a simple kiss. Whether she knows it or not, she comes alive beneath my touch.

"You make me crazy," she says, working her hands under the hem of my shirt.

I pull back and tear it over my head. If she wants to feel my bare skin, I'll make sure there are no barriers between us.

"Back at you."

I find the curve of her neck, suckling the tender skin there. The need to mark her is potent. I want the world to know she's taken. No one but the two of us will know it was me, but that's all that matters.

Between us, she unties the belt holding her robe in place. When it's undone, it falls off her shoulders.

"Reid." The way she says my name has my cock straining against my pants.

"Yes?" I drawl the word, kissing beneath her air. When she shivers, I smile and do it again.

"Y-You know that text you sent me?"

"Mhm," I hum, kissing her long and slow and deep.

She gives my shoulders a gentle shove. "You could taste me again. If you want."

"Fuck, Via." I lower my head. That was the last thing I expected her to say.

"It's okay if you don't—"

I kiss her again, silencing her. If she only knew how much I want her, she wouldn't say things like that.

I continue pressing kisses to her lips, her neck, her

shoulders, building the anticipation. Then I get down on my knees and push the coffee table out of the way. When I slip her pajama bottoms off, I find her bare. Her pretty pink pussy glistens, already wet and begging for me.

"*Reid.*"

"Shh." I part her folds and sink two fingers inside her.

She moans, her head falling back. When I pull my fingers from her body, she mewls in protest, her hazy eyes, so full of need, finding mine.

Without looking away, I put my fingers in my mouth and lick them clean. "Just as delicious as I remember."

Her chest rises and falls rapidly, and her lips move like she might be saying a silent prayer.

Looping my arms around her thighs, I drag her until her ass is practically hanging off the edge of the couch. She rakes her fingers through my hair, tugging at the strands as I settle my mouth on her pussy. If she had any idea how sweet she tastes, she'd have no doubts about why I can't stop thinking about this.

The little sounds she makes encourage me, and when she comes, she screams my name so loud I can't help but smile. Heart racing, I make my way up her body and kiss her with every ounce of passion I feel. If she's disgusted by the taste of herself on my lips, she doesn't show it. She holds my face and kisses me just as fiercely.

When she finally lets me go, I help her back into her bottoms.

And when she's fully dressed again, her cheeks flushed

pink and her chest still heaving, I blurt out probably the last thing I should say to her.

"Go out with me."

Her eyes go wide. "What?"

I smile slowly. "You heard me. I want to take you out. On a date. A real date."

"I ... Reid ..." Her mouth works back and forth. "I don't think that's a good idea."

"Why is that?" I push, curious.

"I—Reid." She cuts herself off and takes a deep breath. "I was married for a long time, and I don't know that I'm ready to date."

"You went on a date with my dad."

She reaches for her robe and tugs it back up onto her shoulders. Once she's covered, she stands and walks to the fridge, the thin fabric flowing behind her. "I was coerced into that by my meddling little sister. It doesn't count." She pulls out a bottle of wine and shocks the hell out of me by drinking straight from the bottle. "This is too much." Pressing a hand to her head, she squints at me. "Why on earth would you want to go on a date with me to begin with?"

Stuffing my hands in the pockets of my jeans, I shrug. "The only answer I have for you probably isn't good enough."

She sets the bottle down and props herself up against the counter. "And what is it?"

"I want to get to know you."

I mean it. I've wanted to know her since the moment I

saw her across the bar. She captivated me. I wanted to know her story. The good and bad. The in-between. All of it.

Laughter bubbles out of her, but when I don't laugh along with her, she sobers. "You're serious?"

"Why wouldn't I be? I asked you on a date the night we met."

She picks up the bottle of wine again and sighs. "What happens if I say yes?"

I stifle a snort. "Then I take you on a date."

"What if I want this to remain what it is?"

I press my lips together, reining in my frustration. "Just sex?"

She gives a single jerky nod in response.

"Then, I don't know. I wasn't lying when I said that's not normally my thing. But I couldn't resist you that night. I still can't." I rub my fingers over my mouth where the taste of her still lingers.

She presses her lips together and hums.

Sure she's going to shoot me down, I hold my breath.

"I'm not ready for something serious."

A.k.a. she doesn't want to get my hopes up.

"Okay." I can bide my time.

"Fine."

The smile that overtakes me is so big it makes my cheeks ache.

"We'll go on one date and see where it goes." She wiggles one finger in the air to drive home her point. "But" —*oh shit*—"I don't want anyone to know."

I school my expression to hide my disappointment. I

don't want to be her dirty secret, not when I want to show her off and shout to the world that I'm hers. "Are you ashamed of me already, angel?" I'm only half joking.

Her cheeks turn the prettiest shade of pink. "This is a small town, Reid, and with our age difference, people will talk. Can you blame me for wanting to avoid that? People are just starting to warm up to me. I don't want to ruin that."

I have a hard time believing that anyone would struggle to like Via.

"All right," I agree. "I can accept being your dirty little secret."

For now.

"Ugh," she groans and brings both hands to her face. "That's not what I meant."

"I know." I close the distance between us and press a kiss to her cheek. "I'll text you about our date. Night, Via."

When she turns her head, I press a lingering kiss to her luscious mouth. She makes a small sound, and instantly, her hands are in my hair, tugging.

She can try to put up walls and tell herself she doesn't actually want to date me, but there's no denying that she's into me. Not with the way her body responds to me.

Reluctantly, I pull away.

"See you tomorrow, angel."

With those parting words, I slip out of her apartment and back to mine.

This time when I climb into bed, I go right to sleep.

twenty

Via

"I don't want you to go." I squeeze my sister tighter, like if I hold her close, then she won't walk away. We've always been close, despite our age difference, but since she's been here, we've grown even closer.

"Don't you dare make me cry," she warns, hugging me back.

We sway from side to side, neither of us wanting to break the hug. Hellos are so much easier than goodbyes.

"When can you come back?" I don't care if I sound like I'm begging.

Izzy releases me finally, but she keeps her hands on my arms like she doesn't want to fully break contact. "Around Christmas, maybe? Mom and Dad are going on a cruise."

This is news to me. The last time we spoke, Mom was still trying to convince me to come for the holidays.

"Oh, that's right." I pretend I knew. "You should come. Maybe by then my apartment will be in better shape and you can stay with me."

The flooring I chose came in, so Derrick's crew is planning to start on that project in the next few days.

"I'd love that." She grips my hands, giving them a squeeze. "I have to go. I need to get through security."

My heart sinks. "I know."

Still, neither of us makes a move.

I hug her again and tell her I love her, then I finally let her go. Taking a step back for good measure, I watch her walk into the airport. Just before she's out of view, she looks back and waves.

"Keep it together," I mutter to myself. "She'll probably FaceTime you the second she's off the plane, and it'll be like she never left."

"Huh?"

Eyes widening, I glance over at the short older lady standing nearby. "Sorry, I was talking to myself."

"Weirdo," she mutters, waddling away from me with a cane in one hand and rolling a suitcase behind her with the other.

Great, it's not even eight, and I'm already being insulted. That bodes well for how my day will go.

On the way back to Parkerville, I stop to pick up coffee and breakfast for Ella and me, since I plan to swing by the bookstore on my way home. I desperately need to place orders for supplies and I need to come up with a name for my shop so I can have a sign made. And that's just scratching the surface of my to-do list. I feel a migraine coming on just thinking about the rest.

Parked on the street in a spot close to the alley, I scoop up the still hot coffee and breakfast biscuits. Inside, Ella is at the front desk, typing on her laptop. When she hears the door, she snaps the lid on the computer closed and slides a pair of blue-light glasses onto her head. Her cheeks are pink, like I caught her doing something she shouldn't have been.

"Sorry," she says sheepishly, picking at a curled edge of a sticker on her laptop that says *don't lose your sparkle*. "I thought you might be my grandpa. He likes to do surprise pop-ins now and then."

"No, just me." I take a seat on an empty stool behind the counter and set down the goods I brought.

"For me?" She brightens.

"Yeah, I wasn't sure what you like, so I got a latte. I hope that's okay. And there's a sausage, egg, and cheese biscuit for each of us in the bag."

"You're a lifesaver," she says, already digging into the bag. "I skipped breakfast this morning because I was running late."

"Happy I could help." I pull out my own wrapped sandwich, my stomach rumbling. "How does this place stay in business?" The second the words are out, I regret them, so I hasten to add, "I don't mean that the way it sounds. It's just that this town is small, and I want to know what to expect since I'm hoping to open my store in the spring."

Ella throws back her head and laughs. "It's a legitimate question." She waves a hand, gesturing to the empty bookstore. "We get a surprising number of online orders. Mostly collectors. I'm sure getting your store up and running is daunting, but in this town, we come together for our people. You'll be surprised by the amount of business you get. You could open an online store as well, right? People could buy, like, art templates or something. Is that a thing? Kinda like paint by numbers?"

I mull over her suggestion. "I like that idea. An online store with stuff like that could work."

In this day and age, with resources like YouTube, I could probably film tutorials. Potentially gain traction that way.

"Oh," Ella claps her hands suddenly, making me jump. "I'm planning a girls' night with some of the ladies—separate from book club. I was thinking Mexican food and margaritas, maybe some dancing." She shimmies her shoulders, knocking into mine playfully. "How does that sound?"

"I'll never say no to a good margarita."

Ella taps her coffee cup to mine. "That's my girl."

I USED TO HAVE VERY LITTLE TIME FOR MYSELF. IT never bothered me, but now that I do have pockets of moments that are all my own, I'm not sure I can go back to not having it.

It's not to say that spending time with one's partner is a bad thing. Despite the demise of my marriage, I don't believe that. But I *do* think it's important for a person to have more than only a job and partner to fulfill them.

Watching a show of my own choosing by myself, or just reading in the quiet, is a pleasantness I long ago forgot existed. After I moved out of my parents' home and went to college, I spent all my time with other people. When I was alone, I was usually too tired to truly appreciate the peace that came with the silence and the room to think.

Now, sitting on my couch with a bowl of popcorn with the historical romance series I've been bingeing pulled up, I feel like I've found my happy place. After spending my days consumed with the renovations and crossing off tasks for the store, I look forward to these moments.

I shove a piece of popcorn into my mouth and wiggle on the cushion to get comfortable, pulling the blanket tighter around me, cocooning myself in.

I'm on the third episode of the evening when I hear it.

A scuttling, scratching sound that instantly has me sitting up straight.

Some kind of critter is in this apartment with me.

Slowly, carefully, I set my popcorn bowl on the coffee table. Eyes wide, like a girl in a horror movie who's about to get her throat slit, I look around without moving my body. The sound is coming from the kitchen, which is open to where I sit. The place is small, so if I stretch my arm out, I can touch the barstool.

That's when I see it.

On the counter, small and gray, searching for food.

Rat or mouse, I'm not sure, because I'm too busy screaming bloody murder. I launch myself off the couch, tripping on my blanket in the process, and dart for my bedroom. Once inside, I slam the door shut. Leaning against it, I struggle to regain my breath. It's like the first day at the bookstore all over again.

I'm on the cusp of hyperventilating as I search for my phone.

Please do not tell me I left it out there with that creature!

Blessedly, I find it stuffed in the pocket of my oversized sweatshirt.

Maybe later I'll contemplate why he's the first person I think of, but right now, I don't hesitate as I pull up Reid's contact information and press Call.

"Hey," he says, his tone infused with happiness. It makes my stomach dip with excitement despite the creature that has infiltrated my apartment.

"Um ... hey."

"Why are you whispering?" All the cheeriness leaches from his voice, leaving only worry.

I scratch the side of my nose, stalling. Do I need his help? Technically, no. I *can* take care of this myself. Am I going to? Absolutely not. So yeah, I do need his help, because I'm chicken shit.

"There's a mouse inside my apartment. I think it's a

mouse, at least. It could be a rat. I panicked and locked myself in my bedroom."

He makes a low choking sound, almost like he's holding in laughter. "You're hiding from a mouse?"

"It's not funny." I cover my face with my free hand. "I *hate* them. I don't want to kill the thing, but I want it out of here. Can you help?"

"Um." He blows out a breath. "Is it okay if I bring my niece?"

His niece. The little girl I saw briefly at Derrick's house. She's young, but old enough to have questions or tell her family about this, but why would she? And even if she did, Reid can surely come up with a reasonable excuse for why I asked for his assistance.

"Just get over here as fast as you can," I say, pressing my ear to my door.

"All right. I'll be there in twenty."

"Thank you." I breathe a sigh of relief and end the call.

I stay sequestered in my bedroom while I wait for Reid to arrive. It feels like a hundred years before there's a knock at the door. It's followed by a text from him, saying that he's here.

Cursing, I smack my head into my bedroom door. I have to leave my safe space in order to let Reid in.

"You can do it," I chant. "It's just a little mouse … or rat."

I gag—like a big, heaving gag.

God, I'm weak.

With a shriek, I open the door and run on my tiptoes

across the apartment. Undoing the latch in record speed, I open it to find Reid standing on the other side, wind-mussed hair and his niece in his arms, clinging to his neck.

"Get in here and catch this thing."

He grins at the awkward little shimmy dance I can't seem to stop. Just that glimpse of the mouse makes me feel dirty, like I'll need ten showers to scrub the dirt and memories from my skin.

He sets his niece down and surveys my apartment. "Where did you last see it?"

I point in the direction of the kitchen counter, my finger shaking.

He arches his brow and huffs a laugh. "You really are scared, huh?"

"You have no idea."

He presses his lips into a thin line, probably to keep from laughing at me again. I appreciate the gesture.

"Do you want to go outside and wait?"

I bite my lip and consider. The cold or the frigid wind? It's a tough decision. "I-I'll be fine."

He arches a brow, not buying what I'm selling one bit.

"Really."

His niece tugs on the bottom of his Carhartt jacket. "What's she scared of?" she whispers, peering over at me from where she's tucked herself mostly behind him. "Should I be scared too?"

"Just a wee little mouse." He crouches so they're eye to eye. "Why don't you protect her for me? Can you do that?"

With a vigorous nod, she shuffles my way. When she's at

my side, she grips my hand and tilts her head back. "I'll save you," she promises with a slight lisp, thanks to a missing tooth.

"Thank you, Lili. That's very brave of you." *Unlike me.*

"If you see it, tell me," Reid instructs, taking careful steps into the kitchen. "Do you have something I can put it in?"

"Put it in?" I repeat, my voice shrill.

"I'll take the little guy somewhere safe, but I need to transport him." He bends down and opens a cabinet.

I jump, half expecting the mouse to come sprinting out at me. "Uh, yeah, there should be a box near the trash can to your left."

He hauls himself up and picks it up. "Perfect." Setting the box on the counter, he lifts his chin and addresses his niece. "Do you see the mouse, Lili?"

"No, not yet." She swings our hands back and forth, grinning up at me with a goofy smile. "Hi."

"Hi, sweetie." I smile down at her. She really is adorable, with hair almost the same shade as Reid's and dark brown eyes. The telltale stain of chocolate rings her upper lip.

Still holding my hand, Lili squats and rubs her fingers together like one might do to draw a cat closer. "Here, mousie, mousie. Come here."

Oh, please, God, do not let her be some sort of mouse whisperer and lure that thing over to me.

Reid might never speak to me again if he witnesses that meltdown.

Having gone through all the cabinets, he clicks on his

phone's flashlight and gets down on his hands and knees to search under my furniture. "Aha, there you are, little guy." He's peering under the couch. The couch I'm currently standing beside.

In a lightning-fast move, I drag Lili to the kitchen. It's still entirely too close, but it's as far as I can go without shutting myself in the bedroom again.

My couch is small, more like a love seat, so Reid has no trouble lifting one side with one hand while reaching under with the other.

But he's not quick enough. With a loud curse, he scrambles to his feet and runs after the mouse.

The mouse that's now headed right for me.

I think I black out. All I know is, one second my feet are on the floor and I'm holding on to Lili, and in the next, I'm on the kitchen counter. Only my feet slip out from under me and I smack my head into the old tile countertop. I hiss at the bolt of pain and bring a hand to my brow, only to find it wet and sticky.

"Uncle Weed, she's bleeding."

I pull my shaky fingers away, and sure enough, I am bleeding.

"Shit." Reid rushes to my side and grasps my face, guiding my head back. "How many fingers am I holding up?"

"Three."

"That's a lot of blood," his niece observes.

"Cloth?" he asks me. "Bandages?"

"Bathroom. Where's the mouse?" I whisper the question like the creature might attack if it overhears me.

"It disappeared," Lili answers. "Poof, gone."

"Great," I groan, my head throbbing. "I swear I'm not normally this accident prone."

He chuckles and pats my knee affectionately. "Wait here."

As if I'm going anywhere now. My head is pounding, and even the slightest move sends pain shooting through me.

Lili takes his place in front of me, tilting her head to the side to take in my no doubt ridiculous state. "You need a princess Band-Aid."

"Yeah, I do," I rasp.

"Uncle Weed, do we need to take her to the hospital?"

Reid returns with a damp cloth and a first-aid kit. "I think she'll be just fine, Lil." He presses the cloth gently to my forehead, dabbing at the blood. "You knocked yourself good," he murmurs.

My whole body heats, and not in a good way. "I'm so embarrassed."

He grins, eyes twinkling behind the frames of his glasses. "Don't be. It happens to the best of us."

I huff and shoot him a glare. "You too have almost knocked yourself out by hitting your head on a counter in an attempt to escape a mouse?"

His smile grows. I want to poke his dimple, to measure how deep it is when he smiles like that, but I keep my hands to myself. Especially since we have an audience. Little eyes and ears tend to be the nosiest of them all.

"Not exactly."

"Mhm. I figured."

"This might sting." He dabs antiseptic onto a cotton pad. "Just warning you."

I hiss the second it touches the cut. "Ow."

"I'm sorry." He blots at the wound quickly, then swipes a dab of ointment over the spot. "All done."

"You look better now," Lili tells me so very helpfully. "No more blood."

"Thanks." I sigh and slump where I'm sitting on the counter. "But the mouse is still in here."

With a chuckle, Reid shoves his hand into his pocket and produces a set of keys. He puts them in my hand, wrapping my fingers around them. "Go sit in my car with Lili. I'll get the mouse."

I don't have to be told twice. Swiping my coat off the hook by the door, I usher the little girl out of the apartment. Once we're settled in Reid's mustang, I start the engine to stave off the cold. Lili sits in the passenger seat beside me.

"You're pretty." She wears the sweetest smile as she tilts her head and inspects me. "Do you like my uncle?"

"He's ... yeah. He's nice." That seems like the best way to answer her.

She considers me for a moment, tapping her glittery pink nails against her thighs. "Are you going to have babies with him?"

I nearly swallow my own tongue, and my eyes threaten to pop out of my head. "Uh ... no. He's just a friend."

"My mom says he needs a girlfriend."

"Oh? Why is that?"

She shrugs and sticks her bottom lip out. "She says he's lonely."

"Is he?" I'm letting my curiosity get the best of me.

"I don't know." she wrinkles her nose. "I'm only four."

I laugh. "Right. Of course."

"Does that hurt?" She points at my forehead.

"A little." I have a headache now, thanks to my clumsiness.

"Do you want me to kiss it and make it better? That's what my mommy does for me. It helps a lot."

"That's okay, but thank you."

"Are you sure?" She puckers her lips. "Just one little kiss?" Holding her thumb and forefinger close in front of her, she waits for my reply.

"Fine, all right."

Lili places a tiny kiss beside the ointment on my forehead. "It'll get better faster now. I promise."

My heart squeezes in my chest at her sincerity. "Thank you."

She beams. "You're welcome."

Waiting for Reid to emerge from my apartment is a test of my patience. The longer it takes, the more I'm convinced my furry roommate will elude him, and I can't stomach the thought of going back in there with that thing.

"You look scared." Lili has tucked her feet under her now. "The mouse can't get you now. You're safe here."

I smile at the little girl. She's really quite amusing. "I know, but I'm hoping he can catch it."

"Oh." Her lips twist back and forth as she thinks. "Maybe, if we cross our fingers really hard, it will help him." She does just that and lifts her brows in expectation, clearly waiting for me to do the same.

I follow suit, crossing my fingers. "Do you think it's working?"

"Mm." She squeezes her eyes shut. "I think so." She opens them again just as Reid steps out of my apartment, box in hand. "It worked!" With a fist pump, she bounces on her knees, then goes to work rolling the window down. It's no small feat for someone so tiny, but she's determined. "You did it, Uncle Weed!"

He grins triumphantly, holding the box up like a trophy.

"You got it?" I shout through the open window.

"I did." He tucks the box under his arm. "You're safe now, promise."

Heart leaping in my chest, I scurry out of his car and run to him, and without hesitation, I wrap my arms around him and smack a kiss on his cheek. "You're my hero."

His face turns the cutest shade of pink.

Behind us, giggles ring out.

In my joy, I forgot about Lili. Oops. I pull away quickly and tug at the bottom of my jacket.

"She kissed you, Uncle Weed."

"Just my cheek," he tells her, strolling to the car. He sets the box on the ground beside it. It's taped shut, and he's poked small holes in the cardboard so the mouse can breathe. He glances back at me and winks, then turns back to his niece. "I kiss your cheeks all the time, don't I?" He doesn't give her a chance to respond before he leans in through the window and plants loud kisses all over her face.

Releasing her, he turns back to me. "I have to drop her off at my dad's, but I'll circle back with something to deter any more unwanted guests."

"Thank you. Seriously. You're a lifesaver."

He grins. "I'm happy to help, Via."

And I believe it. There's no glint in his eyes, no flash of an ulterior motive. Reid Crawford simply wants to help me.

"I'll be back," he says again, like he doesn't want me to forget. "Go in and lock up for now."

I nod. "Bye, Lili."

"Bye." She waves out the window.

I head back up the stairs, and as I reach my door, Reid's Mustang rumbles down the street.

I shouldn't be excited about the prospect of him returning. And I *definitely* shouldn't be thinking about how good his work-roughened hands would feel on my skin. But I can't stop my brain from going there.

Before I can spiral, though, I get a video call from Izzy. She made it home safely, and she's currently showering Wonton in kisses. There's already a deep ache inside me at her absence.

We don't stay on the phone for long since she's tired from her flight and wants to get her things unpacked. Once

I hang up, I return to my show, but with a glass of wine this time. I deserve it after the shock of the mouse and the head injury. Apparently I attract them in Parkerville. The sad—or funny, I suppose, depending on perspective—thing is that I would be far less bothered by a snake than a mouse. I didn't tell Izzy about the incident, mostly because I didn't want to have to confess to calling Reid for help. She'd never let me live it down.

I'm having a hard time keeping my eyes open by the time there's a soft knock on my door.

My heart skips a beat, a telltale sign that I'm feeling more for Reid than I should.

Feelings are such a pesky thing. They can sneak up so easily and without any provocation.

I slip off the couch and wrap my blanket tightly around my body, then shuffle to the door.

On the other side, Reid is eyeing the rickety railing around the landing.

"Don't worry, I'm replacing it." *Like everything else around here.*

Chuckling, he steps inside with a hardware store bag in hand. "Did you know this place was in such bad shape before you moved in?"

"The photos online were a tad misleading," I admit, crinkling my nose, "but I still would've bought it had I known."

"Really?" He sets the bag on the counter and goes about unloading his purchases. "Why?"

Shrugging, I lean back against the now closed door. "It just felt right."

He smiles. "I guess that's the best reason, huh?"

"Those won't kill them, right?" I nod at the contraption in his hand. I might hate mice, but that doesn't mean I want them dead.

He arches a brow in surprise. "I didn't think you'd care, but no, these are live traps. I'll check the traps and release any we catch."

"You're amazing."

He chuckles. "I'm glad you think so. I'm going to put two of these in here and a few outside."

"How much was all of this? Let me get you some money." I turn, ready to waddle back to my room, still wrapped tightly in my blanket.

"Don't worry about it."

I scoff, nearly tripping over the blanket when I spin around again. "I'm sure this wasn't cheap. Let me get you some cash."

"And I'm telling you not to worry about it. Let me take care of you."

Those words, *let me take care of you*, and his firm yet benevolent tone, send a host of butterflies fluttering in my stomach. Have I ever truly been cared for in that way? Maybe in the beginning of my relationship with Chase, but not for a long time. We were always so busy with work. It didn't leave much time for niceties like this.

"I can't let you do that."

He places his palms on the counter. The sleeves of his

sweatshirt are pushed up to his elbows, showing off the massive amount of vein porn he has going on. I could start a social media account and post nothing but photos and videos of his veiny arms and end up with a huge following.

"How about an exchange, then?"

"Like what?" A hint of excitement stirs to life low in my belly at the prospects.

His smile widens. "Not sex, Via. Get your head out of the gutter." *Busted.* "I want lessons."

"Lessons?" I blink, dumbfounded.

"Art lessons."

"From me?" I point at myself, nearly dropping the blanket in the process. "I don't think you need them." If his hummingbird tattoo is any indication, Reid is an incredibly talented artist.

"There's always room for improvement." With a shrug, he turns away from me to place one of the traps on the kitchen counter near where I spotted the mouse. "I want to learn from you."

I can't exactly turn down the bargain, and it would make for good practice…

"All right."

"Cool." He lowers to his haunches and sets another trap behind the couch. "You tell me when, and I'll be here. And you haven't forgotten our date, right? I've been swamped this week, but I should have it figured out soon. Are you free next Saturday?"

Though I try to fight the feeling, I can't stop the warmth that spreads through me. "My schedule is wide open."

He grins and stands, brushing his hands together. "Pencil me in." Grabbing the bag from the counter, he steps up close. "I'll put these outside and be out of your hair."

"Y-You're leaving?" I stutter. Shit. I should be shooing him out the door, but suddenly, I want nothing more than for him to keep me company.

"Yeah." He adjusts his glasses. "I can't have you getting sick of me now, can I?" He winks, making my stomach dip in the process. "I'll see you around, Via." My name is a husky caress on his lips.

He lets himself out but stops and turns just over the threshold. "Oh."

"Yeah?"

"The painting above your couch?" His lips tick almost imperceptibly, like he wants to smile but is trying not to.

My stomach twists and my face heats, but I school my expression and clear my throat. "What about it?"

He full-blown grins then.

Dammit. I wrap my arms around myself, knowing I've been caught.

"Your dress looked great on my floor. Night, Via."

He hurries down the steps and quickly disappears from sight. All the while, I'm frozen in place, struggling to find words. As a lawyer, I'm rarely left speechless, but he has an innate ability to steal every word from my vocabulary.

Reid Crawford knows what he's doing to me, and he's using it to his advantage.

twenty-one

Reid

"Hold on," Justin slides out from beneath the car he's working on. "The chick from the bar?"

"Yeah." I wipe my hands on a rag, but it doesn't help. They're perpetually dirty when I'm at the shop.

Hefting himself up off his creeper, Justin calls out to his dad. "We're taking a break!"

Without waiting for approval, he grabs two beers from the garage fridge and weaves his way up the stairs to the tiny breakroom. It's outfitted with a couch that sags all the way to the floor and a table with matching chairs I'm pretty sure his dad snagged from a gas station that went out of business. The man is a total cheapskate.

Justin sits, and I begrudgingly join him, knowing I'm in for an interrogation.

He pops the cap on the beer and takes a long pull. "Start from the beginning and tell me everything."

With a sigh, I crack my beer open, more for something to do with my hands than a desire to drink. After my mom was killed by a drunk driver, I don't often drink, and especially not in the middle of the workday.

I'm not the kiss and tell type, so I kept my mouth shut when my friends asked whether I brought Via home with me on my birthday. What I do with my dick isn't anyone's business but my own. When they asked about her, I told them we had a good time and left it at that. My friends talk about girls all the time, and it rubs me the wrong way, so I never have. But after I confessed to Justin that I'm struggling to come up with the perfect date idea, I have to give him something.

"She came home with me that night," I confirm reluctantly. Out of all my friends, Justin's the one I trust to keep details of my personal life to himself, so I keep going. "It was great. Really fucking great. I wanted to see her again, but she, uh, she didn't."

With a laugh, Justin brings his beer to his lips and leans back in his chair. "I hate to break it to you, dude, but it could be that you're not as good of a lay as you think."

"Shut up," I groan. "Maybe I shouldn't waste my time telling you this."

"No, no. Go on." He waves his hand. "I'm listening."

"She was interested, but scared."

"Scared?" He leans forward and smirks. "Of you?"

"Not of me," I snap, shoving my glasses up my nose. "Of a ... relationship or whatever our connection could become."

"Like fuck buddies?"

I glare at my best friend. "If you're going to interrupt me every two seconds and spew stupid shit, then I'll go talk to Big Dan instead."

It's an idle threat. He and I both know the last guy I'd ever get advice from is his dad. Big Dan is a cool enough guy, but he's not great with women, and his three ex-wives can attest to that.

"Ha! My dad has shit advice and you know it."

I take a tentative swig of beer, then shove the mostly full can away.

"Why did I even bother giving you one?" Justin gripes, one brow cocked.

I shoot him a shit-eating grin. "You should know better by now."

"Yeah, I should. Anyway, go on. Tell me more about..."

"Via," I supply, reining in my irritation. I told him her name downstairs when I asked if he had suggestions, but obviously, he wasn't listening to me.

Under normal circumstances, my dad is my go-to person for this kind of stuff, but for obvious reasons, that won't be happening.

He snaps his fingers. "Via. Right."

"We ran into each other again." I leave out the part where she was on a date with my dad. That's information I know Justin would never keep between us. "We've seen each other a few times since then, and she finally said yes to a date."

"You're really gonna take her out? She's fucking hot, yeah, but she's gotta be thirty." One side of his lips lifts in a sneer, like even the suggestion of it is gross to him.

I glower. I'm not the violent type, but I'm tempted to throw a fist in his face. "I don't care how old she is. I *like* her."

"Like her, *like her?* For more than sex?" He rears back, his eyes wide.

"Yes." I rake a hand down my face, frustration leaching into my voice. "I hoped you'd give me some suggestions for where to take her, but fuck that." I should have known better than to even bring it up.

"Don't be like that."

"Why not? You're not being helpful."

Justin crosses his arms over his chest and frowns. "You haven't given me a chance."

A headache begins to build behind my eyes. Stupid me for opening my big fat mouth in the first place.

"Seriously, man. I wanna help."

"Fine." I'll give him the benefit of the doubt. "What do you suggest?"

"I don't know."

I have to suppress the urge to shake him. Or, better yet, shake myself. What the fuck was I thinking? *You were thinking you had to talk to someone about her before you burst.*

"Take her to a nice restaurant or something. She's older. She'd probably like that."

I throw my hands up in the air. "Gee, why the fuck didn't I think of that?"

With a groan, Justin picks up both beer cans and stands. "Don't be sarcastic. It's fucking annoying. I'll try to think of something, all right? We gotta get back to work."

"Right." I flatten my palms against the sticky table and push to my feet. "Thanks." My tone hardly invokes any sense of genuine gratitude.

Justin pauses in the doorway, giving me a curious glance. "You're actually nervous about this."

It's a statement, not a question, but I answer anyway. "Yeah, I am."

He hums, his bottom lip stuck out just a little. "Interesting."

I don't even want to touch what he means by that remark, so without a word, I follow him back to the garage and get to work.

I SWEAR I FUCKING BLINKED, AND NOW THE DAY OF our date is upon me. Normally, I look forward to the weekend, but this week, I'd give anything to go back to Monday so I could have more time to figure out what to do.

Now that I'm outside her apartment, I'm seriously questioning my decision.

She's from California. She probably expects a fancy dinner, maybe a wine tasting, but I didn't want to do that. I nixed bowling too. The idea of Via throwing a ball down a lane and eating nachos from a plastic tray is laughable.

Or maybe she loves bowling.

I should've asked.

Stop fucking thinking so much.

Shutting my thoughts off is easier said than done.

My freakout time is up, so I pull the key from the ignition, trudge up the stairs to her apartment, and knock. I'm so fucking jittery that my feet bounce back and forth on the rickety wood decking once I'm at the top. It's like I've never been on a date before.

The flowers! I silently curse myself for leaving them in the car.

I glance back at my car on the street.

Do I risk it?

When the door opens, I have my answer. Via stands in front of me, head bowed almost shyly. Her dark hair hangs in waves my fingers itch to bury themselves in while I kiss her senseless.

But that's all we've been thus far—explosive chemistry and little else. Tonight, my mission is to keep my hands to myself. I can kiss her at the end of the night. That's it.

"Ready?" Her soft tone is completely at odds with the confident woman I know lies beneath.

"Oh, yeah." I shuffle back so she can step out onto the landing. Finally coming back to myself, I take her in. "You look ... wow."

Her coat is unzipped, and beneath it, her purple dress hugs her curves, tempting my hands to rove over every one of them.

Keep your hands to yourself, Reid. This is a date.

She adjusts her coat and purse, a faint blush crawling up her cheeks. "Thank you. I'm not too dressed up, am I?"

"You're perfect."

Her eyes dart up to meet mine, like she wasn't expecting that answer.

"Let's go." I hold my hand out for hers so I can help her down the stairs.

She laces her fingers with mine and blows out a breath. "I know I shouldn't be nervous, but I am."

I'm going to make it my mission to wipe all her nerves away tonight. More than anything, I just want her to relax and enjoy herself.

"I'm nervous too."

Soft laughter escapes her. "We're being ridiculous, aren't we?" Her cheeks go redder, noticeable even in the quickly darkening sky.

"This is different for us."

"Right." She lowers her head. "It is."

I open the passenger door, and once she's tucked safely inside, I round the hood and hop in the driver's seat. Twisting at the waist, I pull the bouquet from the back seat. It's a mix of this and that. I didn't like any of the options at the grocery store, so I bought several and mixed and matched.

"Where exactly are we going?"

I lift one brow and grin. I'm surprised it's taken her this long to ask. "You'll see soon enough."

She eyes me curiously, but doesn't press. Good, because I'm really starting to think this might've been a bad idea. Maybe bad isn't the right idea, but I wish I'd put more thought into it. Even if thoughts of it were all-consuming this week—

"I can hear you thinking from over here." Via's voice pulls me from my thoughts.

"Sorry." I shoot her a sheepish smile. "I'll try to keep the thinking to a minimum."

In a matter of minutes, Via sits up straighter and takes in our surroundings. "Did you forget something at your apartment?"

"No." My heart is pounding an anxious rhythm against my ribcage, but there's no backing out now. "This is where we're going tonight."

She presses her lips together, but her eyes dance, like she's trying not to laugh.

Bad idea. Dammit. I knew this wasn't going to work.

"And here I thought you didn't want to get me in bed again." Her tone is light, amused. And maybe even a little turned on.

I groan. I should've known this is how it would come across. "I don't want to get you in bed again."

Her lips part in surprise as I park.

"Fuck, no, that's not what I meant. Believe me, I want to. I just ... That's not why I'm bringing you here, I swear."

Her lips tilt up the slightest bit. "Then why are we here?"

Nerves slam into me all over again. "I ... uh ... I'm going to make dinner for you."

Why the fuck am I stammering like a teenager on his first date?

Normally, around Via, my natural confidence takes over. But none of our other exchanges have been like this. This one means something. To me, at least. Regardless of whether it's as monumental to her or not, I'm taking this date seriously. As the potential of something more. Sex with Via is great, better than great, but I want to get to know her better. Who she really is underneath it all.

She blinks at me, mouth agape. "You're going to make dinner? Like cook dinner? For me?"

With a laugh, I turn the ignition off. "Who else would I be cooking for?"

"I..." She cradles her hands in her lap. "No one's ever cooked for me before. Not ... not like this, anyway."

I frown and study her. "Your ex-husband never cooked?"

"No." She shakes her head.

I search her face for any trace of sadness but find nothing.

"More often than not, we were both busy and didn't eat together. When we did, we just went out." She shrugs like it's not a big deal.

For a long moment, I watch her, trying to find the right words. "You deserve more than he ever gave you."

"We weren't a good fit for each other." She rubs her

hands down her dress and lowers her head a fraction. "It took me a while to see that. It was hard, the demise of my marriage, but I'm much happier where I am now."

"Are you happy that you're here with me?"

The cold is seeping into the car, but she hasn't made a move to get out, so I don't either.

"I shouldn't be." A humorless laugh escapes her. "You're more than a decade younger than me, Reid. That's a lot. And society ... unfortunately it seems society is far more accepting when the woman is younger than the man than the other way around. But yes, I'm happy that I'm here with you right now."

I blow out a breath. *How do I reply to that?* The last thing I want to do is spook her by saying too much too soon, especially now that I've finally gotten her to agree to go out with me. This thing between us is new, so it's probably not the best time for big declarations, but if she gave me a chance, I wouldn't care what society thought of us. Not if she's the person for me.

I bottle up those words, though, and keep them to myself for now.

"Ready to go in?"

She smiles, nodding almost eagerly. I'm not the best cook. It's a talent I didn't inherit from my mom. But she did teach me some of the basics when I was young. She was in the kitchen a lot, and I liked spending time with her. Tonight, I'm pulling out everything I know in hopes of impressing Via enough to secure a second date.

She lets me hold her hand on the way up to my apartment. Again, she laces our fingers rather than just pressing her palm into mine. I like the way she does that, like she wants to be wound around me.

Inside my apartment, I flick the switch next to the door, flooding the space with light. Then I take Via's coat and hang it on the hook mounted in the entry. My coat joins hers.

"You can sit." I pull out one of the stools for her. "I'll get this started." Rubbing my hands together, I will the adrenaline coursing through my body to abate. The last time this woman was in my apartment, I fucked her so thoroughly I swear her scent clung to me for a week. But that's not why she's here tonight. "Do you want something to drink? I've got water, soda—oh." I snap my fingers. "I picked up a couple bottles of wine too."

When I captured her mouse friend, I noticed a collection of wine bottles, so when I went shopping for this dinner, I got a few options.

"Wine would be great." She flips her hair back over her shoulder and rests her chin in her palm, watching me.

I clap my hands and shoot her a wink. "Wine it is."

I show her the options I chose so she can pick. God knows I have no clue what constitutes good wine. Is it the color? Where it's from? The year? It's all a bunch of gibberish to me.

She points, and I uncork the chosen one. I fill a wineglass, which was also purchased specifically for this evening. I probably would have spent less taking her out to a swanky restaurant, but I wanted to treat her to something unique.

She brings her glass to her nose and inhales, then takes a sip that can only be described as delicate.

"This is great." She lifts the glass in my direction. "Good choice."

I chuckle. "That choice is all thanks to Chuck at the store. Next time I see him, I'll let him know that he has excellent taste in wine."

Her laughter fills my apartment. "Yes, please thank him on my behalf."

I turn to my fridge and pull out ingredients. "I hope you like steak—you're not a vegetarian, are you? Or vegan? Fuck, I should've asked." I drop my head, berating myself for my ineptness. Why didn't I consider asking her beforehand?

Thankfully she puts me out of my misery quickly. "I eat meat."

Relief washes over me. "Good, that's good. This is going to take a while, but I picked up crackers and cheese. We can snack on that while I work." I go about pulling the plate of cheese from the fridge and searching for the crackers I stashed somewhere. She watches me with an amused curl of her lips.

When I've found the crackers and added them to the plate, she picks one up and places a slice of cheese on top. "This will hold me over just fine."

I take a deep breath to steady myself so I can focus on

getting our meal prepared, then I put the potatoes in the oven and rinse asparagus and prep it as well.

"I never knew watching someone cook could be fun." She gives me a slow perusal over the counter.

Damn. Why did I vow to not take things beyond a kiss tonight? The decision seems idiotic now. The desire in her expression as she watches me makes me want to throw out the cake I picked up and eat her for dessert instead.

I clear my throat, hoping to clear away the dirty thoughts too. "I'm glad I can provide adequate entertainment."

"Oh, more than adequate, I'd say." Her eyes sparkle, all traces of her nervousness from earlier gone. Either the wine is helping to calm her or she's decided not to overthink this. If I had to guess, I'd say it's the wine.

I slather the steaks with the garlic and herb compound butter I made this afternoon while I wait for the cast-iron skillet to heat.

"I'm not sure I've ever had a steak made like that."

"Prepare to have your mind blown, then. How do you like your meat cooked?"

"Well done." She cringes. "I know, I know. You're probably judging me so hard. I don't want it *burnt*, but I can't stand the sight of a bloody steak. It makes me want to gag."

I study her, surprised by her defensiveness. Is that something her ex judged her for? Liking her steak well done? "I'll cook it any way you want it, and I'll never judge you. I wouldn't. I'm not like that."

She answers me with a smile and a small "thanks." She

swirls the wine in her glass and takes another sip. "Do you need help with anything?"

"Nope." I turn on the tap so I can wash my hands again. "I've got it."

This was my idea. The last thing I'm going to do is make her work on our date.

"It feels weird not doing anything."

I hesitate, pursing my lips. "Do you really want to help?"

She nods eagerly. "Yes. Put me to work. As much as I like watching you, I want to help in some way."

I have to suppress a groan at those words.

Put me to work.

I can think of a few creative ways I could put her to work. Most of them involve little to no clothes. Like her right here in this kitchen on her knees, taking my cock—

"Reid?"

I jolt out of my thoughts. "I made a loaf of bread this afternoon. You can slice that up. That's about all I need help with right now."

She slips off the stool with a smile. Her purple dress isn't revealing, not in the slightest, but maybe that's what makes it even more enticing. I'm left to my imagination.

Via washes her hands, and I pass her the fresh baked bread, then a cutting board and knife.

"Slice it about this thick." I hold up my thumb and forefinger to show her what I mean. "And butter it on both sides with this." I snag another bowl of compound butter from the fridge and set it on the counter beside her.

"Do you always cook like this?"

"What do you mean?" I ask, gingerly putting one steak in the now sizzling cast-iron pan.

"So..." She shrugs. "Fancy, I guess. You know what I had for dinner last night? Cereal."

"Trust me," I scoop a spoonful of melted butter in the pan back on top of the steaks, "I'm usually too tired to cook like this. Dinner is typically a sandwich or, like you, I end up eating cereal."

She flicks her hair out of her eyes and sets the knife down. "You're telling me you're *not* one of those men who has to have meat with a meal in order to consider it dinner?"

Something about the way she says *men* stirs a sense of confidence to life inside me. I like that she's not downgrading me because of my age.

"No." I laugh. "I don't need meat with my dinner. Sure, it's nice, but I'll live without it."

Tilting her head, she hums. "You continue to surprise me."

I hesitate, then ask, "Is that a good thing?"

She presses her lips together, cheeks twitching as she fights a smile. "I think so."

Leaving the steaks momentarily, I slide the asparagus into the oven beside the potatoes. "After those come out, I'll pop the bread in."

She nods, leaning against the corner counter. "Everything smells delicious."

"Hopefully it'll taste as good."

"You know," she wraps her arms around herself protectively, almost like a cage, "We've had sex twice, but I still don't know a whole lot about you."

"You know more than most."

It's true too. I don't tell just anyone about my mom, or the meaning behind my tattoos. But with Via, I never hesitated. I *wanted* her to know.

"What's your favorite color? And you can't say black." She holds up a finger in warning. "All men want to say black. Pick an actual color."

I try not to grin at her annoyance and fail. "Green. What's yours?"

She mulls it over, like it's not an easy choice. "I like them all, but if I have to pick one, I'd say blue. Like the blue of a cloudless day. It makes me feel at peace."

"What else do you want to know about me?"

Her eyes sparkle like she's been thinking about these questions—and all the things she wants to know about me —for a while. It probably shouldn't fill me with as much satisfaction as it does.

"Favorite food?"

"You can't go wrong with a good burger, but—" I walk away from the stove to pull a bag of lime tortilla chips from the cabinet. "These are my guilty pleasure. I guess you'd classify them as my favorite snack, if we're getting specific here."

"Hmm." She looks the bag over. "Can I try one?"

"Sure." I hold the bag out to her so I can check the steaks. After a quick check, I pull them from the pan and let them rest.

She eyes them with a little frown. "You like yours well done too?"

"Like you, I don't like to see blood coming out of my meat."

She smiles and reaches into the bag of chips. "I'm glad I'm not the only one. Chase—" She snaps her mouth shut and shakes her head. "Sorry. I didn't mean to bring him up."

"Are you over him?" I ask, purely out of curiosity.

She snorts. "Very. But he was such a big part of my life that sometimes it's hard to not bring him up."

"You can talk about him. I don't mind. He's in your past, and I fully plan on being your future."

Her eyes dart to the floor. "Reid—"

"Don't say anything." If she does, she'll only downplay the growing feelings between us. I don't want her trying to squash this before she even gives us a chance to grow. "Please."

With a sigh, she nods and plucks a chip from the bag. She stuffs it into her mouth like if she keeps her mouth busy, then it'll keep her from saying the words on her tongue.

"These *are* good." She goes in for another. "I'll have to pick up a bag the next time I go to the store."

I'm already making a mental note to add an extra to my list.

I don't want our conversation to sour the mood, so I go back to our get-to-know-you questions. "What's *your* favorite food?"

With a laugh, she rolls up the open bag of chips and

puts the clip back on. "It's so dumb, but I *love* a good Caesar salad. Not every place knows how to make a good one, but when they do, nothing else beats it."

"And your favorite snack?" I pull the food out of the oven and pop the bread onto the rack so it can toast.

"Buttered popcorn," she answers, with no hesitation. "The *good* popcorn. The super-greasy, buttery kind from the movie theater. The stuff you pop can't compare."

I might've found this little game amusing at first, but there's no denying that I enjoy having these insights into what makes Via who she is.

With a quick peek in the oven, I grab a mitt and remove the bread.

Via sits back down, sipping at her wine, while I plate our meals. "You want more?" I tip my head at her glass in question. She regards it, a serious expression on her face, for several seconds. "I won't be offended if that's what you're worried about."

Laughter bubbles out of her. "I just don't want you thinking the worst of me on our first date."

I grab the bottle and yank the cork out. "Tonight is about you enjoying yourself."

Because I want you to do this with me again.

She holds out her glass so I can fill it. "I won't have more than this. I don't want..." She looks down, pressing her lips together. Then she takes a deep breath and looks me in the eye. "I don't trust myself with you if I have more."

I stick the cork back in, grinning like the fucking

Cheshire cat. I don't even attempt to hide my smile. I'm too pleased to rein it in. "Afraid you'll be unable to resist me?"

She huffs a laugh. "I'm pretty sure I've already proven that to be fact." She smooths her hair back behind her ears. "With alcohol in my system, I'm scared of what the consequences might be."

"It's okay." I slide a plate in front of her. "You can use me for my body."

Thank fuck my nerves from earlier are disappearing. It took a little time, but I feel more like myself around her again.

"You'd like that, wouldn't you?"

"Oh, absolutely. But I'm not sleeping with you tonight."

I put my own plate down and join her. She looks over at me, brows drawn in offense. "Why not?"

"Because I don't want to have to tell our future kids that I fucked their mom on the first date."

She gapes like a fish, mouth hanging open.

"Careful, now's not the time for me to find something to stuff in your mouth."

Snapping her jaw shut, she shakes her head, her cheeks going pink. "I ... I have no words."

"Good." I point to her plate with my knife. "Eat and let me know if it's any good."

I can see it on her face, the retort she's desperate to voice, but she swallows it down and cuts into her steak. The moan she lets out over the first bite has me pulling in a deep breath to rein in my natural reaction. The primal, sexual sound instantly makes my jeans grow tighter. When her eyes roll back and she moans again, I realize she's exaggerating her response now, trying to rile me up.

Via might not want to admit it, but she loves sparring with me and working me up. There's a fire beneath that quiet exterior. Makes me wonder whether her dumbass ex ever bothered to look, to unleash that wild spirit just waiting to be let loose. Probably not. He had to be a fucking idiot to ever let her go.

"This is the best steak I have ever had, and believe me, I've been to some amazing restaurants."

Pleasure floods me. My mom would be proud that I'm putting the skills she gave me to good use. "I'm glad you like it."

"Like it? I love it. I could easily get used to being spoiled like this. I haven't been eating as well as I should. You've seen my kitchen. It's minuscule, and with so much going on with the building, I've been eating junk food or ordering from the diner." She goes in for another bite, closing her eyes to savor it.

"Say yes to another date with me, and I promise I'll spoil you again."

Her eyes pop open. "I haven't even had a bite of my baked potato, and you're already requesting a second date?"

My answer is quick. Succinct. "Yes."

She squints at me and hums, like she's weighing the pros and cons.

"What do you have to lose?"

She spears a piece of asparagus. "You've already claimed that in some alternate universe, we have kids, so I guess I have that to lose." There's a sadness in the downturn of her lips that I don't quite understand, but I don't stop to ponder it.

"No, angel, they'll exist in this one. I assure you. I'd never talk about an alternate universe when it comes to you."

She clears her throat, an attempt to collect herself. "What are you going to do if I say no?"

I pause, eyes steady on her. "Keep asking."

Her brows rise, amusement curling her lips. "Can't take no for an answer?"

"Oh, I most definitely can, but I know you want to say yes."

She snorts. "How can you possibly know that?"

I take her in, starting at the top of her head and working my way down. "The way you're leaning into me tells me you *want* to be closer to me. And when you lie, your left eye twitches just a little."

She gasps. "It does not."

I raise my hands, giving her my most innocent face. "Trust me, it does."

She lifts a hand like she's going to prod at her eye, but she stops herself.

I take a drink of water, then clear my throat. "As much fun as it is getting to know the little things, I want to know some big things too."

Her shoulders visibly tense, almost curling inward.

"What do you want to know? I hate to disappoint you, but I'm not that exciting."

"Your idea of exciting might be different from mine."

Her fingers dance a beat on the countertop. "I suppose that could be true."

"I want to know more about your love of art."

Her eyes widen. "Really?"

"Yeah. When did you first realize you liked art?"

"Oh, well." She wipes her fingers on a napkin.

That was another purchase I made today. I usually get by with paper towels.

"I guess I was about seven or eight. For Christmas, I got a set of art supplies I'd wanted for months." She smiles wistfully at the memory. "I spent that whole winter break drawing and painting. I'm pretty sure all the walls in my bedroom were covered in various pieces of art by the time I had to go back to school." Tucking her hair behind her ear, she takes a sip of water. "After that, it was my go-to activity in my spare time. I took advanced classes as I got older. I wanted to go to art school, but I wasn't allowed, so I became a lawyer instead. It's what my parents wanted." She gives a small one-shoulder shrug, like she's trying to convey to me that it doesn't matter.

"What do you mean you weren't allowed?"

She chews another bite of steak and swallows before she answers. "They wouldn't pay for college unless I chose a major they approved of."

"Like?" I prompt. How the hell could any parent *force* their kid to choose a career they didn't like?

"Law, obviously." She ticks it off on her finger. "Law school. Any type of science or business."

"And you listened?"

She presses her lips together and makes a little humming sound. "I think I was scared not to. I wasn't in the position to take on the debt on my own, and forgoing college was out, since that was the goal I'd been preparing for my whole adolescence. I thought I had no choice." By now, her shoulders are slumped and her lips are downturned.

Shit. I've made her sad with this topic of conversation when that's not what I meant at all.

"Sometimes parents forget how little life experience kids have acquired by eighteen. That there's still so much left to learn."

"Says the twenty-one-year-old." She laughs in a soft, genuine way. "You make an excellent point. I never thought about it like that. Did you go to college?"

"I went to trade school, actually. Automotive technology. I work for my dad too, obviously, but I learned that skill set from him." I'm rambling, not nervous exactly, but there's a part of me that feels inadequate next to Via. College was never in my plan, but sometimes it feels like I'm less-than because I'm missing that stupid piece of paper.

Via's fork clatters against the plate when she sets it down. "Why do you sound like that's not good enough?"

I snort. "You're a lawyer, for fuck's sake."

She twists her lips back and forth. "Yeah, a lawyer who hated her job. I didn't pursue my passion, and now I finally am. I'd say you're ahead of me in that regard."

"I guess I never thought about it like that."

She gives me a soft smile. "It's easy to think that everyone but you has their shit together, but we're all out here winging it. Even at my age."

I stare, my heart squeezing in my chest. "You're not old, Via."

"Compared to you?" she huffs. "Yes, I am."

Maybe *I'm* the crazy one, because I don't think about the age gap between us.

We finish dinner, and the last of Via's second glass of wine disappears. Once the plates are rinsed, I stick them in my minuscule dishwasher—seriously; the thing is barely worth having, but it does come in handy at times like tonight.

With a glass of water, Via takes a seat on my couch. My date rules still apply, so I won't let her help me clean up.

When all the dishes are loaded and the machine is running, I join her in the living area. "Are you ready for me to take you home, or do you want to stay a while longer? I had something else planned, but I didn't expect it to take me so long to make dinner."

She adjusts her skirt and curls her legs under her. "I guess that depends on what you have in mind. You know, since you said sex is off the table."

Hands on my hips, I let my head drop back. "I really stuck my foot in my mouth with that one, didn't I?" When I lower my head to meet her eyes, my glasses slip down. I need to get them adjusted, not that it'll do much good. I swear every time I do, they're sliding down my nose within a day. That or they're too tight against my head and I have to have them readjusted, only to end up back where I started.

A giggle escapes her. "Maybe, but I appreciate your attempt at chivalry."

"Anyway." I give her my back and pull the item off the shelf. "I thought we could play this." Then spin on my heel so she can see.

She presses her lips together, trying to hide her amusement. "Candy Land?"

I shrug. "I did tell you the first time we met that we could play Candy Land. It seemed fitting."

Smiling, she points to the coffee table. "Game on."

twenty-two

Via

I lie awake in bed the following night, still musing over every detail. It was simple and perfect in every way and by far the best date I've ever been on. I don't need a fancy restaurant or anything that might be perceived as *impressive*. Watching him cook was the sexiest thing I've ever witnessed. It was a struggle to keep my hands to myself. I wanted nothing more than to pull him back to his bedroom after dinner, but I respected his decision to take sex off the table for now. We *should* get to know each other in more than just the biblical sense.

When he dropped me off at home last night, he laid a gentle kiss on my mouth, and I gave him one word before disappearing into my apartment.

Yes.

He knew what it meant instantly.

Yes, to another date.

I'm not sure it's possible for him to top this one, but it doesn't matter. I *want* to spend more time with him. I *want* to know him more.

Does it scare me?

God, yes.

But not enough to stop.

I roll out of bed, head straight to the shower, and twist the ancient, squeaky knob. It takes a few minutes for the water to heat to lukewarm. That's as good as it gets here, I've found, due to the old pipes. I can't wait to have that little problem sorted out. I dream of the day the bathroom upgrade is done and I can stand in a shower for as long as I'd like without running out of hot water.

When I'm finished, I yank on a pair of sweats and throw my robe on over it. All the while, my body fights the need to shiver.

I run a comb through my hair and work heat protectant through it before blowing it dry. If there's one thing I take seriously, it's the health of my hair.

I have the entire day to myself since it's Sunday. I still haven't gotten used to having actual free time. Before, work took up the majority of my waking hours. Chase was a workaholic too. It's no wonder we fell apart. Although, since he was screwing his secretary, I'm not sure workaholic is the correct term for him.

Labels like cheater, philanderer, adulterer would be

more apt, and I'm sure I could find even more creative names for him.

Once my hair is dry, I pad out to the kitchen and pop a coffee pod into the maker. When the delicious aroma of fresh coffee hits my nose, I instantly perk up. When it's ready, I add cream and sugar, mixing it carefully to not make a mess.

With the TV on for background noise, I pull out the boxes of art supplies that arrived a few days ago. I haven't had much time to go through them, but now I itch to unbox everything. I want to sit down, let my mind wander, and *create*. It's been too long since I have, which is laughable, considering I'm opening my own art store. But I've been scared of what might show up on the paper if I do. Emotions are so easily channeled through art.

Besides, I haven't felt inspired since I completed the painting of my green dress.

Until today. Now that craving to put pencil to paper is so strong I can't resist.

My preferred medium has always been paint.

The colors. The mess. Even the smell.

But that's not what my heart yearns to do today, so I flip open the sketchpad, grab a fresh charcoal, and park my butt on the floor.

Sketchbook laid out on the coffee table, I empty my mind and let my hand flow across the page.

It doesn't take long for the strokes and shadows to form a tangible image.

A hand—a man's hand.

Reid's.

I should be embarrassed that my mind wandered to him, but I don't dwell on it. I'm drawing, and that's all that matters.

I work on the sketch for a long time, focusing on the details that I remember—freckles, the curvature of his veins. Eventually I stop to grab a bite to eat and make more coffee. Is the coffee strictly necessary for the creative process? Yes, it most definitely is a vital part.

Sitting down once more, I take a look at what I've created.

I see the flaws—what I could've done better, but I also *feel* the passion bleeding onto the page. For too long, I let this part of myself lay dormant. I tried to suffocate it. I thought if I snuffed out my love of creating, I could fit into these boxes other people so desperately wanted to put me in.

My parents aren't horrible people, but sometimes parents have the tendency to forget that they're raising brand-new individuals, not copies of themselves. I hate that it's taken me this long to put my foot down and live my life for me. It also took the gut punch of Chase's infidelity. But it doesn't matter what brought about the epiphany, just that it happened.

When the sketch is finished, I turn the page and start another.

Again, I don't mean to draw Reid. It just happens.

The curve of his jaw.

The slope of his nose with his glasses sliding precariously down.

That endearingly crooked smile and dimple in his cheek.

I can almost hear him saying, "I think I'm your muse, angel."

I'd scoff at him, of course. Never would I admit to that, but he just might be. Reid inspires me. He's young, but he's more thoughtful, insightful, than most, regardless of age. Those things probably stem from life experiences like losing his mom the way he did and even the situation with his sister. I love that he hasn't let the trials he's been through break his spirit.

Reid is a vibrant splash of color in the dull landscape that is my life.

He's red.

Passion and energy.

He's blue.

Friendly, a rock I can hold on to against the crash of waves.

He's green.

Infallibly positive, with a generous soul.

He's yellow.

The optimistic sunshine on my cloudy days.

He's every color in-between streaked across my blank white canvas.

No matter where the future takes us, my life is better because I met him.

There's comfort in that realization. That I don't have to

put pressure on myself or slap a label on us in order to enjoy it.

I spend the day and well into the evening drawing. It feels so good to let that part reawaken. Despite my decision to open the store, to teach and guide others to appreciate their creative side, I've been suppressing mine. Self-sabotage is an apt description for it. But for some time, I've been fearful of what my emotions might channel onto the page. I'm in a better state of mind now. A lot of that is owed to Reid.

The divorce, the move—none of it was easy, even if it was necessary.

I didn't want that pain and darkness channeled into my art, not when painting has always been something that makes me happy.

Stifling a yawn, I close my sketchpad. My hands ache and my fingers are stained from the pencil, but I feel lighter than I have in a long while.

My phone begins to ring, the sound dulled, so I go in search of it. I'm not sure when I last had it. I've been so focused on drawing today that I didn't have need for it.

Finally, I locate it between the couch cushions.

It's Reid's name that shows up on the screen.

"Hello?" I'm out of breath from the search.

"Hey, I just wanted to make sure you're okay. I texted, but I never heard from you. I was worried."

"Oh." I plop my butt down on the couch. "I'm fine. I've just been drawing."

You, I don't tell him. *I've been drawing you.*

"What exactly have you been drawing?" There's interest in his voice. Like he somehow knows.

I don't want to tell him the truth. It's far too embarrassing. It's like I'm twelve again, scribbling the name of my crush in a notebook.

"A little bit of this and that."

"Will you show me?"

"No!" I blurt a little too quickly.

He clears his throat. "Why not?"

"It's not finished."

It's not a lie, not really. Is art ever truly complete? Not in my opinion. That's what makes it so great.

"You'll show me when it's finished, then?"

I squeeze my eyes shut. *No, I won't.* "Yeah, I'll show you. But only when it's ready."

He chuckles, and I can almost imagine him beside me on the couch. "Okay. As long as you show me one day."

"What have you been up to today?" I counter.

"I watched Lilibet for a while. It was a last-minute thing, but I always have fun with her. We went to the arcade."

I smile to myself. "I bet she loved that."

"Beating me at air hockey was the highlight of her life."

"How much did she beat you by?"

"Too much. She's been learning my tricks."

"She's a cute kid."

"Yeah." I can hear his smile. "She's great."

"How's your sister? Is she still with—"

"The loser? Yeah, unfortunately. She seems to think she doesn't deserve better."

I close my eyes and let my thoughts drift. Was Chase as awful as his sister's boyfriend? I don't think so, but then again, maybe he was, only in a different way. It wasn't until after the divorce that I recognized all the ways in which he was controlling and manipulative and that many of the things he said weren't okay. It's a bit horrifying to realize that I was married to a man like that and still would be if he hadn't cheated. It seems ridiculous, but I'm grateful that controlling bastard cheated on me.

"Sometimes," I begin, "when you're in it, you don't see the toxicity for what it is."

Especially when you started out young and happy.

"Your ex was toxic?"

Of course he's not going to let my comment slide.

"In hindsight, yes." I swallow thickly at the admission. It feels almost like a failure to admit it. "He ... he never hit me. I want you to know that. But looking back at the things he said in the later years of our marriage? He was a manipulative narcissist, and I was too in love with the old him to see that he'd changed. Then again, maybe he was *always* that way, and I was just ... stupid."

Reid is quiet. So quiet, in fact, that I pull the phone from my ear to make sure the call hasn't been disconnected.

"Via," he finally says. "The last thing you could ever be is stupid. You were too good for him, and it sounds like he manipulated you into believing that wasn't the case."

"I don't—"

"Want to talk about him? That's fine. For now. But I

hope you'll open up to me about him eventually. It might be good for you."

"I don't need a therapist," I snap in a way that suggests that maybe I do.

He chuckles, amused at my outburst. How is it possible to be so unfazed by everything? Is it because he's young, or is it just who he is? I wish I could let things roll off my back the way he does.

"I never said you did, angel. But I want to be your friend."

I laugh outright. "I'm pretty sure you want to be more than my friend, Reid."

"That's true." There's that chuckle again. "But it takes a good friendship to establish a solid foundation. I don't want to only be your lover. I want to be your person. The one you go to first. The one you think of when you wake up. The one ... just *the one*." He sounds vulnerable, like he didn't mean to admit that much.

I clutch the phone tighter in my grasp. "Reid—"

"Good night, Via. I'll see you tomorrow."

"I—"

But it's too late. He's gone. I drop my arm, phone and all, to the cushion. His forwardness should scare me. His certainty, at such a young age, is surely false, right?

But didn't I feel confident in my relationship with Chase? I married the man, for Christ's sake!

That fact only worries me more, because if Reid really is sure of me *now*, then what's to say he won't change his mind?

"God, I love margaritas." Ella lifts her glass and takes a long sip through the cocktail straw. It's her second margarita of the night, so things are only getting started.

I dip a chip into the house made salsa. While Ella's on her second drink, I'm on my second bowl of this deliciousness.

"Me too," Jessica chimes in, waving her drink in the air. When it sloshes over the rim, she laughs and licks it from her fingers. "It's nice to go out with you ladies."

Surprisingly, everyone from book club made it tonight. Even Glenda, who sits at the head of the table, talking to the waiter. I think she's telling him to turn the music down, to which he shakes his head and mouths, "I can't do that."

I'm with Glenda on this one. It *is* loud in here.

"There's karaoke tonight," Cassandra says on my left. "Do any of you want to sign up?"

Immediately, I shake my head.

"Oh, come on," Ella says, dunking a chip in the salsa bowl I've commandeered. When she pops the chip into her mouth, I inconspicuously pull the bowl even closer to me. "It'll be fun. *No one* who does karaoke can actually sing. Usually, anyway."

"Right now, we should be figuring out what we're going to eat." I point to my menu. "To soak up the alcohol," I tack on when they give me funny looks. "We're too old for hangovers."

"Speak for yourself." Ella does a little shimmy and takes a healthy sip of her drink. "I'm going to sign up. You in, Cassandra?"

"Absolutely."

They head over to the opposite side of the restaurant. The entire time they're gone, I silently pray that they don't sign anyone else up. Namely, me. My screechy voice will send people running from the building.

"So," Glenda says from the other end of the table, her focus trained solely on me. "Tell me more of your story."

I reach for my margarita and take a fortifying sip. "My story?" I repeat, stalling.

"Everyone's got one—what's yours? All you've told us is that you have an ex-husband and you moved from California. There has to be more."

"Yeah, come on." Jessica reaches for my arm. "Tell us more."

"There's really not much more than that. I was a lawyer, but you already know I'm opening an art store. That was always my dream—art. But I chose to go the more practical route with law." I keep it simple. I don't need to unload *that* situation on my newfound friend group. "Met my ex in college, got married, he cheated, and now, here I am. Truly, not all that exciting."

"Are you dating at all?" Jessica asks. "I take calls for Derrick and manage his schedule. He's single and good-looking. Nice too. I could—"

I shake my head. "We already went on a date."

Ella plops into her seat then. Cassandra hasn't returned.

"You went on a date? With who? Tell us everything!" Ella bounces in her seat like she thinks I've got juicy gossip to spill.

The irony is, I *do*, but I won't tell them about Reid. They'll either be horrified, or they'll be shouting "You go, girl!" I'm not sure which is worse.

"Derrick," I eye the chips and salsa longingly. But I can't stuff my face when I'm the center of attention, so they'll have to wait. "He's the—"

She waves her hand. "We all know who Derrick is."

Right. Small town.

Jessica clears her throat, bringing my attention back to her. "Was the date terrible? He hasn't gone out much since his wife passed."

"It was fine."

Cassandra pulls out her chair, rejoining us. "What'd I miss?"

"Via went on a date with Derrick," Ella says.

Cassandra gasps. "You did? He's *so* handsome. I can't believe you didn't tell us sooner."

I shrug. "I didn't think it was important."

They all talk at once, going on about how this was *very* important information. I'm saved from any more questions when the waiter comes to take our order. By the time everyone's given theirs, Cassandra and Ella are called up for karaoke, and I'm, thankfully, off the hook.

For now, at least.

twenty-three

Reid

When my dad invited me over for dinner, I agreed right away. Dinner at his house meant I wouldn't have to cook. Plus, it's Monday, the worst day of the week. Who wants to cook dinner on a Monday? Not me.

My body aches after a full day of manual labor. I might be in shape, but even my body takes a hit after a workday like the one I had today. I was supposed to be at Via's job site all day, but my dad needed extra hands on another job, so he sent me and another guy over to cover it.

With a grunt, I heave myself out of my car. My legs are like Jell-O. Like I did five-thousand squats today. For all I know, maybe I did.

"Uncle Weed!" A tiny dynamo of a kid slams into me the second I cross the threshold.

With a pained groan, I bend over and pick her up. "Hey, Lili. How's my favorite girl?"

I freeze at the sentiment. Lili's been my favorite girl for so long, but there's another woman in my life creeping up the list. My time with Via today was far too short, but at least I did see her. She's like a drug I need a hit of in order to keep going.

"Good." Lilibet wraps her arms around my neck. "I got to pick a sticker from the treasure box today."

"You did? Why did you get to do that?" I jostle her in my arms, making her giggle.

"I don't know. Because I'm nice."

"That's a very good reason to get a sticker. Where is it? On your shirt?" I start looking for it.

"No, silly. It's too pretty to use. It's in my room so I can look at it."

"Did grandpa take you for ice cream to celebrate?"

She gasps. "No!" She wiggles in my arms, and when I set her on her feet, she takes off like a rocket for the kitchen. "Grandpa! Where's my ice cream for good behavior?"

My dad will curse me out later for planting that idea in her head.

The house smells incredible. The scents of garlic, tomatoes, and other spices fill the air, making my stomach rumble as I head to the kitchen.

"Hey, Dad." I grab a glass from the cabinet and fill it with water. "Dinner smells fantastic. Thanks for the invite."

He smiles over at me, his eyes crinkled at the corners. My dad's still relatively young, but the long, hard workdays in the sun have left him freckled and with more wrinkles around his eyes than he'd probably have otherwise. Though the gray at his temples is probably from raising my sister and me after our mom passed.

"Thanks for coming. I have a few things I want to talk to you about."

Great. It might only be about work, but by the businesslike tone, I have a feeling something more has been on his mind.

"I'll set the table," I mutter. Might as well do something to distract myself from the dread that's suddenly knotting my stomach. "Where's Layla?"

"Showering. She'll be down soon."

"Hey, kid." I snap my fingers at Lili. "Did you wash your hands yet?"

She gives me a pout that tells me she hasn't.

"Wash up and be ready for dinner."

"Grandpa," she whines, "do I have to?"

My dad looks over his shoulder at Lili, who bats her eyes up at him in an effort to win him over.

"No dinner for dirty little goblins. Wash your hands and help Reid set the table."

With a wink, I scoop her up and carry her to the sink. I set her on the step stool in front of it and turn on the water. Squirting a glob of soap into her palm, I remind her of the proper way to scrub her hands free of germs. My mom always drilled it into Layla and me. Sometimes I wonder what she'd think about where we are now. She'd love Lili, of course, and spoil her silly. Though I don't think it's possible to spoil her more than my dad already does.

Once her hands are clean, Lili brings glasses and utensils to the table.

I set out the pasta bowls my dad prefers, and he plates up the spaghetti. I've never had spaghetti that tops his. He makes the sauce from scratch and won't reveal the secret ingredient.

After I've grated fresh parmesan cheese over each bowl, I carry them to the table.

Layla's footsteps are loud on the stairs as she comes down. Even when we were kids, she was constantly stomping up and down the steps.

"I'm starving," she groans. She rounds the corner, still pulling her damp hair up on her head. "Thanks for dinner, Dad."

"No problem," he says, filling the glasses with water from a pitcher.

Sitting down to eat together is nice. We don't do it often enough. Since I moved out, I don't drop by to join in on dinner unless my dad invites me.

Which brings me back to my theory that the invite comes with ulterior motives.

Regardless, I won't turn down a good, free meal.

"How's work?" I ask my sister, twisting noodles around my fork.

She eyes me with an annoyed expression. "It's a job. That's about all I have to say." A sigh rattles her chest.

My sister's life plan went up in flames when she got pregnant. She's made the most of it, even if she can't always see that. She's a good mom too, though she's too hard on herself.

The only thing she's "failed" at is her love life. She consistently picks the worst kind of guys out there.

"I still think you should apply for that blogger job or whatever it's called," my dad pipes in.

"What job?" This is news to me.

Why does no one tell me anything anymore? It's like once I moved out, I lost the privilege of being kept in the loop.

Layla frowns, her fork loose in her hand like she doesn't have the energy to keep a firm grip on it. "It's nothing."

Dad glowers at her. "It's not nothing." To me, he adds, "It's for a blog—"

"Vlog, Dad. She's a *vlogger*. A million people are going to apply for this job. She's super popular. There's no chance I'll get it, so what's the point in trying?"

"What exactly does the job entail?" I ask, sitting up straighter. "Would you have to travel? Move?"

"No. It's remote. I would help with her social media—editing photos, making graphics for her to share, organizing her schedule. That sort of thing."

"Just apply," I tell her. "You have nothing to lose."

Her shoulders slump. "I'm tired of rejections."

"Layla." I set my hands on the table, leveling her with a look. She might be older than me, but oftentimes I feel like her big brother. "The worst that can happen is being told no or hearing nothing at all. The world isn't going to stop spinning. Nothing's going to change if they say no, but if you *are* chosen, everything *could* change. So, again, what do you have to lose?"

She stares into her bowl of spaghetti like it holds the answers to all life's questions.

Sometimes I forget that, once upon a time, my sister had goals and dreams beyond this town. But she chose to stay here and raise Lilibet.

"I'll think about it. Okay? Will that make you happy?"

Lili pats her arm. "Very happy, Mommy. You're gonna do great."

Lili doesn't really understand what we're talking about, but her absolute trust and belief in her mom is sweet. She's a good kid. Layla's raising an incredible girl, despite the odds stacked against her as a young mom.

Dinner's more subdued after that. I'm starting to think maybe I was reading too much into things, but then my dad clears his throat. It's not like an *oh, I've got something lodged in my throat* kind of sound. It's more of a *pay attention to me* sound.

Both Layla and I look at him where he sits at the head of the table. He doesn't make eye contact with Layla, only me. *Great.*

"I wanted to talk to you about something."

"Okay." I slide my empty bowl toward the center of the table. "Shoot."

The urge to cross my arms over my chest is strong, but I fight it. The last thing I need is to go into this conversation with a defensive attitude.

"How much longer do you plan to work part time? It's time to choose. Do you want to settle into working on cars or working for me? It's always been my intention to have you take over the company." He steeples his fingers. "But my dreams don't matter. Yours do. What do *you* want, son?"

I want to shrink beneath his attention, beneath the pressure. That's what I want.

I enjoy carpentry, sure, but I'm not passionate about it, and frankly, I don't want to run the business. My dad's always been open about wanting me to take over, and I've always secretly hated knowing I wouldn't make that dream a reality.

By now I should know what I want to do, have a clear direction. That's what he's pointing out—that it's time to buckle down and say I want to work on cars for the rest of my life, or that I want to let that go and work solely for him until I take over the business.

Layla doesn't know what she wants to do with the rest of her life, and she's older than me, but she has a child, so she has a better excuse than I do.

"Reid?" he prompts.

"Sorry." I shake my head free of cobwebs. "I ... uh ... you know I don't want to do construction. The business ... I don't want it."

I shrink in my seat the moment the words are out of my mouth.

The idea of being a contractor for the rest of my life makes me want to run in the opposite direction.

He lets out a knowing sigh. "That's what I figured you'd

say." Running his fingers through his hair, he presses his lips together. Then he focuses on me again, his expression intense. "You're fired."

"Dad!" Layla yells. "You can't—"

"Why?" My question is calm, curious.

"Because," he leans back in his chair, "if you don't like it, if it's not what makes you happy, then you shouldn't waste your time working for me." He stands then, gathering up his bowl and then Lili's. "You need to focus on what you love. What you're passionate about. So, you're fired. This way you'll have more time to work on cars."

Unfortunately, Big Dan can't afford to bring me on full time, so I'll have to find a second job regardless. Unless, by some miracle, I find a shop hiring for a full-time position.

"I'm doing you a favor." His eyes are sad and his lips are turned down in a frown. He's disappointed that I don't want to follow in his footsteps, but he cares too much about me to put his own desires before mine. "You'll see that."

I dip my chin. "I know."

Layla shoots me a sad look. She knows I don't like disappointing Dad.

I help clean up, and since it's late, I give Lili a hug and say goodbye to Layla and my dad.

"Reid, wait!" he calls after me when I'm halfway to my car.

When I turn to face him, his face is scrunched with worry. Maybe he thinks I'm mad or upset. I'm more resigned than anything. In the back of my mind, I knew this was coming.

"Yeah?" I prompt when he just stares at me in the orange glow of the porch light. The harsh hue makes the tired gray splotches beneath his eyes even more prominent.

He's obviously not sleeping well. Is it because he's been worrying about having this conversation with me? Something to do with Layla? Or something more?

I don't ask, though. Not because I don't care, but because it's not my place to pry into his business. If he wants to talk, he'll come to me.

"You understand, right? I'm not..." He clears his throat. "I'm not doing this to be mean."

I shove my hands into my pockets, drawing my leather jacket more firmly over my body. I should've grabbed an actual coat, but then there'd go my street cred.

"I know." I walk back and pull him into a hug. "I love you, Dad."

He hugs me back, tighter than before, like he doesn't want to let go. "I love you too."

Releasing me, he steps back and watches me walk to my car. His protective gaze doesn't leave me until I drive away. It leaves me wondering, what would he think if he knew I was falling for the woman he likes?

Via might not notice it, but I saw it this morning. The way he looks at her? My own father might just become my competition.

twenty-four

Via

I've been looking forward to this week's book club way more than I should be. Especially after the craziness of margarita night where I *did* get roped into singing karaoke. Even Glenda got on stage. It was a wild night. For me, anyway.

When I moved here, I wasn't concerned about making friends. I had far bigger things to worry about first. I'm so glad I stumbled into the bookstore that day and met Ella. Without her, I would've never been introduced to the book club and all these incredible ladies.

With the paperback for this week's discussion under my arm, I head for the front door.

I shouldn't even bother with bringing the book, since we

spend about five minutes talking about it before the conversation dissolves into other matters, like annoying spouses, tiresome jobs, and the basic goings-on of life.

When I get to the door, I let myself in. The smell of freshly baked cookies fills the room, and the coffee table is covered in a spread of sandwiches cut into tiny triangles, fresh fruit, cheeses, and more.

The book club does not cut corners.

"Via! You're here!" Ella jumps up from the couch and darts over to me. She has a puppy-like energy that I'm envious of. Even on my happiest days, I've never been as peppy as she is.

"Are you sure I shouldn't have brought something?" I whisper. I texted Ella earlier in the week to see if I should bring a snack or a dessert, but she said it wasn't necessary.

"Do you see all this food? Trust me, we're good."

"Stop whispering," Glenda snaps. "I can't hear you."

Ella laughs softly, stepping away from me. "That's kind of the point of whispering."

"Yeah, and I'm nosy."

I have to give Glenda credit for owning up to it.

Ella shakes her head. "Come on, grab a drink and some food."

I do just that, then settle on the couch beside Cassandra.

Lucy claps her hands, startling Glenda, who was too busy scrutinizing the table beside her. For what reason, I'm not sure.

"I'm glad you all could make it. Anything new going on in your lives?"

Beside me, Cassandra smiles. "I got a promotion at work. I'm excited about it, and the extra money will go a long way to helping my husband and me save for fertility treatments."

My blood turns to ice.

I try so hard not to think about fertility—or my infertility—and babies. I thought I'd have at least one child by now, preferably two. But instead, I'm childless, struggling with infertility, *and* divorced. In hindsight, I can see that having kids with Chase would've been a mistake. No matter how precious those children would have been to me, he wouldn't have been a good father.

"Oh, that's so great," Ella squeals. "We should plan a fundraiser for you and Jake in the spring."

Cassandra ducks her head, shoulders curling in. "No, that's okay. Really. It may take a few more years, but we'll get there eventually."

Years.

I'm thirty-two.

And that damn biological clock is always in the background, like a ticking time bomb. It's not dramatic to say I'm running out of time.

I stand up then, all eyes shooting to me at my sudden movement. "Where's your bathroom, Lucy?" I've never needed it before now, so I'm not sure where it's at.

"Down the hall, second door on the left. Is everything okay?"

"Fine," I reply, not making eye contact with anyone as I make a hasty exit.

I find the bathroom easily enough and lock the door behind me. With a shaky breath, I turn the water on, then I let it run. I grip the edge of the sink so tight my knuckles turn white.

I got pregnant twice.

In all our years of trying, I only saw two positive tests. I didn't tell Chase either time. Maybe I knew in my heart those pregnancies wouldn't take. Whatever the reason, it doesn't matter now.

It doesn't lessen the anger I feel toward my own body.

That the one thing it's biologically programmed to do is the one thing it can't.

My own body doesn't want me to have a baby.

It's a maddening thought. One I've screamed and sobbed over. One I've begged whatever entity might be out there listening to take away.

None of it makes a difference.

Not the anger.

Not the sadness.

This is my reality.

Taking several long, deep breaths, I wash my hands. Then I straighten my top, lift my chin, and leave the bathroom. Thankfully, by the time I return to my spot, the conversation has moved on to safer topics.

"Are you okay?" Cassandra pats my knee, frowning.

"Yeah, yeah. I'm fine." I give her a reassuring smile. I hate that she's struggling with infertility, but what I hate more is my cowardice. My instinct to run rather than listen to her story and share my own so she knows she's not alone.

I disassociate for the rest of the time we're together. Ella notices and tries to bring me into the conversation a few times, but her efforts are futile. The normally delicious food tastes chalky in my mouth today, so I barely eat.

When it's finally over, I rattle off an excuse about how I think I might've left my straightener on and make a mad dash to my car to escape. Blessedly, no one calls me out on the fact that my hair is wavy rather than straight today.

I don't often spiral into that broken place anymore. After the divorce, I put my dreams of motherhood on hold and put up steel shutters in my mind. It hurts too much otherwise.

It's hard to want something so badly, something that as a woman I felt I had a *right* to, only to realize that at the end of the day, nothing is guaranteed.

In fight-or-flight mode, I let myself into the apartment and tear off my clothes as I stumble to my room. Never do I get in my bed in the middle of the day, but today is an exception. I crawl beneath the covers, yank them around me, and roll around until I'm safely cocooned inside them.

And then I let myself cry.

"What's wrong with you?"

Leave it to my sister to notice something's amiss the second I answer her FaceTime call.

"Nothing." I let my hair fall forward in the hopes that it'll hide my red-rimmed eyes.

"You've been crying," she accuses, squinting at the screen. "What happened? Did something happen with Reid?"

"No." I shake my head, a humorless laugh bubbling out of my lips. "Reid is great."

Her eyes narrow so severely I'm not sure how she can see anything. "Via." She says my name in a soft voice, like she's speaking to a frightened animal. "It's not Chase, is it?"

I press a hand to my head. It's pounding right behind my eyes, thanks to all the crying I've done today. It's a weird thing, mourning something I want so badly—a vision of a life, a future I'll never have.

"No, God no. It's not about him."

"Then what is it? Are you on your period? Oh my God. You did not watch *Remember Me* again, did you? You *know* that movie always makes you cry."

I shake out two ibuprofen and swallow them with several gulps of water.

"Izzy." I want to snap at her, to tell her to let it go, but where has keeping this to myself gotten me? There's no reward for holding on to pain rather than sharing the burden with others. "I ... I've never told you about how Chase and I struggled to get pregnant."

Her lips part in surprise, and her eyes widen. "Why didn't you?"

"It wasn't your problem."

She frowns. "Via, I'm your sister. You can tell me

anything. The good, the bad, and the ugly. You know you can come to me, right?"

"I know, but I think … I think I was *ashamed*." I lower my head, hating that word. "I know struggling with fertility is nothing to be ashamed of, but it felt—it *feels*—like my body betrayed me. It's supposed to do this one thing," I hold up a finger, "and it just … *can't*."

She's still frowning, her eyes filled with sadness and pity. I can take the sadness. It's the pity that has me wanting to drown my sorrows. "I wish I knew what to say, but I don't."

"You don't have to say anything. I just … I guess I'm glad I'm finally telling you."

I fill her in on the years of negative tests and finally getting a positive, only to miscarry a few days later. And then the second positive, months after the first, when I went to the doctor and was told that the baby was already gone but that my body hadn't started the process yet.

By the time I finish, we're both crying.

"I wish you would've told me sooner," she says off-screen. A moment later, she reappears with a tissue box and Wonton tucked under her arm. "I could've been there for you."

My heart sinks. "I know. I should have."

She blows her nose. "I'm tempted to come back and see you."

As much as I'd love that, I know she can't. "I'll see you soon. For Christmas, right?"

"Yes." She perks up a little at the mention of it. "I've already booked my ticket."

She just left, but already, I can't wait to see her again. Shame on me that it took moving all the way across the country to realize how much I enjoy spending time with my little sister.

"Are you feeling better now?" She worries her bottom lip, like she's not sure if it was the best question to ask.

"A little. I'm still sad."

She sets Wonton down and moves closer to the screen. "You're allowed to be sad, Via. You don't have to be so strong all the time."

That's easier said than done. Maybe it's because I'm the oldest child, but I've always had far more pressure on my shoulders. She went off and started a career in social media influencing without an ounce of flak from our parents. If I'd done the same, I'd never hear the end of it.

"I know," I finally reply with a nod.

"I love you, Via-Mia."

I smile at the nickname. "I love you too, Izzy-Tizzy."

The call ends, and then it's just me again, all alone in my apartment.

twenty-five

Reid

> Via: Are you working on my site today?

I grin down at the phone. I like the way she refers to it as her site.

Fuck, am I so pathetic that I find everything this woman does or says cute?

Yeah, I am.

Great.

> Me: No, I got fired.

I should elaborate, but I don't because, selfishly, I hope

she'll call me. Sure enough, my phone immediately vibrates. My smile only grows.

"Hello?"

"You got fired?" She practically shrieks. "Why? Does your dad know about us? Is that why? Did I get you in trouble?"

Picking up my coffee cup, I chuckle. "No, he doesn't know about us. Not yet, anyway." If I have my way, he'll know about us eventually.

"Then why did he fire you?"

I sigh, pinching the bridge of my nose. "he's doing me a favor, I guess. He knows I'm not passionate about carpentry and he knows I don't want to run the business. And..." I take a deep breath. "He cut me loose so that I'll have more time to focus on what I love."

"Oh." She's quiet for a moment. "That makes sense. How do you feel about it?"

I shrug, but then realize she can't see me. "He's not wrong. I just fucking hate that I'm twenty-one and don't have my life figured out."

She laughs softly. "Reid, you're *twenty-one*. No one expects you to have it figured out."

"Well, *I* do. I bet you knew what you were doing at this age."

She hums. "At twenty-one, I was dating the man I'd eventually marry and on track to be a lawyer. Need I remind you that I'm divorced and not practicing law anymore? I don't think you're making the point that you believe you are."

I stare glumly into my coffee. "Touché."

"When can I see you again?"

Her question makes my heart stutter in my chest. For the most part, I've been the one reaching out, begging for more time with her. The fact that she's asking me? I'm on cloud fucking nine.

"Whenever you want."

"Like now?"

Again, I'm hit with a jolt of shock that makes my heart leap. "If you want."

"I do ... want, that is."

"This won't count as a date," I warn her. "Don't think this gets you closer to getting in my pants."

"Reid!" She laughs. I can almost see how the pink is staining her cheeks right now.

"Bring art supplies. I'm calling in my IOU from the mouse incident."

"You want your lesson?"

"Mhm," I hum, emptying the mug. "I do."

"All right. I'll see you in about an hour. Is that okay?"

"Perfect."

I CAN'T WIPE THE GOOFY GRIN OFF MY FACE WHEN I find Via standing on the other side of my door. She's bundled up in a puffy blue jacket, and she has a matching beanie pulled low to cover her ears and forehead.

"It's cold," she whines, shuffling from side to side. "Let me in."

"Right."

I take the oversized tote bag from her shoulder and step out of her way.

She removes her boots and sets them on the floor beside mine. "The snow came out of nowhere. I swear we've gotten three inches in just the time it took to get from my place to yours."

I arch a brow. "Only three? Disappointing."

She swats my chest. "Don't start."

Shivering, she unzips her coat and drapes it over one of the barstools. She's wearing a sweater, but I still worry about her being warm enough.

"Do you want a sweatshirt?"

Eyes widening, she nods. "Yes, please."

"Let me grab one." I set her bag beside the barstool, then head down the short hall to my room. I just did laundry, but rather than give her one I just hung up, I snag a sweatshirt I wore last night. I like knowing she's going to smell like me. Maybe that makes me a caveman, but what can I say? We haven't evolved as much as we think.

Back in the living room, I find her on her knees with her ass in the air, spreading out art supplies on my coffee table. I have to bite back a groan.

Be good, I remind myself.

Clearing my throat, I hold out the sweatshirt. "Here you go."

"Thanks." She smiles up at me, and I swear my fucking

knees go a little weak. She slips it on and is immediately swallowed up by the fabric. "I wasn't sure what you wanted to learn, so I brought a bit of everything." Picking at the edge of her fingernail, she says, "Full transparency, I have no formal education in art."

I blink at her, fighting a smile. "Via?"

"Yeah?" She sits on the floor and crosses her legs, playing with a string on the sweatshirt.

"You already told me you went to school for law, not art."

Her cheeks redden. "I just wanted to make it clear that I'm not actually a teacher. Just ... someone who loves art and wants to help others who do too."

"I know." I sit too, stretching my legs out beside the coffee table. When our arms brush, she looks over at me, eyes dropping to my lips. Fuck, I want to kiss her. "Besides, art shouldn't have rules. It should just ... be." I shrug, looking over the supplies she brought. The surface of the table is covered in sketchpads, blending pens, paint, brushes, and charcoal.

"I agree." She gathers her hair and pulls it into a ponytail. Her hair is a pretty shade of dark brown, rich with hints of red and violet.

That, I decide, is what I want to draw.

Her hair wrapped around my fist.

I see it in my mind already, the way the strands would flow through my fingers, the colors I want to use to bring her hair color to life—

"Are you listening?"

I press my lips together. "Sorry, I was thinking."

She gives a soft, amused laugh. "I was asking what medium you wanted to start with."

I wet my lips, and her eyes follow the movement, her pupils dilating. "Good ole paper and pencil."

Her breath catches and she lowers her gaze to her lap.

We play with fire every time we're together like this. Keeping my hands to myself feels damn near impossible, but I'll do it. I want her to know that this is more than sex for me. That I like *her*, not just her body. It's hard, though, when even the air seems to crackle with the energy that thrums between us.

Fingers fumbling, she grabs a sketchpad and hands it to me, along with a fresh pack of pencils. I don't need the lessons. I draw well enough on my own. But I'll use any excuse to spend more time with her.

"I thought we could sketch for a while at first. If you have any questions for me, I'll answer them, but I already know you're skilled." She bites her lip, her eyes raking over me.

My body heats at her inspection. She's thinking of the tattoos hidden beneath my clothes.

"All right." I open the sketchpad and lean back against the couch. "Just let me know if you need me to get naked so you can get the proportions correct."

Her jaw drops open and she sucks in a surprised breath. "Reid!"

I laugh. "Sorry, I had to. But if you ever need a nude model for your personal art endeavors, I'm your guy."

"I'll keep that in mind." She averts her attention, like she's afraid that if she looks at me, I'll see something in her expression she doesn't want to show me.

Ah. It hits me then. I smirk. "You've already drawn me." It's a statement, not a question.

"I ... no."

But the way she says no sounds like a lie.

I snap my fingers. "You have. What did you draw?"

Curiosity is getting the best of me. What about me, my body, attracts her the most?

"Reid," she pleads, closing her eyes.

"I want to know." I'm begging now, but I don't care. "Please."

She inhales deeply, her chest rising, and taps her fingers on her jean-covered thighs. "Your forearms." Her eyes drift to where I've got my sleeves rolled up. "Your hands. Lips. The dimple in your cheek. Just ... you."

Maybe it's more innocent than the way I perceive it, but even so, I rejoice. Because she likes *all* of me.

"What would you say if I drew you?"

She rubs her lips together. "I'd be curious about how you see me."

I tap a pencil against the blank white page. "Challenge accepted."

I'M JOLTED BACK TO REALITY WHEN VIA SETS HER pad on the table, stands, and stretches her arms above her head.

"I need to pee."

I open my mouth to tell her where the bathroom is but remember that she already knows. "Help yourself," I say instead, setting my sketchpad down on the couch.

She wanders off, and I manage to wrangle my stiff limbs into a standing position, my back cracking when I'm fully upright.

It's after two, which means I skipped breakfast and lunch. My stomach groans at the reminder.

With the sound of water running in the background, I look out the window.

"Oh, shit."

Via rushes out of the bathroom. "What?"

I wave her over and point at the snow blanketing the ground. The cars in the lot are covered in a layer at least a foot thick.

"That's not good," she mutters. "I should get going."

I grab her arm when she moves away. "Via." Her name comes out in a disbelieving gasp. "You can't be serious."

She worries her bottom lip and peers out the window again. "I can't stay here."

"You don't really have a choice."

She scrunches, making it obvious that wasn't the right thing to say.

"I'll get back home by sheer determination if I have to."

"Via." My tone is stern this time. "You're crazy if you think I'm letting you drive in that. It's still coming down."

We get lots of snow here, but it's coming down quickly and piling up fast. Plus, Via has lived in California her whole life. Despite what she thinks, she's not equipped to handle that kind of drive, and neither is her vehicle.

"I can't just crash here."

I cross my arms over my chest. Classic defensive pose, I know. Sue me.

"Why not?"

She stuffs her hands into the kangaroo pouch of my sweatshirt dwarfing her small frame. "It would be wrong."

"How would it be wrong?" I push. I don't buy that half-assed excuse. She's a lawyer. She should know better than to think that'll be enough to convince me to drop the conversation.

"Reid."

"Via."

I might find this standoff more amusing if I didn't think she was stubborn enough to try to leave. Not that I'd let her in these conditions.

She lets out a defeated sigh. "If I stay here, who's to say something won't happen?"

I smile slowly, my heart rate kicking up a notch. "Is that your way of saying you want to get me naked?"

"You can't deny that when we're alone, that tends to happen."

I take her in from head to toe. I want to move closer, to

hold her hand, but I don't. She's like a cornered, frightened animal, and I don't want to spook her.

"We spent an entire evening here on our first date and I didn't get you naked then, so I think I can resist another time."

She presses her lips together and averts her eyes.

I narrow mine on her, working through why this is such a big issue—*oh.* "You think it's *you* who can't resist *me*?"

She pushes her tongue against the inside of her cheek, making it pop out on one side like she's an adorable little chipmunk. "I can handle myself just fine, thank you."

"Then," I draw out the word slowly, "what's the problem?"

As if coming to a decision, she meets my eye. "What are the chances of your dad showing up to check on you?"

Ah, that explains it.

"Zilch."

"Are you sure about that?"

"Abso-fucking-lutely." I nod, resolute. "He's busy at home with Layla and Lili. He's not going to drive out in these conditions to check on me."

With the heels of her hands pressed to her eye sockets, she mumbles, "I'm being ridiculous. I'm sorry."

"I wish you weren't so scared of being caught with me."

She flinches. "It's not ... it's not that."

"It's exactly that," I say calmly, moving past her to the fridge. My throat is the fucking Sahara Desert after this conversation. "Let me ask you something, Via." I fill up two glasses of water and hand her one.

She swallows nervously, waiting.

"When you went on a date with my dad, were you concerned about *that* age difference? Did you worry about it the way you do ours? Because, based on my calculations, you're smack dab in the middle of us. Eleven years younger, eleven years older."

She takes a large sip of water and regards me for a moment. "I thought about it. Of course I did. But it's different."

"How?" I press. "How is it that different?"

She lets her head drop back. "Come on, Reid, you have to know how society is. You and me?" She flicks a finger between us. "I'd be called so many things—cradle robber, cougar. Everyone would be waiting for you to upgrade me to a newer, shinier model. It's what's expected of men. But if I was with your dad—"

I flinch, because when she says *with* my dad, my stupid brain runs with that image.

"—people wouldn't question it. I *would* be the younger model in that situation. I don't like it. It's just fucking facts."

It would be so easy to get angry, to snap at her, but this is what I asked for. I wanted to hear her reasoning.

"Do you *want* to be with my dad?"

Her face screws up, like she can't believe I'd even ask that. "Would I be here with you if I did?"

I place my hands on the counter, palms flat. I'm making every effort not to get defensive.

"Why *are* you here, Via?"

She looks away, and when she looks back at me, her

eyes are swimming with tears. I hate myself for putting them there.

"Because I wanted to see you." The words are barely a whisper. "Because I like spending time with you. Because I smile every time I see a text from you. Because I fucking *like* you, Reid. Is that good enough?"

In a few strides, I'm standing in front of her.

My hands swallow her face whole as I cradle her soft cheeks. She inhales a shaky breath, one I steal right back when I kiss her.

Slow. I want to take things slow with her, so I don't deepen the kiss, not much, anyway, and I keep my hands firmly on her face. I don't let them wander down to her ass. I don't pick her up the way I want to.

I brush one last soft kiss to her closed lids. Her eyes flutter open and her mouth parts, her lips pinker than they were moments ago.

"You didn't answer me."

I grin at her. "That wasn't answer enough?"

She shakes her head. "I need you to say it."

"It's good enough," I answer, releasing her. "But I don't want to be your dirty secret forever."

"You're not ... that's not what..."

"It's okay." I mean it. I might not like it, but I understand her reasoning. "I'm younger, and your divorce is still fresh. You're not ready to put a label on things. It's okay."

For now. I leave that part unsaid, but it's still there in the space between us.

"Okay," she echoes.

I take her hand, twining our fingers together. "C'mon. I have a frozen pizza in the freezer."

She gives me a wobbly smile, those tears back in her eyes.

"That sounds fantastic."

twenty-six

Via

I could fall in love with Reid Crawford. It's what I think to myself, fighting tears once more. *I could love him harder than I ever loved Chase. This man could ruin me in the best way.*

A movie that neither of us are paying attention to plays in the background while the two of us sit on the floor and eat the pizza he dug out of his freezer. Snow is falling outside, and it's all just so simple.

Simply perfect.

It's a realization for me, that these moments—the quiet pockets of time with a person I care about—are what matter most. Chase and me? We didn't have this, and I didn't know what I was missing.

"This pizza," I hold up the slice I just took a bite out of, "is the best pizza I've ever had."

He smirks, a speck of sauce in the corner of his lip. "Then you've never had good pizza."

I could tell him it's the best because I'm sharing it with him, but I don't want to scare him or myself.

I didn't move to Parkerville, Maine, thinking I would meet someone. And definitely not so soon. But I did.

Our age difference scares me. He's got so many things laid out in front of him to experience. Experiences I've already lived. I don't want to rob him of even a single one of them.

"Maybe it's the company." I put the words out anyway, despite my reservations. "That makes it so good. Did you think of that?"

He grins, adjusting his glasses. "There are much easier ways to say you like spending time with me."

I press my lips together, trying not to smile. Despite my urge to leave, I do like spending time with him. I like it *too* much, which is why I wanted to run away. Reid's presence brings me peace, and that frightens me. I should be my own peace, but when I'm with him, everything else is quiet, and I feel...

I feel like I'm home.

"Are you going to show me your sketches?" I nudge him with my elbow.

He wipes his fingers on his jeans and reaches for his sketchpad. "Take a look."

I don't open it. Not yet. I stroke my fingers over the

cover. "You never asked me questions. I can't say this was much of a lesson."

He reaches for another slice of pizza. "Give me advice after you look, then."

I peel the front cover back, revealing the first page. It's full of small, simple sketches. Outlines, mostly. I'd be stupid not to recognize each one. My fingers. My lips. The side of my face. I look over at him but say nothing, just flip to the next page.

My hair fills the page, bursting with chestnut, red, orange, purple, and even blue hues. I've never seen colors used like this for hair, but the way he blended them together works. It's beautiful. His fingers are entwined in my hair. There's no mistaking the distinctive freckle on the knuckle of his index finger or the lines of his veins.

His gaze sears me, but he doesn't speak, just lets me look.

On the next page, I find the outline of my body. I'm propped up against his couch, sketchpad balanced on my knees. I'm pressing the tip of the pencil to my lips in thought. Even though it's not a fleshed-out drawing, I see it, the vision.

"I don't normally draw people." His voice pulls me from my thoughts. "But I was inspired."

I flip back to the previous page. "Can I keep this one?"

"Sure."

I carefully remove the paper from the pad and slide it between the pages of my own. Is it weird to say I want to frame it?

Outside, the snow is still falling.

Derrick texted me before we put the pizza in the oven to let me know he'd sent the guys home. Apparently the local news is saying this could turn into a blizzard.

A blizzard.

This native Californian doesn't know what to do with that, but I guess it doesn't matter. I'm stuck here with Reid.

Reid stands, grabbing up his empty plate and mine. "Do you want something sweet? I have ice cream sandwiches."

I don't know why this makes me laugh. I guess because of its unexpectedness.

"I don't think I've had an ice cream sandwich since I was a kid."

Gaping, he wanders into the kitchen. "You're having one."

"Do you need help?"

He turns the water on in the sink. "Nope, I'm good."

After washing up the plates, he rifles through the freezer and joins me on the floor again, holding out one of the wrapped sandwiches.

"These make me think of elementary school," I admit. "One year, I won the spelling bee—the class spelling bee, not, like, an actual one or anything—and when my mom picked me up, she took me for a treat. This is what I wanted."

He clears his throat. "How is your relationship with your parents? Is it weird since they wanted you to be a lawyer so badly, and now you've moved on from that?"

I like the way he says it—that I've moved on. I didn't

quit. I didn't give up. I simply chose to take my life in another direction.

"It's..." I bite my bottom lip, curling my fingernail into the edge of the paper and slowly removing it. "Complicated." I guess that's the most accurate way to describe it. "My parents aren't bad people, but they don't understand why I'd quit a stable job and move across the country to a town I'd never even visited. In the past, their disappointment would've shattered me. While I am upset about the lack of understanding, I've done my best to push those feelings out of my mind. This is my life. I'm the one who has to deal with the repercussions of my choices. Not them. My happiness matters more than appeasing others. It took me too long to see that."

"They'll accept it one day." He bites into his ice cream sandwich.

"Maybe or maybe not, and that's okay."

I've accepted that my relationship with them will always be strained. It's not what I want, but the truth is, there is no bridging certain gaps. I can either be okay with what is or walk away completely.

I lick one side of my ice cream, then the other. Reid's eyes track every movement. I don't have to imagine what he's thinking about. I could call him out on it, but I don't. He's shown an incredible amount of restraint, so I'll give him a reprieve.

"I forgot how much I like these," I admit when only half is left.

"They're severely underrated." He wads up the wrapper

into a tiny ball and drops it onto the coffee table. I'm surprised a guy his age even has a coffee table. But Reid surprises me in so many ways.

When I've finished mine, he mutes the TV. "Mind if I put music on?"

I shake my head. "Go head."

He hops up and inspects his record collection. While he peruses his options, I throw away our trash and go to the bathroom again.

I've been waiting for my period to start, so the bit of red staining the toilet paper doesn't surprise me. It's a blessing, I suppose, because it takes away the desire to strip Reid naked and do dirty things with him while we're holed up in his apartment. Having sex while on my period has never been my thing, and even if it was, Reid probably wouldn't be down for it—not with his insistence on waiting. The fact that the twenty-one-year-old possesses more self-restraint than me hasn't gone unnoticed.

I'm washing my hands when Frank Sinatra's voice fills the apartment, bringing me back to the morning I woke up here.

The Via of that morning would die knowing I'm back here now. I was so determined to keep it to one night, to never see him again. The universe had other plans for us.

The door creaks when I open it, but I doubt he can hear it over the music. I ease out, wanting to catch a glimpse of him before he knows I'm back.

He's moving to the music—not really dancing, but more of a sway—while he sings along.

How is he real?

He turns, and when he catches sight of where I'm standing in the archway to the hall, he crooks a finger, beckoning me to him.

I can't stop the smile that overtakes me. I'm grinning like a fool, and when his returning smile lights up his face, mine only grows more.

Reid doesn't have to try to make me happy. He just does.

It's so different from what I'm used to.

I don't like comparing him to my ex-husband, but it's impossible not to, since Chase is my basis for everything.

Chase always thought he had to make big, grand gestures. He was constantly trying to impress me when he already had me. Maybe he was always fooling around behind my back, and that's why. Or maybe it was insecurity that made him feel like he had to keep me wowed. Regardless, none of it matters now.

All I know, in this tiny apartment with Frank Sinatra serenading me and Reid pulling me into his arms to dance, is happiness.

I WAKE UP SOMETIME IN THE NIGHT, SITTING UP AND taking in my unfamiliar surroundings.

I'm in Reid's room. There's a snowstorm.

I can't remember what I was dreaming about, but my

heart is still racing. Shoving the sheets off my body, I stumble out of bed.

Reid insisted he'd sleep on the couch. I argued that we could be adults and share a bed without giving in, especially now that I'm on my period anyway, but he still insisted on being a gentleman.

My throat is parched as I tiptoe my way into the kitchen and ease the refrigerator door open.

"Via?"

Of course he heard me. His apartment isn't even a thousand square feet.

"Yeah, sorry." I close the fridge without getting water. "I didn't mean to wake you."

He rubs his eyes, sitting up, and grabs his glasses from the coffee table.

Despite the disquiet coursing through me, I can't help but take in his shirtless state.

"Is everything okay?"

I nod, wringing my hands in front of me. "Just had a bad dream."

It's dark, and he's cast in shadow, but his tone is full of concern. "Do you want to talk about it?"

I shake my head. "I don't remember it. I was just going to get a glass of water."

Stifling a yawn, he nods. When he stretches his arms above his head, I can't help but watch the rippling of muscles in his torso.

I turn back to the fridge and grab a bottle of water.

Clutching it to my chest, I take him in for another moment before I mutter, "I ... I'm going back to bed."

He dips his head in a nod and swings his legs over the edge of the couch. When he stands, the blanket that was on his lap pools on the floor. Only a pair of thin boxer briefs separates me from the part of him my body aches for. My mouth goes even drier than it was before.

I avert my eyes and head down the hall, followed by the sound of his low chuckle. The door to the bathroom closes behind him while I ease back into his bed. The sheets smell like him—clean and masculine, like musky vanilla and a mix of citrus.

After a healthy swallow of water, I twist the cap back on the bottle and set it on the nightstand. I wish I could remember what chased me from sleep, but I truly have no recollection of what haunted my dreams. Fluffing the pillow, I lie back down and pull the comforter up to my chin.

The toilet flushes, then the sink runs, the faucet squeaking when it's turned off.

When he pokes his head into the room, I can't resist. "Will you lay with me?" I ask, my voice small. "At least until I fall asleep? I promise not to maul you." I hold my breath, anxious about his response. He was so adamant about not sleeping with me before, so I expect an immediate no.

Instead, he carefully steps over the threshold and shuffles my way.

I lift the covers, and he dives in, immediately looping his

arms around me. If I wasn't so tired, I'd be embarrassed over the happy sigh that gusts from me.

He chuckles, kissing the crook of my neck. "Go to sleep," he murmurs, breath warm against my ear. "I've got you."

I curl into his side, laying my head on his chest.

His heart thrums a steady rhythm against my ear, and his thumb rubs slow circles against my arm. It's a small, light gesture, but it brings instant comfort to my body.

My limbs relax, and finally, I sleep again.

twenty-seven

Reid

I wake with the scent of Via's hair filling my nose. Her head is tucked against me, and her breaths are slow and even against my bare skin. I fully intended to slip out of bed once she drifted off, but the soothing rhythm of her breathing and the comfort of her proximity must have put me to sleep.

I rub the silky strands of her hair between my fingers. She hums in her sleep, her hand sliding over my stomach, settling beneath my belly button.

I groan. Shit. Instantly, my dick stirs to life. Covering my face with my left hand, I count backward from one hundred. My decision to take things slow is coming around to bite me in the ass.

When counting backward doesn't work, I silently list the makes and models of as many cars as I can think of.

Via stirs, rubbing the side of her face against my chest. Awareness begins to prickle through her body. I can tell by the way her limbs wiggle.

She stretches her arm above her head, almost smacking me in the face in the process.

"Whoa," I chuckle, ducking away from her flailing limb. "Careful."

She comes fully awake, then, dropping her arm back to her side.

I hold my breath, waiting for her reaction. This was part of the reason I didn't want to share the bed. I was scared of how she might react. If I see regret in her eyes, it'll hurt.

She lifts her head slightly, taking me in. A sleepy smile cracks her lips. "Morning."

"Good morning."

She's blurry, since I'm not wearing my glasses, but she's close enough that it's clear there isn't regret anywhere on her expression. It has me sighing in relief on the inside.

"Is it still snowing?"

I hope not. Not because I don't want her to stay longer, but because I'm ill-prepared to be camped out here for long, especially with another person to feed. I didn't stock up at the store like I should have. In my defense, the weather app said we'd get a foot of snow max. Around here, that's nothing.

"I'm not sure. I'll have to look." I move to slip out of bed, but she tightens her hold on me.

"Don't move just yet."

That's a request I'm happy to oblige.

I wrap my arm around her, rubbing my thumb against her shoulder. The t-shirt I gave her to sleep in has slipped down to reveal her collarbone and the top of her arm.

"I didn't think I liked cuddling," she whispers so softly I'm not sure the words are meant for me. "But I like cuddling you."

I don't like to pry too much into her relationship with her ex. I don't want to come across as insecure or nosy, but after some of the things she's said, I *am* curious about what their relationship was like. At first, I thought things between them were good until that idiot cheated on her, but now I'm not so sure. Maybe she didn't even realize how bad it was until she left.

"Why did you think you didn't like cuddling?"

She traces a finger around my nipple. She's killing me. Seriously testing the limits of my self-control.

Resting her chin on my chest, she twists her lips in thought. "Chase and I ... we cuddled a little early on, but we were both so busy and focused on our goals that it felt more like an obligation than a want. I was so young when we got together, and because of that, I didn't have anything to compare our experiences to. I thought it was normal, and I was mostly content, so I didn't dive deeper into things." She brushes her hair behind her ear, sighing softly. "I convinced myself for a long time that I was okay with how things were. But now…" She trails off. "You've already made me feel more than he did in all the years we were together. That's not an insult to him, even if he deserves it." She wrinkles her nose. "We were a good match on paper, but in reality, we didn't click. I was so angry when he cheated on me. It was the worst kind of betrayal. It sounds crazy, but now I'm glad he did. Otherwise I'd still be stuck in a loveless marriage, not knowing the difference."

"And I'm a selfish prick, because I'm glad he fucked up."

She gives a short laugh. "Trust me, between the two of you, you're not the selfish one." Laying her head on my chest, she whispers, "I really like spending time with you, and that scares me."

I wet my lips, fighting the urge to kiss her. *You haven't brushed your teeth yet,* I remind myself in an effort to douse that desire.

"Why does it scare you?"

She shrugs. "I've hardly known you, but I find myself wanting to be around you and missing you when I'm not. It's weird for me, because when Chase and I were apart, I didn't..." She blows out a breath. "I didn't crave his presence. Sure, I missed him, but it wasn't like this. Not even close."

"I feel that way about you too," I admit. "Let's not overthink it, okay?"

I can already see the wheels turning in her brain. She's thinking about how long we've known each other and the intensity of what's between us.

But why do we have to question our connection? Why does society put so much emphasis on *time*, when what matters most are our feelings? Look how much time she had with Chase, and they weren't the right fit.

"Okay," she acquiesces.

We cuddle for a bit longer before we take turns showering and getting ready. When I finally look outside, the lot still hasn't been cleared.

"I'm going to make egg sandwiches. Sound okay?"

"Sounds delicious." She sits down on the couch, curling her legs up behind her, and when I hand her the remote, she flips through channels before settling on a documentary.

It doesn't take long to whip up egg sandwiches and hash browns. I didn't eat enough yesterday, and the frozen pizza was far from nutritious, so my body is desperate for actual food.

Setting the finished plates of food on the table, I ask her, "Water or orange juice?"

"Orange juice, please." She peels herself from the couch. "I could get used to this. Can you make breakfast for me every morning?"

I fill a glass with juice and set it by her plate as she sits down. "Are you asking if you can move in?" I joke.

She laughs. "It's probably a bit soon for that. Forget I said anything."

I pour my own glass and join her. "It looks like you're going to be stuck here at least most of the day. The parking lot still isn't cleared."

She cracks a small smile. "I'll survive."

My shoulders relax, and the trepidation that's been

swirling in me since her mini-freakout yesterday eases a bit. I don't want her to overthink things. It won't lead anywhere good.

"Your egg sandwich taste okay?"

"Mmm. You're a great cook. Better than me."

I grin. "I'll give you a lesson sometime."

With a laugh, she digs into the hash browns. "Hopefully it's a better lesson than the one I gave you." Worry creases her brow. "Maybe I'm not cut out to do this like I thought I was."

My fork clatters to my plate when it falls from my grip. "Via, listen to me. You're going to be great at it."

She sighs, pushing her plate away like the sight of the food has soured her stomach. "How would you know? I haven't even given you an actual lesson."

"Since we're going to be stuck here for most of the day, I'd be more than happy to play teacher and student with you." My tone implies so much more than the words mean on the surface. I can't help myself.

Mouth agape, she dissolves into laughter. "You're something else."

I shrug. "I try. But seriously, I think we got caught up in just enjoying what we were doing yesterday. You can give me any advice you want."

She cups her cheek, elbow on the counter. "I did all of this on a whim, and suddenly, I'm overthinking it. I've always been a logical person, but I threw all of that out the window when I packed up my whole life and moved here. A lot of what I plan to do doesn't involve teaching. My main goal is to create a safe space where people can uncover their love of art. A place where they can find peace after school or work. I'd love to host wine nights or stuff like that. But I want to be good at it too. I don't want to fail."

I frown, brows pulling tight. "Fail? The only you could fail would be if you didn't try. You're following your dreams for the first time in your life. That's incredible. You should be proud of yourself for that alone."

It bothers me that she's doubting herself so much. For years, she stuffed herself into a box, trying to fit into a role she never wanted to begin with. I suppose that's a hard habit to break.

"I-I guess," she stutters, her eyes full of unshed tears.

I don't want her to cry. She *shouldn't*. What she's doing, what she's done, is more than most would attempt. It's all too easy to grow complacent with what one's been given in life rather than change their situation. I can understand where her stress and worry come from, but I don't want her anxiety to consume her.

"Eat up." I slide her plate closer to her and wink. "Then we can play student-teacher."

twenty-eight

Via

Izzy's shriek is so loud I have to cover my ears to keep from rupturing an eardrum.

"Izzy," I groan when she finally stops screaming. "You don't have to be so loud."

"I can't help it." She dances around, downright giddy. "You're telling me that you were *snowed* in with Reid for two whole days? This is the best news ever."

I'm getting motion sick from the way she keeps spinning with the phone in her hands. "Can you sit down?"

Thankfully, she quickly perches on the couch in her living room. Behind her, palm trees sway outside the window. It's a far cry from the snow piles here. It took a while for the streets to clear—longer than normal, according to Reid.

"I'm sorry. I'm just so excited about this."

"I can tell."

"So, were you naked the whole time or...?" She draws out the last word, wagging her brows at me.

I give her a deadpan stare. "No."

"Why the hell not?" She's back to shrieking. "And why do you sound annoyed about it?"

I roll my shoulders back to loosen the tension. I seriously need to take up yoga again.

I quickly explain Reid's stance on things and how I respect him for that, but—

"But you're horny," she finishes when I'm done.

I give a reluctant nod. "I don't know what it is about him. I never felt like this with Chase, even in my twenties." I pause, then ask, "Do you want to hear about this?"

"Sure, if you need to talk about it. You don't have to tell me anything you don't want."

I take a breath. "My sex life with Chase was good. At least I thought so. Maybe he didn't feel the same. But we were ... compatible." I'm not trying to gross my sister out with details, but I want her to understand how different my connection with Reid is and why it scares me. "It's like this electric current buzzes beneath the surface of my skin when Reid's around. I can't get close enough. I just..." Heat floods my cheeks at just the thought. "I want to rip his close off and devour him. I've *never* felt that way before. On top of all that, I like *him*. He's sweet and funny, and we have a lot in common. When I'm with him, I feel like I'm where I belong."

This might be the least coherently I've ever spoken. I sound like a giddy teenager yammering on about her crush.

Izzy puts the back of her hand to her forehead and feigns swooning. She sobers quickly, though. "In all seriousness, I think you've found someone who awakens your soul. Chase wasn't the right fit for you, but you were content, and frankly, with your lack of dating history, you didn't know better."

She's right. I know she is. It stings a little, the truth in her words.

There's no going back, no way to get back the time I wasted in a relationship that was destined to end and a career that, despite how I excelled, brought me no happiness.

"Don't overthink this thing with Reid," she goes on, like she knows my thoughts are spiraling. "You're allowed to be happy."

I hate that she has to remind me that it's okay to be happy.

"I'm trying not to."

"Good." She smiles. "I love you."

"Love you too."

We end the video call, and I sit on my couch for a moment, picking apart the details of our conversation. Below me, the sounds of hammers and nail guns threaten to give me a headache.

"I need to get out of here."

So I shove my sketchpad, a few art supplies, and my wallet into a bag and scoop up my keys, then head down the stairs.

At the bottom, my feet go out from under me, pulling a scream from my throat.

My butt hits the asphalt with a hard smack that takes my breath away. My bag falls off my shoulder, sending pencils and pens rolling away.

"Ow."

"Is everything okay? I heard—"

Stomach sinking, I close my eyes. I didn't think this moment could get worse, but it does.

"Shit," Derrick curses. "Let me help you up."

Just my luck.

I take his hands and give him a weak smile as he pulls me to my feet.

"I'm sorry. I didn't see the ice."

I don't know why I'm apologizing, and from the way his brows furrow, neither does he.

"Black ice is dangerous." Now that I'm on my feet, he bends, gathering up my fallen supplies.

"Black ice?"

Straightening, he holds out my supplies. "It's a thin layer of ice that's practically invisible. Be careful driving. This isn't the best car for winter around here."

"Great," I groan, stuffing my supplies back into my bag.

"I can take you where you're headed if you need me to," he offers, already reaching into his pocket for his keys.

"No, no." I wave him off. "I'll be fine. I'm not going far and I promise to be careful."

I feel bad that I've been avoiding Derrick. He's a nice man, but the feelings I have for his *son* make it almost impossible to look him in the eye.

"If you're sure." He takes a step back.

"I'm good." I take a cautious step forward, wincing at the pain in my butt. He gives me a questioning look. "Ice and asphalt really hurts your butt."

He chuckles. "Don't fall again. I'll see you later, Via."

He waves and wanders around to the front of the building.

I blow out a breath that fogs the frigid air. I hate that I'm not being fair to him, but I'm stuck between a rock and a hard place.

Once I'm safely inside my car, I crank the engine and shiver. The heat function is already on full blast, but it's blowing cold air, so I turn it back down to give it time to warm up.

I fiddle with the radio while I wait, and once I've found an acceptable song, I put the car in reverse and take my time backing out, terrified I'm going to hit another patch of that dreadful ice.

I'm certain it's paranoia, but I swear I feel the attention of all the guys working on my property. Like they're watching, waiting for my car to wipe out.

I drive a couple of blocks over to a coffee shop Ella has mentioned. I've been too busy with other things to go.

I park on the street and quickly put coins in the meter. The town hasn't bothered to upgrade to the app system yet.

Taking careful steps on the salted sidewalk, I make my way to the front door. Inside, I inhale the scent of freshly brewed coffee, and my system awakens with the knowledge that caffeine is imminent.

"Hey, welcome to Bold Brews. What can I get you?" The girl behind the counter is practically bouncing like she's mainlined a pot of coffee already this morning. Or maybe she's naturally this energetic. If that's the case, I'm jealous.

With a hum, I scan the holiday menu. "A peppermint mocha would be great."

"Awesome." She reaches for a cup and uncaps a Sharpie. "Is that it, or would you like something to eat too?"

"Just the coffee."

"You got it." She taps a few buttons on the screen in front of her, and I hand over cash. Once I've dropped my change in the tip jar, I wander over to claim a cozy spot in the corner so I can sketch for a while.

A couple of minutes later, my drink is ready, so I head back to the counter, then get settled in more comfortably in the armchair. Opening my sketchpad to my most recent piece—a pen and ink drawing of Wonton that I'm hoping to gift to Izzy for Christmas—I settle in and get to work.

There's something about drawing, painting too, that makes time disappear for me. I tend to lose myself in my work, and the world around me fades away. The last dregs of my mocha are cold when I'm pulled back into reality. A group of rowdy guys enters the coffee shop, being unnecessarily loud. Stupidly, I didn't bring my earbuds, so I can't filter their voices out. Up until now, I've been enjoying the soft sounds of the shop and holiday music in the background.

Annoyed, I narrow my eyes on the four guys. When I do, I'm hit with a wave of familiarity. There's no way I know them, but something about them sends a tickle of recognition through my mind. Though it could just be because they're around Reid's age.

Determined to tune them out, I do my best to focus on adding details to Wonton's nose.

The group moves to the side, closer to me, to wait for their orders. One of the guys continues to chat with the barista, the same girl who took my order, and her cheeks pinken in response to his comment.

"Hey," another says, getting my attention. "You look familiar. Do I know you from somewhere?"

I shake my head. "No, I don't think so. Sorry." I look down at my sketchpad, considering getting my things packed up. If these guys are going to hang around, there's no way I'll get any more work done.

"Yeah." He snaps his fingers. "I think I do."

I look up again, frowning. "I'm sorry, but no. I only recently moved here."

"No." He rubs his fingers over his lips. "I've seen you around. Hey, Justin," he calls to the guy who's flirting with the barista. "Doesn't this lady look familiar?"

Justin, I guess, walks away from the girl he was flirting

with. He assesses me, and now the others are gawking too. Way to make me feel like a bug beneath a microscope.

"Yeah," the Justin guy says.

Rolling my eyes and supremely uncomfortable, I shut my sketchpad and shove my stuff into my bag.

"I need to go," I say, shoving to my feet. I grab for my cup and take a step toward the trash can.

"You were at Monday's," Justin says. "You're the chick Reid took home."

My stomach bottoms out.

Oh, shit.

"I knew I recognized you," the first guy pipes in.

My face goes hot under their scrutiny. "Um ... I need to go."

They let me pass, and I shuffle toward my car as quickly as I can on the icy sidewalk. Stupid, no good black ice.

"Via!"

My shoulders tense at the sound of my name.

Dammit. I almost made it out, my hand on the driver's door and everything. I still have my cup in my other hand since in my haste I forgot to drop it in the trash can.

When I turn around, Justin stands outside the coffee shop, hands shoved into the pockets of his jeans. Despite the arctic temperatures, he's wearing a heavy black sweatshirt with a logo on one side of the chest and a beanie tugged low over his ears.

"He really likes you."

Heart flipping behind my ribs, I gape at him, mouth opening and closing like a fish.

He shrugs. "I just thought you should know." He turns and puts his hand on the doorknob, but before he goes back inside, he looks back at me. "He's a good guy, and he's been through a lot." *His mom.* "Don't hurt him. He's happier now than he's ever been, and I think that's because of you."

With those parting words, Justin goes inside, and I get in my car once more.

I sit there for a moment, not quite sure how to process his words. Soon, though, I'm forced to start the car to stave off the cold. Turning the radio up to drown out my thoughts, I drive home.

twenty-nine

Reid

I knock on Big Dan's door, and when his gruff "Come on in" echoes from inside, I obey.

I've been putting off this conversation because I'm pretty sure I know what he's going to say. Regardless, I need to have it. I can't continue working part time and pay all my bills. If I need to find full-time work elsewhere, then the sooner I know, the better.

"Hey, kid." He motions for me to take a seat on the couch across from his desk. The plasticky leather material is ripped in more than one spot, and I'm pretty sure it tears further when I sit down. "I'm sorry I haven't checked in with you in a while. Been busy with office stuff. You know how it is." *I do not, in fact, know how it is.* "What's up?"

"I wanted to talk to you about my position."

"Sure." He leans back, his chair groaning beneath him. "Is there something wrong?"

I shake my head. "No, everything is great. But I'm not working for my dad anymore and—"

He winces. "And you need full-time work."

"Yeah," I draw out the word.

He steeples his fingers, resting his elbows on the table. "Reid, I'm sorry, but I can't afford to have you on full time. We barely do enough business to justify the hours you do get."

I nod. I expected as much. "I understand."

"I'm sorry," he says again. "If I could—"

"I know." With a sigh, I say, "I'm going to be looking for something full time, just so you know."

I'll have to commute at least an hour to find a place that can offer me the hours I need, but I'll do what I have to do.

He nods. "When you find something, let me know."

"I will."

I shake his hand, then head out the door. When it's closed behind me, I groan. My dad was doing the best thing for me when he let me go, but dammit if this situation doesn't suck.

The sketchpad Via left behind for me is now filled with drawings. I guess you could say I've been inspired.

On the coffee table, my laptop sits mockingly. I've filled out numerous applications, and now I'm waiting to hear back. Job hunting is practically a full-time job itself.

I run my fingers through my hair, reminding myself that it'll all work out in the end.

It always does.

If only my dad had let me keep my job until I figured shit out.

He knows me, though. He knows I would have taken my sweet time with the change.

If I can't find a full-time position, I'll have to suck it up and split my time between garages. Maybe, if I'm lucky, I can open my own garage eventually and focus solely on restoration. That's the dream, at least.

My mom always encouraged my sister and me to do what made us happy, and that's what I want.

I wonder, sometimes, what she'd think if she could see what we're doing with our lives. If she'd be happy or proud or if she'd wish we were doing something more. A lump lodges in my throat, but I swallow it down. I don't like thinking that she'd hope we're doing more.

Pulling my laptop back over to me, I do a Google search for garages, this time extending my radius to more towns in the surrounding area. Then I get to work filling out even more applications.

I turn the TV on and scroll through movie options. I

pick one I've seen numerous times, putting it on for background noise.

With a groan, I grab a container of leftovers from the fridge.

My mind, like it usually does these days, drifts to Via. I want to take her on another date soon, but I haven't come up with any ideas. I certainly won't be asking Justin for useless advice this time, either.

When my phone rings, I ignore it. I don't normally screen my calls, but I'm not in the right headspace to chat. I can call whoever it is back later.

But when the phone rings a second time, right behind the first call, my gut tells me something's wrong.

"Layla?"

"Uncle Weed," Lili cries into the phone, the words hard to make out. "He hurt mommy."

I see red. I don't have to ask who. I hate to say I saw this coming, but I knew if my sister didn't dump that weasel, then things would escalate from verbal spats to the physical kind. Not that I could reason with her. Layla has always done her own thing.

"Is your mommy okay?"

Please, please let her be okay.

"I-I don't know," she hiccups into the phone. "He hit her in th-the f-face, and she fell. I called you."

"Lili, where are you?"

From the moment she cried my name, I've been collecting my things—coat, wallet, keys, and shoes. So by the time she tells me she locked herself in the downstairs bathroom, I'm running out to my car.

I call the police on the way.

It's the last thing my sister would want, but that asshole *hit* her, and in front of Lili too. Whether she presses charges or not—and fuck, do I hope she does—I want there to be a record of this.

I break every speeding law known to man on the way to my dad's house. My brakes screech as I come to a stop in front of it, half on the sidewalk, and throw the car into park.

Dammit. This right here is exactly why Dad told Layla this loser wasn't allowed over when he's not home.

Sirens sound in the distance, and it's a good fucking thing they're close. Otherwise I might kill this fucker.

I storm up to the door, only to find it locked. Cursing, I fumble with my keys, dropping them on the ground. I scoop them up and finally locate the right key and slide it into the lock.

"Layla!" I yell my sister's name, panic thick in my tone. "Layla!"

The house is eerily quiet, which only stresses me out more.

I head for the bathroom first, to check on Lili, but stop short in the doorway. The door's open, and my sister is sitting on the bathroom floor, sobbing, her arms wrapped around Lili. She's crying too, clinging to her mom.

Layla's cheek is crusted with blood, and there's a cut across her hairline. From head to toe, I take inventory, searching for more injuries. All seems to be intact, but she's going to have some nasty bruising on her face, and there are bruises on her arm in the distinct shape of fingerprints.

I fist my hands at my sides. "Where is he?"

She shakes her head. "G-Gone."

Anger builds inside me. I want nothing more than to pummel that prick until he's broken, so it's probably a good thing he's gone.

"The police are coming," I tell her. "You need to talk to them."

"I c-can't."

"Why?" The word comes out harsh, causing her to flinch.

"J-Just l-look at m-me. That's w-why."

I assess her, my heart hurting. She deserves so much better than this. Why can't she see that?

"This is exactly why you need to talk to them."

She gives a single nod, tucking Lili's head beneath her neck.

Since I know she's okay, and that Brandon isn't here, I head outside to greet the officers and let them into the house. The ambulance pulled in with them, and the medics head straight to the bathroom once I point them in that direction.

After the police take over, I call my dad.

"Hey, what's up?" he asks. The sound of his truck door closing echoes in the background.

Stomach knotting, I hesitate. There's no good way to tell him his daughter's boyfriend beat her up.

"It's ... uh ... Layla. Brandon came over and he, uh ... he hurt her."

Fuck. I'm stumbling over my words. My brain is still trying to process the situation.

"Is she okay?" The fear in his voice almost brings me to my knees.

No parent—no *person*—is perfect, but our dad has done his best with us. I know without a doubt he loves us with everything he has and would lay down his life in a heartbeat for either my sister or me.

"She's ... she'll be all right." I don't want to say she's okay, because I don't see how she can be after that. "The police are here now. Brandon was gone when I got here."

"How did you know? Did you stop by?"

"Lili called me."

He curses. "I wondered why I had missed calls from Layla. I figured it was Lili making sure I was bringing home McDonald's like I promised. I ... *fuck*."

"You couldn't have known, Dad."

"I'll be there as quick as I can, okay?"

"I'm not going anywhere."

Ending the call, I shove my phone back in my pocket and check on Layla. She's up now, sitting on a kitchen chair while the medics look her over and the cops ask her questions. Her eyes are red rimmed and her bottom lip quivers, but she's trying her best to keep it together for her daughter's sake.

Lili jumps off her lap and runs to me, wrapping her arms around my waist. "Thank you."

Fuck. That simple thank-you cuts me right through my heart. Lili should've never been in the position to have to make that call.

I crouch so I'm closer to her height and pull her in close. I would never forgive myself if something happened to Lili or my sister. As much as I've been frustrated with Layla for staying with Brandon, I would never wish for something like this to happen.

"You're so brave," I tell Lili in a quiet voice. I'm afraid of spooking her after what she's witnessed tonight. "I'm so glad you called me."

With tears in her eyes, she nods. When her lower lip wobbles, it's like a kick to my gut. I squeeze her tight again.

By the time our dad bursts into the house, they've determined that the cut on Layla's head isn't in need of stitches.

"Jesus Christ, Layla." He looks her over, and our dad—the man I haven't seen cry since our mom's passing—falls apart.

Layla's shocked eyes meet mine for the briefest of moments.

"I don't know what I'd do if something happened to you." He hovers over her awkwardly, clearly wanting to hug her but also afraid of hurting her.

"Dad," she sobs. And then he doesn't have to worry about hurting her, because she launches herself at him and hugs him. I haven't seen her hug him, at least not like this, since we were kids.

Layla has always butted heads with Dad more than me. She was more of a wild child, the rebel, so they were at odds. Whereas I had no interest in the kind of shit she got into.

A throat clears, getting my attention. "You're the one who made the call?" I nod. "And you arrived first?" Another nod. "We need to get a statement from you."

"All right. Lili, can you hang out with your mom and Grandpa? I won't be long."

She nods, wiping her tear-streaked face on my hoodie.

Once she's in Layla's arms, I follow the officer over to the corner of the living room and give him details from the time I got the call to when they arrived.

By the time they leave, I'm exhausted. I can't begin to imagine how Layla and Lili feel.

I collapse onto the couch, and Lili climbs up beside me. Heart aching, I wrap my arm around her side. If anything happened to my niece or my sister, I don't know what I'd do with myself. I want to make Brandon pay for this. It would be so easy to get in my car and find the loser, but this is where I need to be. My family needs me.

Dad and Layla talk in the kitchen, voices hushed.

"Are you hungry?" I ask Lili. The last thing on my mind is food, but with the adrenaline wearing off, she might be starving.

She gives a jerky nod in response. The worst part is that she'll never forget this. Shit. What kind of lasting impact might this have on her as she gets older?

"Pizza?"

There's not much I can do at the moment, but if I can

tend to Lilibet and make this whole situation even a smidge better, that's what I'll do.

She nods against me, whispering, "Yes, please."

I place the delivery order through the app while Layla and our dad are still talking in the kitchen.

Prying Lili from my arms, I ask, "Can you stay here for a minute? I'll be right back. I promise."

"Okay," she agrees a tad reluctantly.

I turn the TV on for her before joining the others in the kitchen.

Almost immediately, my dad swings his attention my way. "Did you know?"

My steps falter. "Know what?"

Layla looks away, not wanting to make eye contact with me.

"That he'd hit her before."

My mouth falls open.

"Dad, I told you Reid didn't know." Her voice is soft, almost meek, like all the fight has gone out of my fiery sister.

"When?" I ask her, flexing my fingers at my sides. The blood in my veins that was just cooling is simmering once again.

"Just sometimes." She winces like she finally realizes how bad that sounds. "Usually where no one could see." She wets her lips, her eyes shifting around. "I was scared to leave him. I thought he'd eventually stop."

My dad pinches his brow. "Layla—"

I jump in. There's no point in lecturing her, not after this. She's been beaten down enough today. Literally.

"You're done with him, right?"

"Yes. God, yes."

"Good." The tightness in my chest loosens a fraction at her adamancy. "Are you going to press charges?"

She presses her lips together and ducks her head, but finally nods.

"Then that's all there is to it for now."

I know my dad wants to say more, but he blows out a breath and lets his shoulders sag. He can see that sometimes it's better to say nothing. *I told you so*s won't be helpful in this scenario.

"I ordered pizza since Lili is hungry. Let's sit down and figure out your next steps," I address my sister.

Whether she feels like she needs to move out for safety reasons or wants counseling to sort through what she's been through, we'll support her. That's what family is for.

Layla reaches out to hug me. She might be my older sister, but I've always been the protective one.

She's capable of great things, and maybe now that Brandon won't be holding her back, she can finally achieve them.

thirty

Via

Thanksgiving comes and goes. I spend it by myself, since I'd rather have a root canal than fly back to California. I love my parents, I do, but subjecting myself to their critiques and disappointments doesn't sound like my idea of a nice holiday.

I do miss them, but I just ... I'm not ready to go back.

So, I spend the holiday in my pajamas with my butt parked on the couch, watching cheesy Christmas movies.

I make a turkey sandwich for the occasion and devour an apple pie I picked up from a local bakery. Topped with vanilla ice cream, of course.

Tonight, though, I'm trading out my sweatpants for

something a little nicer. I blow out my hair, then get started on my makeup.

It's my second official date with Reid. It's taken longer than either of us would like, since he has been dealing with family stuff and I've been busy preparing things for the store. My goal is to open in the spring, so we'll see what happens.

Even though we haven't had time for a date, we've met at a café near his apartment a few times so we could catch up in person. Each time, he left me tingling all over from a single kiss.

It still blows my mind that I went from having a one-night stand with this guy, determined to never see him again, to counting down the minutes until I can talk to him in the evenings.

Izzy is my biggest cheerleader, and honestly, if it weren't for her support, then I'd probably be panicking over how much I feel for him already.

Once my makeup is finished, I check my phone. He texted five minutes ago to say that he's on his way.

Shit.

Nearly tripping over my own two feet, I run into my bedroom and hastily sort through my clothes. He told me to dress warm, but does that mean I should dress up but make sure all my extremities are covered? Or are jeans acceptable?

I shoot him a quick text, seeking clarification, and immediately, my phone rings in my palm.

"Via." He says my name low and sultry. "Are you overthinking this?"

"No," I defend. "But you didn't tell me what—"

"We're going ice-skating."

Ice-skating. I can't help but smile. I off-handedly mentioned about a week ago that I'd never been. The fact that he listened and remembered means more than he'll ever know.

"Jeans and a sweater, then?"

"That'll be perfect. I'll be there soon."

I toss my phone on the bed and pull my favorite pair of jeans from the dresser drawer. They've been my favorite pair for years now and for good reason—they hug my body like a second skin, making my butt look incredible.

Snapping the button in place and zipping them up, I turn to the mirror with hands on my hips and assess my lacy black bra. "I wear this all the time," I mutter to my own reflection.

Turning my back on the mirror, I pick out one of my softest sweaters. Between it and my puffy coat and gloves, I should be well protected against the cold.

I'm just putting my shoes on when there's a knock on the door.

"Give me a minute," I call out.

Grabbing my purse, I swing it over my shoulder and pull open the door.

Freshly shaved, dark hair curling beneath a gray beanie, and shoulders hunched against the chilly wind, he looks absolutely kissable.

"Hi," he says, his nose already turning pink from the cold.

I don't say hi back, not with words, anyway. Standing on my tiptoes, I angle in close and kiss him. I'm craving so much more than a kiss, but this will have to do for now.

When I settle back on my feet, he's grinning at me. "Well, hello," he croons. "I like that greeting."

I smile back, a sweet ache forming in my chest. "I've missed you."

It's scary admitting it. That I've grown so attached to him that when I don't see him, I feel his absence. Even so, I want him to know. I haven't been the best with expressing myself with words. It comes from that part of me that was so hurt by Chase. But that gaping wound he left in my heart has closed up thanks to Reid. He's stitched it closed in the shape of his name.

I lock the door and turn, reaching for the railing so I don't slip on the stairs but stop short. My gaze shoots to Reid.

"You put salt on my stairs."

I meant to go to the hardware store and get salt, but I forgot. It's not something I'm used to having to do.

Reid shrugs like it's no big deal. "I had some in my car."

It might seem like a simple thing to him, but for me, it's huge. He saw that it needed to be done, and he did it.

"How's your sister?" I've asked almost every day since he told me what happened. I can't imagine how traumatizing that situation must've been for all of them.

"She's doing better. She's planning to move out soon. I think it'll be good for her to be on her own with Lili."

"How does your dad feel about that?"

Surprisingly, it's not weird talking about Derrick with Reid. It helps that it was only one ill-fated date and that I never had feelings for his dad.

He adjusts his beanie and opens the passenger door for me. I slide inside, and he uses his body as a shield against the cold.

"I think he's sadder than he's letting on. He'll be all alone for the first time."

I frown. "That has to be hard."

Reid shrugs. "I'm sure it is, but it might be good for him. There's more to life than worrying about us. He's put us first our whole lives. He deserves to prioritize himself for a change."

He closes the door, and when he climbs in on his side, he cranks the engine and grins over at me.

"Are you excited about skating?"

I give him an answering smile in return. "You have no idea."

I *HATE* ICE-SKATING.

Or maybe ice-skating hates me.

I hit the ice, ass-first, for the fourth time, as a kid nearby laughs. Not sure I can blame him. Seeing the same person fall this often is probably pretty entertaining. Another kid moves by me, holding tight to a contraption that looks like a walker as she wobbles by.

I need that.

Reid, lips pressed together to hold in laughter, holds out a hand to help me up.

"I suck at this," I gripe, wincing at the sting in my butt cheeks. They're going to be *bruised*. I have no idea how I'll sit in the car on the drive home.

"It's a learning curve."

"This learning curve is a circle."

"A circle?" He chuckles, adjusting his glasses with his free hand. He keeps a tight hold on mine with his other. Not that it does any good. I fall even when he's holding me.

"Yeah, because the curve never ends. Thus, a circle."

He shakes his head, fighting a smile. I'm glad I can amuse him with something other than my fantastic ability to fall.

Swinging around in front of me, he takes both of my hands to pull me along, skating backward while I can't even skate forward.

"I don't know whether you're genuinely trying to help me or just showing off."

He frowns. "Huh? Oh." His brows jump into his hairline. "If I wanted to show off, I'd do so much more than this."

I stick my tongue out at him. "Did you come out of the womb skating?"

His hold on me tightens and he keeps me steady when my legs start to go out from under me *again*.

"Sort of. Around here, skating is pretty popular. I played hockey as a kid."

My jaw drops. "You were a hockey player?"

"Yeah. Through high school. I still play with my friends sometimes."

Book club would have a field day with this information. The last two books we've read have centered on hockey playing heroes. Apparently, the trope is all the rage right now. Ella mentioned hockey butts being superior last week. I dismissed the comment at the time, but now I'm reconsidering, since Reid does have a very nice ass.

"Interesting," I muse.

"I'll have you playing in no time." He glances over his shoulder every so often to make sure he doesn't bump into anyone.

"I doubt it, but thank you for the encouragement."

"You're doing great, Via. You don't give yourself enough credit. You only put on skates a half hour ago. You're ahead of a lot of people."

"Now you're just trying to flatter me. I haven't seen anyone fall as much as me."

He tries to hide his smile. "I wouldn't lie to you. You'll just have to trust me."

His words strike something inside me. After Chase's betrayal, I worried I would never trust again. Certainly not a man. But without even trying, Reid has shown me that I can put my trust in him, and I have.

We manage to make a full circle around the rink without another fall.

"You want me to let go?" he asks.

I want to tell him no. The idea of falling again sucks.

But what's life without a couple of bumps and bruises? The process of getting back up is where the learning happens.

"Yeah. I want to try again."

His mega-watt smile tells me I've made the right choice.

He doesn't drop my hands like a momma bird shoving a baby from the nest. Instead, he loosens his hold at first and waits for me to find my balance. Once I'm steady he moves so he's only holding my fingertips. Finally, he drops his arms to his sides but stays in front of me.

I wobble, but quickly find my center of gravity and steady myself. I'm shaky, there's nothing smooth about me on the ice, but I'm *doing* it.

"Look at me! I can skate!" I don't care if I sound like an excited child. This is something I thought I might never do.

"You're doing great. Keep your arms steady."

"I'm try—"

Before I can finish my response, my feet are sliding out from under me again. My butt hits the ice, my hip screaming in protest.

I suck in a sharp breath and squeeze my eyes shut. "Ouch."

Reid, thankfully, doesn't laugh. Even if I'm sure I present a hysterical sight.

"You were doing great. You just lost your balance."

"Standing on a pair of knives is no easy feat." I take his hands and let him haul me up again.

Gripping the boards along the outside of the rink with one hand, I brush ice off my jeans with the other.

"Do you want to take a break?" he asks, tipping his head at a skater passing by.

I eye the person, but I don't recognize him. Our relationship isn't a secret necessarily, but it's not exactly public either. I don't talk about him with anyone except my sister, and he hasn't told his dad about us. It's not that I'm ashamed of him, but the minute we let other people in on this, it'll open things up for judgment. Reid doesn't care about our age difference, but other people *will* care, and they'll have opinions.

Belatedly, I realize he's asked me a question.

"A break would be good."

Not only does my butt hurt, but my quads are screaming in protest.

Off the ice, we change out of our skates and back into our shoes. I won't be going out there again, and I think he knows it. The bruises forming on my body are enough for the day. We can try again another time. Maybe.

There's a café in the rink, so we head there. We were only on the ice for half an hour, but already, I desperately need water.

"I know this isn't super fancy or anything..." Reid dips his chin, and I swear his ears turn a little pink. "But the food is pretty good. If you want more of a sit-down meal, though, we can go somewhere else."

"Reid." I grab his wrist to still his nervous movements. I don't think he even realized he was tapping his fingers against the side of his leg. "This is wonderful. Seriously. I'm more than happy with getting dinner here."

I've done enough fancy wining and dining to last a lifetime. That's *all* Chase and I did. We never did anything like this—a fun activity together. Nope, just an endless stream of restaurants, which got tiresome after a while.

Reid tugs on his beanie. He's normally so confident, so I enjoy these rare moments where this vulnerable side of him shows itself. It makes what's growing between us all the more real.

"How are you so perfect for me?"

It feels more like a confession than a question. Words dry up on my tongue, so I say nothing in response.

In line, I peruse the menu. Between the skating and my falls, I've worked up quite the appetite.

"What do you recommend?" I ask Reid. "I figure you've spent enough time here to have tried all of it."

"I have." He shoves his hands into his pockets, shoulders curling upward. "The burgers are great. Stay away from the hot dogs. The club sandwich is a good choice, and their fries are some of the best."

When it's our turn to order, we both opt for a burger and fries.

"This was really fun." I slide into a seat at a table in the quietest spot we can find. "I suck at skating, but I've always wanted to do it. I can't thank you enough for letting me experience that."

"You were better at it than you think. Especially since you've never done it before."

"Thanks." I tuck a piece of hair behind my ear. "I tend to expect myself to be perfect at everything."

He chuckles, dipping a fry in ketchup. "I hadn't noticed."

I toss my straw wrapper at him. It falls short, landing beside his tray. "Your sarcasm has been noted."

"You really shouldn't be so hard on yourself."

A little knot of unease tightens in my belly. I finish chewing a bite of my burger and regard him. "Some habits are hard to shake."

As a kid, I always strove to do better. The pressure I felt to excel carried on into my adult life. It's hard to shake something that's so engrained in who I am.

"It's okay to get a little messy." His eyes twinkle, like he has a certain kind of messy in mind. Or maybe I'm reading into it too much since I'm craving him like a hit of nicotine.

My heart beats against my chest at the thought. "Are you going to show me how?" I challenge.

He tugs his beanie off, running his fingers through his hair. "Absolutely. I don't trust anyone else with the job."

We finish up our food, and neither of us says a thing about going back out on the ice.

On the drive back to my place, a delicious tension crackles in the air. He grazes his fingers across my knee every so often, a silent tease I desperately hope he follows through on.

He parks in his usual spot outside my place.

Neither of us says a word or makes a move to get out. The air between us grows heated.

"Reid—"

Hands on my cheeks, he kisses me like if he doesn't, he'll simply cease to exist.

I open my mouth beneath his, and a small sound escapes me. Needy, I try to shift closer to him, but it's impossible with the seat belt still latched.

With shaky fingers, I fumble to undo it.

"Come up," I beg against his lips. "Please."

He pulls away, rubbing his nose against mine. "Are you sure?"

I nod like a damn bobblehead I'm so turned on. "Yes."

It's nearly impossible for us to keep our hands off each other on the climb up the stairs. I giggle like a teenager when he grabs my butt, giving it a squeeze.

It's nearly impossible to hold my fingers steady enough to unlock the door, but when I do, we stumble through, and Reid kicks it shut behind us and turns the lock. In a blink, he has me pinned against it and he's kissing me thoroughly while his fingers work the zipper of my coat. With it unzipped, I wiggle out of it and let it drop to the floor.

His bare hand slides beneath my sweater. "I wanted to wait to do this," he confesses on a breath, his lips skimming down the column of my neck. "I want you to know this is real."

"I know." I kiss him. "I know it's real." There's no denying that this is so much more than a fling. "I know."

The way his eyes light up makes my stomach dip. With a

step back, he shrugs out of his coat and kicks off his shoes. Next to go are his hoodie and shirt. The rippling of his muscles beneath his skin reminds me of the way water reacts when a stone skips across it.

His lips twitch. "Like what you see, angel?"

I don't answer him. Not with words, anyway. Instead, I launch myself at him, desperate for his mouth and the feel of his bare skin beneath my fingers.

He hauls me up and sets me on the kitchen counter so we're nose to nose. I open my legs wider, giving him the perfect space to fit into.

"It's killed me not to touch you like this," he confesses, skimming along my lacy bra beneath my sweater. "Don't think for a minute that waiting has been—"

A sharp knock sounds, and we jolt apart.

Reid looks at the door, then back at me just as there's another knock. Softer this time.

"Expecting someone?"

I shake my head, pulse pounding with a mix of desire and trepidation. "I ... no."

Reid shuffles to the door, holding out a hand toward me. "Just stay there."

I nod, though I'm not sure what the point is in staying where I am since I'm hardly hidden from the door.

"Who's there?" he asks through the door.

"I'm looking for Via," a man replies, most definitely not answering the question.

Reid looks over his shoulder at me, silently asking whether he should open the door.

I shrug, biting my lip. "Don't open it."

More knocking. "Does Via live here?"

"Who wants to know?" Reid asks, his voice deepening with irritation.

Silence, and then, "Her husband."

PART THREE

thirty-one

Via

Reid looks back at me, mouth agape, as if to say, *"Is this guy serious?"*

Now that I'm not so startled, I recognize the voice.

What the fuck is he doing here?

"Chase?" My lips silently form the name.

Reid understands clearly. Eyes widening, he whispers, "Did you know your ex was coming?"

I scoff. "Of course not."

If I *had* known, I would've told him in no uncertain terms that he's not welcome here. Ever. How did he even find out where I live? I didn't tell him I was moving, let alone where.

"Via, I can hear you in there. We need to talk."

Talk? Doesn't he realize the time for talking is way past over? If he wanted to "talk," we had plenty of time for that *before* he cheated. Flying all the way across the country for a *conversation* is more than a little absurd, not to mention presumptuous.

Stupidly, I am curious as to why he's standing at my door in *Maine* and not back in San Francisco.

Reid's face is twisted in annoyance, but there's also worry there.

Shoulders slumping, I sigh. "Let me talk to him."

His eyes narrow, but I can't be bothered by his reaction right now. I'm still too damn confused about what my ex-husband is doing here.

"Are you sure?"

I count to ten silently in my head. "I'm sure."

Do I *want* to talk to Chase? No. I have nothing to say to him. Regardless, he's here, so I might as well find out why.

Reid watches me for another silent moment. When I hop off the counter and lift my chin, making my decision even more clear, he snags his hoodie off the floor and yanks it back on.

Opening the door, Reid stares down my ex. I didn't realize until now, but he has a good three or four inches on Chase. It might not seem like a whole lot, but boy, does it add to the intimidation factor.

"Who are you?" Chase snarls, chest puffing.

I step closer and put a hand on Reid's forearm, ready to intervene.

Chase immediately zeros in on the contact, his lips curling into a snarl.

"He's—"

"Her boyfriend," Reid finishes for me. His fingers brush the inside of my wrist gently, not to lay claim to me, but as a protection of sorts.

"Boyfriend?" Chase sputters. "You look like a kid."

I flinch like I've been slapped. My grip on Reid's arm loosens, but he grasps my hand and twines our fingers together, giving mine a squeeze. Then he releases his hold so he can cross his arms over his chest.

"And you look like a cheater."

Shots fired.

Chase's cheeks turn an ugly shade of red. "Via, can we talk?" I guess he's decided to ignore Reid's presence all together.

In the fading light of the day, with his hair slicked back with gel and his brows drawn low, he looks like a different person. He used to be more carefree and not as stiff. This man is a stranger.

Somewhere along the way, my former husband has become just someone I used to know.

"You came all the way here, to Maine, to *talk*?"

"You wouldn't answer my texts," he says, like this should be all the information I need.

Mouth agape, I blink at him. "Are you serious right now?" I hiss.

Reid shoots a pleased smile in my direction.

"I didn't answer because I have nothing to say to you."

We're *divorced*. We have no reason to communicate. This man has to be insane, and maybe I was too for staying with him for so long, especially since he turned out to be a domineering, gaslighting jerk.

"Well," he throws his arms out at his sides, "I'm here now."

He seriously thinks that means I should hear him out. I don't *want* to listen to him. I'm tempted to shut the door in his face and move on with my life, because how fucking presumptuous can he be to just show up here?

But deep down, I need to hear what he has to say. If I don't, I'll always wonder.

"Reid?" I grip his forearm lightly. "Let me talk to him."

He looks back at me, brow furrowed, and scans my face. "Do you want me to go?"

I shake my head. "Maybe just wait in your car."

Chase snorts. "We'll be talking for a while, kid. Why don't you run home to Mommy and Daddy and have them tuck you into bed?"

Reid looks my ex-husband up and down. "You're even more pathetic than she described."

With that, he lowers his head and gives me a long, leisurely kiss. It's a kiss that's more than PG-13 but not quite R-rated. "I'll be waiting, but take your time," he whispers so that Chase can't hear him. "Say what you need to."

I appreciate that he recognizes this is an opportunity for me to get things off my chest.

With a final peck to my cheek, he slips past Chase, who

doesn't bother to move out of the doorway. If Chase is trying to score points with me, I hate to tell him he's well into the negative already.

"You might as well come in. You've already let enough cold air in as it is."

He scoffs. "You're the one who's left me standing here like this."

"What can I say? I didn't invite you."

He ducks his head, like maybe my words hit their mark. Good.

It's weird seeing Chase in my apartment, in this space that I've made entirely mine. Sure, the renovations haven't begun in here yet, and the place has seen better days, but none of that matters, because it's *mine*. He looks out of place here, like an old lamp that doesn't match the décor.

"Nice place." The sarcasm in his tone is heavy.

It makes me bristle. This certainly isn't considered *nice* by his standards, but I love my apartment.

"Why are you here?" I cross my arms over my chest, staring him down.

It makes no sense. Why would he come all the way here? Why would he go through the effort to find me?

He runs his fingers through his light brown hair. In the months since I've last seen him, he's aged drastically. The lines beside his eyes are much deeper than I remember. And his mouth has been turned down in a frown since he arrived. Maybe things haven't been as fine and dandy with his mistress as he thought they'd be.

"Can't I want to see my wife?"

I narrow my eyes on his manipulative use of the word *wife*. As if because we were once married, he'll always have ownership over me.

"Ex-wife," I correct. "And no, you can't just want to see me. We're not friends."

We used to be, so long ago now that it feels like another lifetime. When did things start devolving for us? When did Chase become so controlling and narcissistic? I don't believe it was always there. Or, if it was, he hid it well.

"Come on, babe," he laughs. "You can't mean that."

I do, wholeheartedly. "Where's your girlfriend? The baby?" I counter. I want this conversation to end. He needs to say his piece and go on his merry way.

"Can I sit?" He waves at the couch. "Or do you have something to say about that too?"

The sigh that comes out of me rattles my chest. My annoyance is at an all-time high, and he's barely even spoken. "Sit."

He does, propping one of my throw pillows behind his back. "What? You're not going to join me?"

I shake my head. The more distance I can keep between us, the better. Otherwise, I might end up strangling him, and I don't want to have to ask Reid to help me hide the body.

Chase huffs a breath. "Fine, stand, then."

"Can you get on with it?" I demand. "You went through the trouble of finding me and coming all the way here, so this ought to be good."

He smiles then, and it's an all-too-pleased with himself kind of smile. "Oh, it was no trouble, really. Your mother was all too happy to give me your address when I mentioned I hoped to reconcile."

My stomach drops to my feet at those words. This man has to be high on something. In what world does he think I'd *ever* get back together with him? And my mother? How dare she hand over my new address? And without even a warning to me after she did. If he went to her for that information, then she has to know that we're not on speaking terms. The betrayal burns hotly beneath my skin.

"Reconcile? You're out of your goddamn mind, Chase. You *cheated* on me." I suspect more than once over the years, though I have no proof. "You have a baby with her."

"The baby isn't mine."

He drops that bit of information between us like a bomb. I don't know how he expects me to react, what he wanted out of this, but I feel nothing.

"Okay," I say slowly, giving him a puzzled frown. "I don't care."

I, blessedly, don't give a shit. What a beautiful thing it is to reach the point where I no longer care about anything regarding the man who betrayed me in the worst way.

Chase scoffs and sits straighter. "You don't care? Didn't you hear me? The baby isn't mine. We can—"

"We can what, Chase? Forgive and forget? We're *divorced*, not separated. And regardless of whether your mistress's baby isn't yours, you still had sex with her. Even if

I hadn't already realized how much better off I am on my own, an affair isn't something I could ever forgive."

I applaud those who can, but I don't possess that ability.

Chase snorts. "You're better off on your own? Look at this shit hole, babe." He waves a hand, gesturing to my apartment while I try not to gag on his use of *babe*. "This place is disgusting."

"It's a work in progress." I don't have to defend myself against him. It's not my fault he can't see the potential.

Chase rubs his hand over his cheeks. "You might not believe me, but I wanted to say I'm sorry."

"Sorry?" The last thing I ever expected from this man was an apology. One that actually sounds shockingly sort of genuine. "For what?"

"I blamed you for our inability to conceive, but all this time, it was me."

My heart twists at that word.

Blamed.

What an ugly word. I was going through the worst time of my life, and all the while, he was blaming me. It goes to show what a piece of shit he is.

"Did you finally get tested?"

Chase refused any kind of fertility testing on his part, and since he was so adamantly against it, when I went on my own, I didn't bother filling him in.

He shakes his head. "No, are you not listening? The baby isn't mine, so clearly, I'm the one with the issue."

Chase *could* have a fertility issue, but I *do*. Not that I'm telling him that. My body and what goes on with it is none of his business.

I let out a long, slow breath. He's been here for minutes, and I already feel exhausted.

"Why did you really track me down?"

"I thought ... I thought you'd want to know."

"Why would I want to know, Chase? Why would I care?" I keep my tone even. It would be all too easy to yell, but he's not worth the effort. It's freeing, knowing that the man who once owned my heart, then hurt me so deeply, now elicits no emotion in me. When he doesn't respond, I ask, "Did you think I'd take you back? That I'd be sitting here waiting for you to show up?"

From the look on his face, that's exactly what he thought. Does he think I'm so weak? That he could waltz back into my life and I'd be happy to pick up where we left off before his affair?

I might not have realized how unhappy I was at the time, but now that I've seen the other side, there's no going back.

"I miss you. Don't you miss me?" His voice takes on this lost little boy quality, like I should be sympathetic to *his* feelings.

"Actually, I don't."

Anger flickers across his face, but I've already heard enough.

"You can go." I flick my head toward the door.

I've heard all I need to from him. There's no point in dragging this out further.

"What?" He laughs incredulously. "I come all the way here, and you're kicking me out?"

"Yes." I leave it at that. The *fuck you, Chase* is on the tip of my tongue, but I bite it back. He'd only see it as a passionate response.

It's fascinating how this man I spent so much of my life with, who I thought I'd grow old with, has become a stranger in a matter of months.

He stands slowly, looking me up and down. "I never knew you could be such a bitch."

Once, those words would've cut me like a knife. Now? I smile.

"If sticking up for myself makes me a bitch, then so be it." I follow him to the door. "Have a good life, Chase."

And, strangely, I mean it.

I've moved past him. My eyes have been opened to his true colors. But I still can't help but hope for the best for him, even if he doesn't deserve it.

He hesitates outside the door, standing in the flickering porch light—I really need to replace the thing, but it'll have to wait until the renovations begin upstairs.

"For what it's worth," he says, letting out a sigh that has his shoulders sagging, "I'm sorry."

I dip my head in acknowledgment. We're not tying up all the years we were together in a pretty bow and promising to be friends, but I suppose this is as close to closure as we'll get. And I'm okay with that.

With one more exhale, he turns and descends the steps.

I never thought I'd see him again—didn't care if I did—but watching him go feels like the end of a chapter.

And when Reid appears, jogging up the stairs, then taking my face in his hands to kiss me, I know it's the beginning of a brand-new one.

thirty-two

Reid

The last thing I wanted to do was leave Via alone with that smug-looking prick. The second he started down the stairs, I couldn't get back to her fast enough. As much as I wanted to confront the fucker, I didn't.

My lips leave hers, but I don't drop my hands from her cheeks.

"Are you okay?" I look her over for any signs of distress.

She glances down. "Yes. I'm still stunned that he was even here, but yeah, I'm fine."

"Do you want to talk about it?"

I won't push her to if she isn't comfortable, even if I am curious as hell about what would bring him all this way.

"Yeah." She nods, stepping out of my hold and grabbing my wrist to tug me inside where it's warm. "I think I should. I think I *want* to." She gives me a small smile.

I blow out a breath and pull out one of the stools at the counter. "You can tell me as much or as little as you want."

She dips her chin, wrapping her arms around herself, and settles on the couch. Despite her assurance that she's okay, it's clear his appearance spooked her. I can't imagine what it had to feel like to be confronted by him so unexpectedly.

"He wanted to tell me that his ... the woman he had an affair with ... it turns out the baby isn't his." She looks away at that. "We struggled to get pregnant, and he blamed me for it. In hindsight, it's a blessing. But I guess in his own weird way, he wanted to apologize. He thinks since this baby isn't his that he's not fertile."

"Thinks? Or knows?"

She shrugs, curling in on herself. I want to go to her, to wrap my arms around her, but she needs space in order to get this off her chest.

"Thinks," she finally mutters. "I, however, know I have a problem." She bites her bottom lip, eyes shining with unshed tears. "My body doesn't like pregnancy. He doesn't know, but I got pregnant twice. Neither one stuck, obviously." She clenches her jaw, sniffling. "There is a small chance I could carry to term if I'm under strict supervision and only with treatments that would keep my body from rejecting the pregnancy. But even then, chances are likely the baby would be preterm. As much as I want to be a mom, that's ... I don't think it's an option for me. I don't want to put my body through that. Physically or mentally. I'd be so stressed through the entire pregnancy. You should know this anyway. That I can't have a baby. In case it's a deal-breaker for you. I wasn't trying to keep this a secret from you, but it's hard to talk about." Her eyes drop from mine to her lap, and she stretches her fingers, watching the way her joints move. When she gives another small sniffle, I can't fucking take it.

In three quick steps, I cross the short distance between us and wrap my arms around her. With a shaky sigh, she tucks her head beneath my chin, letting me hold her.

"There are lots of ways to have kids, Via. Even if you didn't want them at all, it wouldn't be a deal-breaker." I cradle her face in my hands, urging her to look in my eyes and see how serious I am. "I like that you're thinking that far into our future." I can't help but grin.

She rolls her eyes and bites back a smile. "Of course you'd focus on that. We haven't even said..." She turns, trying to look away, but I hold tight, unwilling to let her. I want her to see that I mean what I say.

"We haven't said what yet? I love you?"

When she presses her lips together, I know I'm right. "I'm not going to give you those words yet. Not when I know they'd scare you. But Via?" I bring my lips to the shell of her ear. "When you are ready, I'm going to say it over and over again until the day I die, and I'm going to show you with my body exactly what it means to me."

Her breath catches. Shit, I hope I haven't said too much.

I don't want to push her too far, too fast. Via's strong but still so skittish. She wants to trust me, but she's wary of having her heart—her *trust*—broken again.

I have to tread carefully with her, even if I want to go full steam ahead. She's worth the wait.

"Aren't you listening?" She sniffles, pulling back.

I won't let her go. I won't let her put a wall between us.

"I can't have kids. You can say whatever you want, but you've talked about it before. I can't—I *won't*—take that from you."

"Via." I keep my tone calm but firm. "You are robbing me of nothing. Do you see any kids running around right now? You can't take away something that doesn't exist. But you?" I stroke my thumbs against the soft skin of her cheeks. "*You* are right here. You are tangible. If you walk away from me, I *would* lose you. Don't you see that?"

Lip pulled between her teeth and tears streaming down her face, she gives me the subtlest of nods.

Fuck. The pain in her eyes shatters me. I wrap my arms around her, holding her tight.

Though her intention is selfless, losing her would hurt far more than any other loss I could endure.

I don't let up. Just keep her pressed tight to me. "You have to be tired." The emotional exhaustion of dealing with her ex is enough to have her wiped out, not to mention all the spills she took on the ice. "Why don't you go shower and get ready for bed?"

"A shower sounds nice, but..."

"But what?"

"I don't want you to leave. But after what just happened…" She waves a hand in front of her. "I don't much feel like having sex."

A bemused smile splits my face. "He put a damper on things, didn't he?"

Her shoulders sag. "Like a bucket of ice-cold water."

"We don't have to do anything," I promise. "I'll stay."

It'll make me feel better if I can hold her tonight anyway.

Relief floods her face. "Thank you. I … I don't want to be alone."

She regards the door, her eyes wary. I don't get the impression she's *afraid* of her ex, but his unexpected appearance has to be disconcerting.

Her cheeks suddenly turn pink and her eyes drop. It brings a smile to my lips. Via is confident, a force to be reckoned with in many ways, but there's a part of her when it comes to her sexuality that's almost shy.

"What is it?" I prompt, using two fingers to lift her chin so she's forced to look at me.

With a deep breath in, she straightens and squares her shoulders. "Do you want to shower with me? *Just* shower?"

I hesitate. "Do *you* want me to?"

She nods.

"Words, Via. I need words."

"Yes," she whispers, taking my hand and tugging me down the hall.

As promised, all we did was shower. Her shower is so small that nothing else *could* have happened anyway. I hit my head on the showerhead at least three times. Towel drying my hair, I stroll into her room to find her folding the sheets back. It'll be a tight fit with the two of us in her full-size bed, but I'll do anything to spend the night with her in my arms.

Tossing the towel into her hamper, I stifle a yawn.

"Bed's ready," she announces, letting her eyes drift over me. After the shower, I pulled my boxer briefs back on, but that's it. It's not like I'm going to sleep in my jeans.

"I can see that," I say around a smile.

Her awkward shyness is adorable.

I sit on the side of the bed next to the cleared nightstand. I assume the other side, where a small stack of books and magazines rest, is hers.

Via slides in close and settles on her side. "It's a tight fit."

"I don't mind. It's perfect for cuddling." With an arm around her midsection, I tug her flush against me and roll her over so I'm spooning her. "See?" I press a kiss to the curve of her neck. "Perfect."

She relaxes against me, wiggling her ass to get comfortable.

"Via," I warn. "If I get a boner, it's entirely your fault."

She stifles a laugh. "Sorry."

"Sure you are."

"Shh." She hushes me playfully. "We need to sleep."

I expect to have trouble falling asleep in such close quarters, but in minutes, I'm out, and the next thing I know, daylight is streaming in through a crack in the blinds.

My legs tingle like they're asleep. When I try to move them, sure enough, that tingle turns into a sharper pings-and-needles sensation. Opening my eyes, I discover the issue. Via's leg is draped over mine like she was scared I'd get away from her in my sleep. She's still sleeping peacefully, snoring softly. Trying not to laugh is an effort.

I drink her in greedily. Her face is soft in sleep, lashes fanned out against her cheeks. Her lips are slightly chapped from the cold weather.

She continues to snooze, unbothered.

Her ex's visit shook me up. I hate—I fucking *hate*—that for a moment there, when she asked me to wait outside in my car, I worried she'd come out and tell me she was taking him back. I should've known better. Via's too strong to fall for that asshole's excuses and empty promises.

I ease out of bed, careful not to wake her, and slip into the bathroom. After relieving myself and washing my hands, I steal a swipe of toothpaste and use my finger to clean my teeth. Despite the things we've done, I don't think she'd like it if I used her toothbrush.

Out in her tiny kitchen, I search for ingredients for breakfast, then get to work on pancakes.

I click on one of my favorite playlists on my phone but

keep the volume low, hoping to let her sleep in as long as she needs.

When the pancakes are finished, I stack them and wrap them with foil.

"Hey."

Via's sleepy voice has me almost jumping out of my skin. I spin and pull in a breath to calm my racing heart.

"Good morning. How'd you sleep?"

"Surprisingly well." She tugs on her nightshirt. It's way too big for her and peppered with holes. It's clearly been well loved.

"I made breakfast."

"I thought something smelled good." She gives me a sleepy smile. "What'd you make?"

"Pancakes."

She practically moans at that. "Pancakes sound like heaven right now."

"I'll get you a plate."

With a laugh, she pulls her hair up into a sloppy bun. "It's my place. I should be cooking and feeding you."

I shrug. "I like taking care of you."

I've always taken care of the people I love—my dad and my sister, then Lili, when she came along. It's second nature.

"Still." She shrugs. She pops up on her tiptoes to grab a coffee mug from the upper cabinet, exposing the swell of her ass hidden beneath a pair of pink panties. "I feel bad."

"Don't." I move around her and grab another plate, then divvy up the pancakes. "I enjoy it. I promise."

She sticks a pod into her coffee maker and turns to face me. "I could certainly get used to it."

"What do you like on your pancakes?"

"Butter and syrup, please." She stifles a yawn as a stream of coffee trickles into her mug. When I slather butter on her pancake, then douse it in syrup, she giggles. "Are you going to feed it to me too?"

With a smirk, I cut a bite-size piece. "Only if you want." I hold the fork out, dangling chunk of pancake and all.

She eyes me, like she's fighting an internal battle. Finally, though, she stands on her toes and closes her lips around the tines of the fork. She edges back, licking at the lingering traces of syrup, her eyes locked on me.

Fuck. The sight is insanely sensual.

Lowering again, she grins like she knows exactly how she's made me feel. "Yum."

I drop the fork to the counter and grasp her by the back of the neck. In a breath, my lips are on hers, tasting the remnants of syrup. She melts into me, chest to chest, splaying her hands against my sides like she needs the support to remain upright.

"You're right." I let her go and cut another bite. "That was delicious."

Her breath catches, and her eyes flare with heat.

Her desire is blatant, and I'd like nothing more than to give her what she wants, but after yesterday, she needs time.

"Not now." I brush my nose against hers.

She snags her plate from the counter and sits. "You're such a tease."

With a smirk, I drop into the seat beside her. "You like it."

She glowers at me. She's adorable when she's mad. "I'd like it better if you were fucking me."

Her bold words knock the air from my lungs. *Fuck*. I arch a brow. "Is that so?"

"I want you."

The flames in her eyes unleash my own need. I've been trying to be good, to hold myself back and prove to her that our connection is about more than sex. Last night, I was ready to take the leap, but her dumb-fuck ex put a damper on things. This morning, I expected to find traces of worry etched in the lines on her face. I've been searching for the signs since she appeared in the kitchen but have found nothing but a soft happiness and desire.

I sweep her into my arms, sending the barstool crashing to the floor in the process. Then her mouth is on mine, that delectable sugary syrup taste on her tongue.

Fated—that's what we are.

I knew it when I first laid eyes on her. I have to be patient until she sees it too.

We're right for each other in every way.

In a matter of seconds, we're in her room. I kick the door shut behind us with enough force to rattle the walls.

She laughs, her hot breath on my skin. "Eager, are you?"

"You have no idea."

I lay her on the bed, groaning at the sight of her hair fanned out around her. Her t-shirt rides up, exposing a bit of stomach and her panties.

She looks beautiful.

She looks like *mine*.

And when she dons a sly smile and crooks her finger, I dive over her, catching my body weight with my hands on either side of her head.

Looping her arms around my neck, she licks her lips. "I wasn't supposed to fall for you, but I am."

I smile and drop a kiss to her forehead. "Trust me, angel, you were supposed to."

Without giving her a chance to respond, I put my mouth on her, kissing her deeply.

She moves her hands down my bare chest until her fingers dip just beneath the edge of my underwear. There, she pauses, teasing me with lazy brushes against my bare skin.

"Via," I groan.

"What?" She blinks up at me, the picture of innocence. "I'm not doing anything."

"That's the problem and you know it."

"You want me to touch you?"

I kiss the curve of her neck, and I swear she hums in response. "I want you to do whatever you want."

She grins up at me, and in an impressive move, she wraps her leg around my hips and maneuvers us so that I'm flat on my back while she straddles me. I grasp her waist, but she grabs my hands and pins them beside my head.

Heat swirling in my gut, I arch a brow at her.

"Now I have you right where I want you." She rocks her

hips against me, rubbing her pussy against my hard dick through our underwear.

"And where's that?" I ask through clenched teeth, holding myself back from flipping her over.

Slow, I remind myself. I want to take things slow this time.

To cherish and savor her.

She rocks her hips again. I nearly bite my tongue off.

"Under my control," she finally says.

It takes my addled brain a moment to register her meaning.

Still holding my wrists hostage, she lowers. Her hair tickles my bare chest, my cheeks, before she teases my lips with hers. It's not a kiss, not even close. I groan, closing my eyes in an effort to stay still. To give her this—give her power.

She ghosts her lips back over mine, smiling against my mouth.

She's testing me to see if I can handle letting her take over. I want to touch her so fucking badly. I want to skim my hands beneath her loose shirt, graze my fingers over the smooth skin of her stomach, and cup her breasts. But I need to be patient.

Kissing me in earnest this time fully, she parts my lips with her tongue. All the while, she rocks against me. It's the most delicious kind of torture. Her hands leave my wrists, delving into my hair. Finally free, I grip her hips, but I don't move any higher.

Mine. It's a silent mantra. Fuck, she feels good on top of me.

Sitting up, she pulls her shirt over her head and tosses it onto the floor.

"Via, baby," I groan, digging into her hips. "Can I—" I don't even finish the question before she's nodding. "Thank fuck."

With one arm around her bare torso, I sit so she's positioned in my lap.

I lick around one nipple, then the other.

"Reid." My name is a breathy gasp on her lips. I take my time licking and sucking at her skin. When she's a writhing and moaning mess against me, I lie back and cross my arms behind my head. "What are you doing?" The question escapes her on a guttural groan.

"Letting you take over, angel. My body is yours. Do what you want with me."

"I…" She presses her palms against my abs and searches my face, her confidence waning.

"Don't get shy on me now," I coax. "Take what you need."

I see it, the moment the switch inside her flips. She crawls down my body, tugging at my boxer briefs as she goes. Wrapping her hand around the base of my cock, she strokes up and down. Then she's circling the head with her tongue, taking her time, savoring me. With her hair tied back in that messy knot, I can make out the lust-filled expression on her face. She makes eye contact with me and takes me so deep she gags. She pulls back, saliva stringing from her lips to my dick. With a grin, she does it again. Slower this time. Deeper.

"Fuck, Via."

I count backward from one hundred in my head. The last thing I want to do is blow my load before I get inside that sweet pussy. Waiting has been the sweetest torture, and it's been worth it. It's going to make this all the better.

But—

"Fuck," I curse.

She pops off my dick, eyes wide with worry. "Did I do something wrong?"

"N-No," I stutter. "I just ... I don't have a condom."

She regards me, rubbing her lips together in thought. "I'm on birth control. I'm okay going without a condom if you are."

My heart beats out a fast rhythm behind my breastbone as I study her, looking for any sign of uncertainty. All I see is determination.

Fuck. Is this real life? "I've never had sex without one before."

She strokes my cock and gives me a small smile. "It's okay if you're not comfortable. I promise."

"I really fucking want to. Are you sure?"

She nods. "I'm positive."

Crawling back up my body, she kisses me, slow and deep.

I tease my fingers against the edge of her panties, finding her already soaked. "You're so fucking wet, Via," I growl against her mouth. "You want me that bad, huh?"

"You have no idea." She rolls off me and rids herself of her panties. "I want to feel you over me."

I'm not about to deny my girl her request, so I guide her onto her back and settle my body over hers, elbows pressed to the mattress on either side of her head. She digs her fingers dig into my ass, urging me on. With a groan, I rub my cock against her wetness, then sink in inch by inch until I'm fully seated.

Arching her back, she wraps her legs around my hips. "*Yes.*" Her moan is like music to my ears.

I rock slowly, memorizing the feel of her, how her warmth envelops me and holds on.

"Kiss me," she begs, and I happily oblige.

As cheesy as it might sound, I've been dreaming of making love to Via for weeks, and that's what I do. I see it in her eyes, the shift. She knows I'm right—that we're the real deal. That this is forever.

Even if she still isn't ready to accept that.

It's okay. I'm a patient man, and I know she'll get there.

thirty-three

Via

The store is coming along quickly, all things considered. Derrick thinks it's on track to be done in March.

March.

With Christmas so close, March is right around the corner.

As scared as I am, I'm ready. I feel it deep in my gut that this leap of faith will be worth it. Dreams are a scary thing. So is the risk of failure. But I won't know if I don't try.

The crew paused for a couple of days while they waited for a specific permit from the city, but now that they're moving forward again, actual walls are going up.

"We'll start on your apartment in early January."

Derrick's voice brings me back to reality, and I turn back around to where he stands. "It won't be habitable for a bit, so I wanted to give you enough time to find somewhere to stay. It should take about two weeks to get it all done."

I wince at that. Two weeks is a long time to have to crash at the inn.

"I know, I know. It's not ideal. If I can have it done sooner, I will, but I don't want to make promises I can't keep."

"It'll be fine. I'll figure it out."

Derrick goes on talking, but I'm only half listening to what he's saying. My brain is too busy sorting through all the things I need to get done. And on top of the planning I'm doing for the store and getting temporary housing figured out, Izzy will be back in town for Christmas soon.

"Anyway," he says, smiling at me as my vision comes back into focus once again, "what do you think of that?"

"Of … oh, yeah, sure," I blurt out automatically.

"Cool, I'll pick you up tonight at seven, then."

"Seven? Why?" I draw out the question, giving my mind a chance to replay his words.

His smile falters a little. "For our date. I'm still so sorry about what happened the first time. I've been so busy since then, but I want to make it up to you."

With my heart lodged in my throat, I open my mouth to take back my agreement, but fear gets the best of me. "Yeah, of course. Right. Seven. See you at seven."

Without giving Derrick a chance to question my strange behavior, I turn on my heel and hurry outside. The weather is blisteringly cold, the wind sharp like a slap against my cheeks as I walk blindly down the street.

I have no destination in mind. I just needed to get away from my shop and clear my head. Dammit. I just said *yes* to a date with my boyfriend's dad. My agreement was accidental, but I'm not sure that makes it any better. When I find myself outside the bookstore, I push inside.

Ella looks up from the book she's reading, a smile spreading across her face. "Hey—"

"I said yes to a date with my contractor. Who just so happens to be the father of the guy I'm kind of seeing—who's eleven years younger than me. I'm going to hell, aren't I? I totally am." I throw my head back against the closed door and wince when I smack it harder than I intended. "I'm a horrible person."

"Whoa." Wide-eyed, Ella holds up her hands.

Ugh. I should have eased her into it, but I need advice *now*.

"I'm going to need you to rewind, slow down, and explain all of that again."

I creep toward the counter and lean against it. Exhaustion settles over me like I've just run a marathon. That's how worked up I am over this colossal fuckup I've made.

"You know Derrick, right? The contractor?"

"Well, duh." She tucks a lock of blond hair behind her ear. "Everyone knows Derrick, and we talked about him over margaritas, remember?"

"Right." I wince, rubbing my hands together. "Do you know his son?"

"Not well, but yeah."

"I've been sleeping with his son. We've sort of been seeing each other for a few months now." God, has it really been that long since I first met him? "I went on a date with Derrick. You know that. But that was before Reid and I were really seeing each other and before I knew Derrick was Reid's dad. My sister kind of orchestrated the whole thing." I pause, taking a breath. "Apparently he asked me on another date, and I accidentally said yes."

"Hold on. How do you accidentally say yes to a date?" She shakes her head and huffs a laugh. "And you've been sleeping with his *son*? Damn, this is so much juicier than the book club pick of the month."

Heart sinking, I throw my hands up. "Because I wasn't paying attention to what he was saying." Covering my face, I groan. "What am I going to do?"

She leans back in her chair and snags her phone off the counter. "I think this calls for an emergency book club meeting."

I gape at her as my stomach roils. "I can't tell them about this!"

"Those ladies will have the best advice."

I press my lips together and consider. Dammit. The last thing I want is to become the subject of book club gossip, but I need help. "Fine. Call them."

A COUPLE OF HOURS LATER, I'M PERCHED ON THE hearth at Lucy's house while the ladies take over every seat in the room, forming a circle around me. At this point, I wouldn't be surprised if they pull out candles and perform a séance.

With my heart permanently lodged in my throat, I wring my hands in my lap.

I've caught them all up, and now they're deep in deliberation.

Glenda fixes her attention on me. The look is so intense I swear she can see right through me. "I have a question."

I sit up straighter and swallow thickly. "Okay."

With Glenda, the question could be anything. She could ask whether Reid is allergic to peanuts or—

"Have you slept with the son *and* the dad? I read a book like this once before and—"

Lucy smacks her arm, earning a glare from the older woman. "Glenda, you can't just ask her that!"

"I just did. I'm curious, is all. We've got a real-life smutty book playing out before us. You can't tell me you ladies aren't curious as well."

All eyes shift to me, waiting.

Great, they're really going to make me answer this.

"No," I say, infusing steel into my tone. "I haven't been with Derrick."

Cassandra leans over to whisper to Jessica.

Jessica's response is a little louder. "I totally agree."

"Agree with what?" I ask. I can't help the bite in my tone. They're discussing *my* personal life right in front of me. Plus, Jessica works with Derrick, so that makes this even more embarrassing.

"That you and Reid are like the fated-lovers trope."

My love life is being reduced to book tropes. I guess I should have expected this. I blame Ella for insisting that seeking the advice of our book club crew was a good idea.

"We're not any kind of trope," I insist, slashing my hands through the air. "We're just..."

"Reverse age gap?" Cassandra supplies.

"*Us*," I finish with a huff. "We're just us."

"Well, girly," Glenda wags a finger, "whatever you are, you've just agreed to a date with his dad."

"Thank you, Glenda. I'm aware." The sarcasm drips from my words.

"You have to cancel," Susan says, leaning back on the couch. "It's that simple."

"But what is she going to say?" Anna asks her, gesturing to me. "She can't exactly out her relationship with his son when we don't even know if Reid would be okay with that."

Every comment pulls the knot in my stomach a little tighter.

Tammy snaps her fingers. "Tell him you have cramps. Men are terrified of periods. I've been married for six years, and my husband still refuses to buy tampons for me."

"He won't buy tampons?" Glenda asks in that blunt, gruff way of hers. "Divorce him."

The woman is dead serious.

"I'm not getting a divorce over tampons," Tammy huffs. "Don't be dramatic."

"How am I the dramatic one?" Glenda defends. "I'm not the one scared of wads of cotton."

I mean, she has a point there.

"Whoa, whoa, whoa! Time out!" Ella calls as the room falls into chaos. "We're getting off course here. We're here to help Via, remember? I think we're scaring her." She points at me.

I can only imagine how panic-stricken I look. I'm certainly beginning to feel nauseous.

"Susan is right." She gives me a small, encouraging smile. "You're going to have to call Derrick and cancel."

I cringe. "It feels so mean to cancel on him."

Ella cocks a brow. "Via, you know you can't go on that date."

Shoulders slumping, I sigh. "You're right."

"Take out your phone and make the call."

The ladies start up a chant of "Do it! Do it! Do it!"

So, garnering all the courage I have, I make the call. My stomach churns more violently with each ring.

"Hello?" When Derrick answers, I fight back the urge to throw up.

"Hi ... it's, uh, Via."

He chuckles lightly. "I know. Caller ID is a thing."

I take a deep breath and force the words out in a rush. "I'm so sorry, but I need to cancel our date."

"Oh." The clear disappointment in his tone makes me feel like the shittiest person ever. Derrick is a good guy, but he's not my guy. "Is everything okay?"

"Yes, I'm fine." I grip the phone so tight I all but cut off blood flow to my fingers. I don't have to say more, but I decide to anyway. "You kind of caught me off guard earlier. I didn't think it through before I said yes. I've been seeing someone, and it wouldn't be fair to either of you if I let you take me out."

I close my eyes, heart pounding out of my chest. God, I hope that explanation is enough.

He's quiet for a moment, but eventually, he says, "I understand. Thanks for letting me know."

"Mhm." I hum nervously. "I really am sorry."

"It's okay. Have a good night."

With that, he ends the call. I have the distinct impression I've disappointed him. I can't even be surprised.

It was the right thing to do, but I still feel like a shitty human being for canceling on him. He's a genuinely good guy who deserves to find love. He won't find that with me, but even so, I hate that I've added to the hurt he's already endured.

Ella gives me a thumbs-up. "You did the right thing."

The other ladies chime in their agreement. Despite the uneasiness still flowing through me, I can't help but smile. I didn't have a support system like this in San Francisco. All my friends were *our* friends. Chase's and mine. And most were people we worked with, so none of those relationships were more than surface level anyway.

Lucy stands from the couch. "This calls for wine."

"Yes," I gasp gratefully. "Wine. Please."

It's late, nearing midnight, when I finally park outside my apartment. I stopped drinking hours ago, but we stayed up laughing and talking.

Tapping the lock button on my key fob, I start up the stairs. I'm halfway up when I realize the outdoor light isn't flickering. It's fully lit, and on the top step, Reid sits, waiting for me.

"Reid?"

He looks up at me then, though surely he heard my approach before now. "I fixed your light."

His tone is even, though it's laced with a tinge of annoyance.

"I ... thank you."

He looks at me fully then, and the pain in his expression forces my feet to halt a few stairs below him. "How was your date?"

Fuck.

I didn't even consider that he'd hear about it. If I had, I would've called him the second my call with Derrick ended.

"I wouldn't know," I reply easily. "I didn't go."

His eyes narrow. "Via." My name is a husky growl on his lips, turning my insides to liquid. "Why were you going on a date with my dad?"

I wince. "I didn't mean to say yes. I swear. He was talking about the renovations. I zoned out, and the next thing I knew, he was asking me something, and I blurted out yes. Then, when I realized he'd asked me out, I panicked. I know it looks bad, but I called him and canceled. I explained that I've been seeing someone—"

He grasps me around the legs and hauls me into his body, pulling a gasp from me. "I told you before," he growls, his lips brushing mine with each word, "that I can fuck you better than my dad. It looks like I'm going to have to remind you of that."

He crushes his mouth to mine, rough and bruising. The kiss is full of anguish. God, I'm the worst person ever. I didn't mean to make him feel shitty.

I kiss him back, putting everything I have into it, showing him that he's the only man who matters to me.

"Say it," he demands. "Say you're mine."

A shiver runs up my spine at his possessive request. I *like* it.

"I'm yours."

"That's right, angel." He nips at my ear. "You're mine. Don't forget it again." He stands and carries me across the porch. "Key," he demands.

"In my purse."

He props me against the door, removing the bag from my shoulder. Once he's found the key and shuffled inside with me still in his arms, he sets me down with surprising gentleness and locks up behind us.

He takes off his coat and tosses it onto the couch. His sweatshirt follows it. Then his t-shirt.

He stops there, shoving his hands into the pockets of his

jeans. The move tugs them down so the top of his boxer briefs shows.

The silver chain around his neck glints in the light I left on earlier.

"Take your clothes off. All of them."

This version of Reid is vastly different from the one who made love to me just a few days ago. Though I don't like this version any less. It excites me in a way I haven't experienced before. And I know, without a doubt, that if I wasn't comfortable with this, he would stop in a heartbeat.

But from the very beginning, he's sensed this side of me—before I even knew it was a thing.

Slowly, I remove my clothes, piece by piece.

Reid leans back against the wall, crossing one leg over the other, and watches. His gaze is intense, never faltering.

"I'm sorry for hurting you."

His eyes narrow. "I think you did it on purpose."

My heart lurches. "What? No! I—"

Suddenly he's right in front of me, hand loose around my throat. He tilts my head back, forcing me to meet his stare. "Subconsciously, you wanted this. Wanted me to show you how much better I can pleasure you than any other man."

He seals his lips over mine. The kiss is possessive, deep. I feel it all the way in my soul.

He releases me abruptly, and I stumble.

"Turn around, Via, and put your hands on the wall."

Without a moment of hesitation, I obey. My body responds to his every command. How does this guy, who's more than a decade younger than me, know exactly what I want and need even when *I* don't?

"Spread your legs."

My heart thuds loudly, but I do as I'm told, then wait for what comes next.

I want to look back at him more than anything, but I will myself to stay still.

I nearly jump when his finger ghosts down my spine, stopping just before he reaches my ass. Then his touch disappears. I hold my breath in anticipation of where he'll touch me next.

"Such a good girl," he croons.

A sharp pain erupts in my right butt cheek, pulling a startled scream from me.

I drop my chin and heave in a breath. Though I can't see him, I can feel him crouched behind me, like he's assessing the bite mark he's left on my skin. There's a rustling, and it's killing me not to know what he's doing.

"Can I take a picture?" he asks, his tone soft. "I want to draw this later." He traces his finger around the bite mark.

The urge to say no is strong. The idea of a nude photo of me on his phone is hot, but terrifying. The old me would've immediately said no.

"Only for you, right?"

"Just me."

If I say no, he'll honor my request, but the idea of him drawing me like this sends a wave of desire through me.

Stomach fluttering, I nod. "Okay."

He takes the photo, then rubs my ass, his touch gentle over the bite mark.

My hands are beginning to shake where I have them pressed to the wall. It's harder to stay still than I thought it would be. Craning my neck, I peer back at him.

He smirks up at me from where he's kneeling on the ground. He's still wearing his jeans, but he's undone the belt and button. "Eyes on the wall, angel."

I hesitate for only a second, but from the slap he lands to my ass, my obedience wasn't as automatic as he'd like. My knees join in with my hands, trembling, though for a different reason. The slap hurt, but it also felt strangely good.

For a long moment, he doesn't move again, making me squirm in anticipation.

Just when I'm ready to give in to my curiosity again and look over my shoulder, he presses in behind me, forcing me to spread wider. His mouth is on my pussy in the next instant, stealing a gasp from my throat.

He chuckles, the sound vibrating against my core. He works his tongue against me until I'm on the brink of orgasm, then stops.

The desire unfurling sputters out, and I whimper.

He smooths his palms over the backs of my thighs, up around my butt, and settles them on my waist. Slowly, he rises and presses into me, his jeans rough against my sensitive skin. I bite my lip harder at the feel of his erection grinding against me.

"Did you like knowing I was on my knees for you, even when you're being punished?"

I nod, giving a soft "Yes."

"What were you thinking, Via, saying yes to another date with my dad?" He rolls my hips back against him.

It takes everything in me not to moan. "I-I wasn't thinking. I-It was an accident, like I told you."

"You're never going to let something like that happen, are you?"

"No."

"No what?" He trails his lips down the column of my neck.

"I won't make the same mistake again."

He hums, his body vibrating against me. "That's right. You're mine."

His hands leave my hips. Then there's the sound of clothes rustling. I know better than to look away from the wall, so I let my imagination run wild, picturing the way he's sliding his jeans down and kicking them away. I bet he takes his cock in his hand, squeezes—

I'm pulled from my fantasy when he turns me around and lifts me up like I weigh nothing.

"No condom?" he asks, his focus intense and locked on my face, checking with me to be sure I haven't changed my mind.

I shake my head.

"Thank fuck."

Holding me up against the wall with one arm, he uses his free hand to guide his cock inside me.

"*Oh my God*," I cry, the sensation far more intense than I expected. Maybe because of the position or maybe because he left me on the brink of orgasm moments ago and my body is so keyed up. Either way, it's obvious it'll take very little to set me off.

"Scream *my* name, angel. I'm the one doing this to you. I'm the one bringing you pleasure. Give me the credit I fucking deserve." He thrusts into me harder and harder with each commanding word, until I'm a shaking, delirious mess.

"Reid," I cry, just like he ordered.

"*Yes,*" he groans into my neck. In one quick move, he pulls me from the wall and lowers us to the floor so that I'm riding him. His fingers dig into my hips, his abdominals flexing. "Fuck, Via, you were made for me."

Those words send me toppling over the edge. I fall apart piece by piece, and when I'm nothing but a boneless heap, I collapse on top of him. Reid wraps his arms around me and kisses me while he works himself in and out of my exhausted body until he finds his own release.

We lie, tangled together, coming down from the high of the moment. My heart is beating like I ran a marathon.

Reid brushes my damp hair off my forehead, smiling. "Hi." His sweet tone is in complete juxtaposition to the way he was talking only moments ago.

"Hi," I say back, resting my chin on his hard chest.

"I didn't scare you, did I?" His lips are suddenly turned down and his face is drawn.

"No. You always make me feel safe. I trust you."

He traces his finger over the curve of my cheek. "Good."

"I really am sorry."

His smile grows. "I know."

We lie like that for a long time. When we finally pull ourselves apart, it's only so Reid can tug me into my bedroom, where he makes sweet, gentle love to me, like he wants to make sure I understand that he's capable of loving me in all the ways I need.

thirty-four

Reid

"Mmm, right there is perfect," Layla directs, watching as my dad and I maneuver the couch into her new apartment. "No, no. To your left just a smidge."

"Layla," I groan, dripping with sweat. "Make up your mind."

She purses her lips and shoots me an annoyed look. Lili does the same thing with her mouth when she's perturbed.

"Once you move it a little to the left, it'll be perfect." My dad and I make the smallest move in the direction she wants. "There! Set it down. That's perfect."

Hands on my hips, I arch a brow at my dad. "Tell me again why we didn't pay for professional movers."

"Because, son," he slaps me on the shoulder and heads for the door to get more stuff, "we have enough muscle to do this for free."

I turn to my sister and shoot her an annoyed glare. She sticks her tongue out at me.

No matter how old you get, you revert back to being a child with your sibling.

At least she didn't move into my apartment complex. I love my sister and my niece, but I'm not sure I could handle having them so close. I can picture it now—Lili getting frustrated with her mom and showing up at my door, demanding I take her side. I love that little girl more than anything, but I don't like being put in the middle of things.

Kind of like how I hate that my dad is interested in my girl, since he doesn't know she's my girl. Fuck.

We unload more stuff: pieces of furniture my dad gave Layla, a few thrift store finds, and boxes of books, craft supplies, and Lili's toys.

When we've brought the last of it into the small apartment, I collapse on the couch. "You have too much shit," I complain. "I didn't have nearly this much stuff when I moved."

"Uncle Weed," Lili singsongs, rocking back and forth on her heels. "You said a bad word."

"I did. That was wrong of me. Sorry, Lili."

She holds her hand out. "Pay up."

I sigh, cursing myself. When I was watching her a few weeks ago, I dropped an F-bomb when I stubbed my toe.

The little monster made me pay her ten bucks to keep her mouth shut.

Only this time, my dad and Layla are in the room, watching the whole exchange with barely contained amusement.

"You know," I sit up, pulling out my wallet, "most kids would just run a lemonade stand for cash." I slap a dollar in her palm.

Lili stuffs it in her pocket. "This is easier."

Laughter busts out of me. Freaking kids.

"Why are you paying my kid?" Layla asks, eyes narrowed and arms crossed over her chest.

When Lili spins and pops a hip, I know I'm in deep shit. "Because Uncle Weed said fuck and paid me to keep it a secret. Now I want money every time he says a bad word."

"*Reid.*" My dad closes his eyes and rubs the bridge of his nose. "You can't pay her off so she won't rat you out."

I point at Lili. "Clearly not. You weren't supposed to say anything."

She giggles. "Oops."

Throwing her hands up, Layla says, "I don't even know what to say."

Shaking his head, Dad cuts open a box labeled *Lilibet's Room*. "Reid, make yourself useful and order pizza."

I salute him. "You got it."

He sighs, dropping his head back to look up at the ceiling. I bet he's asking the heavens where he went wrong.

I place the order and opt for pickup instead of delivery since the charge they want to add is ridiculous. I have no problem tipping, but charging a whole other fee on top of that? Nah, I'll drive over there when it's ready and get it.

Before I go, I unpack a few boxes and put stuff into the piles Layla's sorted. She's stressed, and when she's stressed, she micromanages, so I go with it. Along with the tension, though, is a hint of excitement. Living with our dad meant she had help with Lili when she needed it, but this step is one she's needed to take for a long time. Having a place of her own and a work-from-home job we convinced her to apply for with the vlogger is giving her a confidence I thought she'd lost forever.

Twenty minutes in, I peek at my watch. "I'll be right back with the pizzas," I promise, tugging my sweatshirt back on and then shrugging on my coat.

Layla points a box cutter at me from her position on the floor. "You did this on purpose so you could get a break, didn't you?"

"Maybe." I draw out the word.

"Bring me a coffee, *please*." She sets the box cutter down and puts her hands together in front of her in a begging motion. "I need food and caffeine."

I sigh like stopping for coffee is a massive hardship. "If I have to."

"Thank you," she singsongs.

"I want ice cream!" Lili yells from her new bedroom.

"No," the three of us chorus.

"Aw. You guys suck," she grumbles.

I let myself out of the apartment, and on my way to my car, I check my phone, hoping for a text from Via. My notification screen is blank. It shouldn't bother me, I know she's busy, but I *like* hearing from her.

Once I've got the pizzas—one extra-large supreme for us adults and a small cheese for Lili—I head toward the nearby coffee shop.

When I step inside, I spot the back of a very familiar head. I can't control the smile that comes to my lips.

I step up behind her in line and angle in close. "Fancy running into you here."

Via practically jumps out of her skin. "Jesus Christ, Reid! You scared me!" She swats lightly at my chest. "Don't do that."

I chuckle, shoving my hands in my pockets. "Sorry."

She purses her lips. "Don't lie. You're not the least bit sorry."

While she's trying to act perturbed, her eyes are alight. She's happy to see me.

"You haven't texted me today."

She looks away briefly, then back with a shy smile. "You're with your family. I wanted to give you space." Her brows pull down, and she tilts her head. "Why are you here? Shouldn't you be with them?"

"I was picking up pizza, and Layla wanted coffee."

"Well, aren't you a nice little brother?"

I chuckle, adjusting my glasses. "I try."

A throat clears, drawing our attention. "Um," the barista hedges, "it's your turn now."

Via steps up to place her order, and before she can pay, I step around her and order an iced caramel coffee for Layla.

How she drinks iced coffee when it's ten degrees outside is beyond me. I'll take my simple coffee with French vanilla creamer over this any day.

I hand over cash, and while I'm waiting for the change, Via glares at me. God, she's fucking adorable when she's mad.

"What?" I ask with a smirk. I nod to the barista and drop some of the change into the tip jar.

"I was going to pay for it. I could've gotten your sister's too."

We move to the side to wait for our order. "I know you could've, but I *like* doing things for you."

Her shoulders sag. "I ... you really do, don't you?"

"Yep."

"That's different for me, you know. Chase didn't do stuff like that. Not that he didn't pay for my stuff, but you're constantly taking care of me in different ways. You replaced my porch light."

I shrug. It's not a big deal. "Your ex is an asshole."

She presses her lips together in a thin line. "I was so stupid."

"Hey," I growl, tipping her chin up with my index finger so she'll meet my eyes. "Don't say stuff like that. Frankly, I'm thankful for the guy."

Laughter bursts out of her. "Why?"

"Because he fumbled, you found your way here and to me."

I've never considered myself a selfish person, but from the moment I saw Via, I wanted to make her mine. She's the most captivating person I've ever come across. It's no wonder my dad is entranced by her.

"Are you saying we were destined to meet?"

"Mmm," I hum, rocking back on my heels. "I'm not sure I believe in destiny, but if there is such a thing, then yeah, you're mine."

When our order comes up, I snag a straw and put a hand to the small of Via's back to guide her to the door. I selfishly want to touch her while I can. Her sister's coming into town for Christmas, and even though she knows about us, I'm not sure how much I'll get to see of Via while she's here.

Out in the parking lot, I don't let go. I keep my hand on her the whole way to her car.

She leans against her driver's side door and tilts her head back to look up at me. Dark lashes coated with mascara fan against her cheeks. A light pink gloss shines on her lips. Her makeup is subtle, highlighting her natural beauty.

"Do I get a kiss?" My breath fogs in the air, filling the space between us.

"Do you have to ask?" She cocks a brow.

I grin and press my lips to hers. She tastes like strawberries, either because she was eating them before she came to get coffee or because of her lip gloss.

When we part, she unlocks her car and opens the door, standing behind it like a shield against me. It's cute she thinks any barrier could dampen the connection between us.

"I'm not sure if I believe in destiny either," she admits,

her cheeks pink from the brisk cold. "But since I was a little girl, I've done this thing. Where I wish on elevens. When the clock turns to 11:11, it's like a sign. Angel numbers," she goes on. "The night I came to Parkerville, I wished on 11:11 that this move would be the right thing. I think that wish came true when I met you."

She sinks onto the seat and closes the door before I can formulate a response. Her car starts, the sound of the engine forcing me to step away.

I watch her drive away with the dopiest grin on my face.

It wasn't an *I love you*, but it was pretty fucking close.

thirty-five

Via

"This town is magical." Izzy does a spin in front of me and nearly face-plants when her foot hits a patch of ice.

"Careful," I tell her, grasping her arm to steady her as passersby gawk. "You never know where black ice might be."

At the mention of black ice, my mind goes to Derrick. I truly feel terrible for the whole date thing, and I'm still cursing myself for not asking him to just repeat himself. I don't like that I hurt him, even if it wasn't intentional.

I loop my arm through my sister's, lest she attempt that spin again. I picked her up from the airport and dropped her off at the inn to settle in for a couple of hours before we came out tonight.

"I'm surprised you like it here." *I* love it, of course. The small-town vibe is what drew me here in the first place. But I never expected my jet-setting vlogger sister to like it too.

"What's not to like?" she counters. Her smile is so wide I know if I wasn't holding onto her, she'd spin again.

That's something I've always been envious of. Izzy's not afraid to have fun. There's a freeness to her that I never got as the eldest child.

I was expected to follow the rules, get good grades, and excel in a respectable career, while Izzy was allowed to *dream*. Though these days, I'm finally living for myself.

"Look how cute this place is. It has this charm about it."

It does. Every roof is covered in snow, and lights twinkle from the eaves and around the streetlights. Every inch of town is draped in magic.

"When are you moving here, then?" I joke as we near the walk-through light show at the park.

"Don't tempt me. I love it here, but…"

I fight a smile. "But?"

She twists her lips back and forth and hums. "So many of my business opportunities are in LA. If I moved here, it would mean constantly flying to LA. It feels like it would defeat the purpose."

"It would be difficult." It's one of those things that, right now, where she's at in her career, doesn't make sense.

"Funnily enough," she begins, steering me toward the snack stand set up outside the entrance, "I hired an assistant to help me with some of my social media stuff, and believe it or not, she's from a town near here."

"Really? What are the odds of that?" I ask as we settle in line.

"I know, right? Her application stood out for its brutal honesty. The girl has been through a lot. Her story really struck me, and then when I saw where she was from, it felt like kismet. We're going to meet up in person while I'm in town so we can hang out and get to know each other."

"That's cool." She truly needs the help, and it's obvious she's excited. "I'm glad you're finally letting someone help you."

"I struggled with it. I get a lot of criticism for not having a 'real job.' It felt a little pathetic to say I need help with social media." She frowns, looking down at her gloved hands. The tip of her nose is turning red from the cold.

"Not pathetic at all." I bump her shoulder. "You're growing a business."

She sighs, biting her bottom lip. "I guess."

My heart aches at the defeat in her posture. "Is something wrong?"

With such a large online following, Izzy has to deal with people who get a sick satisfaction out of being cruel and tearing her down. My sister is one of the kindest, most genuine people out there, and because of that, she can take mean things to heart way too easily.

"I guess I'm just wondering if it's all going to last."

I frown as the line shifts forward another step. "Where's this coming from?"

"Mom and Dad sat me down and pointed out that the internet can be a harsh place. They think I should have a backup plan. I'm good with money, and I save a lot, but I am young. They're probably right. I should have some idea of what comes next."

I gape at her, my stomach sinking. As soon as she mentioned our parents, I knew they'd gotten in her head. For the most part, they've always been far more supportive of Izzy than they are of me, but at the end of the day, they're still practical people.

"It's not worth worrying about that right now. You're young, and you love what you do. Don't overthink it. Enjoy life the way it is. I promise everything will fall into place."

She looks at me, eyes intent. "Do you feel like things have fallen into place for you?"

I only hesitate for a moment. "Yes. Am I where I thought I'd be at thirty-two? No. I thought I'd still be married," I bark out a sharp laugh. "And I thought I'd be a mom."

The pain that comes with that statement isn't as easy to ignore as it has been in the past.

"Via." My name is a sad exhale. She pulls me into a hug. "I wholeheartedly believe it'll happen for you one day."

I bite my lip to keep the tears at bay. "I hope so."

Squeezing my hand, she says, "Don't lose hope. I can always be your surrogate."

My heart tumbles in my chest with so much force I have to press a hand to my breastbone. "Are you serious?"

"Yeah. I'd do anything for you. If you want a biological child and need me, my womb services are open."

I laugh, beyond thankful for the levity she brings to this situation. I can't imagine ever taking her up on the offer, but I appreciate it, nonetheless. I'm lucky to have a sister who cares so much. "Thanks."

"Any time." She does a little shimmy.

When it's finally our turn, we order two specialty peppermint mochas and the mini gingerbread-flavored donuts.

While we wait for our order, Izzy tugs on her beanie. "In LA, this would be nothing but a photo opportunity." She says it softly, like she's lost in her thoughts. "It's so..." She pulls in a long breath and scans our surroundings. "Vapid. It's filled with people desperate to make it—to be remembered."

She's drenched in a layer of sadness she's normally so good at hiding. But she's letting me see it, letting me in.

"Iz, if you want to leave, you should."

She sighs heavily, her breath fogging the air. "I don't know what I want anymore. That's the problem." Her smile is a mix of melancholy and defeat. "I love so many parts of what I do. I don't want to stop, but when I came to see you in October, this place felt ... *real*. Does that make any sense?"

"Yeah." I smile, my heart warming a little. "It does."

Parkerville is special. It speaks to us James girls.

With our order in hand, we follow the pathway through

the light show. The coffee keeps us warm, and the mini donuts are so delicious we both want more before we leave.

We're on our way back through, almost to the main entrance, when Izzy lets out a shrill scream that has me ducking down for fear we're under attack.

But it's not that at all.

Up ahead of us are Reid, his sister, and his niece.

At first, I think Reid is the reason for her shrieking, but as Izzy runs toward them, it's obvious her excitement is over Layla.

"Oh my Gosh," Izzy says, throwing her arms around the woman. "How crazy to run into you here. It's so nice to meet you in person." She steps back. "I'm Izzy."

"I know who you are," Layla laughs, her cheeks pink.

"Come here, Via." My sister waves me forward. "This is Layla. I was telling you about her earlier. She's my new assistant."

Layla smiles at me. I don't think she recognizes me, and I'm thankful for that. "Hi, it's nice to meet you. What a small world."

"The smallest," I agree, looking Reid over.

He roughs a hand down his face, hiding a smirk. His glasses are a tad askew, and there's stubble on his cheeks like he hasn't had a chance to shave today.

"This is my brother, Reid," Layla says to my sister. "And my daughter, Lili."

"Reid," my sister muses, glancing at me. I keep my face neutral, not wanting to give anything away.

"It's nice to meet you." Reid extends a hand to my little

sister. She shakes it, but I know she's wondering if he's *my* Reid.

When she's not looking, he shoots a smirk my way. I narrow my eyes, silently warning him to keep it together.

"We're on our way out, but I'll see you for lunch, okay? I hope you guys have fun." Izzy wiggles her fingers at Lili, who smiles shyly in return.

Thank God the little girl has been occupied looking at the princess light display around us. Otherwise, I'm fairly certain she would've accidentally ratted Reid and me out.

I walk away before she can take notice of me. Izzy catches up and clutches my arm.

"Is that *him*?" She looks over her shoulder and squeals. "It has to be. He was looking at you like he wanted to eat you."

"Izzy," I hiss.

"Is it?"

"Yes." I make a beeline toward the food stand. I might want to avoid this conversation, but I want those mini donuts more.

"I knew it!" She scans the park again, probably considering following Reid to interrogate him, but he's already out of sight.

"Keep your voice down."

She rolls her eyes. "No one's paying attention to us. Can you believe I hired his *sister*, of all people? Freaking crazy." She takes a breath, and I say a prayer that this will be the end of it, but I know that's unlikely. "He's super hot. Your description didn't do him justice. And the glasses? I think I might be developing a glasses kink." She fans herself, bursting into laughter when she sees the look on my face. "Via, are you getting jealous?"

"No." The word is pure defensiveness. Okay, so maybe I *am* jealous hearing her talk about him like that.

I've never felt possessive before, but right now, I feel like I have those seagulls from *Finding Nemo*, shouting *mine, mine, mine* in my head.

"Do you love him?"

Do I love him?

That question terrifies me.

After what Chase did to me, I didn't think I'd love again. I didn't *want* to. Being that vulnerable again scared me.

But Reid has woven his way into my heart. He's stitched the broken pieces together, mended the cracks and tears. I'm scared to give him those three words, and he knows it. It's why he hasn't spoken them to me. He's afraid he'll scare me away.

I let a man who never deserved me affect how I handle the man who does.

"It's okay," Izzy says when we reach the car. "You don't have to tell me. I already know the answer."

I'm afraid I do too.

thirty-six

Reid

A few days before Christmas, I get a call to interview for a full-time position at a new garage set to open about thirty minutes from home. Out of all the places I applied, this is the one I want most since they plan to do restoration work as well as basic maintenance and repairs.

I hang up feeling excited in a way I haven't been for a long time.

I'm supposed to meet my friends at Monday's in a few hours. The last time I was there was my birthday. The night I met Via. It feels like forever ago—like I've known her my whole life, not just a few months.

Yes, I'm young, but I'm serious about her.

Via isn't just a *right now* kind of thing for me. She's not a fling. She's the real deal. The woman I want to grow old with. I think she sees that too, and it scares her. But she'll get there. I have faith in her—in us.

She thinks I'm too young to know what I want. For other guys my age, maybe that's true, but I know what we have is rare, and I won't let that go because she thinks I need to experience life. I'd rather experience life with her than without her.

To kill time before I head to the bar, I tidy up around my place and shower.

I've been doing a piss-poor job of seeing my friends over the last few months. During my spare time, I prefer hanging out with Via. Not to mention that I'm rarely interested in what they have planned. I've never enjoyed the bar scene, but they threatened to drag my ass out of my apartment if I didn't show tonight. And since Via's spending the holiday with her sister, and I have nothing else to do, I might as well. It'll be good to catch up with everyone.

Monday's is packed when I arrive. I have to circle the lot a few times before I find a place to park. It's not an actual parking spot, but it'll do. I shoot a text to Justin, asking if anyone else is there.

> Justin: Yeah, man. We're waiting on you.

I laugh, shaking my head. Of course they are.

Once inside, I find them at a table off to the left, near the kitchens.

"You made it!" Will says, spreading his arms wide and almost hitting Max in the head in the process.

"We were taking bets on whether you'd show up," Justin says.

I pull out the chair beside him and drop into it. They've been here long enough to polish off half the appetizers scattered across the table.

"Yeah, dude." Lawson leans around Justin. "Where have you been?"

Justin snorts. "Reid's got a girlfriend now, so he's too good for us."

Max shoots me a surprised look. "Since when?"

"Why haven't you told us?" Will drops his elbows to the table and leans forward.

I shrug. "I don't know. It's..."

It's on the tip of my tongue to say it's not serious, but that would be a lie. I don't know how much I want to tell them. I love my friends, but they'll give me shit.

Unfortunately, Justin opens his big fat mouth. "He's dating that woman from his birthday. The older chick. The one we saw at the coffee shop that time."

The older chick. I instantly bristle. That's the best he can do to describe Via? Sure, he doesn't *know* her, but the way he refers to her is so fucking rude. I eye the empty beer glass to his right and the half-full one beside it. This only adds to my annoyance. Despite how my mother died, none of my friends really understand why I feel the way I do about alcohol. This right here is only demonstrating my point.

When people get drunk, they get stupid.

"Her name is Via," I bite out through gritted teeth. "And what do you mean you saw her at the coffee shop?"

Via never mentioned anything to me, and neither did Justin until now.

He crows, oblivious to my annoyance. "He's so whipped for her."

Will, the only one of my friends who has a girlfriend—high school sweethearts—takes in the expression on my face and sits up straighter. "Nothing wrong with being whipped for the right person." He clears his throat. "She was sitting at a coffee shop once when the four of us met up there. Justin's got a crush on the barista. We didn't bother her. Justin just said hi. That's all."

Hi? Somehow, I doubt that. All I can hope is he didn't say something stupid.

"Why didn't you tell us about her?" Max asks.

I turn to him and shrug. "We haven't exactly gone public yet."

Lawson snorts. "Public. What are you? A celebrity?"

"No," I draw out the word, "but my dad tried to date her, so that kind of complicates things, don't you think?"

My dad won't be angry when we tell him, at least I don't think he will be. Regardless, Via is the first woman he's shown interest in since my mom passed. I want him to move on. He deserves that. But I can't help but worry that when he finds out about us, he'll be even less inclined to want to date.

My friends fall silent, a feat that I might later pat myself on the back for.

"Hold on." Max stifles a laugh. "Your dad is interested in your girl?"

"He doesn't know she's my girl."

"This is a soap opera." Lawson chortles, almost choking on his beer.

I lean back in my chair. "I'm aware."

The waitress drops by, so I order dinner, opting to skip the beer. The smell alone is getting to me tonight.

"When are you going to tell him?" Will asks, shoveling nachos onto his plate.

I twist my lips back and forth. "We haven't decided."

"You're serious about her?" The question comes from Max.

"Yep."

"How serious?" This time from Justin.

"Very."

Justin, Lawson, and Max are all wide-eyed and baffled, but Will gives me a knowing look.

"Another one bites the dust." Lawson takes a swig of his beer. "Which one of us do you think is next, boys?"

"Not me." Justin picks up his beer. "I'm not ready for something serious."

Max laughs, pointing at him. "And that right there is exactly why it'll be you."

I'M TIRED WHEN I GET HOME, BUT I TAKE A SHOWER before climbing into bed so I can wash off the bar smell I carried home with me. Once I'm settled under the blankets, I send a text to Via.

> Me: My friends said they ran into you at a coffee shop. I hope they didn't say or do anything to upset you.

I'm not surprised when it takes her a few minutes to respond.

> Via: They were fine. Only one guy actually talked to me.

> Me: Justin?

> Via: That sounds right.

> Me: What did he say?

The curiosity is eating away at me. I probably shouldn't care this much, especially since it'll just piss me off if he acted like an ass.

My phone rings, so I quickly tap Accept.

"Hey."

She laughs softly over the sound of a door closing in the background. "I could feel your anxiety through your texts, so I figured I'd call you."

I groan, crooking my elbow over my eyes. "My friends are idiots. I wanted to make sure he wasn't rude."

"No, nothing like that. He said that you really like me and that you're a good guy. He also told me not to hurt you."

I'm silent. Struck speechless. That was the last thing I was expecting.

"Really?"

"Mhm," she hums.

Her mattress squeaks, and I'm instantly hard at the thought of her lying in her bed. I'm absolutely fucking pathetic, I know.

"It took me by surprise."

"Yeah," I laugh. "Me too. I thought..."

"You thought what?"

I blow out a breath. "Most of my friends aren't interested in settling down, so I thought he might try to scare you off."

"He wouldn't be a very good friend, then. But no. He seems like he genuinely cares about you."

"He's given me a hard time about this more than once, so I'm glad to know that in his own weird way, he approves."

She laughs again. "You worry too much."

I press my lips together so I don't laugh. "Via..."

"I know, I know. *I'm* the worrier in this relationship."

"At least you're self-aware."

She stifles a yawn. "Izzy wore me out today. She wanted to go to this record store to take photos and vlog. Only when I brought it up, she forgot to mention that it was an hour and a half away. I *hate* driving in this weather. I white-knuckled it the whole way there and back while she laughed at me. I offered to let her drive, and that sobered her up real quick."

"I think your sister just likes to watch you squirm."

"Probably." She sighs, and her sheets rustle like she's turning over. "She wants to meet you."

Even though she can't see me, I grin. "She did meet me. At the light show."

"For all of five seconds, and now she won't let it go." I picture Via in her bed, lips pouted in annoyance.

"Do you *want* me to meet her?" I want to be a part of Via's life in every way. I'd love to meet her sister for real, but I won't put that pressure on her.

She doesn't respond right away. The only sound is her soft breathing. "Yeah, I think I do."

I smile to myself. Fuck, this feels like a monumental feat.

"We'll figure something out while she's here."

"Okay." Her voice is small, nervous.

"Don't stress about it, angel."

"I'm not stressing," she says in a tone that confirms that she most definitely is.

"Are you in bed?" I ask to distract her, knowing good and well that's exactly where she is.

"Yes, why?"

Wetting my lips, I put her on speaker and lay my phone on the mattress beside me. "What are you wearing?" I cross my hands behind my head, looking up at the ceiling.

"What am I—Reid, why are you asking that?"

"Play along, Via," I say in that way that I know makes her go weak in the knees.

"I ... are we about to have phone sex?"

I chuckle. God, she amuses me. She might be older than me, but in some ways, she's so damn innocent. "Yes."

"Oh." She swallows audibly. "I'm in my pajamas."

"Be more specific."

"I'm not wearing anything sexy, if that's what you're getting at."

"*Via.*"

"I'm in gray sweatpants and an *American Idol* concert tee."

"You went to an *American Idol* concert?" I shake my head. "Never mind."

"They used to go on tour," she huffs. "I went solely for Adam Lambert."

I laugh. "God, you're cute when you defend yourself."

She groans. "I'm not good at this, Reid. I feel weird."

"I can stop." I won't make her do anything she doesn't like.

"I ... I don't want you to. I'm just..."

"I'll talk you through it, angel. Put me on speaker."

"Okay, you're on speaker now."

"Good girl. Now, I want you to put the phone beside you."

"All right."

"Have you missed me?" I ask, easing into things. With her sister in town, I haven't seen her much.

"Yes," she admits. "With my phone on speaker, it sounds like you're right beside me."

"Just pretend I am, sweetheart. If I was there right now, what would I be doing?"

"I ... k-kissing my neck."

"Kissing your neck, huh? And then what would I do?"

I'm letting her start this off, letting her guide the pace.

"You'd move down my body, pushing my shirt up beneath my breasts so you could kiss my stomach." She sounds more confident now. Without my prompting, she says, "Then you'd slide my legs onto your shoulders and ... and lick my pussy."

I groan and squeeze my dick through my boxer briefs. "You're killing me, Via. Do you have any idea how sexy you are?"

She gives a tiny, breathless moan.

"Via?"

Just her breaths filter down the line to me.

"Are you touching yourself right now, angel?"

"Y-Yes," she moans. "I'm pretending it's your hand and your mouth and—"

"Fuck, baby." I shove my underwear down and stroke myself.

"Are you...?"

"Yeah, I am. Hold on a sec."

I FaceTime her, though I half expect her to ignore the call. My heart pounds when she answers and her face appears.

Her breath catches when she sees that I have the screen

flipped so she can watch me. She bites her bottom lip, but it doesn't hide the quiver. Her eyes are hooded, hazy, as she watches me work up and down on my cock.

"Do you want me to turn my camera?" she asks on a breathy exhale.

"No." The word is a little harsher than I intended. "I want to see your face. Keep touching yourself, baby."

"I'm close," she says. The camera dips a bit, showing off her bare shoulder where her oversized shirt has slid down her arm. When she realizes the camera isn't on her face, she quickly adjusts it. Her cheeks are flushed, illuminated by the soft glow of the lights on the street outside her bedroom window.

"Me too." I twist my hand around the head of my cock, ignoring how ridiculous it is that I'm on the verge of coming this quickly.

"*Reid.*" My name is a moan, a plea, and a prayer all rolled into one.

She arches her neck, and the camera dips again. This time, I get a glimpse of the swell of her breasts.

The little moans that escape her as she comes down from the high of her orgasm snap the last of my control. I groan, dirtying my sheets and hand with sticky white cum.

"That's so hot," she says breathlessly, her eyes glazed over as she looks at the mess I've made of myself because of her. Her bottom lip is swollen from where she was biting it. She looks so fucking kissable.

I tap my screen to turn my camera so she can see my face.

She smiles at me. "Thank you."

I chuckle. "You're thanking me for an orgasm I didn't *actually* give you."

"Just because you're not in bed with me doesn't mean it's not because of you." She rolls over, taking the camera with her. "I'll work out a plan so you can meet Izzy properly. Okay?"

I smile, victorious. This is a big deal for her.

"Okay," I echo. "Get some sleep, Via."

"Good night." She surprises me when she blows me a kiss before she ends the call.

When the call disconnects, I'm left grinning like a fool at the darkened screen.

Fuck, I'm such a goner for this woman.

thirty-seven

Via

Izzy's glee at my discomfort has me tempted to pull over and push her out of my car.

"Can you stop smiling like that?" I gripe. She's making it hard to concentrate on the directions the navigation system is relaying. We're headed to the Mexican restaurant Reid suggested we meet him at.

"How do you know I'm smiling? I'm not even looking at you," she counters.

"Number one, because I have peripheral vision. Number two, because I can *feel* it."

She giggles. "Don't be so sensitive. I'm *excited* for you. I want you to be happy, and Reid clearly makes you happy."

"I'm not being sensitive," I defend, even though I most definitely am.

I don't know why I'm so on edge. This meeting was inevitable, and it'll be fine, but my nerves are rattled regardless.

"You totally are." Izzy's superpower has always been calling me on my bullshit. "I just don't understand why." She turns in her seat and tucks a leg under her. "What are you worried about? Just tell me. Does his breath smell? Does he have a third nipple? Missing teeth? Come on, spill it."

I take a deep breath, easing the car to a stop at the red light. "No, none of that."

"Then what is it?"

I twist my lips back and forth. It's going to sound so stupid when I say it out loud. But with a sigh, I go for it. "I guess I'm scared you'll look at us and realize how much younger than me he really is and have a big laugh about it."

She opens her mouth, but before she can respond, I go on.

"Logically, I know you wouldn't, and it's not even about you specifically. It's just that ... we don't *fit*."

"What do you mean? The two of you have so much in common."

I ease my foot off the brake. "I mean it in more of a physical way. He's only twenty-one. The age difference is obvious, and you know how society is. No one bats an eye when a man dates a young woman. But for a woman to date a guy more than a decade younger than her? There will be judgment."

She's quiet for a moment, watching the scenery out the window. "What does it matter? Last time I checked, you're not in a relationship with society. If you and Reid are happy, then, at the end of the day, that's *all* that matters. The rest be damned."

"You know Mom—"

"Fuck Mom. Dad too, for that matter." Her words shock me speechless. "Live your life for you, Via. Do what makes you happy. You worry too much about everyone else and not enough about yourself."

Leave it to Izzy to slap me silly with the truth of her words.

I exhale a weighted breath. "You're right."

"I'm always right," she says, shimmying her shoulders and brightening.

At the next street, I turn and search for the parking lot. It only takes a moment to spot his Mustang. He must see us too, because he gets out of his car and leans against the door the second we turn in.

My cheeks heat as a memory of our call the other night washes over me. I didn't think phone sex was for me, but Reid changed my mind. Especially after he FaceTimed me and let me watch. The way he stroked himself might be one of the most erotic things I've ever seen.

With a silent huff, I push the memory back to the recesses of my mind. Now definitely isn't the time to be thinking about this.

I shut the car off, trying to ignore Izzy's face-splitting grin in the passenger seat.

"Oh, boy is down bad. Look at that goofy smile he's giving you."

I take a deep breath and get out of the car. Before I left my apartment, I told myself I'd keep my cool, but suddenly, I'm nothing more than a lovesick fool.

The minute I reach Reid, I throw my arms around his shoulders. "I missed you," I murmur into his neck, inhaling that vanilla and citrus scent that I love so much.

He pulls back and gives me a kiss, keeping it light since my sister is present. Wrapping an arm around my waist, he tugs me against his side with a grin.

Then he holds out a hand to my sister. "It's so nice to meet you officially. I'm Reid."

She takes his hand, grinning like a maniac. "Izzy. It's nice to meet you too."

"Are you hungry?"

"*Starved*," Izzy says, like I haven't fed her all day.

"This place has great tacos."

Izzy bounces on her toes and rubs her hands together. "I love tacos."

Reid takes the lead, opening the door for us. Izzy shoots me an impressed look over her shoulder. What kind of guys is she dating if she's that spellbound over a simple gesture?

Inside, a hostess leads us to a table near the back. The place is relatively quiet. Thank God. I'm not sure I can handle any real-world chaos with what a mess my mind is at the moment.

Reid motions for me to slide in first, and then he joins me while Izzy sits across from us.

Once we have chips and salsa and drinks, Izzy sets her menu aside and laces her fingers on top of the table.

"So, Reid, what are your intentions with my sister?"

Beside me, he nearly chokes on the chip. With a finger in the air, he signals that he needs a moment. And when he recovers, he clears his throat. "You're funny. Does this mean you're the one I'll need to ask for permission for her hand in marriage?"

Cheeks heating and heart lurching, I cover my face with my hands and groan.

When I lower my hands, Izzy is smiling. "You got that right."

Suddenly, I have a feeling that Izzy is going to use this dinner as an opportunity to see how much she can embarrass me? As if confirming my suspicion, she shoots me a wink, a chip dangling between her light blue painted nails. "Where do you see yourself in five years, Reid?"

He grins and shakes his head. Searching through the chips, he plucks one out and dips it in the salsa. "Married to your sister and on my way to owning my own auto restoration business."

"Acceptable answer." She steeples her fingers, watching him dip another chip. "I see you carefully avoiding that piece of cilantro in there. I hate to tell you, but that's a deal-breaker. I can't let my sister be involved with a cilantro hater."

He stares at her, clearly trying not to smile, then takes

another chip and makes sure to scoop up the piece of cilantro. He pops the chip into his mouth, keeping his focus trained on her, and makes a point to chew thoroughly before he swallows.

"Does that answer your question?"

Izzy ignores him, looking at me instead. "I like him."

Reid grins, his face lit in triumph.

"Don't let it go to your head," I gripe. "She's been rooting for you from the beginning."

"In fact," she says, pointing at him with a tortilla chip, "you have me to thank for encouraging her to go out and bang a guy's brains out. So you're welcome, buddy."

I cover my face with my hands and slump forward. "Izzy."

She goes on, undeterred. "You guys should make an appearance on my channel sometime. I can tell my subscribers all about how I was your matchmaker and how you owe it all to me."

"I'm sure our parents would love that story," I mutter.

She waves a dismissive hand. "They don't watch my videos."

I arch a brow. "They don't?"

She practically chokes. *"No.* Do you watch them?"

I wrinkle my nose. "No." I feel bad that I don't, but I'm not exactly her demographic. Neither are our parents, but I figured they'd watch them to support her.

The waitress stops by for our order, and once she leaves, I turn to Izzy, expecting her interrogation of Reid to continue.

Instead, she says, "They stopped watching after I did the story time on losing my virginity."

"Izzy." I don't know whether to laugh, cry, or flat-out cringe.

"What? It's true," she says with a shrug. To Reid, she adds, "I'm a content creator if you didn't know."

He chuckles. "My sister's working for you, so yeah, I know."

"I wasn't sure if she'd told you about me. She's awesome."

Reid grins. "I tend to agree."

Beneath the table, Reid finds my hand and gives it a reassuring squeeze. I smile in his direction.

"Ugh," Izzy groans, reaching for her water. "You guys make me sick. All in love and stuff."

In love.

It's blatantly obvious to her, to me too, but I still haven't told him how I feel.

He gives me a smile, one that clearly conveys that he knows how I feel, but that he won't push me to give him those words.

Reid might be young, but he's infinitely patient.

Soon, I tell myself. *I'll tell him soon.*

We were too full on the drive back to my apartment to talk much. Inside, Izzy cues up a new Christmas rom-com.

Before she can hit play, I head toward my room. "I'm going to change."

"Me too." She sets her purse down and pulls out a wad of fabric it's safe to assume is her pajamas.

Laughing, I ask, "You had those the whole time?"

She scoffs. "I wasn't going to have a movie night and stay in my clothes."

With a shake of my head, I shut my bedroom door behind me.

As I change, the smell of popcorn fills the apartment. I don't know how Izzy has room for it, because I'm stuffed.

I'm pulling my pajama shirt over my head when my phone vibrates on my bed.

Scooping my phone up, I find a text message from Reid.

> Reid: I think tonight went well.

> Me: It could've been worse.

> Reid: Your sister is cool. I think she'll be good for mine.

> Me: I hope so. We're about to watch a movie.

> Reid: Okay, enjoy your night.

> Me: Good night.

My bedroom door opens, and on the other side, Izzy's

cradling a bowl of popcorn. "Are you already texting lover boy?" She shoves a handful of popcorn in her mouth and rolls her eyes. "You guys are so painfully in love."

I press my lips together.

"What?"

"I still haven't told him."

"*Via.*"

"I know." I hang my head. "I need to."

"I need to sit down for this." She shoves me aside and drops onto my bed. "Why haven't you told that lovesick golden retriever of a man that you're in love with him?"

I face her, arms crossed over my chest. "Because once I do, there's no going back."

"What do you mean by that?" She digs into the popcorn again, bouncing slightly like she's eager for my answer.

I let my arms drop and wring my hands. "Reid ... he's it for me. I know it in my gut. In my soul. And that's scary. I haven't been divorced long, and I had no intention of getting involved with someone so soon. But he's ... he's my everything. Once I tell him I love him, it's locking in my future with him."

With a tilt of her head, she frowns. "Which you don't want to do?"

I sigh. "I'm not explaining this well. It makes sense in my head."

She sets the bowl to the side and brushes her hands together. "What you're saying is that right now, everything feels like a possibility, but once you tell him you love him, those possibilities will become reality?"

My chest squeezes at the thought. "Basically."

"And that scares you *why*?"

I pinch the bridge of my nose. I'm frustrated with myself. "Because it'll be the best thing I've ever experienced, and if it doesn't work out, I'll be beyond devastated. It would be so much worse than what I went through with Chase."

She's quiet, assessing me while she absorbs my words. "Chase wasn't careful with your heart, but that doesn't mean Reid won't take care of it with everything he has. You know what I see when I look at you two?"

I rub my lips together, nerves taking over. "What?"

"I see a rare, special kind of connection that's visible to anyone who witnesses it. I see the kind of love I could only be so lucky to find one day. What you have with Reid is different from what you had with Chase, and you owe it to him and yourself to stop holding what Chase did to you over this new relationship."

She's right. I know she is. I didn't realize that's what I was doing. Reid isn't Chase, but the fear of being hurt like that has kept me from giving in to my feelings. Reid knows I love him, I can see that he does, but knowing and hearing me say it are two different things.

My stomach flips as an idea strikes me. I sit a little straighter and smile at my sister. "Can you help me with something?"

She raises a brow. "Does it have anything to do with finally telling Reid you love him?"

"It's for his Christmas present."

She stares me down.

I sigh and give her a small smile. "And I'll tell him I love him."

She grins, clapping. "That's my girl."

THE NEXT AFTERNOON, IZZY AND I STAND IN MY mostly empty art store.

"I can't believe I'm doing this," I mutter.

"I can't either." Izzy is browsing the selection of paint colors.

My stock has been building in anticipation of opening in a few months. I'm still filled with anxiety every time I think about it, but I don't doubt my decision at all.

"I think you should use these." She holds up three shades of blue.

"I like those." I motion for her to bring them over to where I have the canvas prepped. It's long enough for me to fit my entire body on. "He better love this."

She laughs, opening the paints.

My chest suddenly feels tight and my palms are damp. Because I'm about to remove my clothes and let my sister paint my naked body so I can lie on canvas and give the hopefully decent result to my boyfriend.

"He's a *guy*. He's going to love it."

I blow out a breath, trying to extinguish my nerves. I used to go head-to-head in the courtroom and not bat an eye, but this has me downright jittery. Giving him this, giving him *me*—my naked body imprinted forever as a piece of art—is extremely intimate in a unique way. When it's done, it shouldn't be obvious to anyone else that it's *me*, but he'll know and I'll know.

And Izzy too, since I need her help.

"Why don't I put on some music?" Izzy suggests, since I'm doing a horrible job at hiding how I feel. "Do you think that would help?"

"It might."

"It's going to be fine. And if you're worried about me seeing you naked … well, I don't have any advice there."

I snort a laugh, and a fraction of my trepidation ebbs. "Thanks, Iz."

She picks up her phone and cues up a playlist. Naturally, she chose something soft and sultry.

"All right," she says, picking up the small paint roller. "It's time to disrobe."

Inhaling, garnering all my courage, I undo the ties of the robe.

Izzy loads up the paint roller with the lightest shade of blue. "You're doing your side, right? Legs, booty, ribs, and breast?" She picks up her phone with her free hand and studies the example I sent her one more time. Then she moves behind me with the roller.

I jump at the cold sensation of the paint on my bare skin. She slathers the parts of me that need to be covered with this shade of blue. When she's satisfied, she works quickly to add in the other shades in the places she sees fit.

"Ready?" she asks, offering me her hands to help me lie on the canvas.

"Yes." I have to get situated carefully so I don't smear the paint. I strategically position one leg on the canvas, then spread out so the side of my boob and my arm are on the canvas. I want it to clearly convey that I'm lying on my side. Sultry and sexy, that's what I want this piece to be.

Izzy helps me up and passes me the robe. Once I've got it wrapped around my body, I assess my work to determine whether it's worth the mess—and possible yeast infection.

"That's fucking hot." Izzy surveys the canvas with wide eyes and a smile. "He's going to lose his shit."

My stomach flutters at the thought. "You think?"

She nods vigorously. "He's a twenty-one-year-old guy. Of course he is."

"It looks better than I thought it would."

"Go wash the paint off," she says, nudging me toward where my coat is draped over a stool. "I'll put this up to dry."

"Thanks for helping me ... and for not thinking I'm crazy."

When the paint is dry, I'll go back and add details that are relevant to us inside it. His hummingbird tattoo. Candy Land. The sign for Monday's.

Izzy laughs. "Honestly, if I'd known this was a thing, I probably would've harassed you about helping me make one."

"Got a secret boyfriend I don't know about?" I joke, pulling on my coat over my robe.

"No, but I wouldn't mind having it for me."

She picks up the canvas and heads to the back, and I head out the door and up the stairs to my apartment.

I rinse the paint off, scrubbing myself thoroughly so no traces remain in unmentionable places. When I'm finished, I find Izzy at my stove.

"What are you making?"

She laughs and turns so I can see the pan in front of her. "Grilled cheese sandwiches like mom used to make us."

I groan. "I can't remember the last time I had one."

"I make them a lot." She shrugs, turning back to the pan. She flips one sandwich, then the other, and peers at me over her shoulder. "It's my favorite comfort food."

When they're finished, she plates them and holds one out to me.

"Thank you for this." I hold the plate aloft. "And for your help with the painting."

With a laugh, she sits on my couch and tucks her legs under her. "You're welcome. Maybe that'll be your niche."

I frown, confused. "My niche?"

Her eyes twinkle. "Erotic art."

"Izzy!"

She laughs and laughs and laughs.

And me?

I smile.

All too soon, Christmas has come and gone. New Year's is around the corner, but Izzy is due in Manhattan for a brand deal obligation. As I pull up to the departure area, my heart sinks a little. I hate goodbyes.

"Don't cry," she warns me, wagging a stern finger in my face. "If you cry, then I'll cry, and I can't mess up my makeup."

Her makeup *is* impeccable. I wouldn't want to mess it up either.

Easing the car into park, I undo my belt, then climb out to help her with her bags.

She slips her tote onto her shoulder and takes her designer suitcase from me. "No crying," she warns again, pulling me in for a hug. "I'll be back for the store opening."

"But that's still months away."

She lets me go and steps back, adjusting the claw clip that holds her hair up. "I promise you won't even have a chance to miss me. You know, it's too bad Reid doesn't have a hot brother. That would *really* encourage me to hurry back." She shimmies her shoulders.

"Izzy," I laugh, shaking my head at her antics.

"It's okay. He has a hot dad. I might be down for the whole DILF thing." With a wink, she turns and wheels her suitcase behind her.

I'm rooted to the spot, trying to compose myself after *that* comment.

She reaches the doors and turns back, blowing me a kiss. "Love you, Via-Mia! Ta-ta for now!"

"I love you too."

She wiggles her fingers, and then she's gone.

Once I'm in my car again, I turn up the music to drown out my thoughts, then I head for home. I already miss her like crazy, and I can't stop dreaming that one of these days she'll move here for good. But I want her to do whatever makes her happy.

Before going home, I pick up a dozen donuts. It's tempting to dig into the fresh, doughy goodness, but I resist. For now, at least.

I pull into the alleyway, avoiding the piles of snow plowed along the street, and shuffle around to the passenger side of my car. I lay the front passenger seat down and maneuver the canvas until it's lying flat. It takes some finagling to secure it properly. The last thing I need is to be smacked in the face with it if I hit my brakes too hard.

With that thought, a wave of horror washes over me. A vision of paramedics finding me inside my car with a canvas that bears the shape of my very own ass and boob enters my mind.

"Via," I say aloud to myself, "you are *way* overthinking this." The likelihood that I'll be in an accident is less than slim, and besides, the canvas is wrapped.

That's just one of the issues that has me spiraling, if I'm honest with myself.

I've been thinking for days about how to convey my feelings to Reid. It's time to open up. For his sake and mine. I have to stop guarding my heart so staunchly. Not when he's certainly won the right to it. After Chase's deception, I was so scared of loving again, of giving someone else the potential to hurt me, but ultimately, I'm only hurting myself if I remain so guarded.

Reid deserves to hear the words, to know how much I love him.

Once the canvas is secured where I want it, I start the drive to Reid's apartment. In hindsight, I should've texted him to make sure he's home, but there wasn't room for logic in my brain while I was freaking out over how completely I've fallen for him.

A man eleven years younger than me.

A man who should be all wrong for me.

A man, who despite everything, has *become* my everything.

I white-knuckle my way through the drive, fighting the urge to turn the car around, drive back to my place, and put off telling him for even longer.

But Reid has been showing me his feelings in subtle ways for months now.

He fell hard and fast.

I fell slow and steady.

Since he's already there and has been patiently waiting for me to join him, I owe it to him to say those three terrifying words first.

When I reach his apartment, I park as close as I can and commandeer the help of a poor man just trying to leave. It takes some clever twists to get the canvas out of my car, but when we do, I thank him profusely. He doesn't give me time to finish before he's scurrying off, probably afraid I'll assign him another task.

With the box of donuts under my arm, I lock my car and heave the canvas under the other.

My heart gallops like a racehorse—partly because of nerves, but also from navigating the stairs. I have to stop a few times to give my arms a break and catch my breath. I'm going to have to start working out, because apparently my muscles are nonexistent.

Reaching his door, I raise my fist and knock.

A moment later, it swings open, revealing Reid in all his dimpled glory. His hair is rumpled like he's been running his fingers through it and his glasses are askew.

"To what do I owe the pleasure?" His voice is a soft, husky croon. He braces one hand above the door and leans in, giving me a quick kiss before I can reply.

My toes curl at the contact.

"I brought your Christmas present."

His face lights up when he notices the wrapped painting leaning against the wall outside his door.

"Whatcha got there, angel?"

I shrug, going for nonchalant. "I guess you're going to have to open it and find out."

Grinning, he steps out, hefts it into his arms, and moves inside again. I follow, closing the door behind me.

"I also brought donuts." I hold up the box.

Spinning, he puts a hand over his heart. "You know just what I love." Patting the wrapped artwork, he asks, "Can I open it?"

I nod, heart racing, and shuck my coat off. "It's yours."

He props his gift up against the wall and rips the paper off like a five-year-old on Christmas morning.

When he's pulled the wrapping away, he steps back to inspect the canvas. "Fuck, Via," he groans, biting his knuckles. "This is hot. Creative too."

I try to hide my pleased smile, but from the twinkle in his eyes, he doesn't miss it.

He crouches down and runs his fingers along the curves of my silhouette on the canvas, taking in the details I added throughout.

He narrows his eyes and hauls himself back up to standing. "This." He traces the curves of my painted body. "Is this you?"

"Yes." My cheeks flush. "Literally."

He blinks at me from behind his glasses. "Like your actual body?"

"Yeah. Izzy had to help me. She painted my body and I had to—"

In an instant, he's in front of me, his hands pressed to my cheeks and his lips covering mine. "I love it," he murmurs when he pulls back.

I put my hands over his. "Really?"

"Fuck, yeah. I'm hanging it above my bed."

A laugh escapes me. "Seriously?"

"Abso-fucking-lutely. I'll do it right now." He carries it back to his bedroom, and I follow.

I stand in the middle of the room while he leans it against the wall and goes in search of his tools. Once he's taken a few measurements, he mounts it, then steps back and makes sure it's level.

"Look at that." He hops down from the bed, hands on his hips as he takes it in. "Perfect. I love it."

He turns to me then, cupping my cheeks again and giving me a long, deep kiss that leaves me wanting more.

I curl my fingers in the fabric of his shirt. I don't want to let go. "There's something I want to tell you." There's a slight quiver to my voice.

Concern instantly fills his eyes. "Is everything okay?"

I nod, heart pounding right out of my chest. "Yeah, everything's fine. I promise. I..." I bite my lip. I'm struggling to say the words. Once they're out there, I can't take them back. Not that I would want to, but this admission makes all of this feel so much more real. We've been living in this Via and Reid bubble, all on our own. Admitting my love for him is crossing a line we can't undo. It'll mean telling his father and facing whatever will come from that. There won't be any more hiding what we are from the world.

"I love you." I put it out there. No take-backs. No more overthinking. No fighting my feelings. It's time I own how I feel.

Reid stares at me, lips parted and eyes wide. "Say it again," he begs, wrapping his hands around my hips and tugging me closer. "I want to hear it again."

I slide my hands up his chest and coil my arms around his neck. "I love you," I whisper. "I love you." Louder this time. "I love you, Reid Crawford. I—"

His mouth is on mine in the next instant, stealing my

words, my breath, my very soul, just like he did on that very first night.

Call it kismet, fate, whatever you want, but our paths were meant to cross in that bar on his birthday. Did I expect to fall in love with him when I went home with him that night? Absolutely not. But the universe knew before I did that Reid is exactly what I need.

He backs me toward the bed until my legs hit the mattress and I'm forced to sit. Reid follows me until I'm lying back and he's hovering over me. His tongue strokes lazily against mine, tasting me.

Pulling back slightly, he regards me, his expression full of wonder. "It took you long enough."

I burst out laughing. It's the most Reid response ever. Sobering, he says, "I love you too."

And then he shows me how much he loves me.

Over and over again.

thirty-eight

Reid

Via's moving into my place.

Well, not technically. It's only while her apartment is being remodeled. Asking her to stay here rather than at the inn like she'd planned was a no-brainer.

"Hi," Via says, standing in the doorway with her bags.

I quickly take the duffel she has slung over one shoulder and the small box wedged under her other arm. "I told you to let me know when you got here so I could help."

"I know." She follows me inside. "But I kind of went overboard. There's more in the car, so I felt guilty asking."

I set her stuff down on my coffee table and pinch the bridge of my nose. "Via." This woman is going to be the death of me. "Never feel guilty about asking for my help."

"But—"

"I love you, okay? And I want to take care of you. Carrying a few bags in is the least of that care."

It's been a week since she told me she loved me, and I'm *still* riding the high. I had been dreaming of hearing those words from Via for a while. I didn't mean to fall so hard or so fast, but I did. I didn't doubt her growing feelings for me, but nothing compares to hearing it.

"I'm sorry."

The apology makes me feel like an asshole. I don't want her to be sorry.

"I don't want to burden you any more than I already have."

"Via," I say slowly, making sure I have her attention. "You are never a burden to me."

"I just feel bad since I'm crashing here and—"

I shut her up with a kiss. Instantly, the tension leaves her body. I don't linger, knowing we have things to get done, but when I take a step back, she stumbles forward like her lips aren't ready to break from mine.

"Can I get the rest in one trip?"

"I'll come with you," she says, tugging at her coat.

I put my own coat on and follow her out to the parking lot. The sidewalk is covered in salt, and it quickly sticks to the bottom of my boots.

"Jesus." The word escapes me when I catch sight of how stuffed her car is. "How'd you get everything in here?"

She plops her hands on her hips, her nose turning

adorably red in the cold. "A lot of trips up and down the stairs."

"You could've called me."

She cocks her head to the side. "Your dad was there."

"Ah." I grab a tote bag filled with art supplies from the back seat. "I see."

Though our relationship is moving into what I would consider serious territory, we still haven't told my dad. I don't want him to be hurt, and Via, despite my assurances, still worries about the age difference.

Fuck anyone who has a problem with her being older than me—even my own father, if it comes to it.

"How's the new job?" she asks, opening the opposite door.

"I like it so far."

When I've got a tote on each shoulder and the box, I round the car and wait for her.

She tugs a suitcase and another bag out of the back, and I can't help but grin. Fuck, she brought a lot of stuff.

She turns, catching my expression, and huffs. "I had to clear out as much as I could."

I cock one brow and take a step toward the building. "I didn't say a thing."

"No, but you had the look." She hip checks the door closed and locks her car.

We fall into step back to the building. The lobby still smells like gingerbread from the display they had up through Christmas. The management office hosted a gingerbread house–making competition and displayed the winners. I never saw an invite. If I had, I would've outdone everyone.

I can't help eyeing Via on our trek up the stairs.

"What?" Her eyes flick up at me. "Why are you looking at me like that?"

"It feels like you're moving in for real."

She groans. "I swear I'm not trying to move into your bachelor pad. I had to take as much as I could since they're redoing the floors and cabinets and everything."

Her ramble is endearing.

"It wouldn't be so bad … if you wanted to move in."

She scoffs as she turns down the hall. "Don't be ridiculous, Reid."

I bristle at that. "What's ridiculous about it?"

She opens the door to my apartment and holds it so I can go in first since my hands are full. I set the box on the kitchen counter and the bags at my feet, then turn to her for an answer.

The door clicks shut.

"Via?" I hang up my coat and hold a hand out for hers.

"It's just too soon. I love you, but I'm not ready for that."

"Why?" I respect her choice, but I want to understand.

She pulls out one of the barstools and sits. "My divorce wasn't all that long ago, and I certainly didn't plan on dating yet, but then you happened." She gestures at me, and I can't help but grin. "I just want to take my time with things. I wouldn't say I rushed into a relationship with Chase, but…" She shrugs. "I was young. I probably should've explored more. Not that I want to do that now," she hastens to add.

"But I need to have my own space and live on my own for a while. Does that make sense?"

Resigned, I nod. "Yeah, I get what you mean."

She leans over and grasps my chin so I'm forced to look at her. "One day."

I smile. "You mean that?"

"Absolutely." She kisses me, then drops back to the stool. "What should we do today?"

I'm such a sucker for this woman. Her use of the word *we* has me wanting to fall to my knees. How her ex ever let her go is beyond me, but his loss is my gain.

"You brought a lot of art supplies."

She smiles. "I did."

I cross my arms over my chest, leaning against the counter behind me. "I wouldn't mind sketching for a while."

"I love that idea. I've been itching to get a few things out of my head and on paper."

"Coffee, first?" I shuffle over to the coffee maker and open the drawer where I keep coffee pods.

"Ugh, yes, please." She slides off the barstool. "I'm desperate for caffeine."

I grab two and pop the first one in the machine.

Via, familiar with my apartment now, pops up on her tiptoes and grabs two mugs from the cabinet.

"You always pick that one." I nod to the one in her right hand.

She clutches it to her chest. "It's *cute*."

I move in closer to her, boxing her in against the

counter. Ducking my head, I brush my nose over her cheek. "I'm glad you find my chicken mug cute."

It was a gag gift from my sister, but I've held on to the stupid thing forever.

"I really do. Look at it." She holds it out so I have to take a step back. "What's not to love?"

Chuckling, I hold my hand out. "Give me the mug."

She pets it, holding on protectively. "Don't hurt it."

"Via," I laugh, "I need it for your coffee."

"Oh." She hands it over. "Right."

I put it under the machine and press start. Within seconds, my apartment fills with the aroma of coffee with a hint of peppermint.

She pulls the creamer from the fridge and adds it, then brings the mug to her nose and inhales. With a sip and a happy sigh, she slides the creamer to me.

It hits me then, how well we work together. It's truly effortless.

I slide the bottle back down the counter and she puts it away.

Thirty minutes later, we're on my floor. We've pushed the coffee table to the opposite wall.

I'm not much for paint, but I find myself drawn to it today. I don't have a particular vision in mind. Instead, I'm adding a riot of bright colors to the paper.

Via is lying on her stomach, using her body as a shield so I can't see what she's working on.

"What are you drawing over there?"

Snickering, she glances over her shoulder. "You're so nosy."

"I'm curious, angel. There's a difference."

With a shake of her head, she lifts the sketchpad and turns it so I can see it.

It's an intricate pencil drawing of angel wings. The details she's added already are astounding. She doesn't see herself as a talented artist, but she truly is. It's a shame she didn't get to pursue art sooner, but at least she's doing it now.

"I want that when you're finished with it."

"What are you going to do with it?" She lays the sketchpad back down on the floor and rubs a finger beneath her nose, unknowingly smearing pencil above her lip. "If you keep putting my art on your walls, you'll eventually run out of space."

"Actually," I hedge, "I have something else in mind."

"Do tell."

"Mm, I think I'm going to keep it a surprise."

She groans. "That's annoying."

I chuckle. "I've gotta keep you on your toes so you don't get bored." I reach over to rub the pencil off her face. When I do, she gasps and pulls back. "Shit," I curse at the dab of paint I left behind. "I was trying to get pencil off. I didn't mean to smear paint on your face."

She doesn't reply. Not with words, anyway. Instead, she dips her finger in the neon yellow paint I was using. And, almost in slow motion, she brings her finger to my face and drags it down my skin.

I chuckle darkly. "Oh, it's on."

I stick my finger in the pink and draw it down her neck and over her collarbone.

"That's cold!" she shrieks, scrambling away. In the process, a glob of paint gets in her hair. "Reid!"

"What?" I raise my hands and smirk.

She lunges forward, yellow-streaked finger going for my throat. She draws a straight line from beneath my chin down my neck.

I smear blue on her forehead.

Then she's got the orange. She shoves my shirt up with her clean hand and spreads the vivid color on my stomach.

I grab her face in one hand, the one with paint on it, and yank her close, then press my lips to hers. She moans into me, and I swallow the sound.

Just like that, I'm hard. I take my shirt off completely, letting her paint my chest with a riot of colors. Blues and pinks and yellows and oranges.

She lifts her arms so I can remove her shirt too. In no time, her ribs are imprinted with the shape of my fingers and hands in shades of peach from the combination of yellow and pink.

When she rolls her hips into mine, I stifle a groan.

"Our clothes are going to be ruined," she says, shaking all that long, dark hair as she rocks against me.

I could come from this alone. Fuck. I close my eyes, naming off car manufacturers in my head.

"What are you doing?" She trails a paint-covered finger

down my stomach. A shiver runs down my spine when she moves it beneath the waistband of my jeans.

"Trying not to blow my load," I grind out.

She laughs. "Then get naked."

"That's only going to make the problem worse."

"Not," she trails her index finger around my nipple, "if you let me take care of the problem."

"*Via.*" I lie back, and she follows me with a laugh, her hair tickling my chest.

"Let me paint you." She kisses my stomach. "My own personal canvas."

I crook my elbow over my eyes. "You're going to be the death of me, woman."

Her next kiss lands at my waistline. "At least you'll die happy, right?"

She undoes my belt with an easy flick and yanks it out of the loops. She throws it, and it lands behind the couch with a clink.

"If I'm getting naked, so are you."

"I will. But not yet." She smiles, popping the button on my jeans. The sound of the zipper sliding down fills the room, making my cock pulse with the need to feel her.

"Angel," I groan. "You're not playing fair."

She laughs, her breath fanning against my stomach. "Never said I would."

I lift my hips so she can shimmy my jeans down my legs.

Palming me over my boxer briefs, she smiles. She's got me in the palm of her hand. Literally.

Little by little, she inches my underwear down. My cock

practically jumps out at her, eager for attention. Laughing lightly, she grasps the base and strokes, flicking her tongue out, barely licking the tip.

My breaths are shaky while she takes her time. When she finally wraps her mouth fully around me, my hips shoot up off the floor. She strokes and sucks, taking me down her throat until she gags.

"God, angel, that mouth of yours."

She lets me go with a pop, her right hand still wrapped around my cock.

"What about this mouth?" she asks with an innocent blink, her lips swollen.

"It's fucking dangerous, that's what."

She releases me and dips her finger into the paint again. She brings it to my lower abdomen and adds streaks of color to the black line work of my hummingbird tattoo. She doesn't just fill in the lines, though. She makes what's already a piece of art her own. As she works, she makes the acrylic paint look almost like watercolor on my skin. She's focused, ass in the air, tongue between her lips like it always is when she's concentrating. I stare at her jean-clad ass, silently cursing myself for not getting her naked already.

"Look at you," she says, sitting back on her knees. "My own little masterpiece."

I look down at the smears of paint all over my body—far more than hers since she's still mostly clothed.

"Come here." I crook a finger at her.

Defiant, as always, she moves, but only an inch closer.

"*Closer.*"

With a wicked smile, she obeys. When her face is in front of mine, I grab her chin and pull her lips to mine. She still tastes of coffee and donuts. With my other hand, I find the clasp of her bra and pinch. It slides down her arms, and she takes it off completely, tossing it aside.

"My turn."

"Wha—"

Cupping her breasts, I swirl my tongue around her nipple. Licking and sucking. She writhes against me. Fingers in my hair. I move to her other nipple and give it the same attention. When my tongue has left a wet trail, I dip a finger in paint and follow the same path. The bright pink stands out sharply against her tanned skin.

"That's cold," she whines, wiggling beneath my touch.

"Keep moving like that, and this is going to be over before we get to the best part."

I lay her back and shuck her pants and underwear down her legs. When she's completely bare before me, I sit back on my haunches and survey her. Her breasts move with every breath she takes, her stomach contracting. A flush spreads from her chest, up her neck, to her cheeks.

Brush in hand, I dip it into the blue paint and slather it on one hand, then the other.

"What are you going to do? I don't have any tattoos."

I grab her hips and haul her into my lap. "If I have my way, then when I'm done with you, there won't be a single inch of your skin that hasn't been touched."

Cupping her breasts, leaving blue paint behind, I grin.

Cleaning my floors will be a nightmare, and there's no

chance in hell that I'll get my deposit back after this, but I can't bring myself to care.

"Are you wet for me?"

Normally, I'd check for myself, but I know better than to put my paint-covered fingers there.

She nods. "Yes. Fuck me, Reid."

I grin. Damn, I love the way she openly asks me for what she wants. Seeing her come out of her shell sexually has been one of the biggest highlights of my life. Knowing that she has that much trust and faith in me makes me feel powerful.

Grasping her hips, I lift her up and then carefully lower her onto my cock. We watch as I disappear inside her one inch at a time. When I'm fully seated, she wraps her arms around my neck, pushing her chest into mine. I slide my hands from her hips up her waist. The paint is beginning to dry on my fingers, so I dip my fingers in yellow paint and add more to my hands while she rocks against me.

"Reid," she breathes my name. "I'm close already." Her whimpers fill the room as she rocks against me faster, harder, riding me to her first orgasm.

While she's coming, screaming loud enough my neighbors can probably hear, I lay her back. Hands on her thighs, I spread her wider and move in slow but steady thrusts. It's killing me to hold back, but I want to make this last.

Gasping, she clutches at the chain dangling from my neck.

Her pussy flutters around me, signaling that she's close to her second orgasm.

She looks so pretty under me.

Via swears she wasn't looking for someone, that she wasn't even thinking about dating. I've never told her the same can be said for me. But the minute I saw her in Monday's, I was a goner.

Hook, line, and sinker.

I knew I had to talk to her. I wasn't planning to take her home with me. I genuinely wanted to connect for a few moments and ask her on a date. But I don't regret how things happened.

She worries that because of my age, there's a chance I'll miss out on life experiences. And she fears that her infertility is an issue.

None of that matters to me.

She matters.

It's *her* I fell in love with.

Our ages?

Inconsequential.

Her fertility issues?

I don't care. There are other ways to have a family if we want one someday.

I knew even before our first date that she was it for me. I have no problem being patient. She said she's not ready to move in with me? That's okay. We'll live together one day.

I see all the destinations ahead of us—the dreams and goals and milestones we'll hit together.

"Reid, I—"

"I know." I skim my hands down her sides, leaving a trail of yellow in their wake. "Let go."

She shudders, breaths ragged as she comes. I fall right behind her, filling her with my release. My strokes slow, losing rhythm as I ride it out. When I'm spent, I roll to my side and take her with me. There's a streak of pink paint on her nose, and I can't remember how it got there. I smooth her hair back from her forehead. We're both in need of a shower, but for now, we lie here, lost in one another. Two masterpieces of our own making.

thirty-nine

Via

As much as I don't want to rush things, Reid is making it difficult not to want to stay here forever. Waking up with him every morning for the past week and a half has been nice.

Easy too.

Nice and easy might not seem like the most glowing review, but it's exactly what I need.

I blink my eyes open to a still-dark room. I don't know what woke me, but Reid is stirring at my side.

"Is that your phone?" he asks, his voice groggy.

"My phone?"

Slowly, the words penetrate my brain. He's right. My

phone is vibrating on the table at my side. It cuts off and starts up again.

A glance at the clock tells me it's a little after five thirty.

No one would be calling me this early if it wasn't urgent.

The sleepy fog dissipates in an instant and is replaced by sheer panic.

What if something happened to Izzy?

I scramble for my phone, but it's not her name on the screen. It's Derrick's.

Reid rolls over, making the bed dip. "Why's my dad calling you this early?"

I ignore his question and swipe to answer the call. "Hello?"

"Hey, Via," he says, his words short and clipped. "I'm sorry to wake you, but you need to get over here. There's ... it's a mess. Just come as soon as you can."

"I'll throw some clothes on and be right over."

I'm already up and out of the bed when I hang up.

"What's going on?" Reid asks.

"I need to get over to my place." I grab a pair of leggings and yank them on. "He didn't give details, but he sounded panicked."

"All right, shit." He rubs at his sleep-mussed hair. "Let me drive you."

I nod shakily. I'm not sure I can drive right now. Not with my nerves ratcheted up to the nth degree.

I've run through a million scenarios by the time I yank one of Reid's sweatshirts over my head and stuff my feet into my boots. Reid, shirt halfway on, passes me my coat and pulls his off the hook too. Within minutes, we're in his car, racing toward my building.

I shoot Derrick a text, telling him I'm almost there.

Reid parks on the street, and I rush out before he has the engine shut off.

By the look of the trucks parked outside the building, Derrick didn't just call me, but his whole team.

I nearly collide with him on my way to the door. He has his phone pressed to his ear, and with his free hand, he grabs my arm, halting me from going in.

"Mhm," he says to the person on the other end. "All right. Thanks."

He hangs up and winces as he slides his phone into his pocket. "A pipe burst," he explains, letting my arm go. "I got a call from Winston across the street. He noticed water seeping out beneath the front door."

I don't know who Winston is, which is probably terrible if he lives across the street, but that's the least of my worries right now.

"How much water?" My vision is going spotty, and I worry I might pass out.

"A good foot or more. The good news is the floor is concrete, but…" He winces again.

But that much water is guaranteed to ruin the newly installed walls. Not to mention the custom counter.

"There's a lot of damage," he says, ushering me inside.

"Via."

At the sound of Reid's voice, I spin, clutching my hands to my chest.

"What happened?" He wraps his arms around me, instantly making me feel a hundred times better. Reid Crawford is my safe place, my home base. Pulling back, he frames my face with his hands. "Is everything okay?"

Now that I know, and now that he's here, my emotions let loose, and the tears I've kept at bay escape. "It's flooded. Almost everything is ruined."

A throat clears behind us, and my blood goes cold.

Fuck. We're so stupid.

In my panic, I didn't consider the consequences of Reid's presence. We've been living in our happy little Reid and Via bubble for the past week and a half, and somewhere along the way, I forgot that most people don't know about us. Derrick is among the first we should've told, but we both held back for different reasons, but now we've stupidly ousted ourselves in the worst way possible.

Reid doesn't let go of my face as he makes eye contact with his dad over my shoulder.

"Hi, Dad."

He says it in a breezy, carefree sort of way, but his lips are turned down with worry and his shoulders are tense.

I turn so I can see both men, though Reid still doesn't release me.

Derrick shakes his head back and forth, confusion furrowing his brows. "I ... I don't understand."

"Dad, I—"

"You're ... you two..." He looks from me to Reid and back again, his jaw slack. "You're together?"

Beside me, Reid presses his lips together and gives a single nod.

"Fuck." Derrick rubs at his stubbled jaw. *"Fuck."* He says it louder this time.

Then he laughs.

Reid eyes me, looking as confused as I feel. Is this man actually amused, or is he on the verge of a mental breakdown?

Derrick yanks open the door and strides inside while the two of us stand out in the cold, dumbstruck.

Seconds later, Derrick pushes the door open. "Get in here."

His command is gruff, laced with hurt and irritation.

Reid grasps my hand and gives it a gentle squeeze.

For now, with the situation at hand, we have bigger fish to fry, and it seems as though Derrick agrees.

There are still a few inches of standing water in the building despite the wet vacs several guys are running. The visible damage to the walls makes me want to throw up.

It feels like all my dreams are going up in flames. Or, more accurately, I suppose, they're drowning in water.

I whimper, fighting back tears as Derrick leads us through the mess, shouting over the noise of the wet vacs and pointing out what needs to be torn out and replaced.

It feels like I'm starting all over again.

"We've got wiggle room in the budget," Derrick says,

guiding us back outside. "I always account for setbacks, but not to this extent."

I nod as panic threatens to claw its way out of my throat.

My budget is blessedly generous since Chase and I split things evenly in the divorce, but regardless, it's going to take even more time and money.

"I'll figure it out," I finally say, voice shaky.

I want to call my sister, to rant and cry to her.

Derrick nods. "Okay, we'll talk about it in a few days." He opens the door to head back inside.

Reid lets go of my hand and grasps his dad's arm. "Dad, we should talk about this."

Derrick keeps his focus fixed on the ground beneath his wet boots. "Not now, Reid. I don't have time for this."

Hurt flashes across Reid's face as he releases his dad.

Without another word, Derrick disappears quickly inside.

Reid shoves his hands into his pockets, and like he can't help himself, he peers into the building, as if hoping his dad is coming back.

He's not. He's disappeared around a corner.

"I can't tell whether he's pissed or hurt or just confused," Reid says, putting a hand to the small of my back and guiding me toward the car.

"Probably a combination of all three."

"Yeah." He rubs his jaw, his breath fogging the air. He opens the car door for me, and I slip inside. Once he's started the car and is pulling away, he speaks again. "My dad has never really been upset with me like this. Sure, I've done some dumb shit on occasion, but nothing too serious. After my mom died, I just wanted to make things easier for him, so I've always watched myself. He had enough going on with work and being a single parent. I love my dad. Hurting him ... it fucking sucks."

A stabbing pain lances my chest. "Reid—"

He holds up a hand. "I'm not giving you up, if that's what you think. My dad and I will get past this. I'm just trying to explain my thoughts."

I rest my hand on his jean-clad thigh. "I'm sorry."

The last thing I want to do is come between them. The whole situation has been crazy from the start, but it was inevitable that we break the news to Derrick eventually. We just didn't think it would happen like this.

We should have told him already. But in an effort to protect his feelings for as long as we could, we inadvertently hurt him more.

Reid sighs. "Since we're out, do you want to get donuts?"

I laugh, taking in the scenery as we pass. Every so often, I catch a glimpse of the ocean down the streets. Since I moved so close to autumn, I haven't gotten to truly appreciate the coastal aspects of the town.

"I can't believe you're thinking about donuts right now."

He shrugs, shifting gears. "I'm hungry."

My heart lifts just a little. "You won't catch me saying no to one of Kathy's donuts."

The line at the donut shop is almost out the door when Reid parallel parks out front. Wow. It looks as though the people of Parkerville are all trying to get their sugar fix before work.

"Stay in here. I'll get the donuts." Reid hops out of the car before I can protest.

The line moves quickly, and when it's Reid's turn to order, he rocks back and forth, full of pent-up energy. Once he's paid and Ms. Kathy herself has handed him a box, he hurries back outside. Snow flurries swirl around so thickly they've dusted the sidewalk in the time he was inside.

Reid slides in the driver's seat and passes me the box, and once he's buckled in, he pulls away.

"Do you want one now?" I ask, raising the lid to see what he got.

Half the box is filled with blueberry cheesecake donuts, and the other half is a mix of glazed and chocolate frosted, along with a lone donut topped with what looks like Fruity Pebbles.

"I thought we could get coffee first and then find a place to park and eat."

"Sounds good to me. Is this one really Fruity-Pebbles flavored?" I point to it before shutting the box.

A hint of a smile creeps up his face. "It was today's special. I thought we could give it a try."

When he pulls into the parking lot of the coffee shop, I undo my seatbelt. "I can go get—"

"Nope, I got it." He's already opening his door and climbing out of the car.

"At least let me pay."

He pokes his head back inside the car. "Nope, but nice try."

A few minutes later, he's back with two steaming-hot coffees.

"You're spoiling me," I say, bringing my cup to my lips. "Yum."

He chuckles. "I think you deserve a little spoiling after the news you got this morning."

Stomach twisting, I lean my head against the headrest. "Don't remind me."

"It's all going to work out," he says, driving toward the coastline. "This town ... we take care of our own."

"But I'm new," I remind him. "I'm not one of you."

He grins at me, raising a brow. "Trust me, Via. You're one of us."

I still don't believe him, but I give him a weak smile, then turn back to the window.

Reid pulls the car into a lot across from a pier. The lighthouse I first noticed when I moved here is to our left.

"I haven't been over here much," I confess.

"There's not too much to do on the water when it's this cold," Reid says, reaching for his coffee. "Come April, the whale watching boats will be running again."

I practically wiggle with giddiness. "Whale watching?"

With a chuckle, he flips open the donut box in my lap. He picks up a blueberry cheesecake and takes a bite.

With a groan, he goes back for another bite and washes it down with a sip of coffee. "I'll take you some time."

I reach for my own donut. It's still warm. "I'd like that."

It's strangely exciting to be making future plans with Reid. Even if that future is only a few months away.

Parkerville, Maine, was a random crapshoot choice. I could've easily ended up in New Hampshire.

Perhaps it's a romantic notion of mine, but it feels like my heart knew the missing piece was here. Not only Reid, but the store, the town, the people.

I've never felt more whole than I do now.

forty

Reid

It's been three days since my dad found out about Via and me.

Three days of unanswered calls and texts.

I've been by his house twice. He wasn't there either time.

He's never flat-out ignored me like this, but I guess there's a first time for everything. He's hurt. Probably pissed off too. He's made it clear at this point that I have to wait for him to come to me.

Pulling into the lot of my apartment, I navigate to a spot near the building. When I cut the engine, I can't help but smile.

I like coming home to Via in my space a little too much.

My apartment has been infiltrated by her things. Her sweater over the back of a chair. Her perfume on the bathroom counter. Candles. God, so many candles.

I didn't know it before, but my small space was lacking those small things that make it feel like home.

I kick the snow and salt off my boots on the welcome mat Via put outside and unlock the door. When I push it open, I'm immediately hit with the smell of tomato sauce.

"Mm, spaghetti," I hum.

Via hasn't heard me yet, not with the music blaring from the turntable. Once I've kicked off my boots, I shuck my coat and hang it on the rack.

In the kitchen, she's swaying her hips to the beat as she stirs the sauce.

She still hasn't heard me when I step up behind her and grasp her hips. She jumps, and the spoon falls from her hand.

"Don't scare me like that." She spins in my arms and swats lightly at my chest.

With a hum, I slide my hands down to the top of the curve of her ass. "It's not my fault you were so into your song." After I've kissed her thoroughly, I take a step back to give her room to work. "Any news about the store today?"

With a groan, she turns back to the stove and picks up the spoon. "They're ripping out all the drywall. They *just* put it in too." She lets out a defeated sigh. "The ladies called for an emergency book club meeting, so after we eat, I'm going to head over for that."

"Emergency book club meeting?" I repeat, propping myself up against the counter. "Sounds serious."

She cracks the oven door and checks on the garlic bread. "You kid, but it could be anything. Anywhere from a cheating spouse to the mailman delivering Glenda's mail to the lady across the street again."

"So," I drawl, "you won't be talking about a book?"

She laughs. "No, we never do. We read them. At least I do, but we usually just..." Her cheeks get pink, and she lowers her voice like it's a secret, *"gossip."*

I chuckle and pull down two bowls, since the spaghetti is almost ready. "Nothing wrong with that. Guys act like they don't gossip, but we're way worse than chicks."

"I told them I was busy with the store, but they insisted." She checks the bread again, then slips on an oven mitt and pulls it out.

While we eat, we catch up on each other's day. It's a simple thing, but I enjoy it.

"I'm leaving the dishes to you," she says, standing and heading for her coat. "I'm already running behind, and I'm scared of what Glenda might do to me." She bends and gives me a quick peck. "I'll be back later."

Before she can reach the door, though, there's a knock.

"Are you expecting someone?"

I shake my head and stand.

She peeks out the window, then turns and mouths, "It's your father."

My dad's here?

With the way he's been icing me out, I figured I'd be lucky if I heard from him for at least a week.

Via opens the door.

"Oh." On the other side of the door, my dad holds his hand up, like he was about to knock again. Dipping his chin, he lowers it and clears his throat. "Are you guys headed out?"

"I am." She smiles. "But Reid's in for the night."

Dad nods, stepping aside to let her pass. He stays there even after she's gone, like he needs permission to cross the threshold when he never has before.

"Come in, Dad." I pick up my plate and Via's and wander toward the kitchen. "Are you hungry? There's spaghetti."

He shakes his head. "No, I'm good." He closes the door behind him and removes his boots, then pads into the kitchen with me.

"You wash. I'll dry," he says, picking up a towel.

I have a dishwasher, but I go with it.

We work side by side to the sound of the water and the clinking of the dishes. Dishes I only own because my dad gifted them to me, among other things, when I moved out. He mumbled something about disowning me if I used paper plates like a frat boy.

The kitchen is small, so he shoos me out while he puts the dishes away. While I wait, I make myself comfortable on the couch. My mind is racing with all the things I should say to him, but when I open my mouth, nothing comes out.

I hold my breath when he grabs one of the kitchen stools and flips it around.

He's still quiet after he sits, like maybe he's waiting for me to speak first. If that's the case, he'll be waiting a long time, because I seem to have lost the ability.

"Via, huh?" He finally breaks the silence.

I nod, still at a loss for words.

He mimics the gesture, lips sealed. "She's a little old for you, don't you think?"

That statement brings my words rushing back. "She's a little young for you, don't you think?"

He winces. "Touché."

My jaw pulses with a mix of irritation and nerves. "I met her before you did. Not that it makes the situation much better, but…" I run my fingers through my hair in an effort to expel the nervous energy coursing through me.

"She never actually wanted to go out with me anyway." He rubs a hand over his jaw and lets out a self-deprecating laugh. "I think her sister pushed her into it. We had a good time, but…" He shrugs. "I could tell she wasn't truly into it. Even so, I asked her out again. She's beautiful and kind and … fuck, I'm lonely."

That last part is like a kick to my fucking gut.

"Especially now that Layla and Lili are gone. It's so quiet. I thought I'd be fine, but I'm not. Maybe I'm just destined to be alone. Your mom was my one great love. Maybe that's all I'll have."

I shake my head. "I don't believe that. There's someone out there for you."

He sighs, crossing his arms over his chest. "I'm getting old, and relationships are hard work." Shrugging, he lets his arms drop. "I'll be fine. Don't worry about me."

Easier said than done. Even if it's traditionally the parent's job to worry about their kids, I can't help but feel that way about him. He's a good person. He deserves happiness. I hate that he was finally stepping out there, and I stole it from him. But Via's mine. She was *always* mine.

"I just want you to be happy," I finally say.

He's quiet for a minute, and when he collects his thoughts, he sits a little straighter. "What exactly is this with her? A fling? Something you need to get out of your system?"

"No," I say, shaking my head steadfastly. "Via is the thing I never knew I was searching for. She's *everything*. I don't give a fuck what you or anyone else might think of me. When you know, you know, and she's it for me. She's not going away. Not now, not ever. So if you're not okay with this, just say so now."

"I ... I'll be okay with it. Eventually. I'm still processing."

"I can give you time." Fuck. It hurts to know we can't just jump back into our easy relationship, but I can respect that it'll take a while for him to come to terms.

He clears his throat and rubs his hands up and down his thighs. "At her age, she's probably going to want kids soon. Are you ready to be a dad?"

Obviously, he doesn't know about her infertility issues. Regardless, he has no right to bring up something like that.

"What Via and I discuss regarding our future and kids is

none of your business. That's between her and me. No one else."

He rears back, eyes wide, then lets out a long exhale. "That was a shitty thing to say. I'm sorry."

"Listen." I rub my hands together and lean forward. "I know this isn't easy, but I love her. I'm *in* love with her. She's not going anywhere. I'm going to marry this woman. I'd make her my wife tomorrow if I thought she'd go for it. You always told me when I met the right woman, I'd know. You were right. I knew it the second I met her."

Gaze fixed on the floor in front of him, he nods.

Eventually, he gets up. "I better head out."

"Dad." I stand too. "Are you going to be okay with this?" He said he would be, but I'm starting to have my doubts.

It's not like I'd break up with Via, but I need to know. To prepare myself.

He sighs, grasping the doorknob. "Like I said before, I'll get there."

With that, he's gone.

It's late by the time Via gets home from her book club meeting. I'm already in bed, alternating between reading and watching bad reality TV. It's a guilty pleasure. One I had to let Via in on since she's been staying here.

I sit up in bed, the blankets pooling at my waist, as she stumbles into the room.

Is she drunk?

If she is, she better not have driven herself home.

Quickly, though, I realize she's crying.

"Hey, what's going on?" I'm up and out of bed, desperate to get my hands on her. "Did something happen?"

She's got her head bowed so her hair falls around her face as she struggles to get her shoes off.

I drop to my knees and help her take them off. "Via," I look up at her, setting one boot aside, "you're scaring me."

"They—" She hiccups. "They want to help me."

Confused, I rub her back and wait for her to elaborate.

"The ladies, Glenda and Lucy and Cassandra … Ella … they want to help with the store so I don't have to push back the opening."

She'd only begun to brainstorm potential opening days when the place flooded.

"I've never … I've never had people in my life who care about me like this before." Her bottom lip trembles.

I cup her face and take her in, wiping the tears away with my thumbs. Not only did her ex do a number on her, but her former friends too. If they can even be called friends.

"I told you this town takes care of their own." I wrap my arms around her, holding her close.

"I know you did." She sniffles into my shirt. "But I didn't expect them to want to pitch and help like this. Glenda even bedazzled a hammer. She was so proud of it."

I chuckle. "That sounds exactly like something she'd do."

She pulls away and shrugs out of her sweater. "I've been so overwhelmed by the water damage, and then these ladies swoop in and want to help me. It's ... wow."

"People care about you."

"Not yet." Biting her lip, she steps away from me. "I need to shower. The girls got a hold of Derrick. They'll be at the store to help tomorrow and Sunday, so I want to be there too."

"I'll come too."

She smiles. "I figured you'd say that."

Standing on her tiptoes, fingers grazing my bare stomach, she gives me a small kiss.

Cuffing the back of her neck, I hold her to me and deepen it.

"How'd it go with your dad?"

I groan and let her go. "Okay, I guess. He's still stunned, but he thinks he'll get there."

"I'm sorry." She bites her lip and averts her gaze. "I never wanted to come between you."

"There's nothing to be sorry for."

And I mean that. I wish he hadn't found out the way he did, but I can't go back and redo it.

"He's your dad, though."

"And we'll be fine."

It'll take time, but we'll get there.

forty-one

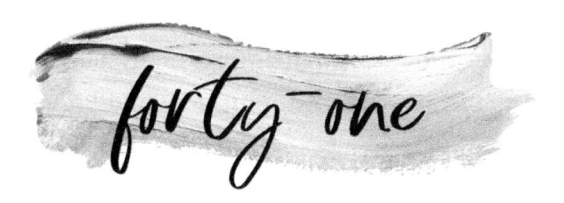

Via

I pause in the doorway, jaw slackening with shock.

"Izzy?" I gape at my sister, who's wearing a pink hard hat and talking to Derrick. He looks annoyed, either by her or because Reid and I have arrived.

"Via!" My sister scurries over and throws her slender arms around my shoulders.

It takes me a moment to hug her back, the shock having rendered me momentarily immobile.

"How…" I pull away from her. "Why are you here?"

"Layla told me the whole town was getting together this weekend to help with repairs, so I flew out."

I squeeze her again as a stray tear leaks out of the corner of my eye, followed by another.

When I let her go, I take in the sight surrounding me. She's right. My book club ladies aren't the only ones here helping. It's *everyone*. The waitress from the diner. Kathy from the donut shop. The gray-haired man I'm pretty sure has a crush on the lady who owns the flower shop.

I scan the room, recognizing so many faces, even if I can't put names to every one. Shit. I should know them all by now. I've been living in my Reid bubble, not really getting to know anyone outside of my book club ladies.

"This is just ... wow." I press my palms to my cheeks and seek out Reid. "I didn't expect this many people."

He throws an arm around my shoulders and tugs me against his side, placing a kiss on top of my head. A couple people notice, shooting curious glances, but they quickly go back to work.

"Are you going to help?" Derrick asks my sister. "I thought that's what you were here for."

"He's grumpy today," she mouths. Then she's off, skipping over to Derrick and giving him a mock salute. "Izzy James, reporting for duty. What would you like me to help with?"

Derrick holds a finger up for each of his directives. "Number one, this isn't the time or place for your blog or photo ops. You got me? No posing. No photos. Just work."

Izzy, ever defiant, sticks a hand on her hip and pouts. "Does this count as posing? Are you going to throw me over your knee and spank me for being a bad girl?"

Derrick's eyes go wide and his lips part. Throwing his hands up, he stalks off, but Izzy runs after him.

"Oh, come on! It was a joke!"

Reid angles in close. "Is it just me, or is your sister flirting with my dad?"

I press my lips together, trying not to laugh. "I think she is."

Straightening, he shakes his head. "I don't know what to say to that."

With a laugh, I tug him over to the table set up with gear. I pass him a hard hat and take one for myself. "I don't think there's anything you can say."

He groans. "But—"

"No." I hold up a hand. "We're not going there. We need to get to work. Show me how it's done?"

He grins at the challenge, dimples flashing. "Absolutely."

By the end of the weekend, my limbs are numb, and all I want to do is sleep for a week. I'm in decent shape. Or so I thought. Manual labor has taught me I have absolutely no strength or endurance. I'm going to have to start lifting weights, because this is downright laughable.

"I'm so *sore*," Izzy says, echoing my thoughts.

I want nothing more than to take an Epsom salt bath, but Reid only has a walk-in shower, and my apartment is still mid-gut job since the repairs to the store took precedent. With the extra help this weekend, we're very close to being back on track. I'll never be able to repay the favor to all of these people, but I'm forever grateful.

"I'm starving," Reid says, rubbing his stomach.

"Wait up!" Ella calls from behind us. The three of us slow our steps and turn. She jogs down the sidewalk, her cheeks-tinged pink from the cold and huffs out a breath when she reaches us. "A bunch of us are getting together at Lobster Shack if you guys want to come."

"*Food.*"

I chuckle at Reid's desperate response and turn to Izzy. "We have to eat, right?"

She shrugs. "I could go for a lobster roll."

"We're in."

"Good," Ella says, walking backward. "I'll see you there."

We round the corner and pile into Reid's car, then head for the Lobster Shack. to get there, the lot already teeming with life.

Inside the restaurant, we find a bunch of tables pushed together, and most of the people who were at the shop are already here.

An emotion I'm not familiar with fills my chest. I think it's the feeling of *belonging*.

Moving to Parkerville was a wild step out of my comfort zone. This was a crapshoot, but luck was on my side, and I've found my people.

Reid pulls out a chair for me, then another for Izzy before he settles into the one on my other side. He swipes a menu and passes it to me.

"You don't need it?"

He chuckles, resting his arm on the back of my chair. "Angel, I've been here a million times."

"Right," I laugh, angling it so I can share it with Izzy.

It doesn't take us long to decide—the menu has about five options total, and each one is a lobster dish.

Laughter reigns, all these people familiar with each other. They care about each other in a way I've never experienced before. I look around the table, trying to put a name to every face.

There's Toby who owns the small gas station on the end of Main Street. Mindy is a stay-at-home mom and our newest book club member—after Glenda asked her if she liked word porn. Beside Mindy, her husband Jake blushed at Glenda's question. I move around the table, proud of my ability to put not only names with faces but tidbits about each of them too.

It's the first time I've felt like a true member of Parkerville. I've found not only a home, but a family too.

forty-two

Reid

Two Months Later

I raise my fist, poised to knock.

The art store's grand opening is tomorrow, and Via is freaking out, so after work, I picked up dinner and flowers.

I haven't seen her much this week. I've been working full time, and she's been busy getting final details for the big event ready.

I still don't know what she's named the place. Other than Via, my dad, ironically, may be the only one who does know, since he hung the sign above the door. The sign that is currently covered with a tarp. Via said she wanted to unveil the name at the grand opening.

Finally, I put my fist to the door and knock.

There's shuffling on the other side, and then she's there, looking more than a little frazzled but still beautiful. Her oversized sweatshirt is speckled with a riot of paint colors, and her normally perfect hair is a mess that's desperately trying to escape her hair tie. Her jeans, though also dotted with paint, fit her like a glove.

I groan. Damn, I want to put my hands all over her. My hunger for her never wanes.

Her eyes get big when she catches sight of the bags in my hand. "Food!" She takes the to-go bags and carries them to her new bar.

The apartment looks nothing like it did a couple of months ago. The floors have been sanded down and stained. The original cabinets—relics from the seventies—were pulled out and replaced. The taupe shade, along with the white quartz countertop, makes the room look so much bigger.

I miss having her stay with me, but I respect her need to have her own space.

For now.

If I have anything to say about it, I'll be putting a ring on her finger sooner rather than later.

Via removes the food from the bags. "I skipped lunch," she says, shoving a stray hair out of her eyes. "I didn't mean to, but I was so busy making sure every detail is perfect."

"Angel," I chuckle, taking off my boots. "It's been perfect for days. I think what you're doing is obsessively fine-tuning."

She pops up on her tiptoes and drapes her arms around my neck.

"Thank you for dinner."

"You're welcome. These are for you too." I hold out the flowers she completely ignored in favor of food.

She takes the bouquet from me with a giddy smile. "You're spoiling me."

I shrug. "Tomorrow's your big day. I just want to support you."

With a quick kiss to my lips, she darts off in search of a glass to put the flowers in.

After dinner, I cage her in against the counter and run my nose up the smooth skin of her neck, inhaling her scent. "Do I get to see the store before everyone else, or do I have to wait?"

"I feel like I should make you suffer and wait." She shudders. "But I want you to see it now."

With a nip to her earlobe, I take a step back. "Good, because I have a surprise for you."

She cocks her head to the side. "More than dinner and flowers?"

"Yep." I nod, trying in vain to bite back a smile.

Downstairs, she unlocks the front door to the store and flicks the light on.

The drab, crumbling building has been transformed. It smells like fresh paint, and the stained concrete floors beneath my feet glisten—at least for now. It won't be long before they're covered in paint. The counter sits to the right of the entrance, and behind it is yet another covered sign.

The wall behind the plaque is painted with rectangles of various colors. Three columns and five rows, so it looks like three paint sample cards. Each color is separated by a white strip with a label. A paint color code, from the look of it, written in Izzy's handwriting.

"When did you do this?"

"Yesterday. We did touchups today. What do you think?" The smile on her face is so damn bright.

She's worried for months about how the store would come together. There were some bumps along the way, but she's done it. The dream she's had for years is finally a reality, and I'm so fucking proud of her.

"It's perfect."

She clasps her hands together. "Do you think so? I'm not sure how well an art store will do here, but I have a bunch of ideas, and the ladies from my book club have already asked if our next meeting can be here. They *never* have it anywhere except Lucy's house, so I feel—"

I shut her up with a kiss.

The Via I met all those months ago was timid. Careful with her words. She was still holding on to that lawyer part of herself. I love the way she rambles now, as silly as that might sound. These days, she voices her worries instead of keeping them bottled inside. She no longer measures her words. Instead, she just exists.

"What was that for?" She laughs when I let her go.

"You're cute when you ramble."

Her cheeks flush. "I'm nervous, that's all."

Taking my hand, she leads me through the open workspace, pointing out each station and explaining its focus. Then she takes me over to the shelves that line one whole wall with pottery waiting to be painted.

"My kiln hasn't come in yet, so I won't be able to offer it yet."

"That's okay. Everything else has come together."

She spins, taking it all in herself. "I can't believe this is mine."

"I can."

"Let me show you my office." She drags me to the back and opens the door to the office.

The walls are painted a light pink, and there's another sign hanging behind her large desk—covered, as well.

"You really don't want anyone to know the name of this place yet, do you?"

She bites her lip, eyes downcast like she's embarrassed. "I wanted you to be the first to know."

I blink. "Does that mean you're going to tell me now, angel?"

She gives a tiny nod in response, stepping behind her desk and flicking a switch that connects to the covered sign. It glows with a peachy hue, but I can't make out the letters through the blanket covering it.

She grasps the blanket but pauses. "I feel like I'm being dramatic for no reason, but here goes."

Tugging it loose, she lets it fall to the ground at her feet.

The LED sign spells out Color Me Happy.

Grinning, I slide my finger into her belt loop and tug her close. "Color Me Happy, huh? I love it."

"It's not too cheesy, is it? I was inspired by ... well, by you."

I rear back, my heart stuttering in my chest. "By me?"

"Yeah, I ..." She dips her chin. "You brought color back into my life. Everything was dull before you. You've made me so unbelievably happy, Reid. When I thought of Color Me Happy, it felt right."

"I love it." I'm too stunned to say much else. Taking her cheeks in my hands, I stare down at her. Her brown eyes are warm, happy, just like she said. There's no sadness clinging there anymore. I've chased it away, and I'll continue to do it with every breath I take. "It's perfect."

"Really?"

I nod. "Don't doubt it. I love it, and everyone else will too."

Stepping away from me, she sits in her office chair. "Can you believe it's all done? I swear I thought I'd never see this day."

"I knew it would come." I stuff my hands in my pockets. "And now, here we are."

She straightens a pen on her desk, the one that's shaped like a diamond on one end. "You said you had a surprise for me?" She's trying not to act too eager, but I can see it in the way she bites her lip to hide her smile.

I swallow back the nerves creeping up my esophagus and tug on my belt.

She puts her hand over mine and stills my movements. "Reid," she laughs, "I love you, but your dick doesn't count as a surprise."

A chuckle escapes me, easing my apprehension. "No, but this surprise does require me to pull my pants down."

She lets her hands drop, brows furrowed, as I slide my jeans to my knees. "What could possibly—"

She gasps as she takes in the fresh ink on my thigh. I've wanted a new tattoo for a while, and the day Via drew the angel wings while we sat side by side in my apartment, I knew that was it. Wings for my angel.

Her throat works and her eyes well with tears. "It's beautiful. It's mine, right? My drawing?"

I nod in answer, a little choked up myself.

"Can I touch it?"

"Not yet. It's still healing. I got it last weekend."

She drops to her knees in front of me to get a closer look.

"It's stunning. They even got the shading right."

I clear my throat, and when she looks up, I caress her cheek. "Just wanted you to know that while I didn't pull my pants down to show you my dick, I can't quite control it when you're staring at me like that."

A burst of laughter leaves her in a hot rush that hits my leg and stomach, which only makes me harder.

I'm absolutely pathetic around this woman.

"Aw, were you feeling left out?" she asks my cock, running a gentle finger along it.

"*Via*," I groan her name. "Don't mock me."

She grins. "I'm not mocking you. I'm mocking him." She pokes it again.

"Via, if you're not nice to him, then—"

"Then what?" she challenges with a glint in her eye.

"Then I'm going to shove my cock down your throat and make you be nice."

"Do it, then."

I blink down at her, speechless. Via shocks the hell out of me sometimes.

"That's what you want?"

She doesn't answer. Not with words, anyway. She yanks my boxer briefs down, letting my cock bob right in front of her face.

Looking up at me with a challenge in her eyes, she crooks her head to the side, waiting.

Then she opens her mouth wide, making no move to touch me.

So, I do as I threatened and shove my cock in her mouth.

When she makes a tiny mewling sound, I swear I almost lose it. Holding her head steady with one hand on her head, I fuck her mouth. She presses her palms to my thighs to brace herself, careful not to touch my fresh tattoo.

When she gags, I slow my strokes, but she shakes her head slightly when I pull out. "Give it to me," she says, lips red and swollen.

Jesus Christ, this woman.

But who am I to deny her?

She takes my cock in her mouth like that's where it belongs and moans, her eyes watering.

"Are you wet?" I ask, my voice deeper than normal. I'm barely holding on. "Is this turning you on, angel?"

She nods. "Can I fuck you in your office?" Another nod.

When I pull back, my cock pops free of her mouth. I haul her up, make quick work of getting rid of her jeans, and lay her out on her desk.

I enter her with a single thrust, finding no resistance. She's *dripping*, absolutely fucking soaked.

"Harder," she begs.

Holding her hip with one hand, I entwine the fingers of the other with hers and give my girl what she wants.

She cries out, already close, and I'm desperate to see her fall over the edge. I keep going, watching in awe as her eyes roll back and her mouth parts slightly.

"Yes." It's a whisper, like if she speaks any louder, I'll stop.

"You're so beautiful when you come." I kiss her neck. "So beautiful." Her cheek. "And mine." I claim her mouth.

She whimpers beneath me.

I bring her to another orgasm before I can't take it anymore. With her pussy spasming around my cock, I finally come. We struggle to catch our breath, holding each other like if we let go, we might fall apart.

When I finally gather my wits again, I tug her down onto the floor. Our clothes are a mess, as are we, but neither of us cares.

Arms around her, I kiss the top of her head.

Fuck. This is just the beginning for us, and the journey? It's going to be fucking incredible.

forty-three

Via

The day has finally arrived.

The grand opening of Color Me Happy. My shop. *I own a store.* It's all mine.

Reid stayed over last night, and he stands by the door of my apartment now. His hair is still damp from a shower I refused to join despite the way he tempted me.

"Do I look okay?" I do a slow turn so he can get a look at my simple cream-colored sweater dress.

"You look beautiful. As always." As he adjusts his button-down, his glasses slip down ever so slightly, and he flicks his head in an effort to get them back in place.

I cross the distance between us and adjust them.

He grins. "Thanks."

I love that he wears glasses. There's something about a good-looking man in glasses that turns me on. In Izzy's words, I have a glasses kink.

"Are you nervous?" he asks, like he doesn't already know I am.

My stomach flips, as if on command. "Absolutely."

"Don't be. It's going to be great. *You're* going to do great." When he looks at me like that, pride shining in his eyes, it's hard not to believe him. "Take a deep breath."

I obey, inhaling until my lungs are full and holding it.

"Good. Now exhale. You've got this."

Again, I follow his orders.

"I've got this," I echo.

He regards me for a long moment, taking me in with just a hint of heat in his eyes. Like he wants to kiss me, but he doesn't want to smudge my makeup.

Downstairs, we head into the building through the new side door that leads straight into my office. This addition will make coming and going so much easier.

Izzy is already inside the store, and when she sees us, she jumps up from the table and throws her arms around me.

"I'm so proud of you."

She's told me this multiple times a day since she returned to Parkerville earlier this week.

"Thank you."

She glances at the clock. "Two minutes to go."

My heart spasms.

There's no going back now.

Shockingly, there's a line outside. Ella, Lucy, Jessica, and the rest of the ladies from book club wave eagerly on the other side of the glass. I wave back, breathing deep to keep my emotions at bay. I'll never be able to thank them enough for stepping up and not only helping with the store, but convincing other people to as well.

Reid gives my hand a small squeeze. "It's showtime."

Heart racing, I step forward and open the doors. "All right, guys. Come on in to Color Me Happy."

I kick the doorstopper down, already overwhelmed by the sheer number of people who pass by me.

"I brought donuts," Kathy says, shoving a stack of boxes into my arms.

"Oh, wow. How much do I owe you?"

"Silly girl," she huffs. "It's a gift. I thought you might want to offer some to customers today."

I am not going to cry.

"Thank you." Despite tamping down on my tears, I can't keep my voice from shaking.

She pats my hand. "You're welcome."

Reid takes the boxes from me and sets them up on a table. Before he walks away, he's sure to snag two. One for him. One for me.

He strides in my direction, holding one out. I'm not sure I can eat it, but I take it anyway with a smile.

"Hey," Derrick says, stepping inside and nodding to each of us. "I didn't want to miss your big day." Without waiting for a response, he moves on to take in the finishing touches he's yet to see.

Reid sighs and takes a too-big bite of donut. He's still upset that his relationship with his dad is strained, but we'll get there. *They'll* get there, at least. I can't imagine a world in which Derrick doesn't have a relationship with his son. They talk, but nowhere near as often as they used to.

My donut nearly slips out of my hand when I catch sight of the couple stepping through the doors next. Reid gives me a puzzled look, quickly taking the donut from me.

"Mom? Dad? What are you doing here?"

I invited them—over the phone and via an official invite —but I didn't expect them to show up. The last time we spoke, they showed little interest when I filled them in on the progress I'd made. Having them stand in front of me feels almost like seeing a ghost.

My mom scoffs. "Did you think we'd miss this?" She looks around with a critical eye. She curls her lip at the paintbrushes floating above us, suspended by clear fishing line. It's obvious she doesn't like them, but she keeps her mouth shut.

I don't answer her question, because the answer would be yes. I was certain they wouldn't bother. "Thank you for being here," I say instead, opening my arms to hug each of them. "This is Reid."

I've told them about him. The last thing I wanted to do was continue to keep him a secret in any way. The disapproval was palpable through the phone when I answered the questions they had about his job and his age. But for once in my life, I didn't give a shit. For too long, I let them keep me in a cage. Let them mold me into what they believed to be the perfect daughter and force me into their version of the perfect career.

I'm finally living for me, and I won't go back.

"Reid," my mom says, looking him up and down. "A pleasure."

Reid presses his lips together, not because he's perturbed, but because he's trying not to laugh. I elbow him lightly.

"The pleasure is all mine." With a wink, he takes her hand and presses a kiss to her knuckles.

"Oh ... well." Flustered, she takes a step away. "I'm going to see your sister."

My dad dips his chin and follows after her. That's typical. He's a man of few words.

My relationship with them will never be picture perfect, but over these months, I've come to be okay with that. It's impossible to make everyone happy. Even the people who share DNA. The only person I have control over is myself, so I've made a conscious effort to focus on my own happiness.

Reid sets our donuts on the counter and takes my hand. "Come on, Via." He tugs me into the center of the room. "Take it all in."

So I do.

The ladies from my book club have taken over a whole table and are painting the small canvases. At another table, some of Reid's friends are checking out the pamphlet that lists the services I offer.

Reid's lips find my ear. "You did it."

"I did." Tears prick my eyes, a buildup of emotion from all these months of working on it amid life's changes—the biggest being finding my person.

Music plays softly in the background, some playlist Izzy chose. I can't believe my store is full of people. I've been focused on the remodel for so long that the reality of today seemed to flee my mind.

But this is what I wanted. A community space where people can get creative.

"Hey," Reid says, winding his arms around my waist. "It's 11:11." He nods at the clock hanging above the doorway that leads to my office. "Make a wish."

I can't fight my smile. "I don't need to."

"Why?"

"Because," I look around at my store, at my new friends and neighbors, my sister, and, most importantly, him, "I already have everything I've ever wanted and more."

epilogue

Via

Three Years Later

The ring on my left hand glimmers in the light.

I love it as much as I did the day Reid and I said "I do" two years ago. Reid would have married me during those first few months I was in Parkerville, but as always, he respected my wishes, so we waited.

I can't help smiling as I watch him run after our son.

The adoption finally went through.

I could've gone through more tests and treatments and God only knows what else to have a biological child, but I didn't want to put myself through that. Not mentally or physically, and luckily, like he always said, Reid didn't mind.

Trevor is six years old. A spunky little boy with a heart of gold. His little sister, Ainsley, sits in my lap, giggling as I bounce her up and down. She's two, and she already has Reid wrapped around her little finger.

Izzy sits beside me, cradling her three-month-old.

We've come so far in a few short years. How vastly different both of our lives look now.

Reid catches up to Trevor and swings him up and into his arms. When he spins, he catches me looking at him and grins.

"Ugh, thank God I have a hot husband too, or I'd be jealous as hell." She smiles down at her baby, caressing her plump little cheek. "Your daddy is the hottest man I've ever seen. If I don't watch out, I'll have ten more of you running around."

She smiles over at me, and I laugh.

Her husband sits on the bench beside her, passing us each a serving of loaded hash browns from one of the food trucks set up for this weekend's festival. Water laps against the rocky shoreline, and Reid and Trevor toss a ball back and forth near it.

The day the shop opened, I thought I had everything I could ever want, but every day since, life has gotten better and better. I have an amazing husband, my store is thriving, my sister lives close, and I'm a mom.

A part of me thought my life was over when I got divorced.

Little did I know it was only the beginning.

Reid jogs over to where I sit and drops a kiss to the top of Ainsley's blond head. Then, with the sweetest smile, he presses his lips to mine.

All those wishes on elevens?

They made me the luckiest woman alive.

UNTIL THEN

DERRICK AND IZZY'S BOOK COMING OCTOBER 2024

I never thought I'd find myself craving the small-town life, but I've grown to hate L.A. and all that comes with it. When a brand deal goes south, I put my life in the City of Angels on hold to move to Parkerville, Maine temporarily. With my sister and assistant living there it seems like the most logical place to go. Until my assistant offers for me to move in with her dad.

Her very hot, rugged dad.

That may or may not hate me after I tried to hook my sister up with him, but she ended up dating his son instead.

Oops.

It was an honest mistake.

I fully expect Derrick to tell me to find another place to bum it, but by some miracle he agrees to let me stay in one of the empty rooms, as long as I do my share, and help keep the place clean and make some meals.

Easy enough, right?

Except I can't stop thinking about Derrick in ways a twenty-six-year-old woman definitely shouldn't be about her forty-four-year-old pseudo-landlord. Who can blame me when he likes walking around the house shirtless and in gray sweatpants?

I'm convinced the feelings are all one way, until I accidentally hear him moaning my name.

acknowledgments

There are so many people that are a part of making this book what it is today.

Emily—it seems silly, but first off, thank you for being my best friend. Who would've thought when we first connected all those years ago on Goodreads that we'd end up here? (Not me!) We've grown together over the last decade (omg how is it that long?!) and I'm beyond lucky to have you. I feel so honored that we get to work together on so many amazing covers. Your talent knows no bounds. You keep getting better and better. It's not often we get to work together on the inside of the book too but when we do it's magic. I always appreciate your insight into the characters and story.

Valentine—I'm so blessed to have connected with you. You have such creative insights into marketing and you're always there when I need to fangirl over our mutual love of the Addicted Series. I love working with you and can't thank you enough for being there for me.

To the whole Valentine PR team—you guys put in so much hard work behind the scenes and believe me it doesn't go unnoticed and is so appreciated. You guys are incredible.

Melanie—I feel so blessed to have found you as a developmental editor. We mesh so well and your thoughts always make my work better. Now that I've found you I don't know what I'd do without you.

Beth, words cannot express how grateful I am to have found you. Thank you for all your hard work on the edits for this book and whipping it into tip top shape.

Cheyenne and KatieGwen—you two have become my best and favorite cheerleaders. I'm so glad I've gotten to know you guys and can call you friends.

Stephanie, Caitlin, and Genesis—thank you for taking the time to beta read this one. Thank you for all your input and loving Reid and Via as much as I do.

Last, but certainly not least, thank you dear reader for being here. Without you, I wouldn't be where I am today. I hope you know how much you mean to me.

Printed in Great Britain
by Amazon